sweet SURRENDER

NEW YORK TIMES BESTSELLING AUTHOR

K. BROMBERG

PRAISE FOR K. BROMBERG

"K. Bromberg always delivers intelligently written, emotionally intense, sensual romance . . ."

—*USA Today*

"K. Bromberg makes you believe in the power of true love."

—#1 *New York Times* bestselling author Audrey Carlan

"Always an absolute must-read."

—*New York Times* bestselling author Helena Hunting

"An irresistibly hot romance that stays with you long after you finish the book."

—#1 *New York Times* bestselling author Jennifer L. Armentrout

"Bromberg is a master at turning up the heat!"

—*New York Times* bestselling author Katy Evans

"Supercharged heat and full of heart. Bromberg aces it from the first page to the last."

—*New York Times* bestselling author Kylie Scott

ALSO WRITTEN BY K. BROMBERG

Driven Series
Driven
Fueled
Crashed
Raced
Aced

Driven Novels
Slow Burn
Sweet Ache
Hard Beat
Down Shift

The Player Duet
The Player
The Catch

The Malone Brothers
Worth the Fight
Worth the Risk
Worth the Fall
Control (Novella)

Wicked Ways
Resist
Reveal

Standalone
Faking It
Then You Happened
Flirting with 40
UnRaveled (Novella)
Sweet Cheeks
Sweet Rivalry (Novella)

The Play Hard Series
Hard to Handle
Hard to Hold
Hard to Score
Hard to Lose
Hard to Love

The S.I.N. Series
Last Resort
On One Condition
Final Proposal

The Redemption Series
Until You

The Full Throttle Series
Off The Grid
On The Edge
Over The Limit
Out of Control

Tangled Hearts Series
Twisted Knight
Threaded Lies

Backstage Pass Series
Sweet Ache
Sweet Regret

Holiday Novellas
The Package
The Detour
Forever More

ISBN: 978-1-967612-07-9

Published by JKB Publishing, LLC

Editing by Marion Making Manuscripts
Cover Design by Y'all that Graphic
Printed in the United States of America

sweet SURRENDER

CHAPTER

one

Hendrix

"Ten. Eleven." I count the twenty-five pound bags of flour for the second time and come up short. "Barney?" I call over my shoulder to the open door where my wholesaler is busy unloading my order in the back alley.

"One sec." His voice is muffled and labored.

I move through my kitchen area, past the long kitchen island lined with stacks of empty cookie sheets and past three industrial mixers. Just as I clear the doorway to the back alley of my shop, he lifts his head. He's short but burly with tufts of salt and pepper hair peeking out from beneath his company cap.

"Sorry. What was that?" he asks.

"My order is short unless you have eight more sacks of flour and ten more of sugar in the back of that van that I'm not seeing."

His grimace should be enough of a warning—one I should expect if the past month is any indication—but I hold tight to my optimism. *Fleetingly.* "You probably need to take that up with the accounting department."

Optimism? Gone.

Accounting department? His wife, Annie.

"Meaning?" I ask, but I already know.

"You're behind on the balance due." He shifts uncomfortably and his Adam's apple bobs. "As it is, Annie had my ass for delivering this much, but it's *you.* We both know you're good for it, but we have bills to pay too."

I attempt a sweet smile but my stomach sinks. "I know. I am good for it. I'm slowly figuring everything out."

Fuck you, Paul.

It's a refrain I've said too many times over the past few weeks. One that makes me feel good even though it also feels like a Band-Aid placed on a bullet hole at the same time. "Tell Annie I'll be catching up on it." *How?* I have no fucking clue. "This . . . all of this caught me way off guard."

Barney falters and then continues to pull off his work gloves. He sets them on the handle of the pallet jack before looking over to me. There's compassion in the depths of his eyes. "I'm sorry this happened to you. Truly, I am." He hangs his head.

"Thank you. It . . . is what it is."

"Yeah, but . . . I saw him here. *With her.* I could have assumed a lot of things, but you'd be amazed at the shit I see so I never said anything. I just figured she was a friend or you guys had an open"—he waves his hands back and forth as he searches for a word and his cheeks color—"thingamajigger. I didn't know and it isn't my place to interfere. Annie's taught me that over the years."

Leave it to Paul to make my supplier feel guilty over his cheating ass.

"It's not your fault. *At all.*" I reach out and squeeze his bicep. "There were signs I should have seen but didn't until it was too late."

Too late, as in opening my front door, walking into my bedroom and seeing Paul's bare ass as he screwed his side piece in our bed, signs.

The sight will forever be burned in my retinas, and the pitching of my stomach still hasn't subsided.

"It's not your fault either," he says, shifting his feet in discomfort. "Paul's a dick. He was before and is even more so now. My Annie always asked what a nice girl like you was doing with a guy like him. Maybe this is a good thing. It might not feel like it now, but it could be."

I smile and nod simply to ease him out of a conversation I'm sure he wanted no part in. "I'll make it a good thing," I say with way more optimism than I feel.

"Good." He nods. "That's what I like to hear. Now, I'll work on Annie to see if I can't accidentally extend some more credit for you. I know you have that big event coming up."

I bite back the sob and release the pent-up hurt and frustration as a sigh instead. It's nowhere near as cathartic though. "I'd be appreciative of whatever you can do. Once I get paid the balance on the event, it'll go straight to you."

And it's true. It will. But then that means I'll be late on my rent and utilities, which puts me in yet another tailspin.

Who am I kidding? I've been living in that endless eddy for the past three weeks.

Barney closes up his truck and heads out while I go back into the bakery. *Cookie Cutter*. It's my labor of love. My dream come true. And while it was one hundred percent my baby—the concept, the implementation, the hard work—Paul had contributed half the start-up capital.

But he took his cheating dick and his helpful money with him when I kicked him out. Now, I'm left with a struggling business that's short on capital, personal bills I can't pay, and a broken, angry heart.

"*Fuck you, Paul.*"

It doesn't feel as good as it once did. The words. The gusto behind them. The anger they barely alleviate. At first saying them was my way to get out the overwhelming emotions—the hurt, the disbelief, the heartache. And it worked.

But the hurt has been replaced by anger. The anger colored in big, bold strokes with despair.

I look around my cookie bakery. Everywhere is bright pastels and happiness. In the signs and awning outside, in the decor inside, and in the obnoxiously happy sentiments and designs on the cookies in the case.

This was all mine—but *unofficially* half his.

I trusted him. I believed him. Who wouldn't after two years together? And now with the shit he packed up and took with him—his clothes, his electronics, his self-help books that clearly worked for shit—one would say taking *his* money back was warranted and it was. What wasn't, however, was the money he took from our *joint* account. *Stole.* The one we started and pooled our savings to qualify for the loan.

And now I'm left in dire straits.

Like the kind of straits that have me wondering how I'm going to deliver one thousand cookies in two weeks' time. I need money for the supplies, and yet I can't make the money unless I provide the cookies. Even more, I can't pay for workers to help me make the cookies because all the money goes to the supplies so it's probably going to be me, myself, and I baking and decorating until my fingers want to fall off. Oh, and I need a bakery to actually make those cookies in, but paying rent when credit is already maxed out is enough to sap anyone's creativity.

Yeah.

Fuck you, Paul.

CHAPTER
two

Gizmo

"**D**ISORDERLY CONDUCT. DRUNK AND DISORDERLY CONDUCT, AGAIN. Criminal damage to property. Misdemeanor assault." Nathaniel looks up from his laptop screen and eyes me over his glasses. "Should I keep reading your rap sheet? Because I can. The list is long and not so distinguished."

My sigh is as heavy as my stare is bored. It's not like he can see it though because my shades are dark and my head is fucking pounding—but hell if last night wasn't worth it. "Your point?"

"My point is it's one thing to be a rock star. It's another thing to be the stereotypical nuisance that goes along with it."

"Just like it's one thing to be a lawyer, Nathaniel, and another thing to be the stereotypical uptight asshole that goes along with it," I say in the same mocking tone that he did.

My brother stares at me with a disdain he's undoubtably felt for longer than either of us can remember. The differences between us have always been night and day. Rebel and saint. Out of control versus fall in line.

"Sure. Fine. Say what you will."

"I did," I say. I'm being an ass, and I know it.

"I like my life," he asserts.

No, he doesn't.

"Ditto." I shrug and earn the same scowl he's been giving me for years. "Is there a reason for this 'meeting' you demanded, or is it just another way to let me know you're perfect and I'm the fuck-up?"

Same shit. Different day.

My combat boots make the only noise in the posh office as I lift them up and cross them on the coffee table.

"My point was your record shows a history of habits, of acting out, and—"

"And I paid the fines asked. I did the community service required." *Jesus Christ. How many times do we have to rehash this?* "I don't get what the big deal is this time around. The courts or whoever allowed me to travel last time. Do your job and they'll approve it again this time."

"Huh." It's the only sound he makes and for some reason, it unsettles me when it shouldn't.

"What is that supposed to mean?"

"Your legal indiscretions are one thing. The nonstop TMZ mentions and photos are another."

"Dude." I chuckle and roll my eyes. "I can't help that paparazzi get paid to take pictures and make shit up."

"What is a judge to think when you say 'I'm on my best behavior. I won't do the same shit I've been doing again'?"

"Who said I was going to say that?"

His chuckle is condescending and so much like our father's that I roll my shoulders and fight the urge to walk out. "Me. Your lawyer. I'm the one who said you were going to say and do that or else I won't represent you."

"Come on." I sigh. "The dramatics are so not like you."

"Dramatics?" he scoffs. "Really?"

Bitterness coats my tongue but I swallow it down like cheap vodka. "Really."

"So that latest story isn't true?"

"Which one would that be?" I narrow my eyes at him and shake my head in disgust.

"Exactly. *Which one would that be?* There are so many posted you don't even know what the latest is."

"There are opportunists everywhere willing to lie for a payday. Willing to say an innocent picture is something bad. I don't have to tell you that."

"And yet the one journalist in particular who keeps the stories about you alive by constantly stirring the pot is causing you the most trouble."

"Lori is . . . Lori is just that—an opportunist," I state about the journalist who has the biggest hard-on for me. "I didn't do shit."

"And there's always an excuse for your behavior."

I bite back my smart-ass remark, my cutdown to blame him when I'm well aware of my own actions. I own them. It's so much easier to blame him.

Hasn't it always been?

"I put in the request to your probation officer like I always do when you need to go overseas. He said he'd bring it to the judge."

"Like he always does," I finish for him, wanting to hurry up this fucking urgent conversation we *needed*.

"Correct. And he did. But the judge who normally approves your travel, your . . . exceptions, without pause, is no longer there."

The first finger of dread slithers up my spine. "So a different judge will approve it. This is Los Angeles. I know I'm not the only musician on probation in this town who needs to travel for work."

"The judge assigned to review your request is an unforgiving prick."

"Seems like everyone in the legal profession is." He takes the barb and my condescending chuckle without so much as a flinch.

"The good thing is I know him."

"Of course you do." I lace my fingers behind my neck like I'm not sitting here talking about my future. "Gotta throw your weight around somehow, huh?"

He groans in frustration, but I know that groan is the last step before he clenches a fist, cocks it back, and plows it in my face.

Good to see he still has some fight left and that the corporate world hasn't completely sucked the life out of him.

"You know, I don't have to represent you, right? I have plenty of business and run a lucrative practice with clients who actually care about their reputations and the outcome."

I grunt. My mood is shit and the dress down I got from the guys last night weighs heavily on me. The assurance I gave them that everything is chill is ringing hollow right now.

"You're not the only successful Gizmodo family member," he says, crossing his arms over his chest. "And yet you sit here with your shitty, *I don't give a fuck* attitude like I owe you. Let's get something straight, I don't owe you shit. You want to help yourself? Fine. You don't want to help yourself? No skin off my fucking back, but I suggest you knock the damn attitude off or you're going to find yourself up shit creek without a paddle, and I sure as shit won't jump into that mess to save your ass at that point."

I hold my hands up and grin. Looks like I'm not the only one having a bad day. I may hate the message but it's not the messenger's fault. *It's mine.* I'll own it but that doesn't mean I have to care one bit about it. "Okay. Fine."

"It's not fine. Far from it, Jase," he says, using my first name. One that few get away with calling me.

"You're right. It's not. Give me the rigmarole. Tell me what a piece of shit I am. That I'm shaming our family name that clearly neither of us cares about. That I'm—"

"How about you admit you're fucking up and don't give a shit that you are? How about you act like you care? Like you're contrite and might have taken the three-year probation you were handed—the one that was a fucking gift—as an impetus to grow up some and be a better man?"

"The last thing I need from anyone, let alone you, is to act like you're my father."

"Then take it from your lawyer," he grits out. "You're going to be hard-pressed to find a judge, let alone *this* judge, to allow you to leave the country. How's that for starters?"

Mic drop.

His voice is so calm, so nonchalant, but he knew damn well that those words would stop me dead in my tracks.

The only thing I love is my band—my chosen family. And my brother, a person I'm bound to by blood and history, sure as shit just got my attention.

"You're lying," I say. Because yes, while I love Nathaniel, I also tend to hate him for things beyond his control. And right now, I loathe him for hitting me where he knows it hurts the most.

"Not lying, no. He's that kind of judge."

"Then be a better lawyer," I throw at him.

The look he levels me with says a dozen different things. *I am a better lawyer. Stop hating me because of our father's choices.*

"Insulting me isn't going to make your situation better. You keep fucking up and aren't learning your lesson. You're on probation and yet another round of pictures were posted three days ago of you in a club with a bottle in one hand and a dozen empties in front of you."

"I was drinking. So fucking what?"

"It's also a violation of your probation."

I scrub a hand over my face in frustration. Three-fucking-year probation for one hotel room. One really bad night where I trashed it after a rough day dealing with my mom and a fucking awful night taking it out on the guys. A night that I've since paid the repairs for, paid the fines for, and done what the courts asked of me. And yet that one fucking night is like a pair of handcuffs growing tighter each and every day.

I roll my shoulders. "It's bullshit. You're telling me that no one else on probation is drinking? Fuck that, Nate. Just—"

"Discretion is a real thing." I go to speak and he holds up a hand to stop me. "Your selfishness, your constant *fuck you* to authority, is going to affect the select few that you care about."

"Yep. Got it." This conversation is just about over.

"That world tour you're planning isn't looking so worldly right now, is it?"

"*Fuck this.*" I stand up and toss the magazine beside me onto his perfectly polished table. "We're done here. I don't want to hear your insults or your—"

"Truth hurts. But you go. Run to the closest bar, down your drinks, run away like you always do when shit gets tough rather than ask me how to fix it."

"I will." I waltz out of his office and past his front office staff. What I'd give to have a door to slam, but all that's in this fucking place is the spring hinges.

Run away like you always do when shit gets tough.

I will, Nathaniel. Just taking an old page out of the Gizmodo family playbook.

CHAPTER
three

Hendrix

"You'll figure it out. I have faith that you will." Paul's voice is in my ear causing goosebumps—not the good kind—to chase over my skin. My hands fist on my design folder as I shift on my feet and look around the line ahead of me in the coffee shop.

"Easy for you to say. I'm not supposed to be figuring anything out. I'm supposed to be baking my ass off."

"Then go do it. Why are you on the phone talking to me?"

Paul's lucky he's not standing in front of me or else it might be a tough task for anyone to remove my fingers from where they'd be wrapped around his throat.

"Because being an adult means you sometimes have to do things you don't want to. For me? That's talking to you and your—"

"The point of this call is . . . what? That you miss me? That you want to reconcile?" His chuckle is pure condescension. "I'm sorry, babe—"

"No. It's that you drained the accounts. That you—"

"Guess you should be a little wiser with who you trust, huh? Your money issues aren't my problem anymore, Hendrix. *Really.*"

"Well, if you hadn't been so busy sticking your dick in your mistress and fucking me over, then I wouldn't be having any problems now, would I?"

With my blood boiling, I end the call with fervor and look up. The man in front of me is coughing into his hand. The woman in front of him is peering back at me with huge eyes. And the man sitting a few tables over, a hoodie up and sunglasses on despite being inside, is grinning without shame.

Shit. I just said that out loud, didn't I?

I put my head down and grimace, but then I figure I didn't do shit wrong—have no shame other than telling the truth.

The line moves forward and as I do, I have the unmistakable feeling of someone staring at me. I glance up and meet the palest blue eyes. Hoodie guy took his sunglasses off and *whoa*, those eyes pack quite a punch. Not just the light color and how they're framed with an abundance of dark lashes, but the curiosity with which they regard me.

I avert my eyes quickly, grateful when the line moves and I place my order. "Is Josie here?" I ask about the owner to the newly hired clerk behind the counter after I pay.

"Um, yeah. Somewhere." She glances over her shoulder to the back, but I can tell by the shake of her hands and the darting of her eyes that she's overwhelmed.

Or just had way too much coffee.

"Don't worry about it. I'll chat with her later," I say and wave a hand as I move for the next in line to order. Josie's Java has been here for longer than I can remember. Whereas my bakery down the street is bright pastels and stripes, her aesthetic is more warm tones and dark browns to match the coffee beans that have been placed in various glass jars across the wall from me.

It's busy today—*when is it not*—so I take the first available table I can find.

Of course, when I sit down and look up, those pale blue eyes are still studying me. He doesn't avert his gaze, just holds mine long enough to make me uncomfortable. Then a group of girls at his back snicker and squeal as they stare at him.

He glances back at them and lifts his chin, clearly basking in their attention. I sigh and look away. It's Los Angeles. Everyone here thinks they're someone even when they aren't. No doubt this guy's the same. Or if he is someone—which I highly doubt—clearly, I don't care.

And yet I look back and hold his eyes for a beat longer.

"Please tell me your day is better than mine," Josie says as she steps into my field of vision and breaks off my staring contest. She sets my iced coffee in front of me and then wipes her hands on the dish towel that's folded into the waistband of her apron. She's about fifteen years older than me with cherubic curls and rosy-red cheeks. She peers at me from behind a pair of oversized, black-framed glasses and her trademark bushy eyebrows that she refuses to pluck. The woman is a legend in everyone's mind but her own, and that's why I've taken to her so fiercely.

I level her with a dubious glare for an answer that has her shaking her head.

"That bad?" she asks.

My smile is quick and sharp. "I haven't found the right contract killer who's willing to maim Paul's nether regions."

"Only his nether regions? Feeling kind today?"

"Cock. Dick. His tiny, little mushroom cap. Are those better?" I ask with a vindictiveness that's not like me. She throws her head back and laughs. "I mean, I keep opening my fridge, hoping to find that whoever robbed that Bank of America down the street last week, stashed the sixty grand they stole there. No such luck. And then there's the small matter of how I'm going to fulfill this gigantic order, so I'm trying to keep it all together without losing my shit."

"So we've moved from the total shock to the anger portion of the getting fucked over by the boyfriend program, huh?" she deadpans.

I laugh. It's the first time I actually have and meant it in the past few days. "Definitely wallowing in the anger portion. But thanks. I can always count on you to lighten my mood."

Another group of girls push their way through the crowd and meet the giggling trio in the corner. I glance their way and then back to Josie. She lifts her eyebrows and shrugs. Business is business even if it is a giggling bunch of teenagers who might split one drink four ways because they're broke.

"At least you have a thousand cookies to keep you busy. You can put on a true crime documentary and fantasize about it being Paul while you shape and mold and decorate them all."

I hang my head and smile as I rock my head from side to side. "Nah.

He's not worth my time." I look back up and meet the kindness in her eyes. "I think it's being blindsided that hurts the most. Like here I was living in my own, completely perfect world—I had my bakery, my boyfriend, my future—all of it mapped out, and in one afternoon, one early arrival home, and *poof*, it's all gone or in jeopardy of being gone."

Josie reaches out and squeezes my shoulder. "It doesn't help and won't make you feel better, but maybe in time, you'll see it was for the best."

I smile but fight back the tears, the ones that feel like a constant ball in my throat that I refuse to let fall, and nod.

"And if not, then we just say what we've been saying."

"Fuck you, Paul," we say in unison followed by laughter.

"I have to get back to work, but I'm here, any time. You know that."

"I do. Thanks, Josie."

I watch her walk off and then allow myself to savor the first sip of my iced coffee. I'm tired and the kick of caffeine is welcome as I open my design folder. I shuffle through sketch after sketch of icing designs for the cookie tops. It sounds ridiculous to have a portfolio for my cookies, but then again, being original isn't exactly the easiest in this town of dreamers and artists.

With a sigh, I turn the page on my sketches. Only in Hollywood does a famous couple hire you to design and provide one thousand cookies for their dog's birthday party, but who am I to judge? A paycheck is a paycheck no matter how strange the work is.

A design idea strikes me and when I look down to my purse to grab my colored pencil kit, a voice nearby says, "Excuse me, miss?"

"Unless you have fifty, eighty—hell, why be stingy—one hundred grand to save my business and cheat-induced insanity, then I don't want any," I mutter as a pair of black combat boots arrives before me. I know who they belong to immediately.

Pretending he's not standing there or that I said what I just said isn't an option, so I take my time with a slow glance up his body to meet his eyes.

And Jesus.

The man is more than just pale blue eyes and a hoodie. He's taller than I anticipated, ruggedly handsome with a sharp jaw and dimples in both cheeks that form as he greets me with a smile.

I seem to have lost my words for a moment as I stare at him with narrowed eyes and parted lips.

"Yes?" I croak.

The roguish smirk on his face says he most definitely heard me. "I think you dropped this."

He holds my business card out to me, but I'm too busy focusing on his honey-coated gravel to respond. My glance down greets me with strong forearms where his sleeves are pushed up to display a sprinkling of intricate tattoos—including what looks like a large pink heart on his wrist.

"Um. Yes. Sure." *Snap out of it.* I reach out and take my card from his hand. "Uh, thanks."

"Cookie Cutter?"

That voice. It's sex on silk sheets. Not that I'd know or anything but . . . never mind.

"Yeah." I hook a thumb over my shoulder as if he knows where I'm motioning. "It's my bakery. Down the street. I bake cookies."

Way to sound intelligent, Hendrix.

"I'm Jase." He holds his hand out and I look at it for a beat before I realize I'm supposed to shake it.

"Hi. Yes." Our hands meet as I attempt to ignore the delicious scent of his cologne. It's clean and reminds me of outdoors. "I'm Hendrix."

"Hendrix?" He lifts his brows and fights a smile I don't quite understand. "Interesting name."

"Yeah, well, blame it on my dad."

"No. I like it. It's . . . *fitting.*"

"Okay." *Whatever that means.* He studies me without shame. His gaze grazes over my features before meeting my eyes again. "Is there something else I can help you with?"

He huffs out a sound. But right before he speaks, an "Excuse me" is said to the right of us.

We both turn to find a tall brunette standing there with a wide smile and gorgeous eyes, which are clearly focused on the man before me. "Hi," Jase says to her.

"I didn't mean to interrupt, but I wanted to . . . you know, give you this." She hands something to Jase. It looks like a folded napkin and he takes it.

"Thanks." He flashes a grin as he glances at whatever's on the napkin, his grin growing even wider before he pockets the note. "I'll keep that in mind."

She does some kind of move—a half curtsy with a dip of her knees while shrugging her shoulders at the same time—almost as if she's hoping he'll take her up right now on whatever it is that he'll keep in mind.

And then she proceeds to stand there staring at him, more awkward than I was being—if that's possible—while being incredibly forward.

"Look"—I interrupt her googly-eyed stare—"whoever you think he is, he's not him. You're just lonely, wishing he were, so I hate to burst your bubble and all, but have some dignity, huh?"

The woman's cupid bow of a mouth shocks open while Jase's dimples deepen. She sputters a response that never quite forms actual words before she huffs and stalks away.

The minute she does, I feel bad. I shouldn't have said that. It's not her fault he's standing there emitting *I'm a celebrity* vibe, while I sit here coping with a shitty day, feeling insecure next to her natural beauty.

"Shit," I mutter and then abruptly stand.

"Where are you going?" Jase's hand is on my arm and the second the two of us realize it, the second we jolt from the connection, he takes it back.

"To apologize to her. I was a bitch. It's not her fault I've had a shit day. Week. Month." I chuckle self-deprecatingly and wonder why this man hasn't already bolted the other way since I'm showing my true—*crazy*—colors right now.

"No. It's fine. Let her go." There's compassion and understanding in his voice that I don't deserve. "I want no part of that."

I stare at his narrowed brows, grateful for the understanding and grace this stranger just gave me but needing to find my footing again.

"No part of what?"

He shakes his head ever so slightly. "Never mind."

"Yeah, well, you need to have a bit more dignity for yourself than letting women fawn all over you like you're someone you're not."

"What does it hurt if it's going to make them feel better or brighten their day?"

"Do you know who *they* think you are?"

"I have a clue. Yes."

"That means this kind of thing happens all the time then."

"It does." He nods and I study him closer. The hint of dark brown hair that peeks out from beneath his hoodie. The gorgeous face. The body hidden by the generic-looking sweatshirt. He could be anybody.

And nobody.

"There are enough wannabes in this town," I say. "Isn't it better in the long run to just be you and not pretend?"

"Depends on your perspective."

Apparently finding my footing means I'm a Grade A bitch.

Shit.

And why is he so damn attractive when he fights that little boy smile on his seriously sexy, grown-man body?

"Forget I said that." I hold my hands up. "I apologize. You didn't deserve that."

He angles his head to the side and those ice-blue eyes hold mine. "You're right. I didn't. And it's a little presumptive to think I'm here asking for your number."

It's my turn to stutter. "I've sworn off men so I assure you I didn't say that. Or even think it."

"Yes, you did. You wouldn't have been so protective of us and our conversation if you hadn't."

"Protective of us?"

"You ran off my admirer." His words are accusatory but his smile and expression are playful.

I don't want them to be playful or him to be attractive or sexy. Charming. That's what he is in the most lethal of ways. He's not my type—so very far from it—and last I checked, I've sworn off men for the time being after *Fuck You, Paul* showed me his true colors.

But he is flirting with me, isn't he?

Get a grip. Being nice is not the same thing as flirting. Clearly, I need an ego boost if I'm thinking some tattooed hottie in the coffee shop is flirting with me when all he did was bring me something I dropped and tell me my name is fitting.

"You're overthinking," he asserts.

"And you're presumptive and—"

"Perhaps." He shrugs. "But regardless of what you say, I know a woman who wants me when I see one."

Jesus. Good thing I wasn't taking a sip of my coffee or I'd have just spit it out. "Did you really just say that?"

His eyes light up. "I did."

"Leave it to a man to think he's the center of every woman's world." I shake my head and take a seat to facilitate this conversation being over. "I take back my apology. You do, in fact, need to find more dignity."

He purses his lips and nods as if the hint to leave me alone has been heard but then taps his finger on the table beside my iced coffee. "For what it's worth, Hendrix, he sounds like an asshole."

"Who does?" My eyes meet his, yet my mind's still repeating the way my name sounds rolling off his tongue.

"Whoever you were talking to on the phone. The man who made you swear off men, I presume." He holds his hands up. "Unsolicited opinion and all."

"You know what they say about opinions." I lift my eyebrows as if they're finishing the old adage for me.

"I do. Funny how willing you were to give yours though, so what does that say about you?"

"Touché. *And warranted.* Like I said, it's been quite the . . . *month.* Thanks for giving me back the card I dropped. I appreciate it."

"Are you blowing me off?"

"I am. Yes." I smile. "Clearly, it's something you've never had happen before, but unlike the rest of them, I have self-respect."

"Glad we established that fact." He gives a definitive nod but there's something about him, that even when he's getting a dig in, I still find myself wanting to like him.

"Me too," I say and take a deliberately long sip on my straw to signal to him that once again, this conversation is over.

What I don't expect is for him to lean down close to my ear and murmur, "For the record, all men aren't cheating assholes." Chills chase over my skin as he pauses. "Some, in fact, are good guys."

"And are you one, Jase?" I ask without thinking.

He leans back so that our eyes meet. The warmth of his breath flutters over my cheek as my own stutters. There's an intensity in his eyes that I didn't expect and a weird want to understand it.

"Depends on the day." As he takes a step back, that grin returns full force. It screams mischief and desire all in one tantalizing and confusing turn up of his lips. And then he walks away, throwing, "Later, Cookie Cutter," over his shoulder as he goes.

I stare after him. I'd like to think it's unknowingly but it's not. I'm no better than the other women and girls in this place whose eyes are glued to him as he walks out the door and onto the street.

He looks both ways for a beat before heading to the left and out of sight.

But I keep staring at the glass storefront and the passersby.

And I keep wondering why my interaction with him feels like it's been the best part of my day—*no, week*—when he's just some random guy in Josie's who's pretending to be someone he isn't.

He's handsome. I'll definitely give him that.

But he's so not my type. Not the tattoos nor the combat boots. Not the cocky smirk nor the self-assurance. Not his effortless charm nor the way he finds it amusing that women think he's someone different. Not *anything* and yet all of those things keep me looking after where he just was.

It's Paul's fault. Has to be.

He's ruined the button-up dress shirt and Oxfords look for you. The clean-cut hair and the unmarked skin.

However, as I force myself to focus back on my design sketches, I catch myself glancing up now and again to check the doorway. *Did that really just happen?*

CHAPTER
four

BECAUSE BEING AN ADULT MEANS YOU SOMETIMES HAVE TO DO THINGS you don't want to.

Hendrix's words repeat in my head. Sure, they were meant for her husband? Boyfriend? Whoever the prick was that cheated on her, but right now, as I clomp my way up the stairs and into my brother's practice, that's what I keep hearing.

And fuck if they don't feel like a rope slowly tightening around my neck.

I take a deep breath and trace the line of the pink heart on the inside of my wrist. The rebel in me fights conforming, struggling against proving my brother right.

But the band member in me knows I can't risk everything my friends and I have worked so fucking hard for.

I pull open the door and walk through the reception area like I own the place despite the dread that drags its way through me.

My brother looks up from his desk and takes notice of me through the glass wall of his office. I have to give it to him. He doesn't lift his eyebrows or smirk like I would if the roles were reversed. He just drops his head back down and finishes writing whatever it is he's writing while I open the door, step inside, and prove his parting words when I left earlier to be right.

I stand there for some time with the pen scratching across the paper being the only sound in the room. He sets it down and then looks up, his blue eyes meeting mine.

"Tell me what I need to do," I say, hands out and resignation like a knife in my chest.

"Did you sleep with her?"

"Who? Hendrix?" I ask, thoroughly confused.

"Who's Hendrix?" No sooner are the words out of his mouth than I realize what I just said. No doubt we have the same confused expressions on both of our faces.

Where the fuck did that come from, Jase?

"She's no one. Long story. And sleep with who?" I ask.

"Lori. The journalist. The pot stirrer."

"No." I shudder.

"You didn't touch something that moves?" He snorts. "Impressive."

There's the snark and condescension. *That didn't take long.*

"So then why is she so pissed?" he continues.

"Because I wouldn't?" I shrug, remembering the endless hints she dropped expressing *her* interest. "Fuck if I know."

"But you do know, don't you?"

"No. I really don't. It could be because I didn't sleep with her. It could be because like we've previously discussed, she's an opportunist. It could be that she gets promoted depending on how many articles she writes and how much interaction they get. And for some fucking reason, the ones about me are a goldmine for her. I don't fucking know. Then again, people choose to do a lot of things in this godforsaken town and none of it really has to do with me."

"And you think that answer is going to satisfy Judge Watkins?" he asks stoically.

Judge Watkins. So the prick has a name. Perfect.

"If I don't know, Nathaniel, then I don't know."

He leans back in his chair and steeples his hands in front of him, fingertips touching and Rolex glinting in the overhead light. "You need a new image."

"Whatever." I roll my eyes as visions of me with zero tattoos in a stuffed suit and glasses flash through my mind. Then I look at my brother and see the same thing and cringe. My chuckle is unforgiving. "No thanks. I'll take my chances."

He waves a hand. "Fine. Do you want to tell the guys or are you going to leave it to me to tell them that they need to find a new drummer for the tour?"

My stomach drops. "They wouldn't do that." My voice is barely audible.

"No? They're just going to let months' if not a year's worth of planning for the concert promoter, for the band, for the staff, for the fans, be all for nothing because you refused to walk the straight and narrow for a few months?"

"The judge will lift the restriction. The last one did for the gigs we played in South America last year."

"Does the band even know your participation is in question or were you keeping that from them?"

Those words are like a knife to my heart. *It's never been a problem before.* But when I look up to meet his eyes, I'm sure he knows the answer—they don't.

"Tickets would need to be refunded. Venues reimbursed. Crews that have spent all this time prepping, out of jobs." He blows out a whistle, clearly insisting on twisting the knife. "I think you need to choose wisely here."

"Fine. Okay. I'll go feed the homeless. I'll try and sign on to do more charity work. I'll make sure the pictures taken of me are there."

"You already do that," he says. "Once a week, you spend the day at the Mission down in the Third District. Everyone who knows you knows that. That's not an image makeover."

"Well, it's better than pictures of me in the clubs, right?"

"There will be no more pictures of you in clubs because you won't be going to any. You're going to find yourself a homebody all of a sudden who prefers to go to charity galas and barbecue in the backyard with friends rather than live it up on the town."

My jaw clenches but I control the urge to tell him he's fucking crazy.

You did this to yourself, Giz.

"Fine. Sure. Why don't you take my balls while we're taking away my manhood?"

"And you said I was being dramatic. Jesus, Jase—"

"I'll post about my trips to the homeless shelter. Make my time spent there more known." The thought makes my stomach pitch—using someone else's demise to make yourself look better—but I can't fuck the band over.

"That's not going to cut it. It's not enough."

"Then what will, Nate the Great?"

He glares at me. He has always hated that nickname. "You're going to get married."

It's my turn to glare at the dropped bomb. I chuckle. "That's fucking hilarious."

"I don't seem to be laughing."

"That's crazy talk."

"In a town full of crazy talk and where nothing is as it seems—according to you and your opportunist photos—it's not so crazy."

"And you're telling me you think everyone's going to buy this shit—that me, Jase Gizmodo—serial dater—"

"The word 'dater' is a bit generous, don't you think?"

"Serial *fuckboy?*" I lift my brows as sarcasm drips from my words.

"Much better."

"Of course it is. Anything for you to put down what I do in my life that you'd kill to be able to do in yours." The animosity stretches between us in a stare full of clenched jaws and unspoken words.

Nathaniel's Adam's apple bobs. "Judge Watkins is as conservative as conservative can be. He's big on family values, not so big on tattoos, and no doubt listens to classical music because even Christian rock is too scandalous for him."

"No doubt he's a hypocrite with a mistress on the side and has a secret fetish."

"And if he did, that wouldn't matter to your case," he says.

"Then find a reason, a conflict of interest, over why he can't make a ruling in this matter."

"That's not how it works. This is a probation request. He has no personal stake in this case that would be grounds for me to ask that."

"Then does he have a daughter or a niece or something I could date? That would cause enough of a conflict."

"You're grasping at straws, Jase."

"Then give me another option here," I all but beg, "because you're making it sound like straws are all I have to hold on to."

"I gave you the option."

"Marriage?" I can barely get the word out. "No, it's not."

"Well, like I told you, I have a good working relationship with Judge

Watkins. I've had a pre-emptive conversation with him over the matter. I explained about the world tour and about how we'd prefer to resolve the matter in the coming months to guarantee that you can leave the country. I asked him what effort of good faith he needs to see from you, to believe that your past record and career doesn't define the man you are despite it doing just that thus far."

"His response?" I already know, but I'm asking anyway.

"He said as a good, Christian man, he knows family is the one grounding force for most troubled men."

"Men like me." Sarcasm drips from the syllables.

"In his jaded eyes, yes."

"Then suggest to him that I'm coming to live with you. *My family and an officer of the court.* And we can be done with this. You can report back that I'm home reading Crime and Punishment every night and teaching Sunday school and then all can be right with the world."

"Abigail agrees."

"Why would you go and talk with her?" I groan. I love my agent to death—she does a great fucking job—but she'd do anything to make her job easier. She loves squeaky clean when I'm a little more grit and rough edges.

"Look. You're a part of BENT," he says, referring to the name of my band, "but you're acting like the only one in the world you care about is yourself. I know that's tough to hear. Even tougher given our . . . *history*, but I'm on your side."

"This is bullshit, Nathaniel. No one gets married to prove to a judge that they're stable. Marriage doesn't equal stability. Look at our family, for fuck's sake." My voice breaks with the desperation I suddenly feel but don't want to admit to.

"I understand your hesitancy—"

"Resistance—"

"Fine. Yes. Resistance." He blows out a sigh. "But this is what he told me he needed to see to know you've made progress. That you've seen the error of your ways and want to better your life."

"Then he's really not as smart as he should be to sit on the bench if he thinks a paper marriage certificate means all my sins are washed away."

Nathaniel clears his throat, but there's something about the look on his face that says there's more. And that look isn't what I want to see right now.

"What is it?" I ask.

"You're right. It would be naive of him to think that if you got married out of the blue that you'd suddenly become a saint."

"What did you say?" I groan.

"I planted the seed is all." He shrugs like it's no big deal, but he forgets that I know him better than most. I know that action and the pinched look on his face says he's already done something. "Watkins thinks that over the past few months you've been slowly falling for your soon-to-be wife. Quietly. Out of the limelight. That she's changed you and you can't wait to marry her and settle down."

"You're fucking serious, aren't you?"

"Dead serious."

If I didn't hate the idea so much, I'd think it was rather genius. Play a part, act like I've done my whole life, and then win whatever reward there is to win—in this case, my freedom to tour overseas.

"But how does me *quietly* falling in love negate the fact that the gossip sites, that Lori, posted more shit about me just this week?"

"Because when all of a sudden those posts stop, when it's you holding your wife's hand as you go out to dinner rather than getting wasted at a club, he'll think you've seen the error of your ways and have grown up."

"This is absurd." I move about the room, needing to abate some of my nervous energy. Needing to knock some sense into myself from agreeing to this ridiculous idea.

"Perhaps, but the answer is pretty clear-cut to him. Show you're settling down over the next few months, and he'll lift the travel restrictions."

"That's some subjective bullshit if I've ever heard it."

"It is. But it's what he asked to see."

"He put this in writing somewhere, right? *Jase marries and therefore he gets to leave the country for work.* Because I gotta tell you, Nate, that doesn't feel like the most secure legal offer if it's just a verbal undertone said in a back chamber without anything to back it up."

It's Nathaniel's turn to be offended but my question is valid. "Nothing's guaranteed, but if precedent prevails, then yes. Judge Watkins and I have been through this before—a little in-chambers negotiation on how I can help my client get the desired result. He hasn't reneged on one yet. He gave his word. I gave mine." He clears his throat. "Don't dishonor my word."

I nod, but every second with this idea in my head feels like acid dripping into my gut. "Marriage. Jesus fucking Christ."

"I know." His voice is softer, more compassionate. "In our family that's like a four-letter word."

"For who?" My back's up and the hurt that underrides everything I do is ignited. "For you? Because last I looked I'm the one who got the short end of the stick, *brother*."

Nathaniel holds his hands up in front of him. "I didn't mean anything by it. I was just stating that I get why you're hesitating."

"You don't know shit about shit." I roll my shoulders. *How could he? I dodge and deflect. Isn't that par for the course when it comes to me?* "Say I agree to this . . . *bullshit*. Who exactly am I going to marry?" Even the word feels foreign on my tongue.

"Someone who has something to benefit from it like you do. A woman who needs your stardom for her own reasons and someone who seems wholesome to make you appear more grounded."

"I already don't like where this is going."

"It's called a PR stunt. It happens all the time. Non-disclosure agreements are signed. Public events are planned and staged. Everyone smiles pretty and plays the part for a set amount of time before irreconcilable differences make it too hard to continue."

"I'm aware. I've seen it with my own eyes—it's Hollywood, after all . . . but you don't think the judge knows this?"

"Which is why I planted the seed I planted. Now it's up to you to water it and make it grow."

I level my brother with a dubious glare. "I'm not a fucking gardener. This is my damn life."

"Then maybe you should treat it as such." His words are a stark rebuke that I let roll off my back. "Abigail and I have compiled a list of suitable women we think would be willing to step into the role. Women we think Watkins would find suitable as well."

I take a seat, prop my elbows on my knees, and hang my head. This is really fucking happening, isn't it?

"We'd make the breach of confidentiality so damning that they wouldn't risk telling anyone that they weren't madly in love with you after a secretive, whirlwind romance."

"Great. I'm so fucked up that you have to threaten a woman to marry me. And in the same breath, how is it a whirlwind if we've been together for months?" I look up and meet his eyes.

"We'd iron out the details obviously, get the story and timeline straight before we went public. I'm just talking hypothetical right now."

"Fucking perfect." I lean my head back and chuckle. It sounds like desperation.

But my brother gives me the moment to think. To hate the idea. Then to come to terms with it. And then to realize how much I loathe the fake bullshit in this town—the one that surrounds me on the daily and that I try to avoid.

"Go home. Sleep on it. Abigail will be here tomorrow at eleven. She's going to bring the three potential business partners with her for you to meet—"

"Christ," I mutter and put my sunglasses back on as if that's going to help the matter. "Business partners? That's the last thing I'd call my fake wife."

"She's going to email their profiles to you later for you to check out, but she's pretty sure she has your type down."

"Sounds so romantic."

"Since when are you into romance, brother?"

"Let me guess, one's a wannabe model, another's trying to get her big break in the music industry, and the other is . . . let's finish out the trifecta . . . is sick of sleeping on directors' couches—to put it politely—and might benefit from changing things up." I stand and shake my head. "No. No. And no."

"We'll find a way to make it work."

"Of course you will." I move toward the door. "And you're insane if you think it won't get out. If you think for a fucking second that she'll keep her mouth shut and the truth won't be posted somewhere before all is said and done, you're fooling yourself."

"That's why there are legal ramifications. A large payment with incentives. Benefits for her. A deal so sweet and damning that no one would ever think of breaking it. Plus she gets you for a few months."

"I'm sure you can tell by my lack of expression how thrilled I am about this," I say drolly.

"It'll work. I know it will. Like I said, we've vetted the women—"

"Easy to say when it's my life and not yours." I pinch the bridge of my nose and make the one decision I can still make in this whole situation. "This is fucking fucked. I'm not meeting with those 'candidates' tomorrow."

"Jase." It's a warning that has me stopping and looking back at my brother.

"No. If I have to play this charade, then I want there to be no mistake with the judge that whoever I'm with is real."

"What the fuck does that mean?"

"I have an idea." I throw up my middle finger as a means of goodbye and then keep walking through the lobby and out the door.

An idea . . . that is brash and ridiculous and definitely not well-thought-out.

Sounds on-brand for me.

CHAPTER
five

Hendrix

THE MUSIC IS LOUD AND MY MUSE IS FLOWING FOR THE FIRST TIME IN days as I swing my hips and pipe yet another sample design on the top of the cookie.

I hum as I decorate, the defiant *screw you* lyrics of my favorite artist like an anthem I can relate to more than anything else in my life right now.

I've shut out life. Paul and his indiscretions. Paul's unabashed theft of my savings. My landlord informing me that my rent will be increasing in two months. The crippling pang of heartbreak that hits out of nowhere every once in a while when I think I've already gotten over it.

So I sing.

I decorate.

I shimmy like no one is watching.

And when the phone rings and it blasts through my Bluetooth speaker, my yelp can probably be heard down the street.

A quick glance at the clock tells me it's after eight in the evening, long past closing time, and so I don't owe it to whoever it is to pick up their call.

But a customer is a customer, so I lower the volume and answer, "Cookie Cutter, this is Hendrix, how may I help you?"

And then in that beat of silence when no one responds, I wage an internal debate over whether I should have said *can* instead of *may* and which one is actually right.

Ridiculous, but a way to fill the fleeting silence.

"Is it true what you said, Hendrix?" The honey-coated-over-gravel voice says my name and I know who it is instantly.

"Jase? How did you . . . never mind." A simple internet search would tell him my phone number since he knew the business name. I'm flustered by the unexpected call, and it takes me a second to gather my thoughts. "Is it true that I said what?"

And while I sound bothered, a small part of me, the part in every single person that heartache can try but can't exactly crush, flutters—for reasons I'd rather not acknowledge.

"About needing money to save your business."

I pause at his words. *Me and my big mouth.* "What are you getting at?" I look around the bakery as if someone is there waiting to prank me.

"I was curious if you were serious. Is money really something you need?"

I laugh self-deprecatingly and it sounds like how I feel—confused. "I'm sorry. I—I just met you, why would I tell you that?"

"Because you want to. Because it's been a shit month, and I'm a nice guy. You know as much as I do that it's killing you not to say, 'Yes it's true,' and then proceed to tell me what a prick that guy you were on the phone with was to you."

"You have an active imagination, I'll give you that." I lean my ass against the kitchen island and smile.

"I do and you know you desperately want to even if it's simply to keep me on the phone a bit longer because you like how the sound of my voice makes you feel."

"And now that imagination has kicked into overdrive."

"So, then what you said was true. You need money to save your company. Why?"

"Why what?"

"Why do you need the money? Do your cookies taste like shit? Are you—"

"They taste like fucking heaven," I say emphatically, drawing a deep, rumbling laugh through the line.

"A woman who believes in herself. I like it. So why don't they sell?"

The man's asking questions that are none of his business and yet I feel compelled to answer him. Maybe it was the kindness in his eyes or maybe it was his undeniable sex appeal—I don't know. All I know is I want to tell him.

"What did the note say?" I ask.

"Note?"

"On the napkin the woman handed you. You want to know my business, I think it's only fair that I get to know yours."

He stutters a laugh, and I can picture that smile and those dimples deepening. "That's fair."

"Then what did it say?"

"Nothing. I paid her to walk up and hand it to me. Its sole purpose was for you to be jealous so that you'd be forced to say yes."

"You're full of shit."

"Most of the time, maybe. But not on this."

I roll my eyes even though he can't see it and shake my head ever so slightly. "Wait. Say yes to what?" Exasperation and good humor tinge the edges of my tone.

"Look something up for me."

My first thought is, don't tell me what to do. My second is, "Why?"

"Because it will make you believe me when I tell you I know how to fix your problem."

"You don't even know my problem."

"I know you need money. Customers. New business. Is that not enough?"

I'm already not liking this topic despite enjoying this conversation. Or more along the lines of, I'm liking who I'm having it with. "Okay. I'll play your game." I wipe my hand on my hand towel and move over to my computer. "What am I looking up?"

"The name Jase Gizmodo."

"Uh—"

"G-I-Z-M-O-D-O or Gizmo for short with a hard G."

I laugh at that. "Noted. Hard G."

"I was teased way too many times by kids who chose to use a soft G."

"I bet—*OH*," I gasp as my screen populates and picture after picture of the man I met earlier, the man whose voice is in my ear, fill the screen in front of me.

Holy.

Shit.

The man from Josie's Java with the ice-blue eyes, the undeniable charm, and the roguish smirk is the drummer of one of the most popular rock bands on this planet—BENT.

Words escape me. I wish they would have escaped me earlier when I told him to have more dignity for allowing women to assume he was someone special. Different. Famous.

He's famous all right.

And if I spent any iota of time wondering what those hinted tattoos looked like, my next scroll down gives me an answer in living color. Images of them on a shirtless Jase—or Gizmo, who the world knows him as. In the image staring back at me, he's standing with his arms out, his muscles defined on broad shoulders and toned arms, with an array of varying tattoos on his arms and chest. The image cuts off at his lower waist but gives the image's intended audience exactly what they're hoping for—the indentations and the deep V just before his hips.

My cheeks flush, and it's Jase clearing his throat on the other end of the connection that reminds me he's there while I'm ogling his body.

"Jase, huh?" I state.

"If I had told you my name was Gizmo—"

"With a hard G."

"Yes, with a hard G"—he chuckles—"would that have made a difference? Would you have known who I was?"

Yes. No. All he had to say was that he was part of BENT and I would've known.

"Hawkin Play or Vince Jennings, you would have known off the bat, right?" he asks, mentioning the band's lead singer and guitarist. "But not Gizmo. You see, drummers never get any love."

There's certain truth to his statement, a raw honesty in it, but I don't sense any animosity in the words. Rather it's more playful, much like his demeanor was earlier.

"Oh, I have a feeling you get plenty of love, Gizmo."

He chuckles. It's low, loaded with warmth, and does something funny to my stomach. "Please. Call me Jase."

I pause, wondering why it feels so intimate for him to ask me to call him a name no one else does. At least it seems so by the screen scrolling in front of me.

"You know I feel like a total ass right now, right?" I ask.

"For?"

"You let me believe that you were some wannabe trying to reel in the women because of it—"

"You believed that all on your own, Hendrix. *You assumed.* I simply chose not to correct or argue with you over it."

"Well, you should have," I state definitively.

"Really?" He chuckles. "In our short interaction, you seemed so *taken* with the male species in general, I'm not exactly positive you would have loved a man you've never met before arguing with you over your very assertive opinion."

I open my mouth to argue but then shut it because he's right. Nail on the head, annoyingly right. "You still should have told me."

"I'll remember that for next time I meet you for the first time."

"Funny."

"I try," he murmurs.

Silence stretches between us as I let it sink in that Jase Gizmodo is on the other end of the phone. And not just on the other end, but the man actively sought out my phone number to call me. *But why?*

"Well, I hate to break it to you, but I don't have any stunning revelation to share with you as to who I am. I'm not famous. I don't do any surprising parlor tricks to wow your friends and make them like me. Hell, I don't even know what I'm saying right now . . ."

"No tricks needed. I like who you are or I wouldn't be calling."

"And why is that again? The you calling part."

"Because you mentioned needing money to save your business—the cookie bakery, I presume."

"You've presumed right." Those words are so hard to say. Failure isn't an easy thing to admit.

I wait for him to ask why, to question why I'd partially put my faith and future in another person's hands—much the same way I've questioned it every minute of every day since I walked in on Paul and the bimbo—but Jase doesn't.

"Okay, well, I might have a way, *an opportunity*, for you to earn what you need to help you stay afloat."

"That sounds shady as shit. 'Earn what I need' spoken from a man I just met."

He barks out a laugh. "You sure don't disappoint, do you?"

"What . . ." Does that mean? *That I don't disappoint?* But the thought dies because I'm still trying to focus on the opportunity he's hinting at that will allow me to *earn* what I need.

And this is where my brain needs to take a rest. I'm a baker. He's a famous musician. The man is calling you for cookies. Probably a lot of cookies. That's the only reasonable answer for this very bizarre, flirty, and coded conversation.

"How big is the order?" I ask.

"Order?"

"Yes. How many cookies do you need? I'm short on staff and supplies—hence my off-the-cuff comment about needing money," I say to simply save face. "So it just depends on the timeline and quantity needed if I could take your order."

"I don't want your cookies, Hendrix." The way he says those six words sounds like the most seductive refusal I've ever heard. He laughs. "Yes, that sounded just as bad as we both think it did."

"Glad I wasn't the only one thinking that. But I am wondering if I should be offended that you don't like baked goods." I pause.

"Something tells me that no single cookie order will net you the kind of cash you muttered at the coffee shop."

"Oh. Okay. So no cookies then?"

"No."

"Then . . . what?"

He clears his throat. "I can't exactly tell you."

"You're offering me an opportunity to make a considerable amount of money but you can't tell me what that is? You do realize that's—"

"Weird. Strange. Yes. And totally not my idea, but Legal says in order to talk about it, they'd need you to sign some documents first to ensure confidentiality is kept."

"A non-disclosure agreement?"

"Yes."

"Just to talk about whatever it is you want to talk about?"

"Yes."

"Again . . . you're aware how odd this sounds?"

"I am. But I'm also aware how easy it is in my line of work to discuss something with someone and then have it splashed all over the internet because the best gossip goes to the highest bidder."

"Like I'd even know who to or how to sell your juicy story."

"You'd be surprised how quickly people come out of the woodwork and what they offer when they know you're associated with me."

That very fact is scary and probably truer than I want to acknowledge. And still . . . very weird to be asked this.

"Is whatever it is you want to do, or me to do, or talk about me doing, illegal?"

"No."

"And yet you're calling me, a woman you just met . . ."

"Look, I know it sounds crazy, but there's a situation and my lawyer and team told me I needed someone to help me with it. They made their own suggestions and none of them called to me in the way you did."

"Called to you?"

"Yes. You were the first person I thought of."

"Why?"

"I'm known for being impulsive." There's humor in his voice but also a good dose of honesty, if I'm reading his tone correctly.

"But we only just met. You don't even know me. I could be a serial killer or a stalker."

"True. You could be although in order to stalk me you'd have to know who I was, and I didn't exactly get that vibe then or now. I think the boyfriend would have been axed first if that was the case, and you were on the phone with him so we all know he's alive."

"There's time yet," I grumble as he laughs.

"And this is why I like you."

"Enough to ask me to sign an NDA to talk about things that we can't talk about so that I can—"

"Yes. *Please.* Are you trying to talk me out of not liking you, because if you are, you're starting to do a good job of it."

"Way to sweep a girl off her feet," I tease.

"So?" he asks, and the hope in the word hangs on the line. I look around at my bakery, at the blood, sweat and tears I've put into this place so far, and acknowledge the real fear that I might lose it all very soon if something doesn't change.

Maybe this chance meeting is the change I didn't know I needed.

"Tell me something," I say.

"Only if I can get a yes or a no after I tell you."

"My name . . . why did you say it was fitting?"

"Jimi Hendrix was ballsy for his time. A little out there, complicated, daring, and beautiful all at the same time. That was also my first impression of you."

Of all the things I expected him to say, *that* was most definitely not it. I hate that tears are welling in my eyes from the answer. How is it that someone has seen me so clearly in such a short time? *And that I love that.*

"Yes," I say.

"Yes, you'll come tomorrow?"

"Yes."

"Why?"

Because I like your answer.

Because it feels good to be seen.

"Because let's face it, if I'm going to become a stalker, I need to start somewhere."

CHAPTER
six

Hendrix

To say my insides didn't do a little flip when I walked into the upscale offices in downtown Los Angeles knowing I was about to come face-to-face with Jase again would be a lie.

They did.

And then I felt like an idiot, holding a box of decorated cookies as I walked into the conference room to find a non-disclosure agreement sitting squarely in front of the seat the receptionist directed me toward.

You don't bring a knife to a gunfight. And you sure as shit don't bring custom-decorated cookies to an NDA-led meeting. *True class, Hendrix.*

I read the NDA with its clauses, its parameters, and its warnings, and hopefully understand enough of the legal jargon to get the gist of it. Just as I sign it, the door at my back opens.

I turn to find Jase standing there in his faded black T-shirt, which is snug in all the right places, and his trademark dimples deepening. "Cookie Cutter. You showed."

Uncertain what I should do, I rise from my seat and hold a hand out to shake his, but it's ignored as he pulls me in for a quick hug. I'm thrown by the action—by the firmness of his chest and biceps as they close around me, by the scent of his cologne, and the murmured, "Good to see you, Hendrix," before he lets me go.

I stand there, a little shell-shocked that he really is this normal, this warm. I've spent the better part of my night and morning becoming fascinated with the drummer Gizmo from BENT, but this is just Jase from the coffee shop.

"Hey." I smile and it feels inadequate as we hold each other's stares for a beat.

The throat clearing at our sides has me snapping my attention away from Jase and to the man standing beside him in an expensive, tailored suit. He holds his hand out. "Nathaniel Gizmodo, nice to meet you."

The similarities hit the minute he says his name. They have the same facial structure, the same build and coloring, even the same dimples, but they're most definitely polar opposites in style.

I take his hand and shake it. "Hendrix Wright. The pleasure is mine."

His smile is as polite as his handshake, but curiosity owns his eyes. He studies me as he moves around the table to the other side from where I was seated. Jase follows him.

"I see you've signed the NDA," Nathaniel says as he pulls the papers toward him. "Any questions?"

"Not that I know of. It seems pretty standard."

"Oh." He lifts his eyebrows. "You've signed NDAs before? Know much about them?"

No. Yes. Only the ones in romance books where the alpha hero makes the sweet, innocent heroine sign them to protect her from telling the world about his taboo and deviant desires.

But I don't think divulging that little nugget will make me look too intelligent or sane at this point in our conversation.

"No. I meant I didn't have any questions. It all seemed pretty straight—"

"Did you bring me cookies?" Jase asks as his eyes grow wide to match the same enthusiasm in his expression. Before I can answer, he's opening the box and grabbing one. His eyes lift to mine. "You did these? The design? The decorating?"

"I did." I nod as I glance down at the various cookies I designed around things I read were important to him—music notes, drum sets, album covers, and the band's name. "Just to prove that you do, in fact, want my cookies." I quirk a brow as Jase laughs.

A glance at Nathaniel has him angling his head to the side studying me, but I can't quite figure out what he's thinking. I'm not sure if that's a good thing or a bad thing.

"When I can't sleep, I bake." I shrug.

"Why couldn't you sleep?"

"Because I was busy googling everything there is to google about you."

"Well . . . that's sobering." He laughs, and I love that he's like this. Unaffected and carefree.

"I already confessed that I wasn't a serial killer so—"

"So you were making sure I wasn't," Jase says.

"Can you blame a girl? I mean, it's the Wild West out there these days."

"It sure is," Jase murmurs as the moment stretches. Smiles play at the corners of our mouths.

"So, we want you to marry him," Nathaniel says without warning.

"What?" I bark out but then realize they're serious. Dead serious.

No.

No again.

And what the hell. One more time—no.

I decorated cookies for hours last night. I may have played BENT's music to get more familiar with their songs. I may have stopped and listened to a particularly difficult drumbeat and thought of Jase and his irrefutable talent. I may have also wondered why Jase wanted to see me—and why I might possibly have to sign an NDA. But this? This was most definitely not it.

Nerves have me sputtering to give a better response and then when I do, something absolutely ridiculous comes out. "Whew, and here I was worried the two of you were into some kind of brother kink where you planned to share me."

I couldn't get two more different responses. Nathaniel's eyes bug out of his head with shock and discomfort. Jase runs a hand through his hair as he chuckles, his eyes suggesting he's game for anything.

Paul's reaction would most resemble Nathaniel's reaction so there's something . . . refreshing about the way Jase reacts.

"It's to repair his image and show he's settled down," Nathaniel states as he nervously turns his wedding ring around on his finger. "To save the band's world tour."

"To make the world and my band, not hate me," Jase says. We both catch Nathaniel start to but then stop the rolling of his eyes. I can't help but presume there's a rift between them, but that's for another time.

Right now? I've just been asked to marry a man I met yesterday. A man who's drop-dead gorgeous and everything I've never found sexy—arrogance, tattoos, rebellion—but do in *this* man. A man who's the exact opposite of Paul and I'm not certain why that seems to be so important—*enthralling*—to me.

"So you're telling me that marrying you would be doing the world a favor?" I laugh. What the hell even is that statement? And how arrogant does one have to be to make it?

"Well, when you put it that way." Jase snorts.

"Be serious," Nathaniel warns him.

"This is fucked up. I can't be serious when it comes to this," Jase says.

"Well, at least we can both agree on that," I say as nervous laughter bubbles up and sounds partly hysterical as it bounces around the room.

This. Is. Crazy. Talk.

"Can I explain?" Nathaniel asks.

"He's the serious one." Jase hooks a thumb at his brother.

"Clearly." I hold Jase's eyes and take in the lifted brow. I surprisingly hate and love this question.

"Jase here has a history of . . . let's just say, acting out."

"I like to have a good time. Sometimes that good time ends up with me having a nice chat with our friendly police officers. Other times, they like me so much, they want me to hang with them in a holding cell for a bit. Nothing violent." Jase holds his hands up. "A few misunderstandings here and there but nothing even remotely near the serial killer realm since that's where it seems you draw the line."

I bite my lip and fight the smile. It's hard not to when it comes to him, it seems. And I know about the trouble he's had here and there—my research last night served me well. "Marriage seems a little extreme though. Like . . . how is a marriage going to save a world tour? And why me when there are probably so many more qualified, carefree women fit to take the role? And how in the hell do you think anyone will buy this stunt? I mean—"

"Miss Wright—"

"She kind of babbles when she's nervous or overthinks. Give her a second to process," Jase says. Both Nathaniel and I look at his brother with the same dumbfounded expressions on our faces.

Why is this even a discussion, Hendrix? The answer is no. Point-blank. End of. No.

"Jase is facing a judgment in the courts."

"I'm on probation," Jase says.

"Which means he can't travel abroad, and therefore can't go on his slated world tour later this year without a judge's permission," Nathaniel continues, clearly irked by his brother's continual interruptions.

"Okay, but wouldn't you have considered this when you planned the tour in the first place?" I direct my question at Jase but don't miss the flicker of a smile at the corners of Nathaniel's mouth. It's obvious I just stepped into some kind of brotherly disagreement and unknowingly took a side.

"You're right, she *is* smart," Nathaniel says to his brother before turning back to me. "The answer is yes, you'd think so, but in the past, the judge signed off without hesitation. It was a given."

"But this time . . .?" I ask.

"New judge. Tighter set of handcuffs," Nathaniel says.

"Figuratively," I murmur more to myself than to the room.

"Yes." Jase smirks as he holds up his wrists. "Figuratively."

"And what exactly are you on probation for? I mean, you're asking me to marry you so it's a valid question, no?"

"Drunk and disorderly conduct. Criminal damage to property—"

"I was drunk and trashed a hotel room," Jase says, impatiently.

"Why?" My question is a reflex that has me cringing the minute it's past my lips.

"Good question and long story," Jase says. "I paid my fines. I did my community service. And I was given a three-year probation term of which I'm one year into." He shrugs. "I didn't hurt anyone. I'm not dangerous. It was just . . . it was what it was. Now I'm trying to find a way around one of the consequences so I don't fuck up my band and my commitment to our fans." His words are apologetic but there's anger somewhere in the mix. Shame too. And I don't know which one is more endearing coming from a man who comes off on social media like he doesn't give a fuck but in person clearly does.

"Okay and getting married is going to help all of this . . . *how?*" I ask.

"The judge's set to make the decision on whether Jase can travel or not—"

"The new judge," Jase says.

"Yes, the new judge isn't exactly thrilled with Jase's behavior and has indicated that he may restrict his access to travel. You can see how that doesn't bode well for a world tour that's set to take place in five months."

"Okay." I draw the word out as I do just what Jase implied I'm trying to do—process this whole idea. I'm not. Can't be.

"But what he did indicate was that he needed proof that Jase has settled down. That he's changed and grown up and has no intention of repeating any of his past behavior moving forward," Nathaniel continues.

"Oh, so he's of the *a good woman will change you* crowd," I joke and roll my eyes, but when I meet Nathaniel's gaze, I realize I just hammered the right nail on the head. "Oh. Perfect. My favorite type."

Jase chuckles like it's an agreement. "The marriage wouldn't be real but at the same time, would be real," Jase says.

"That clarifies things exponentially," I state sarcastically.

"I can see why you like her," Nathaniel says.

"Like, you're serious about this, aren't you?" It's rhetorical and terrifying that he is.

"Unfortunately, yes," Jase says. *Damn.* "I can't let my band or the fans down. I did it. I took the blame. My past mistakes shouldn't ruin everything for everyone else." The playfulness has been replaced by indisputable sincerity. "I assure you, marriage has never been in my plans, so this is just as shocking to me as it is to you. The only difference is I've had more time to process this."

I pinch the bridge of my nose and sigh. Jase Gizmodo of BENT is asking *me*—plain ol' cookie cutter me—to marry *him*, the huge world-renowned star.

Pretend marry.

Marriage of convenience marry, but still marry, nonetheless.

"Miss Wright? Are you okay?" Nathaniel asks.

"How about *no*? To both me being okay and to the question. Just no. On the account of the fact that one, this is crazy-pants shit that actually goes on in Hollywood and two, like, what the fuck, Jase? I just met you." Panic laced with some weird form of excited adrenaline spreads my lips into a smile that I don't feel like I can control.

"True on all accounts," Nathaniel says, "but at the same time, let's remove all emotions from it and look at what it actually is. A contractual obligation. A business agreement."

"With one of the biggest stars on the planet. No big deal." My words drip with sarcasm as Nathaniel nods and Jase grins.

But as our stares hold, I realize that I need to look at this through a different lens. To step back and remember what Jase asked me in his opening greeting when he called me yesterday. At the end of the day, this is about money. "Okay." I pause and I can see Nathaniel's defensive posture relax slightly. Clearly, he's noticed that mine has too. "So we're talking about a business transaction, right? I pretend marry you and in exchange you pay me a fee for this . . . inconvenience?"

"Inconvenience. Yes," Nathaniel says and smiles, his eyes flickering over to taunt his brother. Clearly, big brother is enjoying torturing little brother with my lack of a ringing endorsement.

"I'd like to think of myself as more of a good time than an inconvenience," Jase teases.

I have no doubt that he is just that.

"And you're correct," Nathaniel answers, getting back to business. "There would be payment."

"For how long does this farce last? How much is the payment? What are the parameters? How the hell do you fake a wedding when it's someone like *him*?" I ask the questions as fast as my mind can think them.

"It lasts until my next meeting with the judge, which is in a little over four months. He said if he's seen improvement, or rather proof of change, then it'll be a done deal, permission to travel granted. As for the parameters between you and Jase? If you agree to it, then we iron those out together. There will be minimal staged public appearances, outings where you'll need to accompany Jase, and . . . you'll have to move in with him to sell the authenticity."

Move in with him? I don't know why that never crossed my mind.

"The media is rabid, Miss Wright. They'll run with any reason to not believe this. For Jase's sake and the judge's sake, it needs to, by all intents and purposes, be real."

"Jesus," I mutter.

"You're telling me," Jase says dubiously.

"As far as a wedding, I'm thinking an elopement. Las Vegas is easy, quick, and will fly under the radar. Not too much fanfare, which shouldn't ruin or upset you, and any real ceremony you plan to have someday with a real husband," Nathaniel says in his all-business tone.

Real husband.

"So just pictures?" I ask.

"No. It needs to be legitimate. We'll file for the marriage license, do a small ceremony, leak a few pictures to the press, and then have you guys act all upset that your privacy was ruined. We'll create a backstory that you've been seeing each other secretly for months and that while it was a whirlwind romance, you guys are soulmates, yada, yada, yada."

"But I had a boyfriend. Three weeks ago," I state.

"Then you'll have met a few months ago. We'll paint the narrative that you were friends and once your relationship ended, Jase made a move."

Paul will lose his shit. Top-button-fastened, belt-on-without-exception, stiff-upper-lip Paul who loves rock music, will lose his ever-loving mind.

"It's just that easy?" I ask, surprised. "Feed lies to the press and they run with it?"

"Sadly, it is that easy," Nathaniel says.

I stare at both men with my head nodding and my brain trying to process the ridiculousness of all of this. "And how soon would this need to happen?"

"A few days? This weekend? The sooner the better to establish a record that Jase has calmed his ways," Nathaniel says while both Jase and I physically recoil. *A few days?*

"Oh," I say.

"*Oh* is much calmer than I would put it," Jase says.

"You're the one asking me to marry you," I tease. And then laugh. Anything to mask the nerves jittering through my system.

"And I'm the one over here freaking out about words like wedding and ceremony and the like so you're not alone on that. Believe me," Jase says and scrubs a hand over his face.

"Two hundred thousand dollars," Nathaniel says breaking the silence and knocking me out of my freak-out.

To go right back into a different, yet certifiable other freak-out.

"What?" I ask—*say . . . screech.* I then attempt to smooth over my gaffe with a cleared throat.

"Fifty thousand for each month married and most likely four months, so two hundred thousand dollars will be your compensation with a bonus of another seventy-five thousand to be deposited after one year's time to ensure continued confidentiality."

Did I just hear that correctly? Two hundred seventy-five thousand dollars for a four-month fake marriage with one very hot, very charming rock star?

"What's the catch?" It's the thought that prevails through the shock. "Because there has to be one."

"I'm the catch," Jase jokes but doesn't earn the laugh he's working for. Instead, I'm sitting here blinking as if that's going to help me comprehend what was just offered to me.

"Excuse me a second." I stand abruptly, wishing the office chairs weren't so posh so they'd make a ridiculous screeching noise across the floor—they don't—because I swear they can hear the pounding of my heart in the silence of the room.

"Take all the time you need," Nathaniel says. Flustered and overwhelmed, I push open the door in a desperate search for fresh air.

What. The. Hell. Just. Happened?

CHAPTER
seven

Hendrix

MARRY FOR MONEY.

Marry for pretend.

Marry to help him publicly, that then eases my financial burdens.

It's a no-brainer, right? He's hot as hell. He lives a lavish lifestyle that no doubt I'd never get a chance or pretend to live in otherwise. He purposely picked me.

Oh, and there's one other thing—the *Fuck You, Paul*—component of this. I've never met a pettier person than Paul Flanders, and I have no problem showing him that I can lower to his level.

You want to cheat on me with a waitress from Applebee's? Well, I can move on with Gizmo from BENT who's a thousand times better than you.

But that's bravado talking. The bluster and the ego, but fear is present too. A very real fear of *why the fuck am I even entertaining this crazy idea?*

To save your dream.

To build your business.

To further screw Paul since his parting words were that my cookie business was a pipe dream that would never amount to anything.

I reach for the conference room door, but hesitate, needing one second more. I have so many questions, so many conflicting emotions, so much everything and none of it makes sense.

This isn't me. The spontaneous, *color outside of the lines* person tempted to say yes. So why am I in fact, tempted?

"See? I told you she was cool," Jase's voice comes through the door. "We're chill. And the woman can bake."

I hold my breath, as if they can hear me breathing, and decide to wait another minute and eavesdrop. Nothing is beneath me right now.

"What am I missing, Giz?" Nathaniel asks. "She's not your type—clearly by the amount of clothes she has on alone."

"Hilarious."

"From what I can tell, she's intelligent . . . Wait—did you do something to her that you're trying to pay her off for?"

"You think so little of me."

"Fine. I'll ask it. Did you sleep with her, then?" Nathaniel asks.

"Nope. Not even on my radar. The prissy, preppy ones aren't my type. You know that."

I open my mouth to object, to argue, to what? Defend myself because I'm preppy and heard a comment I wasn't supposed to hear?

And why are my feelings hurt over something I know to be true? I'm a Type A, follow the rules, everything has to be planned girl.

Not to mention, I'm most definitely not the type who I saw on Jase's arm in the photos I looked at last night. Nowhere near the beauty or perfection of the women he's supposedly dated in the past.

This is a business contract. A mutually beneficial agreement. *Which does beg the question . . . will this be believable?*

Maybe I needed to overhear this conversation. Maybe I needed to get my feelings hurt as a reminder of what not to make this into—anything other than a *business* transaction.

With a renewed vigor and my head firmly in the right place, I open the door and walk back into the conference room. "So am I not allowed legal representation for this conversation?"

Both of their heads whip my way, expressions startling either over my question or fear they were overheard. I'm not sure which. "You don't trust us?"

I chuckle, suggesting bravado I don't feel. "That's like asking a sheep if she trusts the wolves surrounding her." I look from one to the other and back and cringe because I know I don't have the funds to hire a lawyer. Hell, I don't even have the funds to make it through the end of the month. And yet at the same time, it's important for them to know I'm not so desperate for money that I'm overlooking any obvious things.

What those are? Who knows.

"Fair." Nathaniel nods. "Would you like to call someone?"

He's called my bluff and now I'm going to have to admit that there's no one for me to call. The only lawyer I know is one of Paul's friends and . . . well, *fuck you, Paul.*

I take my time taking a seat, clasp my hands in front of me, meet their eyes, and say what I've seen people say in movies. "I have demands."

Gizmo lifts his eyebrows and fights a smile. He opens his clasped hands and invites me to speak. "I'd love to hear them."

Think quick, Hendrix.

"I have a huge order to fill. Cookies. I can't miss that deadline. I promised I'd deliver, and I'm only as good as my word."

"Okay. We'll make sure to give you the time you need to do that and organize whatever we need around that," Nathaniel says.

"And clothing. To look the part. I'm not talking Versace or whoever's the popular designer of the moment, but rather just a few upscale basics. All of my clothes are covered in flour or look like an apron." I smile and shrug. "I'm assuming you want someone to represent you properly on the public stage. The last thing I'd want to do is embarrass you with my Target- and Macy's-budgeted wardrobe."

"Reasonable. You'll have a shopping allowance," Jase says. "But for the record, you look great and don't knock Target or Macy's. I like their shit."

I appreciate him trying to make me feel better, but no doubt that threadbare shirt he's wearing cost more than my car payment.

"Like I said, just for basics. A little black dress. Some high heels since I don't own a pair. And whatever else you think I need to look the part for whatever appearances I'd need to accompany you to."

"Probably all of them," Nathaniel says, causing Jase to raise his eyebrows. Clearly, he wasn't warned of that particular detail—or was and doesn't like it. "What else?"

"I—uh—what is the rule on . . ." My cheeks heat as I stare at a man more gorgeous than I remember and recall the feel of his lips near my ear. "The physical." I feel like there's peanut butter on my tongue, making it hard to say those two words.

"This isn't *Pretty Woman*, Miss Wright. The exchange of money for your companionship and public appearances is in no way indicative of requiring sex. My client here is capable of keeping his hands to himself. With that said, there will be times when it's appropriate to share some affection—a kiss perhaps, holding hands, sitting on his lap at a party. Friendly and intimate 'gestures' for both the press and the public to buy that you are, in fact, his wife."

Great. Perfect. Even better.

Oh my God.

"Okay." My voice is barely a whisper and I dare not look in Jase's direction. If I do, I'll either burst out in a nervous and inappropriate giggle or avert my gaze due to embarrassment. "I took drama in high school. I can do the pretend kiss thing. *Easily.*"

"Easily," Jase mimics me with that crooked smirk.

Yes, I looked at him. I looked even when I had no intention of doing so, and now we're locked in that strange staring contest that stirs things inside me—sweet aches and slow burns—when *I'm not his type.*

Not to mention, he is not my type. Clearly. *Be kind to yourself, Hendrix.* This has nothing to do with types and everything to do with money.

"I don't facilitate payments for sex," Nathaniel says.

"And I don't need to pay anyone for sex," Jase adds.

"I doubt you do," I say and roll my eyes as his grin widens. "So, no sex. But this is fake, right? So does that mean no having sex with other people while we're 'married?'"

"Correct," Nathaniel says.

"Come on now," Jase groans. "Celibate for four whole months?"

"If I have to be sexually frustrated, Mr. Gizmodo, then you do too," I snap at him.

"Mr. Gizmodo?" He nods. "Is that what you're going to say when you're mad at me?"

"I'm not mad at you. I just think it's presumptive to assume that you're the only one who has needs. If I have to resist the urge, then so do you."

"Point well made," Nathaniel says.

"Besides, I'm doing you the favor here. I'd rather not be humiliated on a public stage that I'm so horrible in bed, my husband of less than four months can't keep it in his pants."

"Who told you that you were horrible in bed?" Jase asks, missing everything else I said.

"No one," I lie, thinking of Paul and the zingers he landed in that final fight. God, they've done a number on my self-esteem. "I said it merely to make a point."

But Jase holds his glance longer than he should, and that tells me he just might have seen right through me.

And that's unnerving on so many levels.

"You can call me Gizmo. Or Jase. Not Gizmodo," Jase says.

"He hates Jase," Nathaniel chimes in.

"Not when she says it," Jase says, which has his brother looking at him with a curious expression.

"I'll expect the blood tests showing you're clean as well."

"I don't do drugs," Jase says.

"I wasn't talking about drugs." My smile is short but pointed.

Jase sputters out a cough. "I don't have any sexually transmitted diseases."

"Great. Then it won't be hard to get that to me." I shrug. "I'll provide the same. It seems only fair seeing as you want me to live with you."

"Very fair," Nathaniel says as Jase glares at him.

"This conversation is something else," Jase murmurs like he's a bystander when he's the main subject.

"When it comes to the press . . . that terrifies me," I admit.

"Understandably. We'll keep interaction with them to a minimum. You're newlyweds who want your privacy. I'd suspect that your business might get a little busier than normal. We'll get a security guard stationed there to help you keep the crazies at bay and to keep you safe."

"A security guard?" I bark out a laugh.

"Yes. Trust me on this," Nathaniel says. "Granted we agree to each other's terms, we'll instate him tomorrow morning."

"It's not necessary—"

"It is. Just as a prenup is that you'll have to sign along with the contract stating you forfeit any legal claim to his property, wealth, and assets during and after the forgone failure of the marriage," Nathaniel says.

"Of course. What ridiculous person would assume they'd have any rights to it?"

"You'd be surprised," Jase says.

"Then there are the events you'll attend with Gizmo."

Events? Of course. He's a celebrity. The pictures I studied of him last night flash in my mind. Oh my God. That means I'll forever be on the internet linked with him like those other women were. "Like?"

"We'll get you a list but there won't be many. You're a woman who happened to fall in love with a drummer. We'll play the narrative to the press that you're very private and prefer to keep your life and your relationship as such."

"That will only fuel people's curiosity," I say.

"We'll figure out a happy medium. Maybe an interview to give them enough insight to back off. I'll talk with his team about it," Nathaniel says.

"Okay. It's only fair that Jase attends some of my engagements as well," I say.

Jase coughs into his hand in laughter. "Sure. Fine. Aunt Judy's christening? Little Ezra's bar mitzvah? What are we looking at?"

"We're looking at you valuing my time and life and obligations as much as I'm to value yours. Just because you have platinum records framed on a wall somewhere doesn't make you more important than I am."

"No one said it did," Jase says solemnly, almost as if he didn't realize his teasing could hurt my feelings.

"And no, I'm not talking backyard picnics with Grandpa Bob, but if this is to be believed, you have to integrate yourself into my life too. No one respects a woman who gives up everything they've worked for and are working for because they fall in love with a superstar."

"Savvy, beautiful, and self-assured." Jase lifts a brow. "I like it."

"Your flattery isn't going to get you anywhere," I say. *I know it already has. I'm here entertaining this, aren't I?*

"What else?" Nathaniel redirects.

"Will anyone else know the truth? Like, I can't let my family know, can I?"

"I'm sorry, no," Nathaniel says directly. "I understand it's hard to lie to family, but all it takes is one slip, one *I told Sally and she won't tell anyone* and then Jase is in trouble with the judge and the whole purpose of this charade is nullified."

"But my bandmates will know," Jase states, causing Nathaniel to whip his head toward him. "What? They have to. They'll see right through this bullshit if not. It's . . . I trust them with my life."

I don't know the brothers well enough to make assumptions on the look between them, but if I did, it would be hurt. That those words Jase just spoke, hurt his brother.

Nathaniel gives a curt nod, but I can see him struggling to allow this.

"And you pay the taxes," I add.

"What?" Nathaniel's voice sounds surprised.

"My net is fifty thousand a month. You're responsible for the taxes in however you want to cover them. This is California. That fifty would soon be twenty-five, and that's nowhere near enough if you want me to sell this lie like the best of them."

Nathaniel blows out a long, low whistle. "Miss Wright, you came to play."

"No. I know my worth." The comment is matter-of-fact and complete false bravado, but I don't see them noticing.

"Noted, understood, and agreed to."

I fight the gasp that wants to come out. *Why was that so easy?*

"Anything else?" Jase asks.

"There are a million more things that I'm sure I'm not thinking of but . . . I'm a little overwhelmed," I say.

"So that means you need to go home and think about it?" Nathaniel asks, clearly unhappy that I didn't just jump at the chance.

"Something like that," I say.

"Can I ask you a question?" Jase asks.

"Of course."

"Why would you say yes?"

I chuckle nervously. "Other than the money and you're going to help me save my dream?"

"Yes, other than that." Jase's voice is quiet. Curious.

"Because . . . fuck Paul Flanders."

"Who?" Jase snorts.

"My ex."

"Okay." He draws the two syllables out. "Explain."

"You're everything he isn't." Of all of the things I've said in this room over the past hour, that's the most honest of all of them.

"I don't know if that's a compliment or a slight," he says.

"Neither do I," I say quietly.

"Well shit, we're starting this off with a bang," he jokes.

"Don't you believe all relationships should be based on the truth?" I fire back.

"I do. I think." He leans back in his chair and crosses his arms with a shrug. "I don't know, I don't exactly do relationships."

"Then how is this one supposed to be believable?" I ask.

"You're the girl next door—*baker* next door. Grounded. Settled."

"Boring," I state.

"Normal," he corrects.

Normal. That word is like a knife to the heart, reminding me of Paul's bullshit and "hard truths" that he thought I should know about why he *had* to cheat on me.

There's no spontaneity. Everything is even-keel all the time. Normal as normal can be and normal is the death of any person wanting to live life. You were killing me, Hendrix. Little by little. Day by day. This blah *we lived in was killing me. God forbid she made me feel alive again.*

I shake the words from my head, but hell, they still taste acrid on my tongue.

Fuck you, Paul.

"This was your idea? To ask me?" I ask Nathaniel, my voice wavering.

"No." He lifts his chin toward his brother. "It was his."

I look from Nathaniel to Jase. To a man who's truly the opposite of everything I've ever liked or desired. And I do something that I think surprises the both of us.

I reach across the table, pull the contract that Nathaniel had set out earlier, and sign on the dotted line.

"Wow. Okay. What prompted that?" Jase asks.

I meet his gaze and hate the tears that well in mine. "I'm sick of being boring. Predictable. Normal. Maybe it's time I do something unexpected to tip the scales."

CHAPTER
eight

Gizmo

NATHANIEL LOOKS AT ME AND NODS.

"You have to promise me," he says.

"I'm not going to sleep with her. Have no intention to. She's good, real, wholesome."

"Like that's ever stopped you." He puts a hand on my shoulder and squeezes. "But I'm serious. Keep your hands off her."

I roll my eyes. "Thanks for being the pussy patrol, brother, but I can handle my own life."

"You sleep with her, you won't last the four months needed to prove this whole scenario out. Me being the pussy patrol"—he winces at the crass term—"is because you don't date a woman longer than a month once you sleep with her. That's a problem in this scenario. A huge fucking problem. You can't lock your fake wife up in your house when she's miserable because you've slept with and then discarded her."

"I don't do that."

"You do."

"It's mutual though. You make it sound like—"

"No one said you were a bad guy—or even original in doing this. All I'm saying is that this isn't going to work if you sabotage it in the only way you know how."

"People don't stay, Nathaniel. Look at what you did. So why does it matter if I sleep with people and then move on?" My words are a low blow. Ones that aren't warranted. His face pulls tight and his jaw clenches, but he doesn't react to them.

"Promise me, Jase. We're not doing all this hard work for nothing."

"I promise." I roll my eyes, stand, and move about the room.

I don't know how I feel. About this. About the conflict on Hendrix's face or the words she said—and didn't say—that are stuck in my head.

The woman is good under pressure. She doesn't back down or get intimidated when almost all other women would have asked where to sign on the dotted line without a second thought.

But she had many of them. She voiced them.

The terms are negotiated. The contract is signed. The deal is done.

And for a fucker like me who rarely thinks of anyone other than himself, I can't stop thinking about her or her expression when she signed the contract.

And then the concern and regret that glanced through it shortly thereafter.

"I'll be right back," I say to Nathaniel.

It only takes me a few seconds to get to the elevator and out to the parking garage where no doubt she parked. I spot her immediately on the far side of the vacant, dim structure.

"Cookie," I call out as I jog over to her.

"Everything okay?" Hendrix turns, and I'm greeted full force with the reason I suggested her for this in the first place. Her kindness. I know she must be a little overwhelmed and yet her smile is sincere and her hazel eyes are wide with concern as she asks me if I'm okay after everything we just unloaded on her.

"Yeah. Why?" I ask and study her.

Hendrix Wright is definitely not the typical Gizmo type of blond hair, long legs, and a cluster of fake things on her: hair extensions, breasts, eyelashes, nails, fillers, you name it. God love all of them too.

No. She's the total opposite. Natural with light makeup but that's it. Her hair is light brown and it falls in waves down her back. Her eyes are hazel, framed with thick lashes. They could be considered oversized, but that only showcases her every emotion. Her skin is pale, which serves to highlight the dusting of freckles across the bridge of her nose and the blush of pink on the apples of her cheeks.

And then there's her mouth. It's about as sexy as the curve of her ass. Her lips are full and a dark pink, and she has a tendency to bite her bottom lip, which drives me somewhat mad.

"Did I forget something?" she asks when I don't respond to her first question.

"No." I pull up to a stop right in front of her. "I just wanted to make sure you're okay."

She narrows her eyes at me. "Why would I not be?" An unnamed emotion flickers there but it's too quick to pinpoint.

"That was a lot and unexpected and . . . now that you've had a few minutes to decompress without Nathaniel or me staring at you, I just wanted to make sure you're okay." I chuckle. "I guess I already said that, didn't I?"

Her expression softens but her guard stays up. "For some reason this whole past month has been a lot and unexpected so it's just par for the course, I guess." She bites her bottom lip and shifts her feet. "Which like I said, is why I guess I said yes."

"Already getting cold feet?" I tease.

"Isn't that normal before a wedding?" She smiles and looks down at her twisting fingers. Funny how she was so sure of herself in that conference room but now that it's the two of us, she seems nervous.

"From what I hear. I've never been married before."

"Me either," she whispers.

"You sure you're good with this? With . . . everything?" Without thinking, I reach out and tuck an errant piece of hair behind her ear. It's something I've never done before, but it seems Hendrix has that effect on me. Asking someone to marry me. Chasing after them in garages. Tucking hair behind their ears.

"No." She laughs nervously. "I'll be fine. I'm not good at lying. Maybe I should have admitted to that before I signed on the dotted line that come to think of it, wasn't really dotted, but I'm not."

"It'll be fine. We'll stay in our little bubble. You'll get to do your work.

We're currently writing our next album so that will force me to create more since I'll be home more. We'll figure it out. No big deal."

But it's a huge fucking deal. A woman? Living with me? Usually they come for the night, maybe stay for two, and then they're gone. They never live with me.

"I know. It's just . . . weird."

I nod. My bandmates are going to lose their minds over this one. *They're going to give me so much shit.* Here I am thinking about the change to my life when hers is about to get thrown in a blender and turned on without the top put back on. I fear she has no idea what she's signed on for. The life I live and the people who demand everything from me isn't for the faint of heart.

"Thank you," I say softly. Contritely. "You're doing me a huge favor. I promise to try and protect you as much as possible from the outside chaos and noise."

Her smile is brave but she blinks away the threatening tears as she fights the regret brimming in her eyes. "I'm holding you to that."

Let's hope I don't let you down.

That seems to be my MO.

CHAPTER
nine

Gizmo

DROP THE DRUMSTICKS, AND GRAB THE TOWEL I KEEP CLOSE BY TO wipe the sweat off my face and neck.

"You good with that riff?" Vince Jennings, our lead guitarist, asks the three of us.

Hawkin Play, our lead singer, glances over to him and nods. He has a pencil in between his teeth while he scribbles out the lyrics we just figured out with another one in his hand.

Our fourth and final band member, Rocket, sits to the right of me, his eyes closed and head bobbing as he replays the whole song in his head. He's good like that. The lucky bastard can play something once and commit it to memory.

"I like it," Hawke says. "It still needs some tweaking but it has a good feel to it. You fine with it, Giz?"

"You know me, I'm good with anything." I take a sip from my water bottle. "Anything but that crap we put together last time. That was . . . dogshit."

Silence permeates the studio as everyone eyes the other one, waiting for someone's feelings to be hurt, before the four of us start laughing at the same time. "It was definite shit," Rocket says.

"The rhythm was so bad, so off, you couldn't even fuck to it if you wanted to," Hawkin says as he makes a play of jerking his hips spasmodically to make the point.

"I don't need the visual," Vince chimes in. "But you're right. It was fucking horrible and I'm the prick who wrote it."

"Well, it's about time you do something wrong because we were all getting sick of your perfection." I roll my eyes and toss my water bottle his way.

"It's hard to be this good," he says and slides down the wall until his ass is on the floor and his knees are bent in front of him.

This is what it's like when you've been best friends with your bandmates since your late teens. You can fuck with each other, be honest, and know it'll all be okay in the end because we always have each other's backs.

And that's not an easy thing to come by or be a part of in this industry of egos and vultures.

But it also makes what I have to say to the guys that much harder. Stalling, I check the setup of my drum set, as if I haven't already done it a few times today. I drop my rag to the ground and use my foot to mop up the sweat that's dripped there. The studio may be air-conditioned but take after take of this song has me drenched in sweat.

I glance back over my shoulder. Hawkin has taken a seat in the swivel office chair, Rocket is texting someone, and Vince has his head angled up to the ceiling and his eyes are closed.

"You want to tell us what's going on with you, Giz?" Hawkin asks without looking my way.

"Who said there was anything wrong?" I ask.

"Fuck, man. We know you," Vince says. "You don't miss fucking beats to save your life and yet you missed several today. Something is wrong. We know it. You know it. Just spit it the fuck out already."

I drop my head and nod. "Nothing's wrong. I'm trying to fix something before it becomes wrong."

"The tour? The travel? What?" It's Rocket that asks and that earns devastating groans from everyone.

"It's not a problem yet," I lie because it's just easier to break shit to them in pieces.

"Yet?" Hawkin crosses his arms over his chest as Vince tilts his head to the side.

"Jase?" Vince prompts.

"You know, the gift that keeps on giving. *My probation.*"

They all pause. They were there that night at the hotel. After, anyway. They helped me pick up the pieces of myself I was willing to leave behind. They talked me down from the ledge I was teetering on. They supported me through the charges. They know *the why* behind it all and yet here we are, still dealing with the ramifications all this time later.

"What's going on?" Vince's eyes narrow as Rocket steps closer.

"New judge. New hoops to jump through for approval, but we're figuring it out," I say.

"*We're?*" Hawkin asks.

"Nathaniel. Me. Abigail," I say, now clearly having their attention. And so I proceed to explain to them the whole scenario. Nathaniel's talk with the judge. Our discussion over having to get married. My decision to go along with it.

"It's just fucked in all the ways it can be fucked," I say, ending my drawn-out explanation. "It was never a problem before so I assumed it wouldn't be this time. I . . . fuck, I shouldn't have waited until now to ask, but I did and now we know and are trying to fix it."

But their faces say it all. Disappointment. Worry. Stress. Uncertainty. To cancel a sold-out world tour comes with ramifications on numerous fronts.

I try to fix things. "You guys are my family. The last thing I want to do is hurt you or the tour or the fans and so . . . that's why I decided to go along with it."

"Go along with it? *Christ,*" the always-single Rocket mutters. "You sure stuck your boot in that pile of shit, didn't you?"

"Yes, I did," I say, staring at the bottle of whiskey on the soundboard across from me. I'm desperate for it to wash down the disappointment I feel over letting my friends, my brothers, down.

"Look. It's a plan. Not sure if it's a good one, but it sounds like Nathaniel has the judge locked in on this and that the plan will work. Your brother might be a lot of things to you, but screwing you over isn't his style. So go along with it. Fine," Hawkin says, the clear leader in this band of equals. "But to some random woman you met in a coffee shop?" He snorts. "What the fuck, dude?"

"I know. It sounds crazy and—well, perfectly like something I'd do, right?" I ask to which a round of laughs sound off.

"No fucking shit," Vince says and helps himself to that whiskey that's definitely now calling *my* fucking name.

"I promise you, she's chill, normal, and won't fuck up the chemistry or vibe or any of that shit."

"Uh-huh," Vince says, eyes now back to being closed. "Nothing screams opportunist like the rando who's suddenly okay with marrying a strange man for no reason."

I know what he's saying. Even I'd probably think the same thing if the roles were reversed. "She didn't come looking for this. She has no Hollywood aspirations. I'm telling you, you guys will like her."

"How do you know that when you don't even know her?" Rocket adds.

"Kind of like the same way I knew to trust you assholes and your word when you shook hands over letting me in the band way back when," I say. Their expressions relay their disbelief.

Vince lifts his glass toward me. "We're holding you to this, Giz. Your promise to make this work."

"I know. My word is good," I say and hate that my voice almost breaks.

Silence settles in the room as the three guys I care about more than anything stare at me. I won't let them down.

"We know it's good. We were there that night." Hawkin tosses the half-eaten pack of Starbursts onto the table beside him. "But we're going to reserve judgment for this Hendrix chick until after we meet her. That's only fair."

"It is." I nod. "I'll make this right."

I meet each of their eyes to let them know I mean it.

"Fuck. Does this mean we have to throw you a bachelor party?" Vince asks, his eyes wide as we all recall how wild his was. And that's saying a lot with the life we lead.

"Nah, man. We're all good," I say. "Besides, we've been living in one for the past ten years."

"True. Very fucking true," Vince says and walks over, holding the glass out to me. I take a drink. "Thanks for coming clean and doing what needs to be done."

I clear my throat and hate what shame tastes like. "Anything for you guys. You know that."

"We do," Rocket says.

"Never a doubt." Hawkin pushes up out of his seat. "Is the kumbaya moment over? Can we get the fuck back to work now? The plan is to get this new material written before the tour starts."

"Please," I say, thrilled to have this off my chest and out in the open. To have the guys be cool with it.

And what do you know? I don't miss a beat the rest of the fucking session.

CHAPTER
Ten

Hendrix

"**W**HAT DO YOU MEAN, JUST KNOW EVERYTHING IS OKAY?" MY MOM asks in that searching tone of hers that says she's about to jump on a plane to make sure I am, in fact, okay.

And that's exactly why I'm telling her this. I know if she hears reports about Jase and me, or gets calls from the nosy neighbor across the street, Natalia, who sits on her front porch scanning the gossip sites all day, she'll be standing on my doorstep.

"There's a lot going on here, and I just wanted you to know that everything is okay."

"That fucktard Paul isn't messing with you, is he?" she asks. She went from one hundred percent *Team Paul* to *Fucktard Paul* in a matter of a month. Gotta love moms who have your back.

"No. Yes." I sigh and scrunch my nose. "He's being the prick I've learned that he is."

"You're okay though, right? You don't need any money or help or—"

"I'm fine," I lie. The woman lives paycheck to paycheck but would send the whole amount to me if I asked. "It's just . . . I have a few celebrity clients right now so you might hear a few mentions of me or the bakery, and I didn't want you to worry."

"Why would I worry?" she screeches. "That's fabulous, honey. Wonderful. Maybe it'll get you seen by the right people, and the bakery will take off through the stratosphere."

"Perhaps." If I feel this sick to my stomach lying to her, how am I going to feel lying to the world? "Just . . . whatever you hear, just know that everything is okay."

She pauses, and I sure as hell hope that mother's intuition isn't hitting right now. "Okay." She draws the word out. "But that doesn't make me feel any better about whatever it is you're not telling me. I know you, Hendrix."

I clear my throat. "I know. Oh, look. I have some customers coming in. I have to go."

"You're lying."

"No. I'm serious. I have to go."

She makes a noncommittal sound that says she doesn't believe me, but I'm grateful that she lets it go. "Okay. Fine. Make sure to tell them that your mom says you have the best cookies in the world."

I chuckle. "I will."

But when the door chimes, alerting that a customer is here, it's not some random person off the street, *it's Josie*. Today she's wearing polka dots on the top and stripes on the bottom and despite the fact that they should be nowhere near each other, it works perfectly for her.

"Hi," she says as she pushes the door open and then hooks a thumb over her shoulder to the large, hulking man standing outside. "Who's that? I'm thinking I should be alarmed that there's a man standing at your door with a gun on his hip." She glances over her shoulder again. "Right?"

"No. It's—he's—it's just a security guard," I say.

The security guard that Nathaniel said would be sent—though I kind of forgot about him—until I came downstairs this morning from my studio above to find him posted outside with a big smile and a scary-looking weapon holstered on his hip.

"A security guard?" She chews over the words.

"Yes." I act like it's just another day when it's anything but. "His name is Sammy."

"And *why* is Sammy here? Is Paul stalking you? Does some crazed, hot man want you as his goddess sex slave? Do we need to whisk you away for safety?" she asks with a dramatic flair that only she can. Her face falls. "I'm serious though. Are you okay? Why's he here?"

"No. He's—" *What's the lie going to be now, Hendrix?* "The landlord said the alarm was tripped a few times over the past few days. He thinks someone might be trying to break into one of the units. When he told us, one of the other tenants complained they were scared so he hired a security guard for a bit."

She eyes me with curiosity. "So he hired a gun-toting security guard versus a pretend rent-a-cop? I think there's more to the story that he's not telling you."

"There's not. It's fine."

"Sounds like there is to me."

"Sammy's temporary. So far he seems to be a pretty cool guy. Besides, I don't mind him being there," I say. "So what's up?"

Now that look of curiosity turns to pure concern. "I came to pick up my order."

"Shit. Yes." I scrub a hand over my face and grimace. I never miss an order—especially not for Josie who was my first and only customer for a while. "I—it's been a crazy few days. I just lost track of—"

"Apparently." She takes a step closer and waves her hand. "The order doesn't matter. Skip it for all I care but, Hendrix, honey, you never forget things when it comes to your bakery. Are you sure—"

"Yes. I'm all right. I'm fine." I chuckle and point to my cell. "I just got off the phone with my mother who asked me the same thing like twenty times. I'm just tired. I stayed up all night working on the dog party designs—I'm presenting them to the client for approval tomorrow—and somehow an entire day slipped away from me." I laugh to cover up my embarrassment. "How about I run them over to you at the café in about an hour?"

She eyes me again. "You sure?"

"About the cookies or about being okay? How about yes, I'm sure to both?"

Josie reaches out and squeezes my forearm. "Today. Tomorrow. I don't care when you deliver the cookies." She smiles. "But I do care about you."

"I know. And I appreciate it."

And I do. This life I created here with Paul has only ever included his friends, his work acquaintances, his everything . . . save for Josie. And I lost all those friends of his when we broke up. Not one of them has reached out since.

Yet Josie is here every day like clockwork. Checking in on me. Making me laugh. Commiserating with me about owning a small business. Caring about me.

That's a lot in the City of Angels where everyone is from somewhere else and most can't see beyond their own ambition to give a shit.

I don't have a huge army of people in my corner for support, but she's been there since the first day I moved in and it's just how it's been. Her, me, our businesses, and our gossip.

And now she's standing before me with squinted eyes as she studies me. "I'm letting you off the hook right now, but I know there's more you're not telling me. We'll revisit this again."

I let the comment be. It might serve me well once I show up married to Jase as a justification as to why I'm flustered.

After more small talk and non-answers on my part, Josie heads to the café while I slink down into a chair and draw in a deep breath.

The last forty-eight hours have been a doozy. I've packed and unpacked my things about ten times. They're sitting in the trunk of my car while I debate pulling them out and going through them again. What exactly does one bring to move in with her soon-to-be pretend husband when she doesn't even know what's expected of her?

Do you bring books to read because there will be bouts of awkward silence? What about pajamas? Do you bring onesies so there's no temptation to unzip anything to save face from you liking him more than he likes you? Will there be food or does he have a private chef who cooks for him every night?

Then there's the whole fact that I'm going to be married in less than two days. I've been sent a plane ticket, been told where to meet the car and go once I get there . . . but everything else feels . . . *"Ugh,"* I say into the silence.

There's no manual on how to prepare for a fake marriage, nor for the unknown of the next few months.

CHAPTER
eleven

Hendrix

OVERWHELMED IS AN UNDERSTATEMENT.

I glance around the suite at the Four Seasons Hotel Las Vegas and shake my head. It's like a tornado and a hurricane hit the room all at once. The far end of the space holds racks and racks of clothing. When I said I needed a shopping budget to beef up my wardrobe and make me look the part of Jase's wife, I didn't expect to walk into the suite in Las Vegas and find a personal shopper complete with what felt like a whole store to take my pick from.

What I'd expected to find was Jase sitting there with that cocky smile and a *how are we going to laugh our way through this one* expression.

Instead, I was met with a team of people. First, the personal shopper came in and spent more than an hour walking me through outfit combinations and accessories that coordinated with each. I was measured and sized, and then all I had to do was say yes or no like some purchasing agent for an upscale company. If I said yes, it was to be shipped and delivered to Jase's house. If I said no, it was placed on a rejection rack and carted away.

Then there were shoes, purses, and jewelry to accessorize with.

I felt like I was in some bizarre movie where I didn't belong. One where I longed to call my mom and have someone to share this ridiculous scenario with. She'd laugh at how ludicrous this is and gasp with her hand over her mouth before asking me the same thing I'm thinking—*how is this real?*

The guilt in not telling her about this hits hard.

Next were the wedding dresses. More racks of dresses but this time, the choice of color was between ivory to white, the fabric from satin to tulle, and the style from strapless to full sleeves. I shoved my emotions aside and forced myself to look at them as what would fit the narrative rather than what the little girl inside me had always dreamed her wedding dress to look like.

It made the task easier. Less personal. Especially when the folder on my desktop already had saved images of dresses I thought I'd pick from to marry Paul in the near future.

Then came the glam squad. A team of hair and makeup and manicurists waiting to dote on my every need. All I really wanted were two things: to have some silence and solitude so I could prepare myself for what was happening in a few hours *and* to see Jase.

It's like we signed the agreement to do this and we haven't really talked since. Sure, we've exchanged texts about a few things over the past few days, but without his charm and his dimpled smile that convinced me this was a good idea, I'm silently freaking the fuck out.

But I got what I asked for. I'm alone. The room has emptied, the solitude I was seeking now here, but with it came the anxiety the silence brought with it.

"Deep breath," I murmur as I look in the floor-length mirror and my reflection looking back at me.

The dress is gorgeous—and not the me I thought I was. Sounds funny, but true. I'd never thought I'd select a column of soft ivory like this. It complements my curves with a fitted bodice without being overstated, and the back is open so that the fabric pools just above the swell of my ass. My hair has been pulled up and soft tendrils frame my face so that it looks styled but not overdone.

Nerves rattle in a way I didn't expect. So do my thoughts.

I'm getting married shortly.

My mom's going to kill me when she finds out I excluded her from this moment.

My life is about to get exponentially harder and easier all in one big swoop.

I invited this development. I agreed to it.

I take a deep breath. It's too late to back out now—*way too late*—and yet cold feet are a real fucking thing.

On any given day, I'm plain on the Los Angeles scale of beauty—because yes, the land of fame and dreams is different from the rest of the world—but when I look at myself now, I feel beautiful. Maybe I'm allowing myself the grace to feel this way, to admit to it, and maybe Jase and his attention, despite his "normal" comment, are allowing me to see myself in a different light.

A more positive one.

Then again, maybe I'm just overthinking everything in the silence of this room. That's why I'm grateful for the knock on the suite's door.

"Cookie Cutter, you in there?" Jase's muffled voice comes through the door, and oddly, I feel like I can breathe a little easier at the sound.

CHAPTER
twelve

Gizmo

T HERE'S SILENCE ON THE OTHER SIDE OF THE DOOR.

Silence that a part of me wishes remains—that she bolted without looking back—while the other part of me knows this is how I redeem myself in the eyes of the judge.

Both are shitty prospects.

Both have my heart perfectly lodged in my throat regardless of how nonchalant I'm playing this shit.

"Yeah, I'm here," she finally says on the other side of the door.

I'm not sure why I breathe a sigh of relief, but I do. *She didn't leave.* "You okay?" I ask.

"Terrified," she answers as she pulls open the door.

I lose my words. My thoughts. My senses.

Hendrix Wright stands before me in a sheath of ivory, the sun at her back like a halo around her hair, and those expressive hazel eyes begging me for an escape I can't give her.

She's fucking gorgeous.

And feeling vulnerable if that look on her face is any indication.

Hell, if seeing my pretend wife standing in front of me like this doesn't move me in ways it shouldn't.

"Wow," I finally say as she stands there staring at me. "You look . . . stunning. You *are* stunning."

A smile flutters over her pale painted lips as her hands smooth down the fabric at her stomach. "Really? You're okay with this choice? It's okay for your image—"

"Yes." I step into the room without asking and set down the bag in my hand, my eyes glued to her as I take her in. "Most definitely yes."

"Whew. I was nervous. *Am nervous.* I got here and there were all these people and all this stuff"—she waves her hands around at the chaos of the room—"but I didn't see you and that made it harder and me more anxious and then I was alone with just my thoughts and . . . yeah." She blows out a heavy sigh as her cheeks stain pink.

There's something about her little rants that I love. On anyone else they'd come across as crazy and yet with Hendrix, they're adorable. She *is* adorable.

"I'm sorry. I had things to finish back home before I hopped on the jet. They ran long."

"Oh my gosh. Look at you," she says and holds her hands out to me. "You look so handsome."

"I clean up okay," I say.

"Yeah, but you have on a tux."

"A tux is a tux is a tux. Once you've seen one, you've seen them all."

"I know, but you wore one. *For this.*" Her brow furrows and I can see what she's not saying. *For me.*

That prick really did a number on her, didn't he?

"Well, if you have to wear a dress, then it's the least I can do."

"True. Yes. But . . . *thank you.*" She smiles softly and moves to the wall of windows that overlooks the Strip down below.

It's weird—I barely know this woman yet I feel close to her. Maybe it's because she's endearing. Maybe it's because I don't have to worry about impressing her as this is simply business. Or maybe it's because we're both about to be thrown into the same fire and so we share a mutual bond no one else might understand. Whatever it is, the feeling has me walking over to her, standing beside her, and linking my fingers with hers.

I don't know if I expect her to yank her hand back, but I'm relieved when she doesn't.

"How did we get here, huh?" I murmur.

"By plane," she says and we both bark out a nervous laugh at the ridiculous comment. "Sorry. I crack jokes when I'm freaking out. Which I am by the way—freaking out. It's not you though. It's . . . everything else."

"But it is me. I'm the reason you're here."

"Yes, but I like you. It's the everything else that's daunting."

"Define everything else?"

"What is my mom going to say? To think? How is my life going to change? What if we fumble when we kiss at the altar and people can tell it's the first time we've ever done it? I've told everyone—well, my friends and family—that I've sworn off men for a year because of Paul, and now I turn around and get married?" She blows out a shaky sigh that ends in a self-deprecating chuckle and then throws her hands up. "What if, what if, what if?"

I nod slowly. I know she can see it in her periphery, but she doesn't turn or say anything else. "For the record, I'm freaking out too but am well aware being unpredictable is part of my nature. Wanting to get anywhere near a justice of the peace for a wedding is not however."

"Great, so we'll both shock the shit out of everyone while having mild heart attacks ourselves."

I chuckle. "You're funny."

"I'm serious."

I squeeze her fingers. "Should we do some shots to ease our nerves?"

"You have alcohol?" She turns to look at me with wide, hopeful eyes.

"In the bag." I hook my thumb over my shoulder. "I came prepared."

"Yes. Please." If relief was audible, it would be those two words. "I'm good with prepared."

Within a few minutes, I have the bottle of tequila opened and poured into two shot glasses.

"You know it's bad luck to see your bride before the ceremony, right?" she asks as she takes the shot glass I slide across to her.

"Good thing we already know how this is going to turn out." I smile, hold my glass up, and tap it against hers. "To our impending divorce."

"To no future," she adds.

"To life after you're the wife I never dreamed of."

She laughs. "Touché, husband who's definitely not my type."

"No?" I quirk a brow. *Not her type?*

"No."

"Cheers," I say seconds before we toss back the shots. While she might down it like a pro, the hiss she emits after, and her pinched expression that follows, has me laughing.

"Jesus." It must taste like battery acid from her expression, but then she holds her glass back out to me. "I think I need another."

And that has me laughing even harder. This woman is . . . she's something else. "Okay. One more. Then that's it. The last thing we need to be is glassy-eyed and shitfaced no matter how welcome the idea sounds at the moment."

"Party pooper," she says, sticking out her bottom lip.

And if I had to guess, she might already be feeling the effects of the alcohol. *Lightweight.*

"No. Just making sure my soon-to-be wife can stand."

"Pour the shot, Gizmo." She slides her glass in front of me, her eyes holding and challenging mine until I do just that. "I can handle a lot more than you think."

Let's hope so.

I nod and do as she asks. No doubt I can drink her under the table, but we're not going to get to that point today no matter how much I want to.

"What are we toasting to this time?" I ask. She starts to say something and then throws her head back and laughs. "What?" My elbows are on the counter but my glass is being held up, waiting for her.

"Fuck you, Paul," she says with a devilish smirk that lights up her eyes.

"Yeah. Fuck you, Paul. You don't have a clue what you're missing." I wink, tap my glass against hers, and then down the shot.

I welcome the burn. It slides nicely over whatever emotions that look of—surprise, compassion, gratitude—she just gave me conjured up.

"I'm supposed to be a good influence on you." She slides the empty shot glass across the counter so it clinks against the tequila bottle. "Guess I already failed before we even started."

"I live in the failure zone so we're all good."

"What does that mean?" she asks, head angled to the side and those perfect fucking lips parted.

"A lot. A little. Nothing that should be talked about today of all days.

We'll leave my faults for you to discover during our short and disastrous marriage."

The words come out but the inadequacies of my life blare in my own mind. The shortcomings I'm reminded of daily. My dad. My mom. My band . . . who I've let down repeatedly.

"Failure makes you who you are," she murmurs, her smile falling. "Or at least that's what my mom says, and we're not talking about her since I'm about to shock the hell out of her with this one."

"That was a lot of what ifs you had," I murmur as I pour myself one more shot and down it without asking her if she wants one. "And don't worry, I'll charm the pants off your mom so she'll overlook your vow to not touch a man for a year."

"You will, will you?"

"I will. I'm that good."

She laughs as I move around the counter so that I'm near her—there's this inherent need that makes me want to be. It must be the shots or the small insight I gave her about me when I never give it to anyone, but the urge to kiss her, to show her how beautiful she is when she's clearly nervous, is stronger than I'd like to admit.

"What else were you nervous about?" I lean my ass against the counter beside her. "How is your life going to change?"

"A lot." She laughs nervously.

"Perhaps. I'll insulate you as much as possible. You may have signed up to do this, but not to manage the crazy that comes along with it."

"Okay." She bites her bottom lip again.

"If it ever gets to be too much, you need to tell me. To clue me in. The crazy is enough to break someone, and the last thing I need or want is you broken by it, okay?"

"I'll be fine."

She says the words but has no clue what it's like with the spotlight and the world's attention on her. Nor do I want her to.

"Your other what if, about people not believing this, us, because you swore off Paul. People change their minds. Apparently love comes when you're least looking for it—according to whoever said that. Who knew that when I came in to buy some cookies from you I'd become totally smitten with you? Do you know the agony I felt over those few weeks when you were Paul's and all I wanted was for you to be mine?" I flash a grin, rather proud of myself for this scenario. "The day I walked back in the bakery to find you crying over the asshole cheating on you was the best day of my life."

She rolls her eyes. "No one's going to believe that. And no one is smitten after one meeting."

I laugh and reach back for the bag behind me. "They will and this is proof that I can see something and become smitten with it."

"I don't follow."

I pull the ring box from the bag and her startled gasp is about how I felt when I bought the damn thing. "It's not a wedding without a ring, right?" *Why am I suddenly nervous?* "I tried to pick something practical for you since you're always using your hands in the bakery. Something that didn't have a high profile and wouldn't get dough and icing stuck in it or snag gloves if you wear them—"

"You thought of all that?"

"Of course. I want my wife to wear her ring," I tease but damn if those words don't have my stomach flipping as I open the box and hand it to her.

She gasps, her eyes flying up to meet mine and then back to the cushion-cut oval diamond centered in the middle of an infinity band of other diamonds. "Jase. It's—"

"Understated."

"Far from it. It's stunning. Gorgeous . . . *whoa.*"

She reaches out to run a finger over the band where it's nestled in the box. The ring is spectacular but small in comparison to other celebrity wives' standards and yet . . . something about it called to me, much like Hendrix did. It's understated—possibly normally overlooked—but is elegant and classy. It screamed unique and genuine, and from the short time I've known Hendrix, it seems to fit her.

I'm not sure why it was so important for me to get it for her when I could've simply bought a solitaire something or other, but it was.

"Here. Let's put it on you," I say and take the ring out of the box. We both inhale shaky breaths as I slide it on her finger and it fits perfectly.

"*Oh,*" she says, but I have a feeling that *oh* stands for *oh shit.* Oh my God. What the hell are we about to do? How do we stop this train?

Truth be told, I didn't know how to give her the ring. Just like the same situation with a formal ceremony—I probably won't, but just in case I do plan to lower to my knee one day—I didn't want to think of this moment here. The pretend engagement. So I decided to just hand it to her to put on herself but right now it feels ridiculously inadequate and callous.

Maybe that's why I bought her the present—to make up for it. It has to be.

"I also got you something else to go with your dress."

"Jase. The dress, the pampering, is more than enough." She keeps staring at her hand and the ring now on her finger.

"Shush." I tear my eyes off the ring and up to the discord dancing in hers. "But I saw it and thought you'd like it. That it would go with whatever dress you picked out." I pull a second jewelry box out. "Turn around for me."

She holds my gaze for a second but then does as I ask. I'm hard-pressed not to notice how delicate her shoulders and the curve of her neck are as she does so. How smooth her skin is or how incredible her light flowery scent smells.

I lift the multi-stoned diamond tennis necklace over her head, until it rests on her neck, and then fasten it at her nape. Goosebumps chase over her skin and fuck if the sight of them doesn't tell me everything I need to know.

My touch does to her what everything about her does to me. Affected.

Hands off, Jase. Don't fuck this up. You made promises to Nathaniel. Promises to yourself.

She reaches up to run her fingers over the stones of the necklace. "This is completely unnecessary," she says as she turns to face me. "This is too . . . much." Her voice fades as we come face-to-face and well within each other's personal space.

I never noticed the flecks of gold in the hazel of her eyes or the subtle scar just below the hairline of her forehead. And I sure as hell never thought a hitch in someone's breath could sound sexy and yet here we are.

I smile and reach out to run my fingertip over the necklace much like she did. "It looks good on you." My finger trails off the necklace to her skin.

"Thank you." She's breathless.

Fuck.

And close.

"And there's only one way to see about that other *what if* of yours." I lean in closer, my hand moving to rest on the side of her neck, her pulse fluttering beneath my hand as I brush my thumb back and forth over her jawline.

"Which one is that?"

"If we can pull off the kiss."

"Oh." Her throat jumps beneath my hand as she swallows. "I took a theater class in high school. We had to—I can do the pretend way."

"Pretend way?"

"Yes. No tongue." She can barely get the words out.

"Uh-huh." I lick my lips but am too busy staring at hers. She thinks there isn't going to be tongue in this kiss? That I'm not going to steal a taste of her like some bullshit B-list actor? She's fucking crazy.

I brush my lips against hers. Once. Twice. My body hums with desire that's only natural when you kiss someone.

And then she emits the softest sound in the back of her throat. Something about it owns me and begs me to hear it again.

I dip my tongue between her parted lips and deepen the kiss. My free hand slides to the small of her back and pulls her into me while the other remains on the side of her neck.

She tastes like sin and regret. Like surrender and restraint running a race. Like necessity and indulgence warring against one another.

Stop, Giz.

The two words repeat in my mind.

This isn't real.

But her taste is as addicting as I imagined it would be.

When I break the kiss, when I force myself to step back, the only sound in the room is our labored breaths.

And my sudden desire for more.

"Great. Perfect. Guess we proved we could pull it off," Hendrix says in a rush of words as she steps away from me and moves about the room. She picks up an empty water bottle. She fluffs a pillow on the couch. She clears her throat a time or ten. And she infuses cheer into her voice when I can hear the raw unacceptance of what just happened—a kiss for the fucking ages. "Just like theater class."

I throw my head back and laugh.

Thoughts of dragging her back against me fill my head. Ones of messing up her hair and tangling up the sheets a close second after. Ones of proving just how wrong she is about fucking theater class.

Instead, I adjust my hard-on in my pants, grab the bottle of tequila by the neck, and take a swig straight from the bottle.

It's going to be a long four months.

Torturously long.

CHAPTER
thirteen

NOT LIKE THEATER CLASS. NOT EVEN CLOSE.

None of this has been.

Not his kiss I can't stop thinking about in the hotel or the one for the cameras under the chintz-covered arch in the chapel where Elvis married us. It left me speechless and my body filled with a yearning I'm choosing to ignore.

One, I've sworn off men.

Two, Jase Gizmodo is used to playing women. He may be charming and sweet, but I'm under no pretenses that our kiss was more than a kiss to sell the lie, regardless of how damn earth-shattering it was.

Or how much I can't stop thinking about it.

I glance at the diamonds glittering on my ring finger and my head dizzies.

I'm married. *We're married.* And while the ceremony seemed like it should play out like the cheesy B-list movies where the couple gets married in Vegas, it didn't.

Sure we laughed our way through it—the cheesy vows, the Elvis impersonator marrying us, the organ playing as I marched down the aisle—but that's just it, we laughed our way through it.

We had the best time together. Tequila shots and voiced *I do's* followed by *holy shit* as he pressed his lips to mine under the neon lights with Elvis crooning, complete with a corny photograph session after to top it off.

Followed by another shot.

I look over at Jase in the dimly lit elevator beside me. His bow tie is undone and hanging loosely around the unbuttoned collar of his dress shirt. The almost empty bottle of tequila is in one hand while the other is resting politely on my lower back.

He's striking even now as I stare at him and think about the kiss earlier in the hotel room. His lips. His skill. The taste of tequila on his tongue. The way he stole my breath and heated my body in one fell, fucking swoop.

He turns to look at me, the blue of his eyes so light. I don't know what I expected from him after the ceremony—anger maybe over having to get married, aloofness definitely given what I am to him—but it most definitely wasn't the mixture of pride and mischief that I see in them right now.

A slow grin crawls across his lips as he shakes his head. "Sorry for the sucky last name." He pulls me against his side and murmurs, "I've always hated it but now we can hate it together."

"It's not bad."

"Whatever you say, Mrs. Gizmodo."

The sound of those words makes my stomach twist. "You're right. That might take some getting used to."

"I think there might be a lot of that to get used to in the coming days, but we'll figure it out. And if we don't, my house is big enough that when you're mad at me, you have plenty of room to steer clear of me."

"You can just as easily be angry with me."

He angles his head to the side and meets my eyes. "I doubt that's possible."

The elevator arrives at our private floor, but when I look around, it's a different foyer than I remember. "I don't think this is the right—"

"It is." He takes a key card from his front pocket and opens the door, ushering me in before him. "It's the honeymoon suite. Or rather, what my agent, Abigail, requested to be the honeymoon suite. To keep up pretenses, obviously."

"Obviously," I say.

"Who knows what we're about to get. Ready to find out?"

If I thought the room I had earlier was extravagant, this one is that on steroids. The entire penthouse is lined with floor-to-ceiling windows, providing a stunning view of the Strip. The lights that line the wall are colored, but it's the scattered flower petals, the chocolate-covered strawberries and champagne chilled on the table, and the heart-shaped bed with fluffy robes laid out for us that have me catching my breath.

Because if the nuptials and *you may kiss the bride* didn't make this real, seeing all this sure as shit did.

Those nerves the tequila tamed? Yeah, they've come roaring back with a vengeance.

"Oh. Wow," Jase says as he follows behind me. "All that's missing is the vibrating bed."

"Are those still a thing?" I ask, distracted as I move around and peek into the bathroom that's larger than my entire studio.

"I'm sure they are somewhere," he says. "We stayed in some pretty shifty places when we first started out, but I can't say I ever saw one."

"This suite is . . . gorgeous. Over the top. Ridiculous." Completely unnecessary. I smile when I see my luggage is on the far end of the room. Clearly, someone must have packed it up and brought it here for me. I don't know how I feel about that—someone doing things for me. "I'll—uh—get changed. I'm sure you want to get back to Los Angeles and as far away from this as soon as possible."

"Hey." I yelp as Jase grabs my hand and whirls me out as if we're dancing and then back into him. I land solidly against his chest and am greeted by his grin and a flutter in my lower belly. "This is some crazy shit, isn't it?"

"It is," I say and try not to think about his lips being so close. "Probably the craziest thing I've ever done."

"Give it time. You're married to me now. I'm sure there will be more times to stretch those wings of yours." He chuckles as I become fully aware of every single place we're pressed against each other.

"Noted." Why do I sound so breathless? "Um. I'll go get changed. My bag. It's over there."

"True," he says but doesn't let go of me. "It is."

"I'm sure you want to get back home for . . . whatever. In Los Angeles. Away from here."

"Do I make you nervous?" he murmurs, his eyes flickering to my lips before locking on my gaze.

My body wars between sense and desire—neither of which I want to win. This is fake. This whole scenario. We kissed. We got married. *I'm normal* and totally not his type.

"Yes." I smile. "You do. Because we both know that we're standing here thinking about the kiss while knowing the only reason we are is because of the poignancy of the moment. You don't like women like me, and I just broke up with someone after two years so sure, it was a great kiss, but the moment surrounding it elevated it."

"Cookie, no amount of talk is going to dampen my ego. That was a damn good kiss and you and I both know it."

I step back from him, needing to break from his compelling charm. "I can admit it. Easily."

He eyes me as I move about the suite. "What are you doing?" he asks.

"Getting changed." *Anything to change the subject and make me stop thinking about your lips and how soft they are.*

"For?"

"Well, I can't exactly wear this wedding dress on the plane. I'm sure your stylist would prefer it back sooner rather than later."

"Huh." I can sense his displeasure.

I reach back to unclasp the necklace but struggle with it. "Jase? Can you help me with this? I'm sure the jeweler you got this on loan from will need this back as well."

"On loan from?" he asks as I glance over to him.

His jacket is off now, his hands are shoved in his pockets as he rests his shoulder against the wall, but it's the muscle ticking in his jaw that catches my eye.

"Yes. Isn't that how this all works?" I look around but don't see it. "Did whoever move our stuff bring the box up here?"

"That's not how I roll, Hendrix."

"Meaning?"

"When I give gifts, I don't get them on loan from the jeweler, and I sure as shit don't want them back."

Oh. *Oh.* He bought this for me? "But I was under the impression—I thought it was—"

"It's for you. I saw it and was smitten with it." His smile is tight but his eyes soften. "It suits you."

I gulp as my fingers worry over it. This cost a ton of money. I know it had to. "I . . . I can't accept this."

"You did. You will." He moves over to me and studies it for a beat before surprising me and pressing a chaste kiss on my lips. "Now, are we ready to see what the night will bring?"

"What? I thought we were leaving—"

"I know this is fake, but I celebrate all firsts in life. You never get them back so my theory is you better damn well remember them."

"Meaning?"

"Meaning the night is yours. What do you want to do? Have a nice dinner? Eat sushi on a rooftop? Go to a club? Party? Sleep? You tell me, and we'll do it." He holds his hands out toward the windows and the sparkling lights beyond. "The city is yours."

He looks back over his shoulder at me, his grin wide, and I know I'm in serious trouble.

I may have made all kinds of promises to myself, so what is it about him that makes me want to break every single one of them?

CHAPTER
fourteen

Gizmo

MY HEAD POUNDS LIKE A FUCKING BEAT I'D NEVER DRUM.

At least I'd have enough sense not to when the tequila is still wearing off—or maybe still wreaking havoc on my system.

I go to scrub a hand over my face, and the titanium of my wedding band hits me squarely on the brow bone. Talk about being smacked in the face with the cold, hard truth of yesterday.

I'm married.

Fucking married.

Last night flickers through my mind like a slideshow of someone else's life. Someone else's perhaps, yet . . . every moment of it was lived.

"Dance with me," Hendrix shouts above the bruising tempo of the music.

I rise from my seat in the darkened corner of our VIP pod and adjust my hat lower over my face. On any other day, it's okay for Gizmo from BENT to be seen partying in Las Vegas. Just not tonight and not with a woman who has a sixty-thousand-dollar wedding ring on her finger.

People can look back in a week and realize the guy who looked familiar but who they couldn't place really was me, really was here, and really was with his wife, but the plan is for them to remember I looked like I was hiding. That I was trying to have a private moment.

But those thoughts, the careful planning, dissipate as I step up and slide my hand around Hendrix's waist. With my front to her back, I pull her against me so that my lips brush against the shell of her ear when I speak. "I don't dance, Cookie."

She spins around, her lips pink and her eyes alive as she hops up and down to the beat. I try to ignore the jostle of her breasts or how they rub against me as she does. The enticing sight of her body moving in tune with the beat. She smirks and then leans in close to me. "And I don't get married, Jase." She then throws her head back and whoops. "Now, dance."

Then there was the two-a.m. snack run that had us sitting cross-legged on the cement of the hotel balcony with two spoons and a gallon of mint chocolate chip ice cream between us.

"How many other people in this city do you think are celebrating getting married tonight?" she asks around a bite of ice cream while wielding her spoon like a conductor when she talks.

"A lot. A little. I don't think all of them are celebrating though." I take a swig of my beer. It doesn't pair well with the mint but fuck if I care at this point.

"That's depressing." She's buzzed and the little grunt she makes as she tries to dig another spoonful of ice cream out of the container is adorable.

"But true. Accidental pregnancies. An escape from something worse. I—"

"Oh my God." Her eyes widen and the alcohol makes her every expression animated.

"What?" I whip my head over my shoulder toward the suite behind us, thinking someone's in there or something, and it takes a few seconds for the spinning in my head to catch up with the movement.

"Is that what people are going to think of me?" she screeches.

"No. Never." I take another bite. "Yes. Probably."

"Besides, no one's probably going to believe it either. This. Us. I'm the exact opposite of your type."

"I don't have a type." Yes. I do.

"You're so full of shit." We both chuckle as the spoons clink on our teeth and we fall silent. "But we're not fraternizing like that." Her every word is enunciated.

"Correct. It's not in the contract." It may have crossed my mind a time or ten tonight. What she'd feel like beneath me. What those eyes of hers would look like when she came. How her hips would feel gripped in my palms.

"Pretend marriage. Pretend sex." She giggles and rests her head back to the wall and stares up at the sky. "Best relationship ever."

She has a soft smile on her lips and her dark lashes rest against the curve of her cheek. I contemplate the words she just said. The things she just implied.

A best relationship means pretend sex?

What the hell does that mean? It's not my place to ask. Hell, I'm probably drunk and misheard her. Then again, she was pretty fucking clear and my head is full of ways I could show her different.

"Hendrix—"

"Nope. Not talking about it." She giggles again and I can't figure out if she's that buzzed or is using it as an excuse to shove away whatever she thinks I was going to ask.

"Shit. Crap. Brain freeze." She laughs and hisses as she puts the heel of her hand to her forehead and squints her eyes—while digging into the shared container with the spoon in her other hand.

"That sucks. Are you okay?" I lean over and press a kiss to her forehead.

The action is so natural, so . . . just there without thinking, and so is her putting her hand over my entire face and pushing me back while laughing. "I'm fine. I can handle a little ol' brain freeze."

"You sure?" I fall back onto my ass gracelessly.

"Definitely." She reaches over and pats my thigh as ice cream drips off the spoon onto my pants. "It's okay, Jase. You're not my type either."

To collapsing onto the bed as the sky turned a light gray and staring at the room spinning all around us.

"The headlines are going to be ridiculous when people find out," she says.

I turn my head on the pillow and look at her. "Probably run-of-the-mill."

"Run-of-the-mill for you, not for me." She purses her lips, clearly trying to think. "Famous Rock Star Eats Her Cookie."

"Lame." I snort and then laugh. It takes a second for the joke to register as

I'm fucking tired. "It'll say something about how I like to play with big sticks or how you can handle the big stick."

She rolls her eyes and laughs. "How did you not get noticed tonight?"

"I have a lot of practice at it. That, and I'm a drummer. People—"

"In the most popular band on the freaking planet." She reaches over and rests her hand on my forearm. "You sell yourself short. Stop doing that."

I open my mouth to speak and then bite back the history that might just come out with the words. "We should sleep," I finally say.

"Hmm." She's already almost there. "I should change but I'm too tired."

"Same." I start to shift off the bed and she tightens her grip on my arm. "I'll sleep on the couch."

"I'm that irresistible, huh? Think you won't be able to control yourself and jump me in the middle of the night?"

"That's exactly what I was thinking." I chuckle but know the thought has crossed my mind tonight.

"It's okay. I know you want me." Her sleep-drugged voice is as sexy as it is playful.

"I do, do I?" I play along.

"Mm. You do, but you can't have me." She turns on her side so that we're face-to-face on the pillows. Her eyes are closed and her smile's subtle.

"No? But you have my last name."

She reaches out and presses a finger to my lips. "Shh." Her eyes flutter back closed. Just when I think she's drifted off to sleep, she murmurs slightly above a whisper like it's a secret she's keeping from the world. "Paul put cracks in me, but I have a feeling that someone like you would break me. I don't want to be broken, Jase."

"Why would you say that?"

Her ghost of a smile is haunted. "Because I have a feeling that's what you do."

My chest constricts at those words. "I won't break you."

"Promise?" The two syllables slur.

"I promise," I say and sink a little farther into the bed at the sound of her sigh. "Good night, pretend wife."

"Good night, pretend husband."

A soft moan and the slight tug on the sheets beside me have *every* part of me standing at attention. I open my eyes and am met with Hendrix's face close to mine.

And then my eyes travel. Down the V-neck shirt she has on—is that my undershirt?—that's stretched tight over her breasts. The peaks of her nipples are pressed against the fabric, their darkened color sexy as hell.

The shirt's pulled up, baring her stomach and a hint of something white and lacy just above the sheet pooled at her waist.

Well, then. *Whew.*

I shift, my morning hard-on aching now that it has fuel to feed its fire.

She looks like something I could lose myself in. Even with this roaring hangover, I'd gladly suffer if I could get lost in her.

How the fuck is this going to work? I scrub a hand over my face. That promise I made Nathaniel? The promise I made last night? I pride myself on being a man of my word but fuck if I think I'm going to be able to keep this one when my wife looks like that.

It's not fair to ask a man to kiss a woman, to be as comfortable as we were last night, and then not want to fuck her.

It's a normal reaction. A natural one. One any other man would struggle with especially after he knows how goddamn good her kiss tastes.

The difference? I'm taking her home with me. How will that go?

Sixteen weeks without touching her. Sixteen weeks without sex. *Fuck, what was I thinking?*

"Hey." Her raspy voice draws my attention back up to her face, and I'm met with a sleep-drugged smile and eyes that I know for a fact are way clearer than mine.

I don't want to be broken, Jase.

I look at her across the space, her wedding ring sparkling from the sun streaming through the open blinds, and smile back.

"Hey," I murmur but don't move out of the bed like my brain screams I should do.

"Sorry." She tugs the T-shirt down. "I got up in the middle of the night—morning—whatever. My dress was itchy so I picked up the first thing I could find. I think you threw this off and I picked it up."

"No worries."

"I'm probably a disastrous mess." She starts to pat down her hair that *is* going in a million different directions. She has black smudges under her eyes from her mascara, but I can't look away. "I've got morning breath and bedhead and no doubt raccoon eyes. I probably—"

"Yes, you're a disastrous mess." I chuckle as she goes to shove against my shoulder playfully. I reach out and wrap my fingers around her wrist, but her hand remains there and her skin on mine isn't doing my cock any favors. I rub my thumb over the diamond on her finger to calm it down with a cold dose of reality. *Still didn't help any.* "If your husband can't handle you first thing in the morning, then it seems we'll have a serious problem in our marriage."

She snorts. "Can we cite that as the reason for our divorce? Can't handle morning version of spouse?"

"Hmm. Not sure that will fly."

"Yes, you're right."

"Besides, the bedhead is cute." I part groan, part grimace as I try to adjust my cock that's painfully constricted by the pants I still have on from last night.

"Oh," she says with a start, her eyes wide as she glances down again and then back up. She scoots out of bed in a hurry. "Sorry. I didn't mean to—I should have thought about that. I didn't—"

"Relax," I say as I stand up and turn to adjust myself. That only makes matters worse as I know she's watching. I glance over to her as I slide my hands out of the inside of the waistband and hope that works.

Oh yeah, she's most definitely watching.

"It's a cock. It's morning. You're . . ."—standing there with lacy boy shorts and hard nipples beneath my T-shirt. *Fuck, man*—"a woman," I finally say and smile through the grimace. "There are some things a guy just can't control."

"Yes. Um." She flits about the room like she seems to do when she gets nervous. But her eyes shift down to my cock again and back up.

No complaints there.

I hook my thumb over my shoulder toward the bathroom. "I'm going to take a shower." *A cold one.* "Jet's on the tarmac. We can leave whenever you want."

"Jet's on the tarmac?"

"Yeah." I wink. "The Gizmodos don't fly commercial."

"Oh."

The shower is indeed cold—has to be—or I might risk marching back out there and showing Hendrix how hard my cock actually is. I'm tempted to jerk off, to relieve the ache, but think better of it.

You don't jerk off to your fake wife, asshole.

Then again, would that make it a fake orgasm . . . and technically be okay?

CHAPTER
fifteen

Hendrix

W HEN I DON'T KNOW WHAT TO DO, I FIDGET. I MOVE THROUGH THE space and pick up or straighten things or do anything.

And right now, the image of his hard cock pressed against his pants and the scent of his soap in the air has me wanting things I shouldn't want and thinking thoughts that are doing a number on my system.

"Paul put cracks in me, but I have a feeling that someone like you would break me. I don't want to be broken, Jase."

Why the hell would I say that to him? Admit that and open up to him?

I tear open a square, gold foil packet with my teeth and let the empty wrapper flutter to the ground.

THIS is why I don't drink. Ever. Because I open my mouth and say things I shouldn't.

Ugh.

I pull open the balcony door, tear open another packet and tuck its corner beneath an empty champagne bottle.

Why would I give him something to use against me?

I leave another opened packet on the foot of the bed and then another on the kitchen counter. I then take the contents of all the packages, the lubricated latex of the condoms, wrap them up in paper towels and then stuff them in the bottom of the trash can as if they were used.

It's only then I catch movement on the far side of the suite. Jase is standing there with his hair a wet mess, his jeans on his hips but unbuttoned, and his torso bare.

Good thing I'm over here.

"What in the world are you doing?" he asks as he scrubs a towel through his hair and moves toward me barefooted.

I drop another ripped condom wrapper on the edge of the credenza and laugh.

"Cookie?"

"You're a rock star, right?" I tear another wrapper with my teeth and shove it inside the empty champagne bottle on the end table beside me. "Since it will undoubtedly leak somehow, we need to make sure whoever the hotel cleaning staff is, they don't doubt what happened here."

He barks out a laugh as he strolls around the room and takes in the various wrappers I've deposited. "I love the thought, the belief you have that I can perform like this, but if I can fuck that many times in one night, then I'm a goddamn god."

"Exactly." I look up at him and grin. "Only the best public image for my pretend husband."

I love the astonished look on his face and what looks like embarrassment mixed with arrogance. It's the cutest combination that doesn't belong on that body of his. "Or they'll think we had a wild orgy."

"Oh." My face falls and then my nose scrunches. "I didn't quite think of that option. I'll uh—pick them up. I'll—"

"Don't you dare." He reaches out and grabs my wrist to prevent me. "I love what you've done with the place."

We stare at each other across the short distance. What is he thinking? Is he wondering why the "normal" baker he decided to marry is doing this? Am I what he bargained for? Does he look at my lips and want to kiss them again like I do his?

Nah.

Jase is a great guy, would probably tell me he wanted to kiss me again simply to avoid hurting my feelings, but I don't have any delusions of grandeur that he couldn't go out right now, snap his fingers, and have anyone he wanted.

"It's okay, Jase. You're not my type either."

Truer words have never been spoken, but there's something to be said about how much fun we had last night. The laughter. The ice cream. The dancing.

"Where in the world did you get these?" he finally says, breaking the silence, and he lets go of my wrist.

"You got ice cream, I bought condoms." I shrug. "I figured that we needed to stage this better. Sell this convincingly."

"All these condoms and none of them put to good use. What a waste," he jokes as he picks a wrapper up and drops it back down.

"It might be a little awkward bringing someone up from the casino floor while your wife is sound asleep in the bed," I say to play off the pang of hurt that comment unexpectedly causes.

"Hendrix. I wouldn't—"

"Did you really talk me out of getting a tattoo last night?" I ask, wanting to change the subject. The last thing I want him to think is that I wanted to have sex with him. Or think that his joke referred to or implied that he meant me. I mean . . . it didn't, *right?*

It couldn't have.

He's him. I'm me. A kiss is a kiss and a lot different from giving my body to him.

"Yes," he says before my thinking spirals out of control. "You were quite adamant that you get a pink heart like the one I have on my wrist. I thought you might regret it in the morning, considering you've never had one before. And I'm not certain that twenty years from now, when this is all said and done, that you're going to want a reminder of last night."

I hate that he makes sense. "Thank you," I say softly.

Does he really think I'll forget? Or that last night was all that bad? I woke up with a smile on my face despite the headache and feeling freer than I can remember in years. In some respects, as crazy as this whole situation has been, it was exactly what I've needed because of how *Fuck You, Paul,* dismantled my life.

"I'm all for rebelling, sweetheart, but I have a feeling that marrying me is more rebellion than you've ever tried, so let's just take it one day at a time, one hour at a time, before we permanently mark your skin."

I bite my bottom lip and nod. It's reasonable enough. More than. And yet a little part of me—the same part of me who repeats *fuck you, Paul,* every morning—wonders if I'll regret not doing it. Commemorating me living a little.

"I still can't believe you did this." He chuckles.

"Sex." I point to the condoms, wanting to end this conversation. "Drugs." I point to the Ibuprofen bottle sitting on the counter open. "And rock and roll." I point to him.

A grin slides across his lips. "You're something else."

"You ain't seen nothing yet."

CHAPTER
sixteen

Gizmo

Twenty Years Ago

It feels like there's a rock in the pit of my stomach.

No. More like those atomic sour candies that we all dare each other over to see how long we can keep them in our mouths before spitting them out. That's what it feels like. A hundred of those burning a hole in my stomach.

I struggle to breathe. Why does my chest hurt so bad?

"Jase," Nathaniel murmurs as he stands next to me and shakes his head. A warning for me to be quiet.

But I don't look at my brother. I don't respond. Our dad is standing in the middle of the room. His hands are on his hips, and he has a weird expression on his face like when the lawnmower broke, and he wasn't sure if he should fix it or take it to the dump.

And the two of us are standing side by side, barely breathing as if the slightest movement will make him turn his attention toward us.

"It's not that easy, Maggie," he says to our mom. Her eyes are glassy and red from crying. "I have a new wife and a new family. I can't just . . . take both of them."

She says something I can't hear. It's a whisper that has Nathaniel jolting and me looking around to see what I missed.

"Per the court order, we each get one," my dad says.

Mom's eyes flicker over to us and then back to him almost as if she didn't see us. She nods slowly, her voice unemotional and empty when she speaks. "It has said that for the last three years, and yet I've had both, so don't give me any of that *play by the rules* shit now."

"This is inconvenient at best," he says so softly it's barely audible. No doubt he didn't want us to hear it.

He never wants us to hear it anymore. Not since he got his new wife and had his two *new* kids and a life Nathaniel and I wish we had.

"You're not separating us," I say, stomping my feet for emphasis and throwing Nathaniel's warning that we're supposed to be quiet out the window. "You can't take me and leave him here. You don't know . . ." *how bad it gets here.* The last five words scream in my head but never make a sound in the room.

I can't say that in front of Mom.

I can't let her know how bad she gets when she doesn't even know it herself.

But he knows, doesn't he? He lived here so how can he not know?

"I don't know what?" Dad asks, squatting down and turning his attention on me for the first time since the initial stuttered hug and ruffle of my hair. "That you're a handful? That you act out in school constantly? I get the calls from the office too, Jase. Believe me."

"But you never take the call, do you?" I ask. "When's the last time you picked me up?"

"I'm busy working to help provide all of this for you. I can't just leave work at a moment's notice because you can't control yourself."

"Control myself?" I ask through eyes blurring with tears. Nathaniel tugs on my arm, a silent plea for me to let it go.

"Yes. Do you think I can have you at my house when you act out like this? I don't want you rubbing off on my kids."

"We *are* your kids," I say.

His Adam's apple bobs. "You know what I mean."

Yes. You mean you don't want us as your kids anymore. "You don't want us. It's why you left," I whisper. Begging. Pleading. Hating.

I hate that he left us so why do I still want him to pick me up from school?

His ice-blue eyes meet my gaze. I wish I understood what they were telling me. But before I can get a grasp on it, he looks at Nathaniel. "Grab your stuff. We need to get going."

I don't know who gasps louder—me or Nathaniel—but it's the only sound in the room other than my heart pounding in my ears.

My brother doesn't look at me as he bends over and loops his duffle bag through his hand.

And to think we both packed, thinking we would both be going to live with him.

"Nathaniel," I whisper.

He still doesn't look.

"Nate?"

Our dad steps in between us and brusquely takes the bag from Nathaniel before putting his hand on my brother's back and pushing him toward the front door.

"See you in a few weeks, Jase," my dad says without looking over his shoulder.

"Nate!" I shout.

My brother glances over his shoulder and meets my eyes.

Why aren't you speaking up? Why aren't you fighting for me? I'm your brother.

Why is Dad leaving me here? With my crazy mom?

Why isn't Nate trying to get me to go with him?

"I get the calls from the office too, Jase. Believe me. I can't just leave work at a moment's notice because you can't control yourself."

I can control myself. I can.

"I'm sorry, Jasey." My mom wraps her arm around my shoulder and pulls me against her.

I won't cry.

I will not cry.

"I tried to help you. To get him to take you, not because I don't love you, but because I do." She presses a kiss to the side of my head and my body goes numb. "I'm not doing good. I try to but I can't control it."

I hate you.

The thought runs loops in my head, but I'm not sure who I'm talking to: My dad for choosing my brother over me. Nathaniel, the only person who knows what goes on in this house. Or the ugly disease that's stealing, tormenting, and changing my mom's mind slowly.

Day by day.

Minute by minute.

The person who I know loves me but who I'm now tasked with taking care of. *Alone.*

"It's okay, Momma." I wrap my arms around her waist and hold on. "I'm here. I'm not going to leave you." My voice breaks. "I'll always take care of you."

She didn't leave me.

She at least loves me.

But by the time the hug is over, by the time I walk to my small bedroom and shove my duffle bag that was full of hopes back under the bed, she's already gone.

Maggie Gizmodo is sitting on the edge of the couch. She rocks as her fingers rub back and forth absently at the worn corner of the blanket she always keeps close.

Her mind has retreated to the safety of wherever it goes when she can't handle the life all around her.

When it becomes sick.

And when I feel most alone.

CHAPTER
seventeen

Hendrix

IT'S MASSIVE.

Jase's house, that is. Although the thought and the term conjure up a strong visual of his erection in Vegas.

Yeah. Sue me for thinking it but a girl has to fixate on something when her life has been put in a blender and turned on, and to my own detriment, which is what first came to mind.

I shake my head and chuckle at how stupid my thoughts are, especially when I'm standing in a backyard situated on the edge of a canyon. Jase's house is nestled in the Hollywood Hills overlooking Santa Monica with hints of the ocean in the distance.

The house itself is big and bold and overwhelming. It's concrete walls with curved edges and travertine floors that could be so very cold but somehow feel warm and welcoming. The bottom floor feels open and flowy with one end of the house leading down a hall toward where there's a recording studio. The upstairs has one wing with a primary suite that's separated from the other side by a loft of sorts. That space holds all kinds of BENT accolades and other rock memorabilia, and on the other side of it, where I'm staying, has a couple of en-suite bedrooms.

To be honest, I feel like an impostor living in an extravagant resort. I have a closet full of new clothes that don't feel like they're mine regardless of how many times I see them hanging there, color coordinated, and beside a binder from the stylist of how I can use each item.

Then there's all this space and comfort. The peace and quiet and the time to just sit without the bakery downstairs calling to me to come work.

And when Jase is here, regardless of how many times he tells me to make myself at home, I feel like I'm invading his space and privacy. So it's times like right now when he ventures into the city to do whatever he does, that I feel like I can explore.

But I do know what he does, because the past two days he's made sure to find me before he leaves to give me a detailed explanation of where he's going and when he'll be back. The studio. A stop at Nathaniel's office. Then back to the studio before he heads home. For a man who has a reputation that he cares about no one, I'm beginning to think whoever started that rumor has never really met the real Jase Gizmodo.

Or maybe he doesn't want them to.

But he's gone for the day and I'm going to revel in this time to myself. It's been six months of working nonstop toward making the bakery a success and so the past four days have felt like heaven. No early morning wake-up calls to bake. No constant thoughts of how to survive. No need to explain where Paul went to the few regular customers I have.

Just a sign on the door that says closed until Wednesday. *Yes, I feel guilty about doing even that.* But the thought of not having to live paycheck to paycheck for a while and being able to pay Barney and Annie in full in the next few weeks makes it palatable.

So palatable that I even might be enjoying myself as I relax at his luxurious poolside. Who knew I'd get to be so good at pretending?

First, at being blissfully ignorant of the gigantic order I have to fulfill and second, of the fact that there's a diamond ring currently creating a tan line on my finger.

I sink farther into the chaise lounge, welcome the sun's warmth on my skin, and the quiet in my head that hasn't been quieted in forever.

"What are you thinking about?"

I jump at the sound of Jase's voice and instantly panic. "Hi." *I'm in a bathing suit.* "I didn't know you were home." *A bathing suit that is small and ill-fitting and oh, man.* "Why are you here?" *My legs are flat, which means my ass and thighs are spread and probably look like bloated pancakes.*

Oh.

My.

God.

He chuckles, his brows narrowing. "I'm here because I live here?" His pitch goes up at the end of the sentence as if he's not certain whether that's the right answer or not or more like why he's answering it at all.

"Yes. Silly question." My body heats as embarrassment and insecurity hits me. "You said you'd be back at like four." Well after I'd be out of this bikini and in something more . . . covering.

"We finished early," he says.

"I hope you don't mind that I came out here."

His eyes rake over my body as I take the rolled-up towel from behind my head and try to subtly and eloquently cover my thighs and stomach. "Don't cover up on my account."

I snort and keep covering. "I've seen your dates. Toned. Tanned. *Perfect.* You're damn well right I'm going to cover up."

He reaches out and puts a hand on my wrist to stop me. "Hendrix. *Stop.*" His words are a mixture of disbelief, warning, and surprise. "You're beautiful."

I open my mouth to refute him, a response I've acquired over the years to put myself down before someone else does front and center, but the lift of his brows and the disdain in his eyes stop me.

"And no, I don't have to say that because you're my wife."

"Thank you, but I still think you're full of shit."

He sits down on the cushion so that his hip is next to mine, his hand is resting over me and next to my opposite hip, and tsks. "Three days into our marriage and you're already criticizing me." He lifts the beer to his lips and chuckles around his sip. God, *he's gorgeous.* And not just attractive because of his looks or the ink that covers his skin, but . . . his smile, the light in his eyes, the way he looks at me and makes me feel . . . like I'm the only thing he sees.

And I don't know how that makes me feel when clearly right now I'm terribly uncomfortable in my own skin.

But he's sitting next to me, touching me, and I can't stop focusing on how close he is and how charmed I am by him with each interaction.

"You've been busy." I try to sound nonchalant. Try to show that I'm not thinking about how easily that hand he's put on the other side of my hip could run over my bare skin or how it might feel.

"Yeah. Sorry about that. This was all stuff that was scheduled before . . . *this* needed to happen. We're in the middle of a writing phase so sometimes, time escapes us."

"You're working on new material?"

He emits a heavy sigh. "Some days, yes. Other days it feels like we're pulling teeth. And still cool either way."

"Just getting to hear you say that is cool," I say and then worry I just sounded like a fan rather than whatever it is that I am. "But this isn't music for the tour, is it?"

"No. God, no. We're not that insane. The tour is for the last album and old stuff, but we like to write the next one before we head out. Or at least start the process so that we've established a baseline sound for the next release and can tweak it and work on it when we get sick of playing the same shit night after night."

"I always wondered about that. If musicians get sick of playing and hearing the same songs."

"It depends on the day, really. At this point, we don't really have to think when we play our older stuff." He takes another sip. "What about you? Are you sitting out here creating cookie designs in your head?"

"That sounds so trivial compared to what you're doing." I chuckle.

"I'm not creating world peace here. Just music. Just entertainment." That hand I was thinking about? Yeah, he turns it to palm the side of my hip and gives me a good shake. A shake that has an ache firing inches away from where those fingers rest. "Come on now. Why do you always put yourself down?"

"Habit. It's easier. It's—"

"Bullshit," he finishes for me. "You're a business owner. Many people have dreamed of doing that and few do, so don't sell yourself short."

"No, just sell myself to a rock star who needs to get married so I can keep said business open."

"Stop." He shakes me again with his hand on my hip. "No more of that when you're with me. He might have allowed you to do it, but I won't."

Why is that sexy? Jase taking ownership of something that really isn't his?

He dips his head down so we're eye to eye. "Yes?"

"Yes," I grumble.

"No. I want to hear some enthusiasm. Yes, Giz. You're the best husband a woman could ever ask for," he says with way too much cheer.

"Yes, Jase. You're the best husband a woman could ever ask for if she were actually looking for a husband."

He rolls his eyes but smiles so bright it could light up a room. "Now, that's more like it."

"I'm only here to make you happy," I tease.

"Remember that," he says and then takes a sip. "Especially when I tell you that your peace and quiet is going to be disturbed because Halle will be here in a little bit."

"Halle?"

"My assistant. She'll get your schedule and compare it to mine and let you know the events you're needed at and whatnot."

"Okay."

"There probably aren't many, so don't worry about being forced to be with me too much."

I nod as I meet his eyes. Doubt creeps in. "I promise I won't cramp your style."

He levels me with a look. "If I didn't like you or think you were gorgeous, if I didn't think you were sane and intelligent and would make my life easier, I wouldn't have asked for you . . . so stop with whatever I can see going through those eyes of yours."

Am I that transparent?

"Yes. You wear your emotions on your sleeve," he says, answering my own question, startling me.

"It's just a lot to be thrust into. Self-doubt is normal. Self-doubt when I know how cruel women are to other women, especially when they're anonymous behind keyboards and are even harsher."

"Well, raise up your hand and point to your wedding ring if they question it. That's all that needs to be said."

"Until we divorce and they say *I told you so*." He looks at me like I'm unhinged . . . and he's right. I am being just that. But it's been an absolute whirlwind of a week, that I'm surprised my head is even screwed on the right way. It's only natural for me to question, to wonder, and to feel a little unsteady.

I wouldn't have asked for you . . .

He's right. I'm here because he picked me, because he wanted me to be here. I just have to learn to accept it and stop comparing myself to others.

Easier said than done.

But if there's one thing I know about men, they hate a whiny woman and that's exactly what I'm being.

I rest my hand on his arm and squeeze. "I'm being ridiculous. I apologize. I'll work on it."

"It's understandable, you've stepped into a huge role and I'm extremely appreciative. Yeah?" He waits for me to nod. "Okay. Good. We'll probably leak the photos soon too. Just so you know."

"I assumed as much. I planned on heading back to the bakery in the morning, if that's okay? I know the plan was to make it look like we were on a honeymoon, but people know you're out and about on your own so that kind of negates that. Plus, someone had to have seen you in Las Vegas and is bound to say something soon."

"Perhaps. Perhaps not. Regardless, we have a plan. So that big order is coming up?"

"Yeah."

"Can you hire someone to help you? So you're not so stressed about it? I can help out if you need it."

I barely hold back my snort of humor. If the women, young and old, who were awestruck by him in Josie's are any indication, there wouldn't be much help happening. Imagine that in my tiny bakery.

"I'm fine. I've got it handled."

"You should hire someone. To man the counter up front at least while you work in back?"

"Maybe. I don't know." How do I explain to him that I don't have a line of customers that goes out the door or the phone ringing off the hook with orders so I don't need to hire anyone else? Pride has me making excuses. "My clients for the big order are big in the Bollywood scene. I had to sign all kinds of agreements about their privacy. They only wanted me working on their order."

Yeah, that fib isn't going to hold much water.

"They'd know if you didn't ice cookie number five hundred and twenty-two versus if someone else did it?"

Case in point.

"You're right. It sounds ridiculous. I'll figure something out." I lean my head back and close my eyes.

Jase shifts and moves off the chaise. I don't want him to go. While I've enjoyed the quiet and time to myself, it's also rather isolating when you're in a place that's not your own.

I open my eyes to see where he's going and gasp softly when his face blocks the sun and narrows to be my entire field of vision. His hands are on both armrests and his body is leaning down over me.

"I get this feels awkward—the house not being yours and not having your everyday comforts—but use it like it is and let me know what you need so it does feel like yours. I know this ring feels heavy—mine does too—but it's going to be okay. And, Cookie? When you look in the mirror later, try and see yourself through my eyes because you're gorgeous." His voice is back to that seductive silk, and I wonder why he chose being a drummer over lead singer because . . . damn.

My body heats and as much as I want to squirm in my seat to abate it, he's so damn close. He'd know why I was doing it, and I don't exactly want him to know that's how I react to him.

"You better stop with all these compliments," I say. "You keep proving to be the exact opposite of the public persona people say you are."

"What's that?"

"A good guy. A catch. Husband material."

He quirks a brow. "We'll keep this between us."

"Maybe you shouldn't. Maybe you should let the world see this side of you and then Judge Righteous Prick might hear about it."

"Nah. This isn't for everyone to see. Just the people I care about."

Well, that hits me squarely in the chest . . .

"I have to get back to work."

"You're leaving?"

"No." Another flash of a smile that has me catching my breath. "Here. At the house. I'm going to work for a bit. Then hit the gym. Then probably back to writing."

"Okay." I infuse cheer into my voice. He wasn't kidding about not impeding on my life. And while I am fine with that, a simple, "Hey, you want to eat dinner together?" would be nice.

But this is what I asked for, right?

"Jase, you know that you don't have to give me a rundown. You don't owe it to me to tell me where you are every minute of every day."

He pauses and something flashes through his eyes I can't read. He softens his voice and says, "Yeah, well, I know what it's like to wonder if someone's coming home." He shrugs. "It's a habit of mine—good or bad."

So many questions I could ask, curiosities I could satisfy, but I just nod and murmur, "Okay."

"Okay?" He chuckles and then stills when he looks up before looking back down at me. "It's not a bad thing to be informed."

"I never said it was. I just don't want you to feel like—"

And then without any warning, Jase leans over and cuts the comment short by brushing his lips over mine.

My lips shock open and he takes the opportunity to slip his tongue between them and meet mine.

It's only been a few days, but the reminder of what his kiss tastes like and how it makes me feel comes roaring back like a tidal wave about to pull me under.

Thoughts evade me as I slide my hands around his neck, thread my fingers through the hair at the nape of his neck, and pull him closer to me.

I forget to breathe and that this is pretend because all I can see and feel and want is Jase.

And before I can fully process the plethora of feelings the kiss caused—desire, confusion, want, disbelief—it ends.

His smile is crooked and his eyes are dark with desire when he looks at me, as our labored breathing mixes with the sounds of birds chirping.

"Jase?" I ask when my synapses fire.

"Making sure we're still good to sell this." He winks and his words jar me.

"Oh. Of course." My words sound as jilted as I feel. *Can't a guy give a girl a warning?*

He takes a few steps back and scrubs a hand over his jaw as he stares at me.

"What's that look for?" I ask.

"You may have been one of the most random decisions in my life, Cookie Cutter, but I lucked out."

"Why's that?"

"Because damn, girl, you can kiss."

And without another word, he turns on his heel and heads back into the house. I stare at his distressed blue jeans and black T-shirt-clad back as he goes.

I'm never going to survive this.

Not when kisses like that are going to be the norm and me being left without any sort of relief is part of the plan.

Talk about torture . . .

CHAPTER
eighteen

Gizmo

"**Y**OU REALIZE YOU ALWAYS HAVE SHITTY TIMING WHEN YOU CALL, right?" I adjust my hard-on in my pants as I stare out the window at the pool where I left Hendrix moments ago.

The urge to go back out there and finish what we started is real, but Nathaniel's voice in my ear is like cold water splashed in my face.

And a reminder of what I promised him.

Regardless, and at my own discomfort, I accomplished what I set out to do when I went to talk to her, so at least there's that.

"What's so shitty about it? I can't possibly be interrupting a groupie giving you head—"

"It was one time and she wasn't a groupie." I roll my eyes. She was *kind of* a groupie, but I don't think he cares much about semantics. "Besides, part of the deal was me abstaining, so I'm pretty sure you're implying I've already cheated on my wife when I haven't."

"Shocker." He snorts.

"Fucker," I respond.

"So much hostility," he jokes, although I can imagine his hands held up in surrender. "Jesus. I was simply calling to check in and see how it's going."

"That's mighty kind of you to take time out of your visit to Dad's house to think of me." The vitriol in my tone is lightened with the chuckle I emit but fuck if I don't still feel it.

"I told you that you were welcome to come with me."

Over my dead fucking body. The physical recoil I have to him even saying it doesn't surprise me. "Yeah, well, you also told me I had to get married. You're asking for a lot for me to do one, let alone two, things that you ask."

"It's not like you think it is," he says quietly.

"What? Marriage? No shit."

"No. Dad."

"Hmm. I bet." My disinterest is plain as fucking day. *Not like I ever got a chance to know myself.* "Is there a reason for this call, Nathaniel? The judge reach out and say I'm granted freedom? The probation officer give you an update? You miss my sarcasm? What?"

He clears his throat like he's prone to do before he gives me a lecture but then pauses. "Like I said, I was just calling to see how everything was going."

"It's good. Fine. *Whatever.*" Another glance out the window has me questioning my sanity and what exactly that *whatever* entails. Hendrix is flipping over on her stomach and undoing the back of her top to avoid tan lines.

Every juvenile fantasy boys have had about running out onto a beach or pool and yelling *fire* to get a free glance of tits runs through my head.

"Good? Fine? Whatever? That doesn't exactly sound promising," he says, oblivious to my childish but very real thoughts.

"It is. It's nothing. Just frustrated with work stuff."

"Okay." He falls silent for a beat. "You're not already questioning your choice of a wife, are you?"

"Yeah. Definitely," I murmur absently as she adjusts the bottoms of her suit to highlight even more of her ass. *Jesus.* "She's itching to get back to her work and I need . . ." Another adjustment that has me looking even closer.

"Finish the sentence, Jase. You need what? Her to be gone so you can have the privacy to fuck somebody else?"

"Christ, Nate. Do you actually think that's all I think about?"

At times. When a gorgeous woman is living under my roof. *Perhaps.*

"If it's not, that's the image you portray."

"Image. Not reality."

"Great. Then I don't have to worry about Hendrix suing you for misconduct."

"Always thinking the best of me, aren't you, brother?"

"No, just looking out for you." I can imagine his shrug. "You went from she's the one for the job to sounding not so sure, so in my head she's cramping your style and you're pissed about it."

"How about I went from single to living with someone in a matter of days? How about I have to suddenly worry about another person's feelings and how they're probably going to get hurt by all of this when it's not her fault in the first place? How about stuff like that, huh? It's a fucking lot."

"Welcome to being a grown-up," he says sarcastically. I refuse to acknowledge the silent dig. He didn't fight when his life was chosen for him. I didn't have a choice. I've had to fight for everything from *that day* forward. "Why though, Jase?"

Because I made a promise to you not to touch her and right now, I sure as shit feel like breaking it.

CHAPTER
nineteen

"**U**GH."

It's my first and only thought when I see the caller ID on my phone say "Mom" on the incoming call.

If I pick up, then I'm already lying to her.

But nothing has broken yet and so it might be the last time I actually talk to her without the burden of guilt that's fast approaching.

Wedding pictures will "leak" by Friday, at least that's the plan, and so with that knowledge, I opt to answer and have a much easier conversation.

"Mom. Hi. How are you doing?"

"Honey? Are you okay? I called the bakery and the message said you were closed for a few days. Is something wrong?"

Shit. "I'm fine. Good. That was from a few days ago. I've been there. I just forgot to change the message."

"But you were closed? Why? What's wrong? You haven't taken a day off since you opened. Do I need to come out and take care of Fucktard for you?"

I chuckle. "No, Mom. This has nothing to do with Paul. I have a big order coming up and needed a few days' break before I start on it."

She makes a noncommittal sound that says she doubts me. "Okay, but how are you going to pay bills if you aren't open?"

She doesn't know that Paul drained our accounts. That would have resulted in a lecture about how I put my future in the hands of a man. She'd then want to come and save the day when she doesn't have the money to save the day with in the first place.

And she doesn't know I'm being paid to now be Mrs. Jase Gizmodo. That would open a whole other round of questions about what services I'm being paid for exactly and . . . now, I comprehend why Nathaniel required that no one else know.

It makes it easier and harder at the same time.

"I'm good. I promise. This order is huge and I inflated the prices so I covered the days off."

"You sure about that or are you just giving me lip service?"

"I am. I promise."

"And here I was all worked up because Nosy Natalia—you know my friend who lives across the street and obsesses over her gossip sites all day— swears there was a picture of you in one of them."

My heart jumps in my chest.

"That's ridiculous."

"I said the same thing, but honey, she showed me the pictures and I can see why she thought that. They were taken at a distance but I'm telling you, that girl is your doppelgänger."

If my mom thinks it . . . someone must have taken a picture from our night out in Vegas. Truth be told, I'm surprised one hasn't been posted or bought by tabloids sooner.

"Right down to the bikini she was wearing," she continues as I pause mid-motion. "It was almost identical to the one you wore on our girls' trip a few years back. Such a unique pattern it was. I knew it wasn't you though. What in the world would you be doing in the backyard of a mansion in Los Angeles?"

Each sentence of this conversation is getting ostensibly worse.

Bikini? Backyard of a mansion?

My hands begin to tremble, but she speaks and answers the question before I can even put words to it. "Some musician's house no less. You don't even like tattoos and you could see he had plenty of them as he bent over and kissed her."

My body flushes with a heat I've never experienced before.

It's happening. I knew this was coming, that people would know, but . . . in my bikini? In my most vulnerable state?

"Mom, I have to go," I say, trying to keep my voice as even as possible.

"I'm all for letting loose and frolicking and the like, but Natalia was saying how it looked a lot like those pictures from the Playboy Mansion way back when."

"It wasn't there," I say without thinking, not realizing I just gave her a nugget to bite on.

"It was . . . you?" Confusion peppers her voice.

Welcome to the club, Mom.

"I'll explain later. In the coming days, just remember what I told you the last time we talked."

"That you're okay?"

"Exactly."

"This isn't sitting well with me."

"You're talking to me. You hear that I'm fine. It's a picture in a bikini in a friend's backyard. That's all."

"Hmm," she murmurs.

"Now I do have to go as I have a potential client coming in and need to get ready."

We end the call on my lie, but I'm so overwhelmed as I scramble to social media, search Gizmo, and see picture after grainy picture of Jase and me in his backyard.

The bottom I was worried about dropping out, does just that.

I can't look away.

There are pictures of me standing and picking my swimsuit out of my ass. There's another of Jase sitting beside me. One where he's turned toward the pool with a huge grin on his face as if I said something funny. The last one is of him kissing me as my hands dive into his hair.

Oh. My.

The same types of pictures I've scrolled through and judged before.

"Jase?" I ask as I move through the house, grateful his house staff is gone for the day. "Jase?" This time my pitch escalates and I pick up my pace, almost feeling desperate to find him.

"Hendrix? What's wrong?" he asks as he steps down the hall where his recording studio is and moves toward me. His brows are knit and tone is laced with concern.

"They know. The public knows."

"Calm down." He sounds like the voice of reason. "What are we talking about?"

I shove my phone at him and jab my finger from my free hand at its screen. "There. Right there."

He purses his lips as he studies them before his lips crawl into a slow smile. "Perfect."

"Perfect?"

"Yeah. I tried to position us so they'd get a good angle with it."

It takes a second for his words to sink in, but the minute they do, I feel like I've been slapped in the face. "What do you mean that you tried to position us for a good angle?"

"My publicist set it up. The tip to a photographer that I had a woman at my house. Where to go to catch a good photo." He shrugs. "And they did their job."

"Of me in a bathing suit? You set it all up, planned a paparazzi shoot, and didn't think to tell me?" I screech.

He shrugs again. "What's the big deal? If I'd told you, then you would have looked their way and made it obvious that we set up a PR stunt. It's not like they know who you are or anything. You still have your privacy for a few more hours yet."

"Lucky me."

"God, can we cut that crap?"

"You tricked me." *With a kiss that left me reeling.*

Who is this man?

Tears burn in my eyes.

After all the kind words of affirmation he threw at me, it would be reasonable to believe he kissed me because he wanted to.

It's a business arrangement, Hendrix. You forgot that, didn't you?

"Better get used to the exposure, Hendrix. This is what you signed up for."

Clearly the honeymoon is over. I thought I was getting to know the true Jase.

"Isn't it?" he asks.

"I didn't sign up to be lied to. Not once did you think about—"

"What's the big fucking deal?" he shouts. "In two days, everyone is going to know we're married. At least this way it doesn't look like you were some wannabe groupie I picked up in Vegas."

"Wow. Just feed into my fears, why don't you."

He pulls down on the back of his neck and groans. "You didn't have to say yes to this."

And like any person fighting with someone for the first time, you don't know where lines can and can't be drawn or just how dirty your opponent is willing to fight.

"And you didn't have to bring me in to help solve your problems." My tone is even despite the racing of my heart.

He groans and moves about the space like a caged animal who's at war with himself.

"Look." His sigh is heavy as he lifts his hands and drops them. There's regret in his eyes but only a hint of it in his words when he speaks. "I did what I had to do. It's not that big of a deal so quit making it one."

I stare at him, hating the tears welling in my eyes. I'm hurt, when I really shouldn't be. *But he blindsided me today, and I hate feeling like I'm on the back foot. Humiliated.*

It's a business arrangement, and you've learned something about your fake husband today. *He won't always include you, despite the bullshit he fed you about ensuring you know where he is.*

"I'm not making it anything, Jase." It's a partial lie. He kissed me by the pool and for the smallest, tiniest sliver of time, I believed in the tenderness. *I won't again.*

You don't kiss when you don't want to—*just because.* Well, Jase Gizmodo does. *So, keep your guard up.*

"I have shit to do," I mutter.

"Hendrix—"

"Don't." I hold a hand up. "Like you said, it's not a big deal." My tone says differently. And with those words, I turn and head back down the hallway to my bedroom without looking back. Jase calls after me, frustration in his voice, but he doesn't chase after me.

I don't want him to, either.

CHAPTER
twenty

Gizmo

YOU'RE AN ASSHOLE.

A Grade A, certifiable asshole, Giz.

I close my eyes and rest my forehead against the pantry door. I don't need a fucking therapist to point out what I did.

Pushed to see a reaction.

Pushed to see if she'd leave.

Pushed to see if she'd stay.

Pushed . . . because that's all I know how to fucking do when my guard is up.

Did I have every right to have the pictures taken? Hell, yes. It's my house. It's my backyard. It's my fucking privacy.

But not telling her? The waiting to see how she'd react when she found out? The purposeful slip of letting her know I booked that photographer? The absolute dickish reaction just now?

Yeah, that was all asshole shit that I did to test Hendrix.

To see what she's made of even though it's probably too late given she's already married to me.

To see if she'd stay when the going gets rough. *Fuck.*

I scrub a hand over my face. It's too goddamn early in this venture to test someone. To push them. To see how hard they'll push back.

But why? Why do this with a woman I'm not supposed to care about or worry what she thinks? Isn't that why I chose her in the first place?

The gorgeous wallflower from the coffee shop with bills to pay isn't supposed to cause any trouble and yet . . . I kind of want her to.

Fucked up, I know.

Even more fucked up . . . *I like her.* Or what I know of her so far. And I want to know her more.

"Fuck," I mutter.

I head to the fridge to grab a beer.

And then I go to my studio to do the only thing that's ever quieted the noise in my head.

I go beat the shit out of my drums.

CHAPTER
twenty-one

Hendrix

I STAND OUTSIDE THE STUDIO'S OPEN DOOR AND LISTEN TO JASE AS HE plays through different lyrics and sounds. Each time he replays it, he either tweaks a line or changes the chord going with it.

I'm the least musical person on the face of the planet so no doubt even that description of what he's doing is incorrect. He talks or hums when he can't finish lines. All I know is it sounds like he's trying to make something sound like what he's hearing in his head and is getting frustrated by it.

"I built these walls, stone by stone
Told myself I'd walk alone
Love was just a hmmm-hmmm-hmmm
One more spark, one more flame
But then you —"

He stops and mumbles to himself, "I need to figure out a line to sing here," before picking right back up and singing the next lines.

"Sweet surrender, I'm falling now
No more running, no more doubt
Take my heart, don't let me go
Hmm-Hmm-Hmm"

Eating crow is never fun and yet this is what I need to do.

I came into this situation knowing exactly what it was—a deal, an agreement, a way to better his image and my bank account. It's not Jase's fault that I liked the man I thought he was and misinterpreted the kiss. *Again.*

I've been corrected and while I still think he was in the wrong for not telling me about the photographer, my footing has been reaffirmed and I know squarely where I stand.

Jase Gizmodo is a flirt. While it's probably innocent in nature, it's just how he is, he doesn't understand that casual kisses and crooked smirks aren't the norm . . . *for me.*

Or that a man who looks like he does and can sing like he can is a hard one not to like.

With a deep breath, I step into the doorway to try to right the wrongs from earlier. It's the least I can do since we're stuck with each other for the next few months.

Jase is sitting so I'm met with his profile. He's shirtless with his hair falling on his brow as he hunches over an acoustic guitar. He holds a pencil between his lips as he nods at whatever he's been writing on the scribbled sheet of paper in front of him. A keyboard is to his right and a computer that looks like it has some kind of program open is to his left and angled in my direction.

That reminder that I can't crush on him just hit hard and heavy as I stare at him in his element.

"Hey," he says when he catches sight of me. "Give me one second. I don't want to forget what's in my head."

"Of course." I stay where I am, conscious that this is his inner sanctum and he may not want me here.

He hums through a few more notes as his fingers hit the keys on the keyboard before setting the guitar in its stand and looking over to me. His expression is stoic. "Did you need me?"

"You play all these instruments?" I ask and move into the studio, completely impressed.

He nods as I reach out and run a finger over the cymbal so that it moves. "I do. Well enough to get by but drums is my main instrument."

"That's admirable. I can't even play one let alone three. I mean, what are those things that kids take home in grade school that parents despise?"

"A recorder?"

"Yeah. That." My smile is automatic at the thought of how hard I tried to play that damn thing. "I think my mom may have 'accidentally' thrown it away." I glance his way. He's standing on the opposite side of the room, arms crossed over his chest, watching me as I move around the space.

"No doubt you drove her up a wall playing it."

"Definitely. Did you drive your parents crazy practicing the drums?"

His smile is quick but strained. "Something like that."

It's a non-answer but I don't push. He's uncomfortable talking about his family—that's obvious—and if he wants to tell me, he'll tell me.

"Your dad?" he asks.

I shrug. "Never knew him. From what I've heard about him, don't think I want to."

"Sorry."

"Don't be. You can't miss what you never had, right?" I say the words, the ones I tell everyone, but it doesn't lessen that small pang I get. It doesn't ease that curiosity over why he didn't want me.

"Doesn't make it any easier," he says softly.

"Perhaps." I run my finger across several keys of the keyboard, the sound harsh despite the beauty of the individual notes. "I don't mean to bug you."

He moves to the opposite side of the room now, almost like he's purposely keeping distance between us, before taking a seat on the stool behind his drum set. "Didn't bug me. I could probably use the break."

"Writing some of the new stuff?"

He nods. "Yeah. It's just a song."

"I like it." I wave at the doorway. "I mean from what I heard, anyway."

"It's shit."

"I have a feeling you'd say that about any song regardless of how good it is. You're hard on yourself."

"Someone has to be."

"Can we talk about before? Earlier?" I ask.

"It's over. I don't hold grudges over petty shit," he says and then hangs his head for a beat before looking back up at me. "I know. I get it. It wasn't petty to you. But grudges aren't my style."

"That doesn't mean I shouldn't apologize about my freak-out earlier. I know you're used to your privacy being invaded, but clearly I'm not. It was hard finding out that you're the one who orchestrated it. You're right with what you said though—that I signed up for this—but I was too blindsided to see it. It's apparent that I need to get thicker skin or stop—"

"Worrying about what everyone thinks and own everything you are?" He lifts his eyebrows. "Pretty much."

"Easier said than done." I roll my eyes as I come back near him and his drum set. "I'm far from perfect and I look at this whole thing as a growing experience for me. I'm going to make mistakes and am adult enough to admit it, so can you just accept my apology so we can move on?"

"No."

"No?" I cough out a laugh.

"I won't accept it. I should be the one apologizing. I should have told you what was going on, and I didn't because I selfishly wanted it to look authentic and real and like you actually like me."

"Actually like you?" *Is he for real?*

"That's what I said."

We stare at each other across the space. It's obvious we're both trying to make this unexpected, awkward situation work.

"Fine. We'll call it even. You apologized. I apologized . . ."

"But?" He lifts his eyebrows and fights the smirk playing at the corner of his lips.

"But don't mistake me trying to find my footing in this new setting as a chance for you to be a dick." He barks out a surprised laugh and then reins it back in. "I didn't like the man who showed up in the hall earlier. The one who sought out ways out to be rude and hurtful. It was almost as if you were putting me in my place for reasons that validated you, but that I sure as shit didn't understand. He was a prick and nothing like the man I've gotten to know and like."

His grin returns. "You're sexy when you're angry."

"I'm sexy all the time," I joke, completely uncertain where that came from.

His laugh roars through the studio. "There's that confidence I need to see more of from you."

"Whatever." I roll my eyes as my cheeks heat.

"I'm serious. Let the world see this woman, the one I get, and not the crazy one who you were earlier."

I nod. "Touché. Point made."

"Fair is fair," he says as he approaches me and holds his arms wide. "Now we need to hug it out."

"Hug it out?"

"Yes. What two self-respecting adults do when they own their mistakes."

And before I can refute him, he engulfs me in his arms. I'm met with the scent of his cologne and soap, with the warm feel of his bare skin against my cheek, and the firmness of his arms as he tightens his grip on me.

"You need to loosen up, Cookie. Wasn't that part of you agreeing to do this?" He leans back so his face is within inches of mine and reminds me solidly of how damn handsome he is. "To live a little? To not be *normal?*"

"Wanting to be photographed in a bikini is not living a little, Jase. It's terrifying."

"No, but not giving a fuck is." He winks and then throws his head back and laughs. "So let's go. Lesson number one in Operation Live-A-Little—"

"Operation Live-A-Little?"

"Yeah." Those boyish dimples deepen. "My way to make you live up to the rashness that made you accept my very romantic proposal."

"We're not doing this." I roll my eyes.

"We *so are,*" he says, imitating me by rolling his eyes and then winking at me. "C'mon." He tugs on my hand and brings me with him over to the drum set.

"I think you're crazy," I say but a smile is on my lips.

"Perfect. That's better than being a dick or a prick or whatever you called me." He takes a seat on the stool behind his drum set and holds out his hand to me. "You know you want me to show you how to play."

Maybe I do. Maybe I don't. All I know is that I don't want to go back to my room or the emptiness of the gorgeous house beyond.

"I don't have a musical bone in my body."

"Everybody does. It just takes the right person to bring it out of them."

"And you think that would be you?"

He purses his lips as he studies me. "Your husband is a man of many talents, Hendrix."

And the way he says those words, the double entendre, has my body heating.

This time when he tugs my hand, he does it so I stumble and am forced to sit on his lap. "Oh," I yelp as he helps to position me, my legs straddling one of his thighs.

First the hug.

Now me on his lap.

Someone is playing with fire.

I'm not doing a particularly good job of remembering to separate church and state right now. I mean, what red-blooded, normal woman would when they're sitting on Jase's lap with his body framing hers?

His chin brushes over my shoulder and his breath ghosts against my ear, making me forget every reason I should get up and move. "It's simple, really. Playing the drums. Just a bunch of motions with your body to create a desired outcome, both of which are guaranteed to make you feel." He reaches to the table behind where we're sitting and holds out two drumsticks. "Here."

"This is ridiculous," I mutter and hold the sticks awkwardly.

His chuckle vibrates against my spine even though I'm desperately trying to keep space between us. "It's only ridiculous because you're making it that way."

His hands slide over mine and adjust my grip. They're warm. Strong. A little rough from years of playing.

"Loosen up, Cookie," he murmurs, voice thick with amusement. "They're not weapons."

I scoff. "You don't know that."

"Ah, yes. The serial killer notion returns." He chuckles, and the sound wraps around me like a song. "You're going to have to let me lead you. Help you. Control your movements. Yeah?"

"Mm-hmm." I don't trust myself to speak. I'm so very aware of his every breath and my every nerve.

"The snare. The hi-hat. Kick drum . . ." he continues with his quick lesson of the various parts to the set, using our connected hands to point to each one as he goes.

"You think I'm going to actually remember this?"

"You're a drummer's wife, knowing them is a requirement."

I start to say something, to make a quip much like he does, but then, without warning, he lifts my hands and brings them down in a steady rhythm.

My words fail as I try to follow what he's doing.

It's useless and yet we're creating a rhythm. One that I actually like. I'm under no pretenses that my skill has anything to do with the sound—he's the one moving my hands with the tempo and location to hit—and yet I have an odd sense of satisfaction.

The sharp *crack* of the snare drum jolts through me as we hit it and then he drops our hands to the tops of my thighs.

"See?" he says, his lips brushing just behind my ear. "Not so hard."

Easy for him to say. My body is hyperaware of him—his chest pressed against my back, the solid weight of his thighs beneath mine, the slow inhale and exhale that keeps time better than any metronome could.

"All right, let's try it again. Another something simple." He guides my left hand to the hi-hat, my right to the snare—at least I think that's what they're called. My lesson was quick and his presence is distracting. "One, two, three, four—" He taps his foot against the pedal, the steady thud of it matches the beat he whispers against my skin.

I try to follow along, but I'm awkward and my arms move like I'm fighting off an invisible attacker with zero grace.

Jase groans playfully and chuckles. "Jesus, woman, you're as stiff as a board."

"Says the musical prodigy who can probably just hear something and play it," I say.

"No. That's Rocket," he says, referring to his bandmate. He shifts slightly, and I jolt when his fingers graze my waist. "See? There's your problem." His voice dips lower, teasing. "You're too tense, Cookie. Drumming's all about letting go. Feeling it."

I huff. This is clearly not my forte. "And how do you suggest I do that?"

He tightens his grip around my waist and pulls me flush against his chest—the exact position I was avoiding.

Heat blooms across my skin as chills tighten my scalp.

"Easy," he murmurs. "Stop thinking."

His hand skims up my arm, causing my breath to hitch. He adjusts my grip again, fingers lingering longer than necessary.

"Close your eyes," he says quietly.

I hesitate.

Jase presses a lazy, barely-there kiss to my shoulder, but it's enough to make me question if he did or didn't. "Trust me," he murmurs.

That's the problem. *I do.*

But last time I trusted someone I was blindsided.

I let out a shaky breath and surrender as my world shrinks to the warmth of him behind me and the steady rhythm of his heartbeat against my back.

"Now," he whispers, "this time just feel it."

I strike the snare, then the hi-hat, my body falling into the pattern he set. Jase's voice guides me through each motion, each calamity of notes that sounds nothing like his did.

Or maybe it does. I can't tell because Jase is the master of distraction with how his lips brush against my temple as he continues to count out the beat.

For a short span of time, I finally hit the components, the pieces, the whatever the sequence is called, in the right order and it sounds *kind of* decent.

"Attagirl," he says. A smile tugs at my lips as his arms tighten around me ever so slightly. "Told you I could teach you."

I turn my head to meet his gaze. His blue eyes flicker with something dangerous. Something enticing.

Something I've told myself is simple flirtation from a playful man and nothing more.

But this doesn't feel innocent. Not the way his body frames mine, not the fact that I'm sitting on his lap, and most definitely not that weird, panicky feeling in my chest.

My heartbeat stutters and my fingers go slack on the sticks.

"You're losing your rhythm."

"You're distracting," I mutter and turn my attention fully back to the sticks in my hands and the set in front of me, but my mind is racing with all the thoughts I shouldn't be having. That I can't be having . . . and yet they're there anyway.

"Good. That's just what I like to be."

"I, uh . . . I should probably let you get back to what you were doing. I shouldn't have interrupted your creativity."

"Hmm," he says but rests his chin on my shoulder instead of leaning back to let me escape.

Because it would be an escape. From the tumultuous tornado he's just sent every nerve ending in my body into. I've kissed the man, I know how that wreaked havoc on my system, but this quiet, in-control, ridiculously skilled persona gives him an undeniable sex appeal.

Just when I tell myself that I know there's nothing between us, that his flirting is innocent and simply who he is, he goes and does *this* and muddies the waters for me.

"Jase." I shift so we're almost face-to-face. I don't know why I said his name, don't have a reasonable explanation other than maybe it's my way of reminding myself of the situation. Of what can't—what shouldn't be. But when my eyes flutter up to meet his, there's no mistaking the darkening of his pupils and the bob of his Adam's apple.

He's . . . *gorgeous*. Like this. In his element. It calls to me on levels I can't comprehend.

"Hendrix." His voice is soft. Deep. Hesitant yet heavy like he wants to ask what he knows he shouldn't.

The moment stretches as my body burns bright with ache and need and confusion.

"Jase? You back there?" Halle's voice calls out from somewhere in the house and shocks me off his lap.

"I've gotta—I need to . . . yeah." I give up trying to pretend I have my cool about me. "I've got to get some work done." I hook a thumb over my shoulder like a dork as if he didn't know where I'd be going.

"Work?"

"Yeah. Baking. I bake." *Brilliant, Hendrix.*

The smile playing at the corners of his mouth says he thinks as much. "This is going to be a problem, isn't it?" he asks, his head angling to the side and his tongue licking out to wet his bottom lip.

"What is?" I ask.

"Jase?" Halle calls again.

"Back here," he says loudly, but his eyes never leave mine. "Wanting you and not being able to have you."

"Oh." *Oh.* OH.

I stand there in the doorway, shocked by his words with my pulse pounding in my ears. I need to say something more—something literate—but I don't think I can.

Every part of me wants to say he's joking, flirting, but the expression on his face says otherwise.

Halle's footsteps are coming closer.

"I'll let you get used to the idea, Cookie. Pretty sure you're a look before you leap type of girl whereas I just leap. There's a reason I'm the one in trouble." He lifts his eyebrows as Halle steps in and halts momentarily, clearly sensing there's something going on here.

"Hi. Sorry. Am I interrupting something? I can go out to the kitchen," she says as she moves across the studio and sets her bag down in a subtle attempt to let us finish whatever our moment was.

"No need to," Jase says as a smile crawls over his lips and I step out of the room, desperate for a moment to think clearly.

I move down the hall toward the kitchen as Jase's voice floats after me. "We were just mapping out what we've coined to be Operation Live-A-Little. I think Hendrix might need time to get used to the idea."

"Oh? What's that?" she asks in her chatty way.

But I stop listening to their conversation because I'm too wrapped up in my own head. Too fixated on one sentence Jase just said.

Wanting you and not being able to have you.

Fuck.

CHAPTER
twenty-two

EXHAUSTION HITS THE SECOND I STEP OUT OF THE STUDIO. WHEN I'M within those four walls, I'm invigorated. Motivated. But the minute that door opens, the moment the music and creativity stops, I'm spent.

That and maybe—*just maybe*—I'm waiting until I know Hendrix is asleep. I pushed every limit I could earlier without breaking them. My body remembers all too well the feel of her ass nestled up against my cock, and it hasn't exactly forgiven me yet.

"Christ," I mutter as I pad down the hallway toward the kitchen in bare feet. I roll my shoulders, muscles stiff from playing too damn long.

But hedging my bets seemed like it worked. The house is quiet, the kind of silence that makes you feel the space all around you. Makes you want to create noise to break it up and at the same time tiptoe so as to respect it.

I've had some of my best creativity runs in this kind of silence but not tonight. Nowhere close. My mind was too occupied with Hendrix and the softness of her skin and her intoxicating scent.

When I reach the kitchen, I stop short.

There's a place setting on the island with something wrapped in tinfoil next to the plate. As I approach, I find a note scribbled on a torn piece of paper beside it.

Thought you might be hungry. Here's to celebrating another first. Our first fight. Our first make-up. Our first successful Operation Live-A-Little. Food is in the warming drawer. Don't say I never do anything nice for my husband.

-H

A smirk tugs at my lips. *Smart-ass.*

And as much as she might be, she's the one who took the time to be considerate. To take care of me after a long day's work.

Can't say anyone has ever done that for me before. Or rather, maybe I've never given someone the opportunity to do that.

There's something to be said about that, but my brain's too tired to recognize it.

I peel back the foil, and the scent of garlic bread hits me. My mouth waters as I move to the other side of the island and pull open the warming drawer to find a plate loaded with pasta and what looks like a bolognese.

Jesus. The woman knows a way to a man's heart.

Have I eaten since breakfast? *Hell.* No wonder I'm starving.

I grab the plate, sit down and dig in. Homecooked meals are a rarity for a guy like me. Sure, I have a chef prepare meals for me and leave them in my fridge, but it's not like this. Not even close.

This is a million times better than what I normally grab with one of the guys. We're the take-out kings when we're writing an album, but they're crazy if they think I'd share any of this with them.

The first bite is as good as the food smells. The woman can bake *and* cook. Lucky fucking me.

My phone vibrates on the counter. *Thirty something missed texts? Fuck me.* I skim through the ones that matter as I eat and fire off responses to the guys and their bullshit razzing over why I'm MIA. Most of which have to do with Hendrix. A majority of them cruder with each unanswered text.

Fucking assholes.

But I finish my texts and my food with a grin on my lips.

She should have told me she cooked. I would have eaten with her. Kept her company. The thought strikes as I'm washing my dishes, and I realize how inconsiderate I've been to her.

I asked Hendrix to pack her life up for me and yet, I haven't made any adjustments to mine. If the roles were reversed, I'd revel in the solitude and the silence I've left her to have. I'd spend all day in my head creating music or drinking beer by the pool and relaxing.

But she's not me. She's without her comforts, without her normal surroundings, and honestly, she's forbidden to really tell anyone where she is. So does this feel like a prison to her? Being cooped up in this house where everything is someone else's and that someone else never seems to be around?

Yeah. No doubt it does.

It doesn't matter how nice a house is, the walls can still feel like confinement. I know that for a fact. That's how I first felt when stardom struck and I was struggling to adjust.

But then she goes and does this.

I scrape a hand down my face and exhale harshly.

I promised Nathaniel. I told him I wouldn't touch her, wouldn't complicate shit. I need her to help me pull this charade off and the last thing I want to do is fuck things up.

But damn if she isn't making this difficult to stand my ground.

I said what I said to her earlier though, didn't I? I talked the talk. I saw her reaction—wide eyes, hitched breath, pebbled nipples—with my own eyes.

She wants me just as bad. I'd hang one of my Grammys on it.

A four-month fling? Nothing serious. Nothing deep. She said she's sworn off men so I know she wouldn't be clingy and ask for more. The only thing I'd have to worry about is it ending sooner than our marriage does.

At least that's my reasoning as I take a shower, brush my teeth, and get ready for bed. But that reasoning ends up carrying me down the hall, past the dimly lit loft area, and toward her cracked bedroom door.

I push it open a few inches. She's curled on her side, the blankets twisted around her legs, and one arm tucked under her cheek. In the faint glow of the moonlight spilling in through the window, she looks . . . soft. Vulnerable.

A strange sensation tightens in my chest but I ignore it. The woman cooked me dinner. She's uprooted her life for me. Of course I have a soft spot for her. Care for her. What guy wouldn't?

Walk away, Giz.

Thoughts of her on my lap fill my head.

Walk the fuck away.

Of my hands on hers. Of the surprise in her eyes when she got it right.

I shift my feet and when the floor creaks beneath me, she stirs to life. *Shit.*

"Jase?" Her lashes flutter as her eyes blink open. She frowns, then pushes up onto her elbows. "Did you need something?"

I rub the back of my neck. "Hey."

"You're aware you're standing in my doorway like that serial killer thing we talked about, right?"

I huff out a laugh and lean my shoulder on the doorjamb. "Funny."

She stares at me for a beat, then tilts her head, voice softer. "You okay?"

No. Yes. Hell if I know.

"Thank you for dinner. You could have come gotten me. I would have eaten with you—celebrated that first with you."

"I didn't want to bug you. Plus Halle was still here, and I don't know that dynamic and—"

"You're rambling."

"I tend to do that."

"So I've noticed," I say softly. "Thank you. That was . . . unexpected. Thoughtful. Exactly what I needed after a long day working."

Her smile is soft but I can't read her eyes through the darkness. "No need to thank me."

"There is, but if I say it again you'll be stubborn and argue," I tease.

"You should have thought of that before you married me." She smiles.

Silence stretches between us, filling the darkness. *What is it about her . . .*

I should leave.

I've thanked her for dinner. Now I should get the hell out of here before I do something I can't take back.

Maybe that's why I'm still standing here though, in the dim glow of her room.

Hendrix isn't just my fake wife. She isn't just a temptation. She's a risk.

And fuck, that makes a man like me want her even more.

"Is there something else on your mind?" she asks.

I shrug, feeling like a fish out of water. "I'm far from perfect, Hendrix. I was rude to you earlier and—"

"And you already apologized. No grudges, remember?"

"Yeah but . . . I have a way of testing people. Pushing them to see how they'll react."

"You mean if they'll run," she says evenly.

I nod. The admission is easier when the dark masks the shame in my expression. "Maybe I was doing that to you."

She smiles. It's bright and brilliant and so very obvious in the darkness as she holds up her ring finger. "Well, this makes that kind of complicated, huh?"

I appreciate her ability to see I'm uncomfortable and add levity to the moment. "True."

"I'm still here, Jase. It takes more than that to scare me off."

Why do those words lighten the pressure in my chest? "Parents really know how to fuck a kid up sometimes," I say. *Why the hell did I just say that?* "I should go." It's my turn to be flustered. "Sorry to wake you. I—I just wanted to thank you for dinner."

"Don't go." Her words stop me. There's a quiet plea in her voice almost as if she too, needed the interaction that I went looking for. "Stay. Talk to me."

CHAPTER
twenty-three

Hendrix

H E LOOKS LIKE A DREAM. ONE MARRED WITH SHADOWS BUT THAT OWNS
the light somehow. His arms are crossed and a pair of sweats hang loose
on his hips.

His eyes say yes, but his body falters, hesitating at my request.

Probably much like mine did earlier when he dropped that bomb on
me. The *me wanting you and not being able to have you* part.

I scoot back against the headboard, tugging the blankets over my lap.
Sleep has been hard here. Sure I crash into slumber at some point, but these
hills are too quiet, too still.

I'm used to the city—the hum of traffic, the rumble of trash trucks, the
occasional scream of someone cussing their ex out on the street below my
apartment. That? That's a lullaby.

"Can't sleep?" I love his voice like this. A little low, a lot rough from what
I can assume were his hours in the studio.

"No. It's too quiet here."

A smirk tugs at the corners of his mouth. "I can yell profanities down the hall. Play the drums outside your door. Go on long, rambling delusional tirades to make noise. Would that help any?"

"Tempting," I tease.

"I know a thing or two about tirades. I promise I could unleash one like you've never heard before." He shrugs and gives me that boyish smile.

I huff out a laugh and pat the bed beside me. "Come sit. Tell me about the song you were working on."

His jaw ticks. "It's shit."

"So you said, but to my untrained ear it was beautiful." I pat the bed again, not wanting to be alone anymore. "Please?"

Jase moves across the space and stops at the foot of the bed. His eyes hold mine, almost as if he's questioning my request and his response to it when he was the one responsible for the sexual tension vibrating between us.

He exhales, drags a hand through his hair, and then takes a seat at the foot of the bed, the mattress dipping with his weight. "I can't seem to get it right."

I frown. "Get what right?"

"The song, the lyrics and beat," he says, his expression unreadable.

"Isn't that part of the writing process?"

"Yeah, but . . . we have a contest between the four of us—Hawke, Vince, Rocket, and me. Each one of us has to write a song for each album. We've been doing it ever since our first debut album years ago."

"Four best friends competing at the highest stakes. What could go wrong?" I say sarcastically.

"Exactly. And over the years, at least one of theirs have topped the charts. I'm the only one who hasn't." He snorts. "This time, I want it."

"I thought drummers didn't like the limelight."

"I said we were underappreciated." His lips curve. "I didn't say that we don't love the limelight."

I shake my head. "Why are you so hard on yourself?"

His eyes meet mine, something flickering there before he looks away. "It's not sounding the way I want it to. Something is missing. Besides, saying it was shit isn't being hard on myself. It's called being honest."

"I liked what I heard."

He chuckles, but it's not his usual cocky laugh. It's self-deprecating.

"No. What Hawke and Vince write is beautiful. Effortless. And Rocket has this inherent knack for kick-ass bridges. Mine . . . it sounds like a struggle."

"Maybe that's how it's supposed to sound." I study him, watching the tension in his jaw. "Maybe that's who you are. Beauty often comes after struggle."

His gaze snaps to mine, sharp, like I hit a nerve. Then, just as quickly, he laughs it off. "You have no idea."

Maybe not. But I know enough.

A yawn sneaks up on him, and before I can process what's happening, he lies back on the bed, his head right beside where my hand is resting on the comforter.

I stiffen.

And then, slowly, I let myself relax.

My fingers drift to his hair before I can think better of it, threading through the freshly showered strands.

I shouldn't be doing this. Touching him. Not with the words spoken earlier, the needs they stirred in me, and a flimsy cotton tank top and my tiny shorts as the only barrier.

But when Jase exhales, when the tension in his shoulders falls with the sound, I hate to say it, but my chest constricts even though I don't want it to.

What is it about this man that's gotten under my skin so quickly? With Paul it took weeks before I went out with him let alone slept with him. But Jase is proving to be an exception with his boyish smile and need to celebrate firsts. And then there's the way his body felt against mine as he taught me how to play the drums. My body and mind are at war with each other, but both are shouting *what if?*

"That feels like heaven," he murmurs.

Don't do it, Hendrix. You've just had your heart broken by Paul. You were just betrayed and screwed over. Don't let that justified weakness open you up to being hurt again.

This is how it started with Paul, did it not? Sweet. Kind. Apologetic after an argument. Compliant when they're a little too brutal with their words.

I squeeze my eyes shut and try to forget.

"I'm so sick of this shit, Hendrix. You want and I give but what do I get in return? Nothing. Nada. A failing bakery and a girl who fucking sucks in bed."

Paul's voice echoes in my head. Words I knew to be untrue at the time but that I allowed to wear me down until I started to believe them. I shove it away.

"You're thinking too hard over there," Jase says and reaches out to pat a hand on my leg beside him. But when the pat is done, he doesn't move his hand.

Operation Live-A-Little.

This is temporary, is it not? My being here with Jase? The man stated he wanted me and here I am debating morals when I need to just say fuck it and do exactly what Jase suggested—live a little.

"Jase?"

He hums, his breath warm against my bare thigh.

"What did you mean when you said you couldn't? With me?"

He stills.

For a long moment, he doesn't answer. Then he sighs, rubbing a hand over his face before shifting onto his side and tilting his head up to meet my gaze.

"I promised my brother," he murmurs. "That we wouldn't cross the line." He swallows. "Or rather, that *I* wouldn't."

My chest tightens. "Why?"

His lips press together, like he's debating telling me the truth. Finally, he exhales. "Because I have a way of ghosting people once I do. You know, the typical guy thing. Chase until you get what you want, get it, then push them away."

I hum, tracing a slow pattern against his scalp.

I appreciate his honesty. The truth in his words. And maybe the underlying whatever it is that he's not speaking. I hear his admission—that he's a player—but that's not what I see and I want to understand the why behind it.

But that's for another time. For when I can sit and tell myself I'm trying to justify why I want this man when I swore off wanting men.

Bite the bullet, Hendrix.

"That would make it difficult to carry out our pretend marriage if we weren't talking."

He huffs a laugh. "True."

"I mean, if you want press, I'm sure the icy glares from the newly wedded wife from across the room at one of the functions we're scheduled to go to would do it."

"No doubt."

"But I don't exactly think that's what Nathaniel and your agent were going for when they set this up."

"Definitely not," he says as his own thumb begins to rub back and forth over my thigh.

I hesitate, then push. "But wouldn't it make it just as difficult if we avoided each other at home, but had to be all lovey-dovey in public and . . ."

"Why would we avoid each other at home?" he asks.

I take a deep breath and pray I'm not wrong in how I'm reading him or his comments because if I am, this is going to be morbidly embarrassing. "Because we both felt the same way. Because we both wanted to test these waters. Because the *wanting* goes both ways."

Silence.

Jase sits up, shifting into a seated position, studying me across the dim light. His blue eyes darken, something heavy settling between us.

His tongue darts out between his lips as my pulse begins to race. "Ask me what you're going to ask me, Hendrix."

My throat is dry. "We already completed our first task in Operation Live-A-Little . . ."

"Hmm."

"And it seems I didn't promise your brother anything."

His jaw tightens. "Ask me." His voice is raw, almost desperate.

I'll let you get used to the idea, Cookie. Pretty sure you're a look before you leap type of girl whereas I just leap.

I swallow. "What if I don't need to get used to the idea? What if I feel the same way that you do?"

He freezes.

I swear the air gets thinner, the space between us charged with *heat.* Need. Not that we'd admit that out loud.

"Why?" His voice is barely a whisper with more gravel than honey this time, and it tugs on parts of me deep down.

Because I want to feel beautiful and wanted and sexy. Because you make me step outside myself and see someone different from what I see and I love how that feels.

"No reason."

He doesn't believe me. I can see it in the way his fingers flex against his knee, the way his gaze burns into me. "That wasn't a lot of time to think about it."

I force a smirk. "Maybe I'm sick of thinking about things."

He reaches out and links his fingers with mine. "Then why are you nervous? I can feel you trembling."

"Because you're intimidating."

His brows pull together and he chuckles. "I'm gonna need more words than that, Cookie."

I exhale slowly. "It means . . . clearly, you have more experience than me, and . . . I'm bound to not live up to what . . . never mind."

Jase snorts, shaking his head. "My first inclination is to tell you you're being ridiculous. My second is to ask who the fuck made you think that?"

"Forget I said anything."

He leans back, studying me like he's trying to unravel something. His expression darkens, his body going rigid. "Who?"

I force out a laugh, but it sounds brittle. "I—"

"*Fuck You, Paul.*" He says the three words like a curse, dragging a hand through his hair. The muscles in his jaw tick, and his body tenses.

I can't meet his eyes. My fingers in my lap look more interesting than anything else here.

He exhales sharply, and in the deafening silence, shifts to face me. He lifts my chin up with his finger so that I'm forced to meet his eyes. For the first time since I've met him, he looks like he's barely keeping it together.

"Was it?" he asks.

"It's not relevant."

His chuckle is low and unforgiving and the warning in it, or the look in his eyes as he holds mine, has chills racing over my skin.

"How about this? I'm going to make it my mission to fuck the remnants and Paul and all his criticisms right out of you. And when I do, then you'll know just how goddamn relevant it is."

CHAPTER
twenty-four

Hendrix

BEFORE I HAVE TIME TO THINK OR RESPOND OR REACT, HIS LIPS CLOSE over mine in a kiss that's teeming with inspiration and predicated on what feels like anger.

It's exactly what I both craved and feared it would be. What I knew it to be but stepped into with a knowing eye. It's hungry and toxic and so fucking addicting.

The scrape of his stubble. The warmth of his tongue as it interlaces with mine. The brush of his fingertips up my cheekbones to cup my face. The muted sighs as we move straight past those to pleading moans.

"Jase." It's a whisper to myself. To him. An acknowledgment that I don't want to think and yet my body has already leaped over the cliff without looking.

"Let me," he murmurs against my lips and his hands thread through my hair and hold my head in place. "Let me erase him." His eyes hold mine seconds before he lowers his head to lace a long series of open-mouthed kisses down the curve of my shoulder. "Let me show you." Another tantalizing kiss on my lips. "Let me." The slide of his strong hands down my back to the bottom of my tank top and then pulling it up and over my head. His strangled groan when he leans back and takes me in is . . . everything.

"Fucking hell, Hendrix." His words are grated restraint. The tensing of the tendons in his neck a visual confirmation of the grip he has on his control.

He runs a hand down the side of my face and over my chest. The subtle roughness of his drumstick-calloused hands a contrast to the smoothness of my skin. But it feels like everywhere he touches catches fire. My nipples harden and ache as his thumbs brush over their peaks. Goosebumps start and are then chased over my skin by the heat he creates.

His mouth leaves mine in a brutal dismissal to travel down my neck. His lips become teeth, his tongue turns merciless as he tastes every inch of skin between my collarbone and my breasts.

It's heaven. It's hell. It's both at once and neither separately.

He lowers his head to take each nipple in his mouth. To tease and suck and lick as I arch into him, lost in the sensation and increasingly feeling as if I'll never find my way back again.

I don't even want to.

I'm exactly where I want to be.

His hands are on the flimsy fabric of my shorts, tugging them down my legs until I'm bare before him, stripped down both literally and figuratively. I should feel exposed, but instead I feel powerful. *Alive.*

Especially when he emits a groan that tells me everything I need to know about how he sees me. How he wants me. How he desires me.

"Spread those thighs for me, Hendrix." His eyes lock on me and then dart back down to my thighs as he pushes down his sweats.

My breath hitches when his cock springs free. It's thick and hard and my body aches to feel it.

"Let me see you. Let me savor you." He kisses his way up the inside of my thigh. Each touch another ignition of embers begging to burn hot. Each slide of his tongue like gasoline on the fire he's stoking.

And then when he gets to the apex of my thighs, he swipes his tongue ever so slowly up and down the seam of my sex. My hips buck as sensations streak like fucking lightning through me. "Jase." I cry out his name but only as a means to beg him to do it again.

But when I do, he chuckles. He swirls his tongue around my clit before sucking on it. He tucks two fingers and then three into me as my body welcomes every sensation he evokes and controls.

He's impatient but unhurried. Desperate but controlled. It's a contradiction that's uniquely Jase. Just like the relentless determination he has to break through every barrier I put between us.

It's working.

I never should have doubted that it would.

His mouth is an addiction in and of itself. The way he teases and tastes me. The way he praises me and encourages me.

But it's when he leans back up on his haunches, when that cocky smirk has his dimples deepening, when he says, "You're tight as fuck, Hendrix, but I'm pretty sure you'll be able to take all of me," that I'm pretty sure I died and went to heaven.

I'm not used to dialogue during sex. To being turned on by words. To being made to feel wonderful because of those words.

"Jase," I beg.

"No. Not yet." His lips return to my skin as his fingers continue to work in and out of me, his thumb on my clit adding friction and pleasure. "He's still on your skin. He's still in your system. Come for me, Hendrix. Loosen that pussy so when I fuck you, you'll be able to take all of me. You'll be so full you won't remember what anyone feels like but me."

"Jase," I whisper again, this time more of a plea. This time hoping that my voice alone will make him snap. Will push him to give me what I want—him. Inside me.

In every part of me.

A knowing smile pulls at his lips, like he's aware that even though I think I still have control, I've already surrendered it to him in full. He keeps a steady pace with his fingers as I moan and writhe beneath him before finally letting one word slip from my lips. "Please."

His fucking smirk grows. His dimples deepen. "That's my girl," he says and then shifts back up my body, positioning himself between the thighs he's determined to keep spread apart. "Glad we're on the same page."

My fingers tangle in his hair as he kisses me again, as he swallows my moans and whispers them right back in an echo of need and want and desire. When I feel the hard press of his cock against my pussy, I ache for more.

He pulls back to look into my eyes, his gaze dark with something that feels both dangerous and thrilling. "You ready?"

I nod before I even realize I have, desperate and needy and so fucking alive. "Yes." My voice is soft, but the words hang in the air like a challenge.

I bite my bottom lip as he eases into me, his eyes fixed on mine, gauging every reaction. Savoring every whimper. It's slow at first, torturous and exquisite. Testing of limits. Relishing in sensation.

Pain flirts with pleasure in that way that makes me crave more of both. The stretch he creates. The heat of him. The way he fills me.

"Can you take a little more of me?" he begs as he shifts his hips and pushes even farther into me.

My head dizzies and my nerves sing with a headiness like I've never felt before.

When he's all the way in, when I'm gasping to form some version of coherent thought, he stills with a groan. "Fuck, Hendrix," he says, and it sounds like a prayer.

He stays like that, so deep inside me, that everything else fades away until all I feel is him. Until all I know is him.

He begins to move. Slowly. Firmly. Stretching me in every way imaginable until it feels like there will never be enough of him inside me because nothing has ever felt this good or this right or this perfect.

"Jase." It's only his name on my lips. It's only his body I feel.

My mind becomes a haze of incomplete thoughts. Of praise I want to say and directions to what I like. Of pleasure like I've never felt before.

"Fuck," he grunts as he begins to pick up speed, as his hips get faster and rougher and more desperate with each thrust. The sound of our skin slapping together barely audible over my pleas for more, for harder, for faster. *For simply him.*

I cling to him as everything blurs together: my need for air, my desire for more, my want to make this last forever and then the urgency to claim my orgasm.

I'm gone and lost, my body moving with a mind of its own to get closer, to sink deeper into the sensation he's creating.

The world is reduced to just us: heat and skin and friction. Until it feels like we're both catching fire. Until it feels like we're both burning. Scorching. Consumed by each other and how alive we feel.

"Come for me, Hendrix," he demands just as my vision starts to fade, just as my pulse starts to race even faster than it already is. "Come for me before I lose my fucking mind."

He works harder—hands and lips and cock and . . . just everything. So that when my orgasm slams into me, there is no point of return.

There's no saying I don't know what good sex feels like anymore.

It's just him driving me to plummet over the edge without any ability to hold myself back. There's nothing else in those few euphoric moments but us—panting, grasping, climaxing—tangled together and lost in sensations.

I tremble through the last waves of pleasure as he comes shortly after. My name is a groan on his lips. It's a promise for more and a plea for this pleasure to never end.

He collapses on top of me, still inside me, and we stay like that, catching our breath as the world slowly comes back into focus around us.

"Jesus," I breathe, tracing lazy circles on his back. "I think . . ."

"You're not supposed to be able to think when I'm done with you. Or walk. Or—"

"You think you're that good, do you?" I tease.

He nuzzles into my neck, a low chuckle vibrating through his chest. "Are you complaining, wife?"

"No. Definitely not."

CHAPTER
twenty-five

Gizmo

WELL, *SHIT.*

That most definitely wasn't supposed to happen.

I stand beside the bed where Hendrix is breathing softly. Moonlight streams across her face. Her lips are parted and with each rise and fall of her chest, the sheet slips off a little more.

I'm conflicted.

I broke my promise to Nathaniel. If I should be good for something, at least it should be that, right?

But hell, if what just happened wasn't worth every ounce of guilt, then I don't know what was . . . because *Jesus Christ.* This woman is something else.

Delicate and determined.

Sexy yet uncertain.

A siren begging to be released.

There were glimpses of that, little snippets of her not wanting to care about making noise or getting lost in the sensations. And then it was like she'd realize she was and would then rein herself back in. Almost as if I don't want her to have a good time or feel or come or anything of the sort.

The urge to reach out and brush her hair off her face surprises me, so I don't.

But damn. Just damn.

I'm pretty sure she just issued a challenge to me that she doesn't even realize she laid down.

To finish undoing whatever the fuck Paul did to her. Seems to me that he made her feel less than in all aspects of herself—her body, her sexuality, her confidence.

I've got enough shit on my own plate. A song to write. An album to put together with the guys. A tour to prep for—hopefully. And yet, something makes me want to add this to it.

Hendrix is doing a massive thing for me. Isn't this the least I can do? Help her find her confidence before we "divorce" and part ways? Help erase her ex's bullshit from her system?

I have three and a half to four months with her. More than enough time. Have some fun. Have a lot of sex. We would both leave better than when we started this.

I'd say that's what a good relationship does but fuck if I even know what one is. Never had one. Never wanted to.

The hand I scrub over my face smells like her skin—light . . . floral— and with a hint of pussy. I grin. Every man's fucking dream.

I take a step back from the bed, from her, and know sleep won't come now. Not after that. Not after tonight.

Time to go back to the studio.

CHAPTER
twenty-six

H AVE A GOOD DAY AT WORK, WIFE.

Have a good day writing, husband.

The imaginary conversation I had with Jase when I left the house this morning plays through my head like I'm trying to justify why, when I woke up, the bed was empty beside me.

He doesn't owe me anything. Not a kiss goodbye. Not even his presence in the kitchen. And clearly not a warm spot in the bed beside me.

That's not to say I wouldn't have minded seeing him this morning before I left.

This is just fun. Just a fling. Just me using him as a rebound to figuratively rinse the taste of Paul out of my mouth and yet . . . last night was incredible.

Operation Live-A-Little started off with a massive bang. *Literally.*

I can't stop thinking about it, about him, and the snapshots flash through my mind over and over and over.

And how I came harder than I ever have in my life. Like . . . whoa.

My ring still feels foreign, heavy on my finger, and it's more noticeable than ever as I unlock the door from the inside to greet Sammy. I've wondered if he should perhaps man the back entry where I come in each morning and leave every night, but I'm sure all of this is unnecessary anyway.

"Morning, Miss Wright," he says.

"Morning, Sammy."

Because I am Miss Wright to everyone still for a little bit longer before I am known as Mrs. Gizmodo.

That thought combined with the memory of his hands on me, of his tongue—*good God the man has a great tongue*—and his cock make my body heat.

Just sex, Hendrix.

Sex, to date, has been "meh." But sex with Jase? It was *I want to tell the world* sex. Spectacular. *Those multi-talented fingers certainly knew how to bring me to orgasm. Three times.* Now I understand why some people talk about sex as if it's some be-all and end-all thing.

I throw my keys on the back counter and draw in a deep breath. So much to do and so little time. The metal racks lining the far wall are stacked with sheets upon sheets where I left the cookies, all five hundred of them, to cool last night before I left. I have another bazillion to go. As much as I'm behind, I'm on course with my lateness and have a plan to finish by the deadline.

That's funny. I'll be stressing and working all night long at some point, but at least I like to trick myself into thinking I know how this is going to go.

Just as I tie my apron on and wash my hands, a text alerts on my phone. I pick it up and smile when I see it's from Jase. He may not have been in the bed when I woke up, but he's texting . . . and that counts for something.

> Jase: Will be in the studio most of the day with the phone turned off. Then to run errands. Be home around 6.

> Me: You don't owe me a schedule.

> Jase: I know. Habit. Feel free not to respond when I do.

> Me: I'll be at the bakery. Probably super late.

> Jase: Have a good day, wife.

> Me: Write a kick-ass song, husband.

My smile widens as I reread the texts, loving that my pretend conversation in my head just became a real one.

The thought carries me as I get the front of the store set up—lights on, flowers situated, music playing, open sign lit up—before I get baking.

No sooner do I have the butter and sugar in the mixing vat does Josie come through the door at her whirlwind pace.

"You're ignoring me," she says with her trademark cheer that I wish I had more of. "You took days off without telling me. You came back to work but haven't come and seen me or gotten a coffee. Should I be offended and sad that you're sipping mai tais by the pool with someone else other than me?"

I freeze, pausing adding brown sugar to the vat, my heart hurtling into my throat.

Did she see the photo in the tabloids and guess it was me? Does she know?

That's impossible. She can't. But one look at her, one locking of our eyes, and the urge inside me to say something, to someone, claws at my insides like it's a very real thing.

I can't hold it in anymore.

And she's so observant it won't be long before she notices the ring anyway.

The least I can do is break the news to her face-to-face rather than her find out from the papers. Besides, it'll be my litmus test on how believable my lies are.

"Don't be offended. There were no mai tais. There was tequila though and we both know how you can't tolerate that."

"She's starting with jokes. That means she has something to tell me."

"What?" I chuckle.

"When you're afraid I'm going to give you a dead honest opinion—"

"I expect nothing less."

"Remember that." She waggles a finger in my direction and then finishes her thought. "You crack jokes to lighten the blow."

I turn and add the mixture of dry ingredients and then move toward where she stands at the edge of the kitchen. I grab a rag and wipe my hands on it, purposely keeping it over my left ring finger. "So, you're right. I do have something to tell you."

Her eyes narrow. "Your tone is concerning." I laugh nervously. "If you tell me you're pregnant with Fucktard's baby, I'm going to need a minute to swallow the litany of obscenities that will take over my mind before I can speak."

"No. God, no. It's nothing like that." I wipe a hand over my brow. "Jesus. Thank you. Anything I say now is tame compared to that."

"So . . . ?"

I grip the back of the chair and inhale. "So I don't want you to find out through the media."

"That's . . . ominous. And intriguing." She leans back, studying me as her brows arch. "Why would the media write anything about little ol' you?"

My fingers tighten around the chair. "I got married this past weekend."

She stares at me, deadpan. "Yeah. Sure. And I'm the fucking Pope."

I don't say anything, but just chew on my bottom lip, waiting for it to hit her.

Her mouth drops open. "Wait. I mean . . . there's no way you're serious."

I nod, my pulse thumping.

Her eyes bulge. "What the actual fuck?" she hisses, grabbing my wrist and yanking me closer. I can see when the other part of my comment breaks through the shock. "I'll ask again, why would the media know about it?" Her tone is cautious, questioning, and disbelieving.

We do live in the City of Angels where celebrities are on every corner—or rather in every café in my case—so it's not a far-off assumption for her to make that I just might have married someone famous.

"Who?" I didn't think her eyes could widen any farther but they do.

"You're not going to believe it even when I say the name."

"Try me."

I take a breath. "You ever heard of the band BENT?"

She blinks. Then scoffs. "Okay. You're funny."

I don't say anything. Instead, I slowly pull the towel off my hand where it rests on the top of the chair so that the diamond can glint in the shop's bright lights.

Josie freezes. Stares. Then—

"Wait. No." Her head rocks back and forth. "OH MY GOD." She looks over her shoulder at where Sammy is standing outside and then back at me as it all connects. "Which one? Gizmo or Rocket? The other two are married. Their wedding photos were posted all over the place." I don't fight the smile that spreads on my lips as she moves toward me, reaching for my hand and ogling the diamond on my finger. "Rocket? Less tattoos. More mellow. Ridiculously handsome. A tad more reserved if you can call a rock star reserved."

I remain silent, the smile still there, and let her work through it all in her head.

"Gizmo?" Her eyes narrow. "The man is gorgeous. Sexy. A little reckless for your taste. The exact opposite of Paul. Well, I mean, both are but he's even further in the sliding scale of preppy accountant to bad boy if that's even possible." Her cheeks flush and she rolls her eyes. "My God. You're so full of shit. You have me sitting here trying to pick a husband for you when you're just trying to get me all worked up, aren't you?"

"I'm not. No." This is rather amusing. "The ring is real."

She studies it again, a sound of approval falling from her lips as the lights hit the diamonds and cast prisms around the room. "He ain't joking with that rock." She looks up at me. "Hendrix?"

"Hmm?" I play coy.

"I need a name, Wright."

"It's Jase. *Gizmo.* Whatever you want to call him—"

"You're shitting me?"

"No." I shake my head back and forth.

"You're *shitting me.*" Her voice escalates to a screechy pitch. "Jase fucking Gizmodo?"

I wince. "Shh." I glance over my shoulder at the security screen door at the back of the bakery because there's no way her voice isn't carrying out there. "Keep your voice down."

"Don't you dare tell me to keep my voice down when you just dropped a goddamn bombshell in my lap!" She yanks me in for a hug of all hugs, squeezing the breath out of me as she jumps up and down.

"I can't breathe." I laugh. Seconds before she pushes me away and grabs my hand again with a renewed fascination over it.

"That is a ridiculously expensive rock."

"It was two minutes ago too."

She waves a hand at me. "Yeah, but that's when I was convinced it was fake despite what you said." She studies it again and then looks up at me breathless. "How—why—WHEN? I mean what the ever-loving fuck, Hendrix—"

I hold my hands up. "I know. Outwardly I've been lamenting Paul and how bad he's screwed me over with the bakery but somehow this was slowly happening." *Please believe me.* "What started with a run into each other outside your coffee shop a few months ago, ended up with him calling me for an order of cookies. That order turned into a conversation. A little flirting. Oddly enough we have a lot in common. We were friends—have been friends for the past three months. I thought what I was feeling for him was more of a thrill because another man was paying attention to me and hearing me and validating how I felt about things . . . but then a few weeks ago, he kissed me and—"

"That must have been one earth-shattering kiss for you to go and get married."

"I know. It sounds crazy," I say, finishing the lie we'd rehearsed over and over. "It wasn't planned. The wedding. It was impulsive and the most reckless thing I've ever done but . . . it made me feel alive, Josie. Like . . . for the first time in as long as I can remember."

She studies me as the shock gives way to hearing what I'm saying. She nods as if she understands and her incredulous smile softens. "When did this happen? *I need details.*"

"This past weekend. We were in Vegas and . . . and we joked about it, then the joke turned to driving to the chapel and—"

"And Elvis married you?" she barks as she pushes the call that comes through her phone to voicemail.

I nod. "Yes. Not the wedding I'd ever thought I'd have but . . . it was perfect nonetheless." My smile is genuine because it really was a great night.

The dress. She's not going to believe it was spur-of-the-moment when pictures are leaked and I'm in a wedding dress. Think.

Think.

"I mean who knew me pointing to a wedding dress in the window of a boutique in the hotel was going to turn into him daring me to try it on. Then he gave me a look and said, come on, let's do it. Leap without looking. Live a little . . . I mean, I think I'm still in shock."

Stop rambling, Hendrix. Rambling means lying. She knows you well enough to notice that.

She shakes her head. "I'm digesting all of this. Slowly. I might need a minute."

"I'm still digesting it too." I snort.

"It's all so sudden. You didn't think of waiting? I mean . . ."

I shrug. "I know. I've thought of all that since then but honestly, Josie, it just felt right. Maybe it was fast because of who he is. And . . . maybe, and probably more so, because of Paul. He made me feel like I was nothing when Jase, he makes me feel like I'm everything." My voice drops. "I know this isn't like me—to be impulsive like this—but it felt good and right and so I acted out for once in my life."

"The fact that you're dead serious is mind-boggling. And fucking awesome at the same time," she sings.

"It's been . . . a whirlwind to say the least, overwhelming and isolating, and I've been dying to tell someone." *Even if it means lying to a woman I consider my best friend.*

She raises her hand. "I'm your girl for all the juicy details. But . . . Hendrix. HENDRIX." She releases a long breath, then starts ticking things off her fingers. "So let me get this straight. Jase Gizmodo. Rock star. Infuriatingly hot. Tattooed, talented, ridiculously rich."

I roll my eyes. "Yes."

She keeps ticking off her fingers. "Cocky as hell. A man who can wink at a woman and make her forget her own name."

I roll my eyes, again, last night front and center in my mind. My name wasn't exactly forgotten but damn if all thoughts didn't leave my head. "You're going a tad overboard."

"You married that. *Him.* What the hell, Hendrix?" Clearly it's sinking in and settling now with her.

I exhale and smile. "I did."

Her phone rings for a second time and she pushes it to voicemail. "So why keep it a secret?"

"To minimize the drama that comes with it. He likes to keep his personal life as private as possible. Plus, we know people are going to dig into my past when they find out who I am. No doubt the fact that I just got out of a relationship will be brought up. Then there's the snap decision to get married—"

"Which is so not like you but that I'm loving for you."

"And just so we can keep our privacy a bit longer before we're surrounded by prying eyes and chaos."

"I can understand that. Appreciate it." She squeezes my hand. "Thank you for trusting me." She smiles. "Gizmo is one lucky man, Hendrix. And I am sure he knows that, which is why he was so quick to marry you. A secret friendship. Sigh. It's so swoony, and it's what you deserve."

I smile as my chest aches in the best way.

"You didn't get a shower or a bachelorette party or any of that stuff."

"That's okay. I don't need it."

"I'm doing something for you. When this is all out and people know, you're going to get that damn party you deserve." Her phone rings again and she groans as she looks at it. "It's the café. Something must be up. I have to go."

"Of course."

She pulls me in for a quick hug and then throws her head back and laughs. "This is the craziest shit I've ever heard." She turns and heads toward the door. "Absolutely bonkers and I love every single moment of it for you."

I watch the door shut behind her, and for the first time, breathe what feels like a sigh of relief.

Josie was my first test if I could pull this off, and other than my mother, probably one of the hardest because she knows me so well.

And I did it.

She believed me.

So there's that.

And she never once told me I was stupid. That, I appreciate, more than she could ever know.

Now it's time to bake and ice some cookies.

CHAPTER
twenty-seven

Gizmo

"**H**E'S LATE," VINCE SAYS WHEN I WALK INTO THE STUDIO.

"Giz is never late," Rocket says and looks at me. "You're the most on time fucker of all of us and yet you're late."

"I got a haircut."

Laughter rings out. "You're so full of shit you stink, Giz. You have swagger," Hawkin chimes in as he shifts behind the soundboard.

"You're swaggering." Rocket snickers.

"Yep. No doubt. Someone definitely got fucking laid last night," Hawkin says.

"What the hell are you talking about?" I throw up a middle finger with one hand as I throw my keys and wallet on the console beside the drum set and go to the fridge. A glance at my watch says it's eleven, which only spurs on the debate whether I should decide on the beer or water.

It's a hard fucking choice.

Write drunk, play it back sober.

But we're going to be here long enough that I opt for water.

And when I do the guys throw up their hands and cheer. "Again . . . what the fuck?"

"You're hydrating. That means it *was* great sex," Vince says.

"Phenomenal sex that you need to recoup," Rocket adds.

"You sure you don't need Gatorade to replenish those electrolytes you lost?" Hawkin completes the trio.

I shake my head and laugh. "You guys are assholes."

"He's not denying it," Vince says. "There's that."

"I'm not confirming it either," I say.

"Which is confirmation in and of itself if I've ever heard one," Hawkin says.

"So . . . let's hear it," Rocket says, propping his boots up on the table like he owns the place. "Are you fucking her yet or what? If you're gonna play house then why not reap the benefits of it, right?"

I take a sip from my water and now, really wish it were beer. The four of us share just about everything so my hesitation is strange. Hendrix isn't some band groupie I'm going to never see again—or that they won't either.

It's weird. I want them to respect her. To not think about her like they do all the other women we've met, had, and been done with over the years.

She's different. The situation is different. That's all.

"You guys are being dicks," I mutter and move toward the back of the studio where my hand-scribbled notes are laid out.

"We're being dicks?" Hawkin scoffs. "From the head dick himself when it comes to giving us shit about women."

"Dude, whatever. It's not like that. She's not like that. I told you, she's doing me a favor here—"

"A lot of favors apparently," Vince mutters as he takes a sip. He was smart and went for something stronger than water. They all bark out laughs.

"Fuck you all," I mutter and question my own want to protect her from this kind of shit. *And this is just good-natured fun from the people I know.*

"No need to get defensive about it," Rocket says through his smirk.

"I'm not. Can we put this time to good use and get started please?" I ask.

"Let's just hope you had more rhythm with your hips than you've had in here the past few sessions," Hawkin teases.

Vince's chuckle pulls my eyes over to his. While Hawkin might be the leader of this band, Vince is the silent force behind it. Or rather, *has become* over the years. "You are being defensive," he finally says from where he's leaned against the wall, watching me like he's already picked apart every one of my tells.

No doubt he has.

"Word's going to be out soon enough—now that the pic of you with her at your pool has surfaced—so what's the big deal?" Hawkin asks.

I focus on rubbing the condensation off my bottle. "Because she's not just one of . . . whatever, can we start please?"

"Why? You have some hot piece of ass to get back home to when we're done?" Rocket jokes, but it's Rocket and rather than be mad, the comment tugs at the corners of my lips and has me shaking my head. "Because you have to actually see her the morning after, the month after, two months after, and so now you have to know her as a person and don't like the idea of us wondering how good she is in bed?"

"Dude." I scrub a hand through my hair. "Hawke and Vince are both married. I doubt they're looking because their wives are awesome. So that would mean we're talking about you, and she wouldn't touch you with a ten-foot pole." It's my turn to grin. "Ugly fuckers aren't her type."

"We all look the same in the dark. Some of us are just a little more blessed than others," he says and we all laugh.

"When do the wedding photos leak?" Vince interjects, clearly seeing Rocket needs a distraction or he'll keep going and when he keeps going, sometimes some shoving occurs.

"Please tell me you guys took some cheesy-ass photos with Elvis or blue suede shoes or something," Hawke says.

"*Please*. I need this bullshit to be commemorated so we can blow up pictures of it in future years and harass the fuck out of you for it," Rocket says.

No doubt the fucker would too.

"Apparently any day. You know how it goes. Shop for the right price. Have an influencer post they have some big inside scoop. Create some buzz, and then people clamor for the pic when it's 'leaked,'" I say.

"So the charity benefit will be a fucking madhouse then," Hawkin says.

"No shit," Vince murmurs.

And I should be worried about it. About Hendrix and how she's going to take the onslaught of attention I've grown accustomed to. Those should be my concerns but my mind is on last night. To her on my lap, her body flush against mine, the drumsticks in her hand. Then her on her bed, thighs spread wide and the part of her lips and gasp when I pushed into her.

Jesus fucking Christ.

I take another sip of my water, ignoring the way Vince is still staring at me like he already knows what's in my head.

"It's probably the best place for us to be after. The media will be a madhouse but there are so many celebrities slated to be there that security will be tight and the media will be managed. The last thing I want to do is feed her to the dogs right away because you two fuckers both know how brutal they can be."

Vince and Hawkin give knowing nods. They might be razzing the fuck out of me, but their wives were once the ones the media were desperate to sell pictures of and write shitty things about, so they get it. They know what I'm trying to protect Hendrix from.

"True," Vince says. "What other events is she coming to?"

"Lucky for us, our calendar is pretty clear so that's a blessing in disguise," I say

"The lockdown, the stay home order before a tour," Hawkin murmurs. And he's right. This is our MO. Before a tour, we are at home as much as possible since our own beds will be a distant memory for some time. It allows us to stay on schedule—write new material, rehearse for the tour, and ground ourselves before the chaos and wear and tear commences.

"Yeah. It's great timing if there's such a thing."

"So?" Rocket prompts as he plops down on the leather couch on the far end of the studio. "We need details. Is she any good?"

I nearly choke on my water. "Excuse me?"

Rocket grins. "At playing the drums." He pauses just long enough for the innuendo to sink in. "*Obviously.*"

I glare at him. "You're an asshole."

"Yeah, yeah." He waves a hand. "You avoiding the question?"

I lean back, smirking. "What do you think?"

Hawke whistles low, shaking his head. "I think if you *were* fucking her, you'd be way less fun to mess with right now."

"Or way more fun." Rocket grins. "I bet he's already in deep. He's not used to respectable women. She got you whipped yet, Giz?"

I scoff. "Not even close."

Vince finally speaks again, voice calm. Too calm. "You lying?"

I don't flinch. Don't waver. Just smirk and tip my bottle toward him. "What do you think?"

They all laugh, and I let them, playing along. Because the truth?

That's a whole different beast I don't think I'm ready to mess with yet.

It was just sex.

Just a little twist in the sheets between willing participants.

Just a little fun while we're stuck in this together. But one thing's for sure.

Her ex was a fucking idiot.

CHAPTER
twenty-eight

Hendrix

THE SCENT OF CINNAMON AND VANILLA CLINGS TO MY SKIN, SEEPING into my clothes, my hair, probably my damn soul at this point. The industrial mixer hums in the background, a steady rhythm that should be soothing but isn't, only because I'm drowning in icing and the long wait between when one color dries so I can do the next.

Time is not my friend right now. Not when another order just came in and I'm determined to get the dog birthday cookies done and take on this new order.

I may have money being deposited in my bank account, but I learned in the past few months that "rainy days" are a real thing and I need to prepare for them accordingly. Slacking off now isn't an option.

The bell above the bakery door jingles.

A little thrill shoots through me. Customers aren't exactly chomping at the bit to come buy my cookies and so any chance I get to possibly gain a new one is exciting.

And that statement alone shows how new I am at this whole thing.

I wipe my hands on my apron and peek over the counter. A woman stands near the front case. I can't tell whether she's more interested in the cookies or scrolling through her phone—which is a common thing these days—so I stand there politely and wait so I don't distract her.

But as she scrolls, she keeps glancing up at the menu above my head and then quickly back down every few seconds in a way that has me taking notice.

Then it dawns on me. She's not looking at the menu. She's looking at *me*.

Another jingle at the door. Another shuffle of feet into Cookie Cutter.

Then another.

What the hell is going on?

Sammy meets my eyes through the front glass window, almost as if to ask if I'm okay. I nod to which he does the same in kind.

They're customers. Why would I ever need help with that? It's exciting. Exhilarating. *It's income.*

"May I help you?" I ask the first woman in line who's still standing there with a flush in her cheeks and her phone angled up as if she's taking a picture of the menu.

But before she can answer, another group of women in their late teens or early twenties file in. The five of them huddle together, whispering loudly. *Are you sure? Do you think? I don't understand how she did it?*

They murmur to each other, their gazes flicking in my direction before snapping away when I catch them.

My stomach twists.

I know.

I *know* before I even reach for my phone, before my fingers start fumbling to unlock the screen.

The photos have leaked.

My fake wedding. My fake husband. My private moments.

The world knows.

My hand trembles as I scroll to find the pictures, but it doesn't take long.

They. Are. Everywhere.

Jase's hand on mine. His lips ghosting just above my skin. The stupidly intimate way he tucked a loose strand of hair behind my ear like he's been doing it for years. It's all been captured, frozen in time, and sold to the world like a goddamn blockbuster premiere. A perfectly crafted moment, staged just right, and yet with so many good, personal memories behind them for me.

It's fake. It's nothing.

And yet, the tightness in my chest tells me I'm lying to myself.

But now, it's out there for the world to devour. To criticize. To question.

For a second, an electric thrill zips through me.

It's real now. *We* are real. Even if it's just in headlines, in speculation, in tabloid gossip. It feels big. Overwhelming. I am officially Hendrix Gizmodo to the world.

Then the panic sets in.

I am not ready for this. *Will I ever be?*

But definitely not today. Not when my entire counter is covered in half-finished cookies already earmarked for an order and not enough cookies made for an influx of customers.

Customers? Not really. More like looky-loos.

A bead of sweat drips down my back.

"Can I help anyone?" I ask as if nothing has changed when inside I'm absolutely panicking. They just keep staring as if I'm going to suddenly break out into song and confess all my deepest, darkest secrets. Or how big Jase's cock is. I have a feeling they'd want one more than the other. I force a polite smile as I fight the nervous bout of laughter threatening to bubble up. "We have all different types of cookies. We have coffee and tea."

"Is it true?" someone shouts out, getting a murmured consent from the rest of the crowd as the door jingles for a third time in as many minutes.

I don't have to ask what she means. *Is it true you're married to Gizmo?*

I smile and purposely run my hand through my hair so that the diamond shoots prisms of light all over the room. The subtle gasps that ring out are all the answers I need to know that they caught the subtle hint.

There might even be a muffled sob mixed somewhere in there.

I fight the smile that threatens to break through. But that smile lasts only a few seconds as some of the women file out, muttering.

"Total bullshit."

"I'm prettier than her. What the fuck does she have that I don't?"

"Talk about average. Like . . . what the fuck, Giz?"

I can't do this right now. And I sure as shit am not going to let their cruel, jealous words ruin the incredible high from sex with Jase last night. Or the myriad of feelings that sex has created this morning.

And while I recognize their cattiness for what it is, that doesn't mean each time another group of women come in, another set of comments is spouted off, that it doesn't erode that joy a little more.

Bit by bit.

Hour by hour.

I force my attention back to my work, trying to ignore the whispers, the way I *feel* people watching me, like I'm a caged animal at the zoo.

By the time the day ends, I'm wrecked.

Not only am I wrecked, but halfway through the day, I put a sign on the front case that if they're going to stay longer than five minutes, they have to purchase something.

Despite the sign, I greet everyone with a sugary-sweet tone that would make my buttercream jealous, aware of how my every action and words can be twisted on social media or posted if someone might secretly be recording me while doing so.

But those purchases used up all my inventory for the day and had me siphoning some from the order I'm working on in the back so that I have items to sell.

And that makes me even further behind with my order schedule and with trying to figure out how I'm going to bake extra cookies for the store tomorrow because no doubt, the news will spread and more people will come.

It's not necessarily a bad problem to have. It's great actually. I just need to look at it as a little bonus to this whole prelude because when we divorce, no doubt I'll be dubbed as having the worst cookies in town or some juvenile shit like that.

But by closing time, I'm spent. My hands ache, my back is stiff, and my hair—what's left of it after I stress-yanked my ponytail loose about a hundred times—is coated in a fine layer of powdered sugar. Or is that flour?

Who knows?

Who cares?

No doubt there will be some pictures of me hitting the internet today and I'll be far from glamorous in them. The thought bugs me, but then again, isn't that part of my appeal to Jase? That I'm normal, everyday-ish?

The best part of the day is when I lock the doors and focus on what I need to do without distraction. Finish the damn dog cookies. And maybe drink a glass of wine while doing it.

CHAPTER
twenty-nine

Jase: Need a ride, wife? I hear today was quite the day.

The irritation bubbling in my chest cracks just enough for a laugh to escape.

Of course, he'd be this smug about it. Of course, he wouldn't care that the media just plastered our faces everywhere. Or that his wife looks like a hot mess—ponytail falling, makeup faded, expression tired—as she works all day. He's used to this. The stares. The sense of feeling like a caged animal.

The admiration.

Different from what I was on the receiving end of today because it comes with the territory.

I hesitate, thumb hovering over the keyboard, when another text comes in.

Jase: I come bearing food. Don't make me eat alone. What will the media write if they see that? He's bad in bed? She can't take it all? I mean . . .

Damn him. I crack a smile and some of the exhaustion eases from my shoulders. I look at the cookies all around me. The empty spaces where they were when I started this morning and now need to be replenished. The eggs sitting in the fridge and the flour in its bins waiting for me to take them out and make more. I know what I'm going to do before I even type.

Me: You're insufferable.

Jase: And yet, you're gonna say yes.

I sigh, shaking my head and groaning. This is going to put me back even further and yet . . . how can I say no? How can I—

Beep. Beep.

The horn sounds off in the back alley and echoes through the closed security screen door. Before I can even reach it to see what's going on, Sammy is there opening it for me and looking around.

I will say it's definitely nice not to have to worry about leaving here at night. For the most part, the neighborhood I'm in is safe, but between the alley, the shady characters that sometimes loiter in it, and now all of Jase's curious fans, having Sammy here is a definite bonus.

But the thought vanishes when the car comes into view.

Sleek. Black. Expensive.

The passenger-side window rolls down, and there he is—Jase, one arm slung over the steering wheel, his hair a little mussed, like he's been dragging his fingers through it. The streetlights catch on the ink lining his forearm, the silver glint of his rings.

How is it possible to have forgotten how gorgeous he is? How is it fathomable that I would have ever looked at him and thought he wasn't my type?

Perfect case of don't judge a book by its cover.

And in this case, he's temporarily mine.

He smirks, like he already knows the kind of day I've had.

"Need a ride, Cookie?"

I roll my eyes, but I can't help the way my lips twitch. "Hmm. I'm pretty sure my husband might not be too thrilled with the idea of me getting in the car with some dark and mysterious man."

"I think I can take him."

"Really?"

Jase taps his chin, considering. "In fact, I know I can." He looks over his shoulder and then back to me. "Quick. Get in before he finds out."

He winks and I shake my head. Within seconds I have the bakery locked up, my purse in hand, and yank open the passenger door and slide inside. *God, is this the first time I've sat down today?*

His scent wraps around me instantly—clean, musky, and just a little like leather.

Jase looks at me for a beat, eyes flicking over my flour-dusted shirt, the tension still clinging to my shoulders. His voice is the exact opposite of how he looks when he speaks, "Rough day?"

I sink into the seat, letting my head fall back. "You have no idea."

His smirk fades into something almost . . . compassionate. He reaches for the radio, scrolling through stations until soft rock filters through the speakers, like he knows I need something easy.

Like he actually *sees* me.

And just like that, the panic I've been holding on to all day loosens its grip. With him, I feel safe from this chaos. Or if it's not safe, then maybe the feeling is understood. Regardless, he gets it and that's comforting in and of itself.

Jase puts the car in drive and gives me some time to let the fact that today actually happened—that this *is* happening—without speaking. I close my eyes and just let the music soothe me and find an odd contentment in him quiet beside me.

"We were in the studio all day. I didn't have my phone on because . . . simply because I'm not used to having anyone need me." He pauses but I keep my eyes closed, lulled by the sound of his voice. "I didn't realize news had hit until we went to leave."

"Well, it did," I murmur.

"You didn't text me."

I open my eyes and study him as he drives, pondering his statement. "Was I supposed to?"

"No. Yes. I don't know." He glances my way and then back to the road. For a man who always seems sure of himself, he's suddenly lost his footing. It's cute.

"What does that mean?"

He blows out a sigh like he's trying to find his words. "You're a fascinating woman."

"Oh?"

"You have bouts of insecurity but then today happens—your whole life shifts—and you just, according to Sammy, handle it like a goddamn pro. That takes a lot of guts and a shit ton of fortitude. I'm proud of you." He reaches out and puts his hand on my thigh and squeezes to reinforce his words. "I guess I thought you'd text because you needed me to come and . . . I don't know. Help you? Rescue you?" He huffs out a laugh and removes his hand from my leg to run it through his hair before setting right back on it. "That sounds ridiculous. I'm fully aware."

"That's sweet of you. I was so busy, I didn't have a single second to spare. Besides, what are you going to do other than make the situation more chaotic?"

"I know but helpless doesn't look good on any man and that's how I felt today when I found out you were fending off everyone on your own." He glances over at me and his Adam's apple bobs.

"It was chaotic but I'm pretty sure that will be the norm for a while."

"But you said it was busy? That's good, right? More sales? More business?"

"Yes, the Gizmo effect apparently."

He chuckles but I keep thinking about his hand on my thigh and how his thumb absently brushes back and forth like it's a habit. And that makes me think of his hands last night and exactly how capable they are.

I try to refocus. To redirect.

"Hey. I thought you said there was food?" My stomach growls as if on cue. The car doesn't smell like food and I turn around to look behind us at the seats. There is nothing.

"We're almost to the restaurant."

"Jase?" I look out the window for the first time and see we're in the Wilshire Boulevard area and cringe.

"The hottest new couple has to be seen now, don't they? Or at least that's what I'm being told."

"Jase." The first time I said his name it was a question. This time was a warning. "You couldn't have given me a little heads-up?" I grumble, yanking down the visor mirror to assess the damage. Flour dusts the front of my shirt, a smudge of buttercream clings to my wrist, and my hair is still twisted in a messy knot, ponytail, something or other from working.

Jase smirks from the driver's seat. "Where's the fun in that?"

I shoot him a glare. "You could've at least let me change. I look like . . . I just wrestled a sack of flour."

He shrugs, totally unbothered. "You're with me. Who cares?"

And totally like a person used to being adored even when a picture is taken that paints him in the ugliest of angles.

He looks ridiculously good in his black tee and leather jacket, like he just casually rolled off the cover of *Rolling Stone*.

I groan, slumping in my seat. "They're gonna think you picked me up off the street." *I look exactly like the mess the mean girls said I am.* I'm feeling blindsided . . . again. And desperately trying not to care.

And failing at it.

"Well, that might put a dent in the whole *make Jase look wholesome* thing we're aiming for if I'm picking up prostitutes for dinner."

"Whoa. I mean homeless. Not a prostitute," I joke and slap at his leg. "Thanks a lot."

He grabs my hand so I can't hit his leg anymore and glances at me, his lips twitching. "Nah, they're gonna wonder how the hell I landed the hottest woman in this restaurant."

My stomach flips. It's ridiculous that it does because I live in reality and know exactly how I look—like a hot mess—while he's trying to boost my ego. And yet, I find myself biting my lip, fighting back a smile.

Right up until we pull in line for the valet in front of The Vine. It's an upscale restaurant that screams we take reservations three months in advance with paparazzi permanently camped out across the street with their cameras.

It's the place to go and be seen, and Jase is doing just that—being seen. Showing off his new wife for the world to see her.

Fuck.

Just fuck.

CHAPTER
thirty

Gizmo

THE FLASHES ARE BLINDING THE MINUTE THE VALET OPENS MY DOOR. I hold a hand up in a wave and move around the hood of the car, slower than normal.

"I've got it," I tell the valet who's about to open Hendrix's door. I'm there in seconds and when I do open the door, Hendrix is sitting there, eyes wide, and the only way to describe her expression is shell-shocked.

She stares at me, eyes blinking and body frozen in place. It's a look of terror mixed with exhaustion, and I do the only fathomable thing to do to wipe that look off her face, and the one thing I've thought about doing way too many times today—I lean in, cup her face, and brush my lips ever so gently against hers.

It takes a second for it to register to her, but I feel the minute it does. Her body startles and her lips react. The noise outside grows louder and the flashes grow brighter.

I can't do this to her. Not on her first full day as a spectacle. Not after a hard day's work. And most definitely not when she isn't feeling the best about herself.

Screw Abigail and her requirements to be seen—*the sooner the better.* Hendrix deserves better than this.

"Stay there," I say when I lean back, her eyes searching mine.

"I don't—"

But I cut her words off when I shut the door, keeping her inside. The valet looks at me oddly. "Change of plans," I say as the cameras go off a million times more before I climb back behind the wheel.

No doubt this will be posted and misconstrued a dozen different ways in the coming hours on social media, but the last thing I need to do is throw Hendrix into the fire the first night.

What an ass I was thinking this would be right.

"Jase? I thought we were going to dinner here."

"We were," I say as I pull out of the circular driveway and back onto the road.

"Was that considered a PR stunt?" she asks, concern woven into each word.

"The kiss?" I ask as I look over my shoulder before changing lanes.

"Well, I know that was. I meant—"

"No." I stop at the light and lean over and kiss her softly again, shocking the hell out of me and twisting up my insides even more than they already are. "That was because I wanted to. It's been a long fucking day and the thought of kissing you has been front and center in my mind."

"Oh."

I love when she makes that sound, that startled *oh* that she uses for a myriad of responses. "The restaurant? Yes. I had plans to take you there, but honestly, that's not what you wanted and it wasn't fair to ask that of you after a long day of work. So now we're going to share the want."

That would have been feeding her to the wolves. Is she beautiful? Fuck yeah, she is. But after a long day of work, tired and flour-covered, the "Hollywood standard" would have eviscerated her. I thought up Operation Live-A-Little to bolster her self-esteem, to make her see herself how I do—gorgeous, driven, funny, honest—and parading her around when she didn't feel her best would have done the exact opposite.

"I get we're married and all, Jase, but you just lost me," she jokes and then lets her head fall back against the seat again. But I like how she angles it there so she can look at me. I like the feeling of her eyes on me like I'm the only thing she sees.

"I'm hungry. You're hungry. We're both tired. Let's skip the fancy and go for what will hit perfectly." I end the comment with perfect timing as I pull into the drive-thru line at In-N-Out Burger.

"Really?" Her eyes widen and she perks up in a way that tells me this was the right decision.

"Yes. Really. But"—I hold a finger up—"pretty sure I can top The Vine."

"No way," she gasps.

"Yes way."

CHAPTER
thirty-one

Gizmo

THE CRASH OF THE WAVES BEYOND IS LIKE A SOOTHING SOUNDTRACK to the crinkle of the paper bag every time we reach in to grab another couple of fries.

We're backed into a parking spot at the beach. There are other people milling around, but the night is moonless, and while that prevents a view of the waves, it also prevents people from recognizing me.

And I'm beginning to realize I might have needed this just as much as she did.

There's a rush that comes with being recognized. A feeding of my ego that becomes addicting after you've had it for so long. But this is simple. Real—just like Hendrix—and I mean that in the best way possible.

"This is heaven," she says as she takes a sip of her drink and leans back against the back part of the seat from where we're seated in the cargo area of my SUV.

"I am definitely not complaining." I chuckle when I finish chewing. "This was our staple when we first started—before we made it. The burgers are cheap and the beach is free and man, that goes a long way when you're broke."

My mind flashes back for a second. To the long days and endless hours trying to make something of ourselves. To this being our only hope, our only chance to be the men we saw in each other when our own parents didn't or couldn't see it themselves. The laughs we had on this beach. The memories. The arguments. The baring of our souls to one another. BENT was forged in this sand.

Funny how a woman who isn't supposed to be a part of my life but now very much is, made me see that.

"You went quiet there for a second," she says, knocking her knee against mine. "Where'd you go?"

"To back when the only thing I ever had was dreams."

"Dreams are good," she murmurs and rests her head on my shoulder.

"They definitely are." I pause. "So tell me about yours. Why a bakery? Why cookies? Why that instead of, I don't know, becoming some famous pastry chef or whatever?"

"I like the quiet."

I snort. "Cookie, I hate to break it to you, but I think you married the wrong guy then."

Her body shakes with a soft laugh.

"Clearly." She exhales slowly. "I liked being by myself as a kid. My mom and her husband at the time fought a lot. He was fond of the bottom of the bottle and that led to some pretty horrific fights. Going into the kitchen, putting music on and creating something was my way of shutting out the noise until he sobered up. I also wasn't his, and I always felt like I didn't belong anywhere, but in the kitchen, I was in charge. I could create and get mad at my imaginary helpers." She chuckles. "And then when I walked into the family room with whatever design I had made at the time, it forced them to abandon their bickering and praise me instead. Kind of self-absorbing and prolonging the inevitable divorce when it all came down to it, but when you're younger, you're only thinking about the here and now."

"So they ended up divorcing?"

She nods. "It was for the best. They split. My mom was finally happy again and the fighting stopped. He moved on to a new wife, a new life, and while I wasn't exactly a big fan of his, I was jealous that I didn't have a 'real' family. One I could bring home friends to after school without having to explain why I didn't have a dad. That kind of thing."

Her words hit me squarely in the gut. A silent reflection of my own life, my own situation, and it takes everything I have to not press the heel of my hand to my breastbone. The last thing I need or want is to bare my scars to the world. That would be a telltale sign her words just picked a scab off one of them.

"I'm sorry."

"Yeah, well, so am I, but being sorry doesn't change shit so I've moved on."

"Divorce cookies," I murmur to which she laughs.

"That's about right."

"So you baked as a distraction." I smile.

"I did. As I got older, I became known for it. At first it was for friends' birthday parties. Then it was for teachers wanting this or that. I worked at a bank during the day and then baked from my apartment at night. It was a lot."

"And how did Cookie Cutter start?"

"Mmm," she says and then falls quiet. I have a feeling Paul is about to enter the picture. *The fucker.* "A bakery was always the dream. A successful one. Paul was sick of me working at both jobs and not being able to give him the quality time he deserved."

"I'm reserving judgment here, Hendrix, but if you love someone, you support them even when their dreams overshadow you for a while."

She angles her head up to look at me. Her expression tells me she doesn't understand how someone like me could say that. I'm not even quite sure that I understand it if I'm honest.

"For as much of a prick as he turned out to be, he did encourage me to officially start the bakery. Find the location with the loft above it and get friends who were mechanical to help me repair some of the mixing vats I have when I bought used ones. And when the banks wouldn't approve me for a small business loan, he stepped up and used some of his own money."

"Hmm."

She laughs. "I know that sound. I *feel* that sound. I'm grateful for the help he gave me but that doesn't erase what he did."

"Fucking someone in your bed?"

"That and the draining of our bank accounts before he left." *The fuck? He took her money?* Even my dad, despite his complete assholery, didn't steal from Mom when he left us.

I blow out a long, low whistle. No wonder she is, was, in dire straits. How the fuck did her ex think she could run a business with no capital? *Did she sign a contract with him? Was it illegal for him to do that?*

Nathaniel would have a field day with this but it's out of my wheelhouse.

"You know that's completely fucked, right, Cookie?"

"Hmm." It's her turn to make the sound.

"Did he get back all of the money he put into the company?"

"Nowhere close."

"And he hasn't asked for the remainder?"

"There were fights. Plenty of fights. But you can't give back something you don't have, and he can't ask for the things that aren't officially his."

I nod, letting the crash of the waves fill the silence, and hope that's where it ends for her. For him. *Unless he decides to come after her for the rest.* Shit.

Fuck you, Paul.

"Back to the cookies. Paul is . . . the past and—"

"Fuck him."

She snorts. "Exactly. *Fuck him.* I like creating things. Making people happy with something as simple as a cookie. To eat. To save. To commemorate." She chuckles. "Now I just sound stupid. Enough about me." She shifts so that she's cross-legged and facing me. "How'd BENT start?"

I smirk. "A bet."

She blinks. "A bet?"

"Yeah. Rocket and I were drunk off our asses one night in some shitty garage—we were teenagers trying to act way cooler than we were. He swore I couldn't learn to play drums in six months."

"Six months?"

"Yeah. The bet was that I had to learn and play them in a contest the local club was holding. I told him if I did, then he had to break up with his girlfriend because I liked her." The memory and his cockiness have me smiling.

"By the smirk on your face you won the bet."

I nod. "I did. I won the girl. Apparently, she liked drummers better anyway, so it was only a matter of time before she broke up with him, but . . . that helped things along." I chuckle. "God, he was so pissed at me. We got in a fistfight over me winning the bet. And as fate would have it, the guy who broke us up was Hawkin."

"Wow."

"Yeah. You're telling me. He and his friend Vincent were starting a band, mostly to get women, and then . . . somehow we were decent."

"More than decent."

"Not at first. My God." The endless rehearsals. The fights over each others' girls. The fights over the songs to play. "We had a rough go for a while. I think all of us questioned if we'd even work. But then we became friends. And that led us to caring more. To becoming better. Then better became good. Played a few gigs. Got lucky to be in the right place at the right time."

She shakes her head, grinning. "You make it sound so simple."

"It was way easier than dealing with life at home." The words come out before I can think them through. Before I can stop them.

And now I'm left with my ass hanging in the wind and facing a conversation I really don't want to have.

CHAPTER
thirty-two

Hendrix

I F DISCOMFORT WAS A VISUAL, IT WOULD BE JASE GIZMODO IN THE HERE and now. Lips pulled tight, eyes averting, and hands crumpling up all the wrappers and putting them into the bag.

Anything to avoid me asking why he just said what he said. *It was way easier than dealing with life at home.*

"Your parents divorced or together?" I ask, taking a shot in the dark.

"Divorced. Dad not around. Just like you. Sucks but . . . my mom and me, we did our best."

"Not Nathaniel?"

He winces. "He lived with our dad."

"Oh. I'm sorry. I didn't mean to—"

"Why Paul? What was it about him that pulled you to him?"

I stiffen, more because Paul is the last person I want to talk about when I'm sitting here beside him versus his obvious change of subject.

But I'll give him time. Trust is earned, not given, and for a man who's in the public eye, no doubt everything he says is up for sale in most cases.

"Paul." I sigh. "He seemed so well put together while I was all over the place. Worked at a big accounting firm while I was struggling to find my way. He was kind and flirty and made me feel seen when I'd never had that before. In hindsight, I realize that he was good at manipulating situations and controlling narratives so that 'I'm sorry' was a constant refrain on my lips even when I knew I'd done nothing wrong. He made me feel like I was never enough, you know? Like everything I did was somehow wrong. But I think that was part of his thing—if you make someone feel inferior, then they're easier to manipulate and control."

Jase's jaw clenches. "He ever hurt you?"

I swallow. "Not physically. No. I'd never allow that." I say the words but know damn well that emotional abuse can be just as damaging. But I'm working on that. On owning my mistakes, loving who I am, and how I'm not the inadequate woman Paul painted me out to be.

Jase leans forward, presses a kiss to my cheek, and whispers, "If he ever comes to the bakery again, you tell Sammy right away." His voice is casual, but there's an edge to it, something protective and sharp that makes my stomach flip for an entirely different reason. "He'll make sure he's removed promptly."

I clear my throat and nod. "Okay. He won't come back." Then again, when he finds out that I'm married, he just might. "My turn."

His lips twitch. "Hit me."

"Why no girlfriends?"

He smirks, but it doesn't quite reach his eyes. "I don't do well with relationships."

"That's not an answer."

He exhales, running a hand through his hair. "I push people away. Always have." His fingers drum against his thigh. "Being in the band . . . it's chaotic. It's loud. I got used to never really letting anyone in."

I study him. "You let your bandmates in."

"Yeah." He grins. "But they're stuck with me. Contractually."

I roll my eyes. "So you're saying I should've negotiated a better prenup?"

He smirks. "Might've been a good idea. You never know, I might try to take you for all you're worth when we divorce."

I throw my head back and laugh. "Take away. You won't get much."

"Once you start selling your divorce cookies there will be."

"What?"

"Divorce cookies. Breakup cookies. I don't know. We celebrate everything else in life, why not home in on why you started in the first place? Help people celebrate cutting ties and moving on?"

"You have a point." A very good point. Too bad they'd never sell.

"See I'm good for more than just sex."

"Are you?" I murmur.

"Are you doubting me, Cookie?"

"I mean, I don't have much to go off yet," I tease. He clears the trash out of the way and pulls me onto his lap so that I'm straddling him.

My breath hitches. My heart races.

His eyes meet mine and arch up with the most mischievous gleam.

"Operation Live-A-Little?" I ask.

"No, this one's called Jase-Needs-A-Lot." And with that, his mouth crashes down onto mine.

His hands splay across my back, pulling me in against him and then hooking around my shoulders to hold me in place as he kisses me senselessly. Our breaths mingle as tightly as our bodies, but I'm all for drowning in his air.

We might be pretending to be married but this doesn't feel pretend. The want between us. The need to sate it. The undeniable sparks when his fingers skim over my skin.

Sure, it's fresh and new and that makes it more exciting but there's a genuine connection. A camaraderie. It can't be more than that because we've only known each other for a short time, but it's something for sure.

And when his lips slide down the curve of my neck, when his hands delve beneath my waistband to find me wet for him, whatever my thoughts are on that cease to exist.

Because all I can do is feel. All I can do is want. All I can do is take.

"Someone will see—"

My reluctant protest is stymied by his lips meeting mine and his hands sliding their way up my back to dive into my hair. "No one will notice. It's dark. And getting caught adds to the thrill."

"Jase—"

"Are you going to argue or are you going to pull your pants off one leg and ride my cock till we both come?"

Jesus. Well . . . when he puts it that way.

I stare at him as my heartbeat thunders and my pussy aches fiercely. He must know the minute my desire wins over my concern—it must be written all over my face—because the second he sees it, he dives back in for another kiss.

And that kiss is breath-stealing and desperation-inducing.

There is no turning back if I wanted to because Jase ignites something in me sexually that I've never known.

We're a mass of frenzied movements. Each one getting us closer to the ecstasy I know he can provide my body with.

I'm caught between the chill of the air and the heat of his hands, and I don't know which is more intoxicating. His fingers work me over, taking their time, dragging out my anticipation until urgency has me sliding my hands beneath his pants and finding his cock. It's silky and hard and has my own ache sweetening.

I lose myself in the urgency of it. In the taste and feel of him. In the hard lines of his body and the desperation in his own touch as his mouth covers my nipple through my shirt, wetting it with his hot tongue, making me gasp and arch against him.

"Fuck," I groan, my head falling back as his teeth bite at my nipples and his cock pulses against my hand as I work him up and down.

In several unskilled movements, I have one leg of my pants off and he has his own pushed down around below his hips. I'm straddling him again, one hand threaded through his hair as my mouth takes and takes while the other readies him for me.

His fingers find me wet for him and tease across skin that's already sensitized from his touch. He tucks two inside me and twists until I'm nothing but a throaty moan holding on tight and begging for more.

"I need you," I manage between breaths. "Want you."

"You're going to remember this," he says roughly, as his fingers pull out, the feeling of emptiness they leave behind suddenly replaced with his cock. His hands are now on my hips guiding me to sink down slowly onto him.

And once he's inside me and bottoms out, everything becomes a blur. Motions. Sensations. Muffled cries of pleasure.

The roar of blood in my ears blocks out every other noise except for his murmured praise in my ear.

"Take that cock, Hendrix."

My world narrows to the man beneath me and the way he fills me so completely.

"Ride me. Fucking ride. Harder. All the way down."

His teeth graze my collarbone, and I forget how to breathe.

"Fuck, you're so tight for me. So wet for me. That's my girl. Just. Like. That."

I'm right there on the edge, seconds from tumbling over when headlights flash across us.

"Don't you fucking stop, baby."

I freeze in fear but it's too late. I'm already lost to the pleasure and can't hold back the frantic movements of my hips.

"Fuck, yes," Jase groans as I grind down on him. "Take it. Every goddamn inch."

He hooks his arms beneath mine and around my shoulders as he holds me in place, thrusting into me in a relentless rhythm.

I feel him swell inside me seconds before I fall apart around him. My body stills for half a second as my orgasm rips through me, and I throw my head back with an uncontrolled cry of his name.

His hand clamps over my mouth to stifle my cries, but they are still loud in the quiet night, getting lost in the crashing waves feet away.

His other hand wraps around my waist and holds me to him, against him, guiding me up and down as my body spasms around him.

But it's his body that's tensing now. It's his cry out for more as he comes with a fucking sexy, feral groan that has my nipples tightening.

The headlights slow as they pass, and the car's engine purrs into our awareness just before it zips out of sight.

"Jesus, woman," he mutters as we both tremble with the aftershocks and our breaths are still hitching. Despite being in a public place, neither of us makes a move to separate or get our pants back on right away.

I rest my forehead on his shoulder as he runs his hand up and down the length of my back.

"I'd be remiss if I didn't say that was some really good In-N-Out."

It takes him a second to get the joke.

To snicker.

Then to throw his head back and laugh before grabbing both sides of my face and kissing me appreciatively.

"Yes. It damn well was."

CHAPTER
thirty-three

Hendrix

I GLANCE THROUGH THE SHOWER DOOR, OUT INTO MY BEDROOM AT THE clock hanging on the wall and cringe.

It's so freaking late.

I'm going to be so exhausted tomorrow, but I'm on the tail end of this big order so I'll get it done.

Live like a rock star. Isn't that what Jase had said on the way home? Work till you crash standing up. Steal a few Zs. Then get back up until you crash again.

No wonder rock stars die young.

I just finish twisting my wet hair up into the towel when I hear my cell phone ring. That's mine, right?

I think.

It has to be.

Where did I leave it?

Within seconds, I wrap another towel around me and am jogging down the hall to find it. No one calls at this time of night unless it's an emergency. No one.

Just as I skid to a halt on my wet feet into the kitchen, I find Jase there, shirtless, of course, with my cell phone to his ear.

"It's a pleasure to meet you too, Ms. Wright, but now that I think of it, you have a different last name than Hendrix. Oh. You changed it back so it'd match. That makes sense," he says.

My eyes bug out of my head as his cheeky grin meets my horror. "No," I gasp.

Jase holds up his hand for me, as if he's got this under control, before he continues speaking. "Your daughter is . . ." His eyes scrape up and down my long legs and desire heats in his eyes when there's no way he can already want me again. "*Incredible.*"

Those words along with the look in his eyes have my heart fluttering in my chest.

He's not supposed to make me feel this way. His words aren't, the looks he gives me shouldn't, and yet since the first moment we met, hasn't that been what's been happening?

"I know, I know," he says as I am dying to hear the other side of the conversation and try to motion for him to put the call on speaker. He just grins, his dimples deepening, and keeps it to his ear in an act of playful defiance. "And we apologize for not including you in the big day. I know to you it feels like it was impulsive and reckless but—" His eyes light up as he listens to her. "Yes. I agree completely. Sometimes you just can't stop love when it's as strong as ours." He chuckles and lifts his eyebrows at me like my mother is out of her mind. *She very well could be.* "Well, Nosy Natalia is right. She's quite the social media sleuth. Hendrix and I met and it's been a storm brewing beneath the surface over the months waiting for the right time to erupt."

"*Erupt?*" I mouth to him and groan.

"I'd like to call it more of a surrender of our wills. *A sweet surrender,*" he says and when his eyes find mine, the softness in them hits me squarely in the gut. "But your neighbor is wrong. Hendrix isn't pregnant. This wasn't a shotgun wedding for that reason." He nods his head. "Hmm. Yes, well, she definitely has a temper and a lot of fight in her, but that's part of the reason I love her. She learned her lesson with Paul—" He laughs. "I stand corrected— *with Fucktard*—and she won't ever allow herself to be treated like that again. And sure as shit, not by me."

There is a pause as I adjust my towel, drawing his eyes again.

"One hundred percent agree." He nods and his eyebrows furrow. "I'll keep that in mind."

"What is she telling you?" I whisper-yell, partially dying inside over everything she's *oversharing* with him.

By the time he hangs up, he'll probably know who my first kiss was, that I wore braces forever, and was a total dork in high school.

His grin just widens when he knows I'm curious. "I know. Definitely." His eyes meet and hold mine again. "She said yes and I had to jump at the chance before she realized I wasn't worthy of her."

He laughs loudly but sincerely. Clearly, my mom has turned on her own charm with him because his cheeks are heating and he's running a hand over the back of his neck.

"She does work too hard. But sometimes dreams are that way. Hmm, yes. But don't worry. I'll be convincing her to hire some help for the shop so she can breathe a bit easier." He barks out another laugh. "And yes, to have more time to make grandbabies for you, although I'm a firm believer in enjoying your marriage first."

My face feels like a furnace just exploded in my head and no doubt my cheeks are beet red. My mother is talking to Jase about sex. About babies. About . . . can I just die now?

Please.

"Sounds good. I look forward to officially meeting you too. We'll figure it out. I promise." He holds the phone out to me and I shake my head violently. I am not prepared for the lie-fest to my mother. Especially when I'm standing in a towel and his eyes are as hungry as they are. "She's right here. Yes."

I level him with a glare as he hands me the phone. I push the mute button. "I told you not to give it to me."

His grin falls lopsided. "I'm just hoping you get so wrapped up in talking to her that your towel falls loose."

I roll my eyes and laugh. Such a guy. But damn his words make me feel good. I unmute the call as I hold the towel in place with my other hand. He made me talk to my mom. He's not seeing shit.

"Mom. Hi. I knew you'd be calling."

"You said for me to know that you were okay. You didn't tell me you were marrying a rock star," she screeches. "I'm beginning to think we don't communicate well."

"Oh, Mom." I sigh, but my smile is real. As is the pat on my ass that Jase gives as he walks by.

"*Oh, Mom,* is right. You're lucky I don't hop on a plane and visit you right this minute to give you two a huge congratulations hug. Now you better tell me everything and not leave a single thing out, or I'm going to make that threat a reality." She tsks. "You tell me you have some huge order to fulfill when in fact you were planning a wedding."

"I do have a huge order. One thousand cookies for a dog's birthday party. That was planned. The wedding . . . not so much."

"About that. I'm going to need some more details to understand this." Silence falls on the line. "I'm waiting, young lady."

Oh boy.

Let the lying commence . . .

CHAPTER
thirty-four

Hendrix

THE DAYS BLUR TOGETHER. BETWEEN THE CONTINUOUS ORDERS COMING in and the influx of people who suddenly care about my bakery—mostly looky-loos hoping to catch a glimpse of Jase when he's never set foot in here to begin with—I barely have time to breathe, let alone revel in this newfound, albeit temporary, success.

Jase was right. I need help. I can keep up with the orders, but it's the orders and the customers and the ridiculous questions being asked—so someone can snap a sneaky pic of me—that I can't do.

So I placed an ad for help—one for an experienced baker and another for a storefront clerk. Needless to say, none of them seem like they hold any validity. From the ones I've sorted through on my computer in front of me, most of them are from women whose qualifications seem to be "Die-hard BENT Fan" and "Future Mrs. Gizmo."

It's ridiculous.

It's exhausting.

It's unfathomable.

But isn't that how this whole experience has been? It's not like I've had a ton of time to sit and actually acknowledge that I'm in a marriage of convenience with a rock star.

I mean, I have. I had the whole wedding and a few days at his house to come to grips with it, but now that the world knows, it's a completely different ball game. There's a whole lot of mental gymnastics to navigate.

I close my laptop, stand, and then catch my reflection in the bakery's front glass. My hair is still up in a messy bun, I have a little flour on my cheek, and my apron has streaks of icing on it. I look exactly how I always do after a long day of baking and creating, with one exception.

The massive diamond on my finger.

The ring that Paul notices immediately when he walks through the open back door like he owns the place. I recoil immediately at the sight of him.

Really should have gotten that key from him. I'm regretting telling Sammy that I was done for the day and that he could leave. Is it so bad I just wanted some time to myself in my own shop without eyes on me?

Yes. Apparently, it is.

Jase is going to be furious with me for it.

"Oh. Look. She's actually bothered to show up today," he sneers as he leans his ass against the counter and takes up residence opposite me.

Funny how you can love someone with your whole heart, talk about making a life together, a future, and in a matter of weeks all you feel is disgust when you see that person again. And I most definitely do feel that when I look at him in a place we built together.

"I've been here every day last I checked."

He holds a finger up. "Every day except for when you ran off to get married, huh?"

"Was that before or after you were fucking Applebee's in our bed? Because I was under the impression that right there negated you getting to have a say about anything in my life."

"You're—or maybe the lack of *you*—is the reason there was Applebee's in the first place."

"Save it." *Don't let him get in your head, Hendrix. Don't give him an inch.* "It's probably best that you leave, Paul."

His expression twists with something dark. Anger? Jealousy? Entitlement? "Nah. I think I'll stay. Especially since you've been avoiding me."

I cross my arms. "Avoiding you? Um, *no shit*. You typically avoid your ex when he's a cheating piece of shit." Besides, the only text I received today from someone other than media trying to get an "in" with me was Jase sending me his usual rundown of where he's going to be. Paul will have to try harder than that if he thinks I'm going to bend to him again.

Paul scoffs. "Hilarious. You want to talk about cheating? You're parading around like some little trophy wife, acting all innocent. How'd you even meet him, huh? When did you find the time to screw Jase Gizmodo? I'd ask how much he's paying you for the sex, but then again we both know you're not that good—"

"Get out." Words bubble up in my throat—besides the fear of being found out—but I don't allow either to come out.

"Come on, Hendrix. This is total bullshit. There's some sick game being played here, and I just can't figure out what it is. Are you paying him? Like is this your scheme to make this shitty bakery a success? Is it more than that? Because, it sure as shit isn't because he wants you."

"I'm going to say it again, Paul, and then I'm going to call the cops. You need to go." I walk over to open the door and point to the alley.

Big mistake.

Because the diamond catches the light, flashing between us. Paul has my wrist gripped in his hand in seconds. His eyes narrow as he studies it, the vein in his forehead popping out. "Hmm. Seems you *are* whoring for him." He flashes a nasty smile. "Guess I could always take back what's owed to me." His eyes drag up and down the length of me. "One way or another."

"Let. Me. Go," I grit out. Paul is all bark and no bite, but that doesn't mean fear isn't snaking down my spine. *What is he actually capable of?*

Paul's chuckle is maniacal as he tries to pull me against him with one hand while the fingers of his other are on the ring on my finger.

Before I can react, the bell above the door chimes, and then suddenly, Paul is no longer touching me. Jase comes out of nowhere and has Paul pinned against the wall, his forearm against Paul's throat and his face inches away.

"That's my wife," Jase growls. "Stay the fuck away from her. Do. Not. Ever. Touch. Her. Again."

CHAPTER
thirty-five

Gizmo

'VE FELT RAGE BEFORE.

I've swung fists and broken bottles over heads and on bar tops.

I've let my anger get the best of me more times than I can count.

But this? Seeing that fucker's hands on Hendrix? Sensing her fear as she struggled against his grip? This is completely different.

This is lethal.

I've never wanted to harm somebody more than I do right now. *How the fuck did he get past Sammy?*

Paul wheezes beneath my grip, his hands grabbing and fingers clawing at my forearm for an easier breath. "I'm going to sue you for everything you're worth."

I press harder, my pulse pounding in my ears. "Try me. I have a lawyer who eats pricks like you for lunch," I say, knowing damn well Nathaniel is more Paul than he is me, but the thought's fleeting as I remember where those hands of his just were.

"Fuck you," he grunts out.

"Call her a whore again. See what happens," I threaten.

"Jase." Hendrix's voice is quiet but firm. It barely cuts through the haze in my brain. She places her hand on my arm and pulls back. A subtle reminder where I am and what the fuck I'm doing. *You can't.*

I hear her words, I know what she means—that I can't afford more bad press, a lawsuit, a scandal. It's so tempting to get lost in the noise and forget that there's a highbrow judge already looking for a reason to believe I'm a reckless asshole.

But her hand tugging on my shoulder has me stepping back from the brink.

I slowly release Paul, and he sidesteps me, coughing as he glares at Hendrix, his voice hoarse when he speaks. "This isn't over. Not by a long fucking shot."

I step into the space between them. "Good," I taunt while I force my hands to unclench and not give in to the urge to plow it into his face. "I'm always down for a good ass-kicking. Until then, Paul, it's time for you to leave."

Paul hesitates, his jaw clenched, motivation clearly undecided, before nodding and then going out the door.

Hendrix exhales shakily. "I'm sorry. I didn't mean for you to—"

"To protect you?" I turn to face her fully, temper still running hot. "That's my job."

"No. It's not. That was my fault and—"

"And if you apologize again, I'm going to get even angrier than I already am."

"Thank you then?" Her cheeks are flushed and her eyes are wide with concern.

I force myself to take it down a notch. Hendrix has never seen me like this, and in some respects, I don't want her to. "Hey," I say, my voice softening. "You don't have to thank me for anything."

"You didn't have to step in."

"Yeah, I fucking did."

She shakes her head. "No, you didn't. You have too much on the line. You need to think of yourself. Of why we're doing this."

"He was assaulting you, Hendrix. I should be calling the police on the prick. He had his hands on you," I yell. "And where the fuck is Sammy?"

She throws her hands up in defeat, almost as if she knows I'm going to be upset with what she says next. "I told him to go home. Convinced him I was done so I could have a moment of peace to myself. It's my fault Sammy's not here, Jase, not his. Don't be mad."

I study her as my pulse races alongside my fury. "I'm not mad but . . . there's a fucking reason he's here. To keep you safe." I reach out to shake her shoulders in frustration but stop myself.

His hands were on her.

The thought sickens me.

"He didn't assault me," she lies. I can see it clear as day in those eyes of hers. She was scared. Wasn't sure what the fucktard was capable of. That makes my blood boil even more.

"Don't make excuses for his behavior."

She reaches out and grabs one of my arms with both of her hands. "I'm not. Please. He's just angry. Going through the emotions of finding out we're married. That I traded up for a much more successful, sexier man."

"Now you're slinging bullshit, Cookie." But she put a smile on my lips and lowered the temperature slightly.

"Maybe." She shrugs and presses a kiss to my shoulder. "Possibly." Another kiss. "Regardless, I'm extremely grateful of the timing of your arrival. Nothing happened. You protected me. I just don't want you to get in any further trouble when we have so many eyes on us and one in particular that makes all the difference."

"Yes. Fine. Sammy is—"

"Not going to get in trouble for doing what I asked of him. But . . . I won't do it again."

"Promise?" I ask.

"Promise."

I nod and run a hand through my hair.

What if I'd been too late?

For the first time in a long time, I don't care just about myself. Yeah, I need to be on the world tour and make this all work, but seeing the fear in her eyes? Seeing his anger—his aggression—completely focused on her? It *enraged* me. Have I ever felt that before?

No.

Hendrix Wright deserves the affection of someone far better than me, but she's managed to wind herself around my heart.

I care about her.

And damn if that's not a mindfuck for a selfish prick like me.

CHAPTER
thirty-six

Hendrix

WAKE UP ALONE.

Again.

Not that Jase and I are sleeping in my bed together on the regular or anything, but after sex . . . sometimes we fall asleep tangled together. Sometimes he keeps a respectable distance. Regardless of how we fall asleep, by morning his side of the bed is always cold.

I don't know what I think of that. Like, we're doing everything a married couple does so maybe it would be nice every once in a while to not wake up alone.

Or maybe it's for the best and a perfect way for us to keep our great sex life from creeping over the line into the emotion realm.

Then again, I think my toes are already dangling over that line despite telling myself daily that it's not going to happen.

But who could blame me?

The man is everything he said he wasn't. Considerate. Caring. Attentive.

This whole scheme may be all about looking good for the judge and to his benefit, but time and again Jase has adjusted on the fly with my needs and wants and best interest in mind.

He reversed his plans to take me to a flashy restaurant, picking up that I'd felt completely underdressed and would have been embarrassed.

Then there's Jase's chokehold on Paul to protect me. The image of Jase pinning Paul against the wall is burned in my mind. I've never seen someone so enraged on my behalf.

Not that I'm one for violence, but it felt nice to be protected. To be cared for enough that someone wanted to.

And how could I forget the texts I receive whenever we're apart. The rundown of his schedule and where he'll be so that I know when to expect him. It's thoughtful and comforting in a sense to know he's considerate of my time.

His compliments? Of my body and our time in bed? Yeah, that's not something I'm used to. His praise of my business and my drive to make it succeed? So vastly different from what I'm used to hearing and yet each time I do, I stand a little taller.

Jase Gizmodo is slowly helping me get my confidence back. Confidence I never knew I'd lost until the day I looked over in Josie's and met those ice-blue eyes of his.

Am I giving him anything in return, though? Yes, he laughs a lot when he's with me—we do have fun together. *Is that all I'll be for him when this ends? Just a fun person to pass a few months with?* Maybe I should be content with that, but it's hard not to hope that I mean more to him than a warm body at night.

So even with the bed cold beside me, I shuffle down the hall, rubbing my arms against the early morning chill, toward his voice. It's hushed, low, almost as if he's being polite and trying not to wake me.

I turn the corner just in time to see him at the window, shoulders hunched over, head angled down. He has a shirt halfway on, like he started to pull it down but got lost in the conversation so he forgot to pull it the rest of the way down.

I don't know why the sight jars me, but it does. His words even more so.

". . . I know. I'll figure it out. I'm coming. I'll be there in a few."

A pause.

"Yeah, I know. Just give me some time. I'll handle it."

He's talking to someone in a voice I've never heard before. Quiet. Earnest. *Like he's keeping a secret.*

I don't know what to think.

The words from a few nights ago echo in my head. *I push people away once I sleep with them.*

Keeping a secret or cheating on me . . .

I step back around the corner and tiptoe back to my room. The doubt comes with every step. Am I going to be shamed yet again? Jase getting caught cheating on me on a public stage will be painfully real.

Knock it off, Hendrix. Clearly he has a life outside of you.

That's all this is.

But when the front door slams a minute later, I spend a ridiculous amount of time waiting for my phone to buzz. Waiting for the usual text to come through that tells me where he'll be today.

It doesn't come.

Not as I lie in bed and stare at the ceiling.

Not as I get in the shower to get ready for work.

And sure as shit not as I unlock the back door of the bakery with a good morning nod to Sammy.

I can't help but let the unease twist my stomach or the unsettled thoughts own my head.

With a sigh and a bakery loaded with new orders impossible to fulfill, I shake my head to try and rid all my overthinking.

This marriage is fake, Hendrix.

That's not a newsflash. *It's not something you didn't know.*

It doesn't matter where he goes or who he talks to.

You're made of tougher stuff than this, Hendrix.

Just keep your heart out of this "business arrangement" and you will be absolutely fine.

You will not be a cliché, because you won't allow yourself to be.

Easier said than done.

CHAPTER
thirty-seven

Gizmo

THE SHELTER IS BUSY.

I stand behind the serving counter, my baseball hat low over my eyes, my long sleeves hiding the tattoos snaking down my arms, and my hands sweating inside the cheap, plastic, serving gloves they give us to wear.

People stand quietly in line. Some have their heads down as they shuffle their feet when the line moves, others make a comment or two to their line neighbor, while others have various outbursts as their mental illnesses overshadow the ghost of who they used to be.

There's no judgment here at the shelter, no requirements on appearances or grooming. They serve everyone and don't ask questions.

I spoon the macaroni and cheese onto the plates that are held out to me. A few of the people make small talk with me as they move through the line. Many don't. I smile and meet their eyes all while scanning every face that walks through the door.

And while I do this once a week when I'm in town, the director called me this morning to say she finally spotted her again. That she was here in the shelter for food.

That my mom was here.

I haven't seen her in months.

And the need to lay eyes on her, to make sure the shell of the woman, who I still love very much, is okay? Absolute.

"Jase," the director says from behind me. "Let me take the line. Why don't you go take a plate over to the table near the door?"

"Okay. Thanks."

My heart lodges firmly in my throat as I trek across the warehouse space toward the petite figure turned into herself at the far table. She's in all dark colors except for a fuchsia scarf that's wrapped around her head, holding her matted hair out of her face.

Her clothes are mismatched but her shoes don't have holes in them. Healthy feet are especially important when you're on the streets—or so I've learned over my endless hours here. Eyes that used to hold so much light look up to meet mine. They're glassy and vacant but kindness still flickers in them along with the softened smile she gives me.

I force my own smile because seeing her like this is always the toughest part. "Hey, Maggie." I don't call her Mom. I learned that lesson the hard way years ago. Most days she doesn't know who she is let alone the fact that she was a mother. Other times she knows it but not the specifics. Both are devastating to me. "I thought you might want some food."

"Who told you that?" she barks at me, her eyes flickering around the space. Paranoia owns her most days.

"The director." I motion across the room. "She knows you don't like to stand in line with all the "smelly" men as she calls them, so she asked me to bring this to you."

It's brief but I see a flicker of relief in her eyes. "Thank you."

"Do you mind if I sit for a minute?"

She grabs her bag to her chest and hugs it tightly as she eyes me like a thief wanting her goods. "Why?"

"Because my feet hurt and I thought you might want someone to talk to."

"You can sit. But I don't want to talk." She stoops her head low and whispers, "The voices might hear if we do."

The voices who took you from me.

I nod as I slowly take a seat, careful that any quick moves will put her on the defensive so that she might act out or run away.

It's happened before.

Each time with her is a new lesson to learn. A new set of rules her mind has conjured up but that no one else knows the answer to.

Once seated, I glance at her hands. They are clean for the most part so I hold close to the fact that she's able to wash somewhere at least.

"Eat. *Please*," I say.

"Did you do something to it?" She narrows her eyes at me, her voice loaded with skepticism. "Did *they* tell you to bring it to me so that I'd get sick?"

"No, ma'am." *It's me, Mom. Jase. Can you see me? Do you know it's me somewhere lost in your mind?* "It's the same food everyone is getting only I gave you a little extra because I know you like the biscuits and fruit."

The things she can store in her pockets and save for a later time.

"Thank you." She takes a few bites and then sets down the fork as if she's waiting to make sure I didn't just poison her.

"Is it good?" I ask, desperate to make conversation with her.

She looks at me, then past me. "I have a son, you know. The most beautiful boy. He's going to be famous when he grows up."

I clear my throat and grip the edge of the table, my heart splitting apart piece by fucking piece.

"I need you to go so he can sit down." She makes a shooing motion with her hand as I fight the burning tears. A glance over my shoulder tells me there's no one there, but she's already muttering to whoever she sees in her head. *Already talking to her son.* Her imaginary one.

She doesn't know who I am.

Not today.

I murmur something, anything, to hold on a bit longer, but she's already drifted back into her own mind.

Fuck. I hate this.

It's the same every time, like an addiction I can't shake but that only destroys me more each time I see her. I dig a hand into my pocket and slide the envelope across the table to her.

She jerks her bag back. "I don't want anything from you," she spits out.

"It's money. Get yourself a hotel for the night. Take a shower. Sleep in a bed."

"They did send you, didn't they?" She flings the envelope off the table and it flies against the wall with a thud.

My heart lurches in my throat as her agitation and paranoia grows.

I take a step back. Then another, putting my hands up as I go. If I leave she'll stay and eat. If I don't, she'll run and disappear without any warm food in her belly.

I can't breathe. The pressure in my chest is crushing as I frantically try to get outside. To draw in fresh air.

The minute I turn the corner and am around the side of the building, out of sight of everyone, I press my hands to my knees and let loose a ragged, pathetic sob.

It's not like she remembers what she's lost. It's still all right there for her. In her tormented mind. In her memory.

It's me who lost everything.

It's me who remembers what I used to have.

It's me whose scars have just been ripped open yet again.

I don't realize I've called Vince until his voice cuts through the static in my brain. "You okay, man?"

No. No, I'm not.

"Can you come get me?"

CHAPTER
thirty-eight

Gizmo

"**Y**OU WANT TO TALK ABOUT IT?"

I stare at the glass of whiskey in front of me. I've lost count of how many have been poured, but it's definitely a number on more than one hand. "Same shit. Different day."

"Nah. It's more than that," Vince says in that quiet, steady tone of his I've grown to count on.

"Sometimes it's just too much. That's all. No more. No less." I throw back the drink. The burn is well past gone, but it does nothing to dull the panicked look in my mother's eyes that stays front and center in my mind.

"I don't want anything from you," she spits out.

"It's money. Get yourself a hotel for the night. Take a shower. Sleep in a bed."

"They did send you, didn't they?"

"I get it. I hear you."

"I know you do," I murmur. Vince dealt with his own demons in his past when it came to his dad, and so I'm well aware he knows the hurt a parent can inflict.

But it feels different when that parent has no choice in the matter. Vince's dad was an abusive asshole. My father chose my brother. My mother . . . didn't have any say in the matter because her mind ate her whole . . . bit by bit. Day by day. Year by year.

"You got to see her?" he asks as he pours me another glass.

The bar may be no more than a dark hole in the wall, but the bartender gave us the bottle and has left us alone.

"Yeah." I shake my head and replay the whole interaction in my head. "She's never going to get better, has never wanted to, and yet every time I get that call, I hope that she has."

"I'm sorry, brother."

I shrug, too fucking angry that there's nothing I can do differently. "It is what it is."

"What about Nathaniel? Do you ever bring—"

"No. Not happening." I purse my lips and don't voice the fears that run rampant in my mind. The ones that have already built up a scenario that she'd see him and know who he was instantly. The son who escaped. The one she rarely saw. And then there'd be me, the son who took care of her as best as I could and she wouldn't recognize me at all. "He doesn't understand. He . . . she's mine to take care of. Always has been."

He puts a hand on my shoulder and squeezes. "No one does," he says softly. "But just like me, that doesn't mean he can't be here for you."

Fuck.

Fuck my mom's sickness.

Fuck my brother.

Fuck my father for leaving his ex-wife to get sicker and sicker without caring a fuck about her.

Or me.

I close my eyes a beat and let the room spin. *I hate this.* The anger I still feel and that momentary dash of hope I get each time I see her. The one that says maybe this time will be different. Both are stupid fucking emotions.

"That's the last one, Giz. We have the gala tonight."

"Fuck," I hiss out. Just what I fucking need on top of a shitty day.

"Yeah, well, I'll call Doc Evans to come sober you up."

I nod. Won't be the first time for him to administer us saline IVs, won't be the last. "I don't want Hendrix to see me like this," I mutter.

Vince stills beside me. I'm coherent enough to see the awareness hit him. "Well, fuck me. Never heard you say that before."

"Say what?"

"You care what she thinks."

"She's my fucking wife. Of course I care what she thinks." She's the only ray of sunshine in my fucked-up day. Yeah, she'd love to see me right now. Just like this. Huh. A fucked-up son of a fucked-up mom.

"Yeah, well, I'm beginning to think she's more than just that." He sighs and throws some bills onto the bar for the bartender.

She can't be more than that, Vince. She'd never want more than the contracted time anyway.

Fuck.

CHAPTER
thirty-nine

Hendrix

STYLISTS AND MAKEUP ARTISTS MILL ABOUT THE GREAT ROOM OFF the kitchen as they pamper and ready me for the charity gala tonight. It's our first official event as a married couple and, of course, Jase already coordinated for the same glam squad he sent to Las Vegas to get me ready. I'm grateful for the familiarity and am well aware they're all gossiping about us being newlyweds, and that's great for the rumor mill that no doubt is secretly going on.

The dress we've picked out is stunning. It's a deep purple with a low-cut neckline that tastefully hugs my curves. My heels are high with red soles and I question if I'll be able to walk in them without falling flat on my face.

"That's what your husband's arm is for," the manicurist said when I told her I was probably going to wobble on them until I fell over.

I glance again at the door, that paranoia over where Jase went earlier still front and center. He hasn't responded to any texts, picked up any calls, and he's still not back yet.

When I hear boots clomping down the hall, I have to bite back the relief that floods my voice when I say, "Jase?"

But the first face that comes into the room is none other than Vince Jennings, Jase's bandmate. His arm is around Jase who is unsteady on his feet.

Relief floods me that Jase is here and whole and okay, but at the same time, I'm a bit pissed that we're in this position to begin with. I take him and his disheveled appearance in and hate that I'm disappointed in him.

This is our first night out as a couple, showing the world who we are, and this is how he prepares for it? I guess the marriage idea is a little more traumatizing for him than I expected it to be.

I shift my attention to Vince.

"Hi." I say the word and then realize how stupid it sounds, but at least I stop short of officially introducing myself. I have an audience of women who *should* assume that since I married Jase, I'd have already met his bandmates.

It seems by the way Vince takes in the room around me that he understands this too. "Hendrix." His eyes hold mine and he just nods as our unofficial introduction to one another.

It's a weird feeling to be stunned by who his friends are when he's of the same status, but I have to admit if there wasn't worry mixed with relief, then I might be a little more starstruck.

"Cookie," Jase says, the syllables slurring as he tries to take a step and Vince steadies him.

He's not just drunk. He's blitzed drunk.

Fucking perfect.

Anger fires in my blood. Memories of growing up with my alcoholic stepdad flash back.

"You're home late. Again," my mom yells. "And you reek of cheap perfume. Who was it tonight?"

"Oh shut the fuck up, Sandra. You're such a stuck-up bitch. Can't a man have a night to himself every now and then?"

"Right. Clearly, you've forgotten I'm your wife. Again."

"And you wonder why I don't come home," he yells.

I hate when he does this to my mom. I hate the fighting. I hate how he treats her. If the walls weren't paper-thin, I wouldn't have to hear it at all. So, I do what I always do when I need to hide. I grab my headphones and head toward the kitchen. I have a new recipe I want to try and now seems like a better time than any.

I think I've blocked so much of those days from my mind, but it comes back with a vengeance when Jase meets my eyes. There's defiance there, shame, and an unfettered not giving a fuck. *Guess there's my answer.*

And the chuckle he emits? The one that almost sounds apologetic over whatever he's done? That guts me.

"Tiger can't change its spots," he says. "Told you I'd fuck things up when they're going good. Push. Push. Push."

Vince sighs and mutters for him to shut up before looking back at me. "He had a rough day."

"So I see," I whisper, grateful the glam squad has quietly gone about their business with their heads down as I feel my past creeping up on me. My stomach knots. I don't know whether to be angry or heartbroken, but the sight of Jase like this—reckless, lost—hits a deep and raw space in me.

"Even with everything tonight, you let him get like this?" I can't help the accusation in my voice, but I'm hurt and can't hide it.

"He's like this and not worse because of me. There's stuff . . . there's a history here." He pauses and sighs. "I have the doc on the way. He'll give him an IV to sober him up. It'll help."

"Great. Fucking perfect," I mutter. He does this so much he has a doctor on standby? I'm in way over my head if that's the case.

"I've got it under control. He'll be good for tonight. I promise," Vince says as he helps him to the other room.

I stare after the two of them, trying to hide my disillusionment. I also feel mortified, because what does this say to the glam squad around me? But I steel my shoulders and straighten my spine. You're not his confidante, Hendrix. You're only in his life for a short time, and you can handle this.

A few minutes pass when another set of footsteps trek down the hall. A man in his late fifties with a button-down dress shirt and medical bag in his hand smiles stiffly before heading to where Vince calls out to him.

I sit in my chair as finishing touches are put on my makeup, my hands clenched into fists, unsure whether I should stay where I am or be in there with Jase.

But the ache in my chest tells me exactly what I already know.

I care. *Too much.* I won't be a fool this time. I'm not oblivious to the red flags. I won't give Jase my heart, but I do care.

And the thought is as terrifying as it is comforting.

CHAPTER
forty

Hendrix

WITH ITS ELEGANT GOWNS, CRISP TUXEDOS, AND CAMERA FLASHES, the gala is a glittering spectacle of wealth and power, a world so far removed from my own of flour and sugar that it feels like I've stepped into someone else's life.

In reality, I have, but that's beside the point.

Every detail is meticulously curated—the extravagant floral arrangements, the cascading chandeliers, the waitstaff moving seamlessly through the crowd with trays of champagne flutes.

And yet, despite the opulence, all I can think about is the man standing beside me.

Jase looks flawless. Not a trace of the broken man I saw just hours ago. No resemblance to the impassioned apologies he offered several times on the way over here.

My questions over what happened remain unanswered. My need to know got lost in the sadness in his eyes that he tried to hide with quiet smiles, brushes of his lips against my cheek, and his praise for how I look.

But something did in fact happen and no matter how well Jase Gizmodo cleans up, pressed and polished in his tuxedo, it doesn't erase it.

I glance over at him again and wonder how he was able to turn it around so easily. It's almost as if he was born for this.

Maybe he was.

As he interacts with those around him, he laughs in all the right places, nods at the perfect moments, and then turns on that charm with his effortless grin. The same charm that easily won me over.

He's introducing me to everyone we meet or who greets him. He's doting on me with his attention when others are looking our way, but I can see the mask slip every once in a while.

It's in the way his smile doesn't quite reach his eyes. It's how Rocket or Hawkin or Vince make a point to come and talk with us for a few minutes at a time, whichever one's turn it is unassumingly studying Jase's face to make sure he's okay. But there are some moments when Jase goes somewhere absently and then gives a little shake of his head to bring himself back. He's here, he's present, but it's a struggle to find his way back.

But I applaud him for it and hate that he has to do it at the same time.

As the night wears on, his spark comes back bit by bit. Eventually, the mask slips off completely and we're all treated with the Jase Gizmodo we all know and love with his sincere laugh and wide smile.

A warm hand presses against the small of my back, guiding me through the room. His touch is light, almost absentminded, but I'm well aware of it and him beside me as are all the eyes in the room.

"So you've met the guys. Thoughts other than how you married the wrong one?"

I chuckle. Our introductions were brief and amid others so there was a subdued greeting like we know each other. But I still noticed their assessing stares and felt their silent judgment as they wondered what kind of woman would marry a guy she'd never met before.

And while it was slightly uncomfortable, a part of me was grateful that he has friends who look out for him since it seems no one else does. There is clearly genuine closeness between the four of them that I didn't sense he has with Nathaniel.

"You're staring at me, Cookie," he murmurs, his breath teasing the shell of my ear.

I stiffen, instantly defensive. "I am not."

"You are," he counters, his voice low, teasing. "If I didn't know any better, I'd think you actually like looking at me."

I roll my eyes. "Don't flatter yourself."

But the way his lips curve tells me he doesn't believe me. Worse, I don't believe myself.

"Maybe I just wanted to make sure you were okay. You know . . ."

"I'm fine. Good to go. Never better."

"And of course when you say it like that, I'm supposed to believe it." We walk a few more feet and I tug on his arm looped through mine. "Jase?"

He stops and sighs heavily. It takes a second for him to meet my eyes and when he does, I can see the reluctance in them. "There are times when a man needs some grace, Cookie, and today was one of those times."

I nod, my bottom lip worrying between my teeth. "I'm worried about you is all."

"I know. And I'm sorry that I did that to you. That I made you worry and doubt and question why the fuck you said yes to this." His smile is a flash of apology.

"No. Yes." I chuckle. "Maybe. My own past didn't help the situation."

"I'm okay. I promise you that I am."

"What happ—" I wave a hand at him as he smiles at someone passing by. "Never mind. It's not my business to pry."

"Look, I had some unexpected news about a family member that threw me. It wasn't the first time I got news like that, and I'm certain it won't be the last. It just knocked me off my feet for a bit. I called Vince. He picked me up. We had a few drinks. Got it out of my system. It's over and done with, tucked back away, okay?"

"Okay," I say. I've had a whole day to stew on where he went and with whom, and even though I could feel hurt and angry, I've tried to remind myself that our lives are not intertwined forever. Down the track, even in five years' time, today won't matter. *It's a blip on this temporary radar.* And I can deal with it.

He leans forward and brushes a kiss on my lips. I'm sure it's for show but like most of his kisses, this one makes me melt a little. *I'm wiser to what this is, but he's still a damn good kisser.* I've also realized I'm happy to be his friend. A real friend.

"You could have called me," I whisper. "I would have been there for you, no questions asked."

His eyebrows narrow ever so slightly as our eyes hold and before he can respond, a statuesque blonde in a dangerously low-cut black dress approaches us. She offers Jase a sultry smile but completely ignores my existence.

"Gizmo," she purrs, reaching out to touch his forearm. "It's been too long." The look in her eyes is much more than a comment. *It's an invitation.*

He smirks, his usual charm slipping into place. "Madison. Looking beautiful as usual."

"As are you, Gizmo. We should get a drink. It's been *far* too long."

"You think?"

"Oh, I do. I know just the place too."

"Hmm," Jase responds, smiling.

As I watch their interaction, a strange tightness settles in my chest. Interesting. He's just finished apologizing to me for his behavior today, and now he's flaunting his past lovers. *You were right to keep your heart out of this, Hendrix.* The way she leans into him, the way her fingers trail lightly along the fabric of his sleeve, makes my blood heat, though. She's being so brazen, knowing he's married and pursuing him anyway. *How do women get off on that sort of bitchy behavior? Why don't they stick up for each other?*

Jase glances my way, amusement flickering in his gaze. He knows exactly what he's doing. And dammit, he's an asshole, but I don't see that he's into Madison. *He's playing a game.* All right then.

"So, this must be the lucky woman who tamed the untamable Gizmo." Madison's voice is a sugarcoated barb as she finally acknowledges me. She extends a perfectly manicured hand, her smile anything but warm. "Madison Sinclair."

"Hendrix Gizmodo." I shake her hand, gripping just a little too tightly.

An innate jealousy flares within me. Yes, this is all pretend, but I am in fact sleeping with the man so the spike of emotion would seem normal.

She laughs, her gaze flickering between Jase and me like she's piecing together a puzzle. "Well, aren't you full of surprises?"

Jase tilts his head, clearly enjoying whatever game she's playing. "Always."

She looks familiar and for a second, I try and place her as a celebrity.

But then it hits me where I've seen her before—in one of the many photos I found online of Jase. She was on his arm.

So it's no surprise to me she's trying to let me know she staked her claim before me. That she has slept with my husband. So do I make a discreet comment and let this go? Let the woman feel good about herself for "putting me in my place"? Or do I make myself visible, act my part for the appearance's sake? After all, when this is over, there's no doubt in my mind that Jase will be back to sleeping with every *Madison* who offers.

I shift closer to Jase, placing a hand on his chest, feeling the solid warmth beneath my palm. "I recognize you. You've been one of Jase's dates before at an event like this." My smile is quick and my voice is loaded with sweetness. "Who did you come with tonight, Madison? I can't imagine you came alone."

Jase goes completely still, all but choking on his next breath.

Madison's smile falters slightly.

And for the first time tonight, I feel like I have the upper hand. Like I found my backbone and am finally on an even playing field.

Jase recovers quickly, wrapping an arm around my waist and pulling me against him. His lips brush my temple, lingering just long enough to send heat rushing through me. "She's a quick learner," he murmurs against my skin.

I know it's all part of the act, but when he pulls back, I see something new in his expression—something unreadable, something dangerous.

Desire.

Pride.

Want.

As Madison makes a polite excuse and melts back into the crowd, I exhale slowly and try to regain my composure. Jase watches me, his gaze darker now, sharper.

"That was interesting," he muses.

I arch a brow. "What was?"

His fingers brush against my hip, slow and deliberate. "You, getting jealous."

"Please." I snort. "I was just playing the part and letting her down gently."

"Killing her with kindness?"

"Can't be called a bitch when you're sweet and complimentary, now can you?"

"True but you can still be jealous." His voice is smooth, teasing, but there's something else beneath it—something unsettling.

"Whatever." I roll my eyes.

"Excuse me for a moment? I need to use the restroom. Will you be okay on your own?"

"Fine. Yes." I watch him walk away and draw in a deep breath.

"Ah, there she is," a smooth, confident voice says. "Thought he'd never leave your side."

I turn to find Quinlan, Hawkin's wife, standing before me, a champagne flute in her hand and a warm, knowing smile on her lips. Beside her, Bristol, Vince's wife, tilts her head, assessing me.

"So," Bristol says with a knowing smirk. "How's the bakery?"

They know the truth, but lucky for me they seem okay with it and are playing the game.

Just like I am.

I clear my throat, gripping my clutch just a little tighter. "Busy," I say with a polite smile. "Flour-covered hands aren't exactly gala-friendly, but I'm here. I'm trying."

Quinlan chuckles, lifting her glass to her lips. "I get that. I used to think I'd never fit into this world either. But you'd be surprised how easy it gets after a while."

I raise a brow. "You mean it stops feeling like everyone is watching and waiting for me to fail?"

Bristol laughs. "We're not that lucky. They're always watching. The trick is that you stop caring."

I exhale, stealing a glance at where I last saw Madison. "That easy, huh?"

"Not easy," Quinlan corrects. "It's brutally hard, but necessary. And it's majorly worth it for your own mental health."

Bristol leans in conspiratorially. "A tip from someone who struggled at first? Ignore the comments, the gossip, and the fans who think they know everything about your relationship. They don't."

I nod slowly, taking in her words.

"Also," Quinlan adds, "if you ever need to vent, drink, or just take a break from being Gizmo's wife, we're always a phone call away."

"We're the BENT Bitches and we mean that term in the most loving of ways."

That unexpected warmth settles in my chest, easing some of the tightness I've had. I've spent so much time trying to prove I belong, so much time worrying about where I fit into this new, bizarre world, that I never considered the possibility that maybe—I didn't have to do it alone.

I let out a breath, finally relaxing as I meet their gazes. "I think I'm going to like having you two around."

Bristol grins. "You don't have a choice. If they're brothers, we're definitely sisters."

I laugh, and for the first time tonight, I feel like maybe I can handle this after all.

"Oh, shit. Giz is coming back," Bristol says and laughs. "We weren't here."

"Nope. If we weren't here then we can't be accused of corrupting you," Quinlan says as she gives Jase a quick hug and kisses him on the cheek. "It wasn't our fault. We promise."

"It's always your fault," he teases, his grin genuine, as they walk toward their husbands. "I see you met the BENT Babes."

"Bitches," I correct and wink. "Get it straight."

But before he can respond, a waiter appears, offering Jase a drink. He hesitates for half a second before taking it, his fingers tightening around the glass. I see the conflict in his eyes, the flicker of something unresolved.

I reach out and take the drink from his hand before he takes that first sip. "Maybe we hold off on this after earlier?"

I know it's not my place to say it, to ask it, but I need to know whatever happens next tonight is real and not because of alcohol.

Jase narrows his eyes at me, but then his expression shifts, almost as if he realizes he's two halves to a whole now—at least publicly anyway. He doesn't argue against my request. Rather, he just lets me take the glass and set it on a passing tray.

"Thank you," I murmur.

"Facing one of these sober. Now, that'll be interesting." He chuckles sarcastically but when he links his fingers with mine and squeezes, that's all I need.

He's giving me a concession.

A huge one, apparently.

And that says a lot about the kind of man he is.

CHAPTER

forty-one

Gizmo

"Y OU GOOD, BROTHER?" VINCE ASKS.

I glance his way and want to grit my teeth at the way he's studying me, looking for any signs of . . . what the fuck ever, but then again, he is the one who came and got me. He didn't push for more answers than I gave him. He just fucking knew what I needed because of where I was. "For the tenth time, yes. I'm good." I slap a hand on his back.

"Wouldn't be doing my job if I weren't checking."

"Yeah, well, that doesn't mean I have to like it."

He barks out a laugh. "None of us like this touchy-feely shit. I get it. You get it. I'm just glad you're doing all right."

Am I? I wasn't five hours ago.

"Yep. I'm doing all right." Especially as I mull over Hendrix's words too. *"You could have called me. I would have been there for you, no questions asked."* I have no doubt that she would have—*she's that kind*—but why put extra stress on her when this is only temporary?

"I'd be doing a helluva lot better with a drink in my hand, but I promised her," I say with a lift of my chin in Hendrix's direction and then a growl I don't even realize I emit as another man walks up to Hendrix. I can't fucking blame them. Not when she's wearing that deep purple dress that hugs her curves just like I'd prefer to be doing instead of being across the room thinking about it.

Madison comes nowhere close to touching what Hendrix has.

"Her," he says with a hum in his throat that I want to ignore. "I remember what it was like to say shit like that—*her*—when it came to Bristol. Like you want to pretend that fucking ache in your chest isn't there but you can't fucking ignore it."

"I'm not ignoring shit. She's here for . . . a set time. We're simply enjoying that time."

He snorts. "*Enjoying.* That's a word. So is, *I don't want Hendrix to see me like this.*" He says my own words from earlier back to me. The ones I uttered when I was a fucking mess and Vince wanted to bring me home.

"Those are several words but we know math isn't your strong suit, so I won't hold it against you," I joke.

"Yeah, well, those several words told me a lot about your headspace when it comes to you and—" He lifts his chin much the same way I did and then winces.

I follow his line of sight and roll my shoulders as another man—an actor—approaches Hendrix.

"You look like you're ready to rip someone's head off," Vince says.

"Shut up," I grunt.

"Is that where we are with this now? Already?"

"What the fuck does that mean?" I ask, but don't look his way.

He laughs, clapping me on the back. "Man, you've got it bad."

I don't respond. Because he's not wrong.

Rocket saunters up, grinning as he takes a sip of his scotch and looks where we're looking. "Gotta hand it to you, Giz, you sure as shit know how to pick 'em. I mean, she's fucking hot and funny and—"

"You met her for ten minutes. Back off, fucker."

He raises his eyebrows and looks at me. "Remember that bet way back when? The drums for breaking up with my girl?"

"How could I forget? She was good at a lot of things," I say to wipe the smug look off his face.

"Yeah, well, I think it's time to reciprocate that bet. When your time is up with her, maybe it's my turn to have your seconds."

Fury flashes instantly in a way I've never experienced before. My glare is nothing compared to how tightly clenched my fists are. "Don't even fucking think about it."

Rocket raises his hands in surrender, his chuckle drawing others to look our way. "Relax. I was just messing with you."

But I'm not laughing. Because this isn't a joke.

Across the room, Hendrix glances my way. Our eyes meet, and for a moment, I forget that Rocket and Vince are standing there or that no doubt, Hawkin is somewhere close by about to chime into their razzing.

You could have called me.

Those words ring in my ear. They were sincere, and despite the fact they came from someone I definitely hurt earlier, she said them as a woman trying to help me right a wrong.

A lump forms in my throat and I struggle with these foreign feelings. I don't quite understand them.

Then my phone buzzes.

Hendrix: Why are you looking at me like that?

I smirk.

Me: Like what?

Hendrix: Like you want to cause a scene.

Me: Maybe I do. Sounds par for the course.

Hendrix: You're supposed to be on your best behavior. Remember?

Me: And you're not supposed to be charming every man who comes and talks to you.

I watch her smile curl up as she reads the text.

Hendrix: Maybe this is all part of my master plan.

Me: Master plan? To do what?

Her eyes widen slightly, a flush creeping up her neck. And damn if I don't want to drag her out of here right now. All I can hope is that the text she's typing me gives me a reason to do just that.

Hendrix: To find somewhere very soon, very near, where you can put that smart mouth of yours to good use.

Me: Are you asking what I think you're asking, Cookie? Say the words. Tell me what you want.

Hendrix: I want you to fuck me, Jase. Hard. Fast. In this dress. Against a wall. On the floor. Bent over. I don't care so long as it's soon.

Me: Is that so?

Hendrix: Maybe I want to fuck the Madison Sinclair right out of you. Operation Live-A-Little.

Jesus. Fucking. Christ.

I reread the text again to make sure she really just sent that to me. That she really just said that.

Yep.

She sure as fuck did.

My cock stirs and I don't need anyone, let alone these fuckers, to see it. "I'll be right back. Hendrix needs to be rescued." The lie is quick and easy and is greeted with chuckles from the guys.

But I don't care. All I see is the purple dress. All I can think about is slipping it up over her hips, bending her over, and sliding into her tight pussy.

Operation Live-A-Little is the best fucking plan I've ever had.

Hands down.

I reach Hendrix in seconds—her lips parted, eyes darkened, and cheeks flushed—and grab her elbow with a little more force than necessary.

More like desperation.

"Let's go," I mutter.

"I thought you'd never ask," she taunts.

CHAPTER
forty-two

S HE'S LAUGHING. THE SOUND IS THROATY AND PURE SEDUCTION AS her fingers lace with mine, and we move quickly, dodging people as we search for somewhere to have our own little party.

I tug her into the elevator, punch the button, and the doors slide shut with an agonizing slowness. Her breath catches when I press her up against the wall, pinning her there with my body. My lips are on hers in an instant, her kiss tasting like sparks begging to ignite, as her fingers tangle in my hair and pull me closer.

She tastes like mint and want and Hendrix, and I don't know how I'll ever want anything else.

"Upstairs. There has to be somewhere upstairs to go."

"There's always this elevator." She nips my bottom lip and tugs on it.

"You're crazy," I murmur against her mouth. And I fucking love this side of her. Brazen. Daring. Asking for what she wants.

"I'm serious," she whispers, and it's all I can do not to rip that damn dress off right here.

The elevator dings and we stumble into the hallway. A quick glance around shows me a women's lounge and I grab her hand, practically pulling her there.

"If anybody's in here, I suggest you go out!" I yell and am greeted with the glorious sound of silence. No sooner do I lock the fucking door behind us and my lips are on hers again.

My hands pull up the hem of this stunning purple dress.

My fingertips skim over the lace beneath that drives me fucking insane.

Then from one beat to another, we're a blur of limbs and heat. Of want laced with greed and desperation edged with need.

"I need you in me, Jase." Another kiss as her hands undo my pants and pull my cock out in an act of much-appreciated desperation. "Right here." She bends over and braces her hands on the vanity, meeting my eyes in the reflection of the mirror in front of her. "Right now."

I stroke a hand up and down my cock as I take in the sight before me. Hendrix bent over, the globes of her ass bare, and her pussy dripping with arousal. Begging for me to fill it. To own it. To claim it.

"I want you to watch me while I come," she murmurs. "I want you to walk back into that ballroom after this, to be in that room with everyone, and know I can still feel you inside of me."

"Fucking hell, Hendrix."

"Fuck me, Jase."

I crash into her, the sensation almost as blinding as her words. It's a rhythm with no grace, all hunger that drowns us both. Her fingers grip the edge of the vanity like it's the only thing tethering her to this moment, to this world, and I'm lost in the pulse of wanting her more than I've ever wanted anything.

The frantic sound of skin on skin echoes around us, blending with the ragged sounds of our breaths. It's raw and real and hot as fuck. And I lose myself again and again to the feel of her. To the scent of her. To knowing she's fucking mine for as long as I want to have her.

She pushes back against me with every thrust, a silent demand that pulls me closer and closer to the edge.

"Harder," she gasps, her voice wavering with want.

I reach around and find her clit, slick and swollen and begging for attention. The first stroke has her shuddering beneath my hand, her moan raw and ragged and full of need that kicks me into overdrive.

"Like that?"

The mirror shows her face—the pleasure etched in every line of it—and makes me want to give her more. To take more.

"More," she pants out, urging me to trail a hand up her back and tangle it in her hair. She gasps as I pull it, because it only serves to seat me deeper in the process.

"Yes," she cries out, her voice breaking around another moan. My fingers work her clit in the rhythm of our bodies, faster and harder, until she's trembling beneath my hands. "Just like that."

She comes undone all around me. Her body arches as I watch her reflection. She's wild and stunning and everything I never wanted but can't seem to step away from now.

The sight of her shattered like this and by my hand sends me right over the edge with her.

"*Fuck. Yes.*" It's a half-growl, half-shout, seconds before my world goes black, then white, as consuming pleasure blazes through me and leaves me wanting more. Of her. Of this.

Always more.

We stay like that for a moment—her lips parted, eyes shut tight, skin flushed—while I feel like I've just been to battle and come out victorious on the other side.

My pants are still around my ankles and her dress is still up over her hips when I slip out of her and sigh. She turns to face me, and the disheveled look in her hazel eyes makes me want to take her all over again.

She straightens her dress, and fuck, if that isn't an image that will fuel my fantasies for years. Lips swollen, hair wild, cheeks flushed.

"Guess we need to figure out how to celebrate this kind of first, huh?" Then she throws her head back and laughs.

CHAPTER
forty-three

Hendrix

NOW WHAT?

That's the question I keep asking myself as we drive home in the limo from the gala. Something has shifted, changed, and I don't know what exactly that is.

It's in Jase's silence as he stares outside at the world passing by.

It's in the energy crackling between us. It feels different. More undeniable. More real.

My go-to in these situations is to crack a joke, to lighten the mood with something silly, but I don't say a word. It's like an inexplicable line was crossed, and I don't know how to navigate that.

So I let the silence stretch, and a suffocating weight settles between us.

Did I do something wrong?

I thought the sex was fun and flirty . . . definitely the hottest thing I've ever done . . . but did something happen after that when we went back to the party for the short time before the car came?

When we step inside the house, the tension only thickens to the point that I can't stand it anymore.

"So what gives?" I ask. My heels are in one hand and I hold them up as I shrug. "What did I do wrong? Why are you not talking?"

Jase just looks at me like a tiger casing his prey, and I'm not sure if I should be unnerved by it or turned on.

But his lack of words wreaks havoc on my nerves.

"Hello? Say something. Anything?"

"Not a big fan of all the men talking to you tonight."

"Pot? Meet kettle," I say and roll my eyes. He can't be serious. Madison was far from the only woman hoping to get beneath him tonight.

"Still. Not a fan."

"Then maybe you shouldn't have picked me for a wife, huh?" I don't know why I'm raring for a fight. Maybe it's because I feel like I've done something wrong and I'm trying to create a defense, just in case.

Stupid, but in the moment, true.

"I didn't say there was a problem with it. I said I wasn't a fan of it," he says stoically.

"You can drop the jealous husband act. No one's here to watch."

He takes a step toward me, hands in his pockets. "It wasn't an act."

"Then what is your problem? Why the cold shoulder? Why—"

"Will you shut up?" he says as he yanks me against him and slants his lips over mine in a kiss to rival all kisses. In a kiss that could start and end wars. It's full of hunger and heat and want and desire.

One hand fists in my hair, tilting my head back so I have no other place to look than into his eyes—so that my entire world becomes him in my line of sight—and his other hand holds me firmly against him.

"I'm quiet because all I can think about is wanting to do that to you. All fucking night. I want to kiss you and taste you and fuck you. And even after today—after earlier—you're still fucking here. I don't know what that means to me. I don't know what to feel, because I don't deserve it. *But you are still here.* So I'm trying to not question it so I don't push you away. That's the last fucking thing I want to do right now."

His rush of words, his startled confession, is mind-bending to me, and a part of me wishes he'd been drinking so I can blame it on that, but he hasn't.

He knows what he's saying.

And it's what I think I need to hear, but in the same breath what I'm terrified to hear.

Something happened to him today. Something that he won't discuss with me. He was vulnerable and instead of me being put off by it, I didn't budge.

That's all he's talking about.

That's all he's implying.

And even I don't buy the lie.

But he's looking like he is—with emotion welling in his eyes and his chest heaving against mine—and I want more. Of him. Of whatever this is. Of the madness that we are together.

I reach up and run my palms down both sides of his cheeks, framing his face there. I feel the muscles in his cheeks turn up as he offers a stuttered smile.

"I'm here, Jase. Right here. Right now. That's what we have, right?" His breath hitches, just barely, but I catch it seconds before I brush my lips to his. "Need me. Take me. Want me. Use me."

That's all it takes to reignite the still-smoldering fuse.

My lips crash against his as we move down the hall. His hands grip my hips like I'll disappear if he lets go.

The kiss is fire and fury. It's the pent-up tension unraveling between us in a single touch of our tongues. He pulls me closer, backing me against the doorframe. I'm desperate to feel every inch of him.

"*Jase.*" His name—one word—means so many things.

What is this?

How did this happen?

Why do I feel so strongly for you when I shouldn't?

He rests his forehead against mine and sucks in a ragged breath, clearly trying to process his own questions, his own wants. Or simply trying to come up with reasons why this is a bad idea when it feels so goddamn good.

"Tell me to stop," he murmurs. "Tell me I'm crazy for wanting you this bad."

I open my mouth to speak, to give him the answer I think he wants to hear—it's just sex, just physical—but it feels like so much more than that.

And both of us are terrified to admit it.

So I hide behind that fear.

I choose to show him with actions instead.

I slide a hand slowly back up his chest, up the side of his neck so that I can fist it in the short hair at the back of his neck, and then I lean in to kiss him again.

"You're not crazy," I murmur. "Far fucking from it."

CHAPTER
forty-four

Hendrix

I WAKE UP TO AN EMPTY BED. *Again.*

The sheets are cool where Jase should be, and for some reason, the reality of it gnaws at me. Last night was . . . too much. An overload of sensations, of unspoken emotions, of well-intended actions.

It was an overload of noise that contradicts this silence. I'm left alone with my thoughts, tangled in a mess of emotions I don't know that I want to sort through.

I roll onto my back, staring at the ceiling. My body still hums with the memory of his touch, of the way he looked at me like I was the only thing that mattered. Like I was real.

And yet, like every night we spend together, when I wake up, he's gone.

I should feel relief, right? This is pretend, it's going to end, and so this is just my reminder of that.

But that doesn't abate the hollow feeling I have or lessen the lie I'm telling myself. *I don't just like the man.* I've downright fallen for him.

Fuck, man.

Just fuck.

The scent of coffee drifts through the air. It snaps me from my thoughts but only because if there's coffee, he's still here.

I slip out of bed, grab his discarded dress shirt from last night, and pad barefoot toward the kitchen.

Jase is standing at the counter, his back to me, a mug in one hand, the other running through his messy, still-damp hair. He looks good like this—undone, bare, real. But there's tension in his shoulders. What's so heavy that it surrounds him now?

"Morning," I say softly.

He turns, his eyes locking onto mine, and for a moment, neither of us speaks. There's too much unsaid between us, too much weight pressing down on what should be simple.

"Morning," he finally says, his voice rough. He watches me for a beat, then gestures to the coffeepot. "Made enough for you."

It's a small thing, a simple thing, but it makes me smile.

I step forward, pouring myself a cup, trying to ignore the way his eyes track my every move. "About last night . . ."

Jase exhales heavily, setting his mug down. "What about it?"

"You'd had a rough day. I pushed you. We . . . I don't know. I don't want you to . . ."

He offers me a lopsided smile, those dimples deepening in each cheek. "Are you saying you regret it? And if so, which part particularly? Fucking in the women's lounge at the gala or riding my face here at home?" He takes a step toward me and slides his hand down my chest where his shirt is unbuttoned.

My body heats immediately. I've never believed that such a visceral reaction was a real thing. I always thought it was pretend shit for movies or romance novels.

Then again, aren't I living in a pretend world right now?

He leans in closer. I can smell the soap from his shower. "For the record, I don't regret a goddamn thing." He winks and presses a kiss to my cheek as if this is the most normal conversation in the world. "And neither should you."

"Oh."

"I love when you make that sound." He pats me on the ass. "I have to get to the studio. I had an idea this morning, which is why I'm up so early."

"Baker's hours," I tease.

"Seems fitting." He hisses as his coffee burns his tongue. "Dinner at home tonight? Together?"

I falter in taking a sip. That's the first time he's asked something like that. "You're not meeting up with the guys to write?"

"Are you telling me you don't want to have dinner with me, Cookie? I mean, I'm a man. I can take it if so, but my ego's going to be a little bruised."

"No. That's not . . . I just figured that's who you're normally with. Since you're writing new material." I try and talk my way out of sounding like a jilted lover jealous of his bandmates. That wasn't my intention. My comment was more reflexive at his surprising request.

"True, but tonight I want to eat with you. I'll even cook."

I level him with a dubious look. "You? Cook?"

His grin is lightning quick. "I'm a man of many talents."

"I'm well aware."

We stare at each other across the distance. Our smiles are wide but the look we exchange holds a quiet acceptance that we're slipping into different territory? That this has gone from a contract to friendship? That we enjoy each other's company outside of the twisted sheets?

I don't know but it's doing funny things to my insides and catching me off guard.

"Yes. I'd like to have dinner with you. I don't know how late I'll be though."

"That's okay. I can wait." He raps his knuckles on the counter. "Have a good day at work."

I take my first sip of coffee as my head spins from the whirlwind that is Jase Gizmodo.

"Oh, and Cookie?" he calls over his shoulder.

"Yeah?" I look after his very fine ass walking down the hallway.

"You look sexy as hell in my shirt. Make sure to have that on later when we get home."

CHAPTER
forty-five

Gizmo

My daily check-in with Sammy told me she was going to be exhausted when she finally got home.

An endless line of customers. Some media trying to sneak its way in the bakery and score an interview with her. Fangirls hanging out in the alley hoping for who knows what with her.

I swear she'd rather walk barefoot over broken glass than ask for help. That's going to change, starting with tonight.

With me doing this for her. Because my world she's stepped into is a lot for anyone to handle, especially for someone not used to this life like I am. So when she walks in the door in a bit—her shoulders tight with tension, her usual fire dulled by the weight and stress of the day—I know tonight'll be just what the doctor ordered.

Relaxation without any strings attached.

And yeah, maybe that comes in the form of me ordering her favorite takeout, but still, the effort is there.

As are the ideas I have in mind to keep this growth sustainable for her once I'm out of the picture. The uptick in customers is great for her now, but how does she sustain this when all is said and done? What will make her stand out from the other cookie bakeries in town?

I'm working on it. I have thoughts about it. I just need to figure out how to put them in motion.

Her headlights hitting the windows tells me she's home and draws me away from my wandering thoughts and back into the conversation happening against my ear.

"Hey, I have to go, Hendrix is home."

"Okay." Nathaniel draws the word out, curiosity tingeing its edges, but doesn't ask anything more. "Like I said, things are looking good. Judge Watkins likes what he's seeing and is buying the ruse. Keep it up and he'll feel more comfortable lifting the travel restriction."

"'Kay. Thanks for the update. Good to hear it." I say the words, absorb the good news, but am distracted.

"Love you, brother," Nathaniel says.

I pause. Hear the words, feel their sincerity, but don't necessarily feel comfortable saying them back. "Talk to you soon."

I hear the door open, followed by the shuffle of her bag hitting the floor.

"In here," I say as if she doesn't know where the kitchen is.

She enters within seconds, her tired hazel eyes darting between me and the takeout containers spread across the table. Then, slowly, they drag over my bare chest.

That slight hitch of her shoulders is all I need to see to know that shirtless was a good choice. For me. For my chances at something later. And to give her a little something to focus on other than her long day.

Mission accomplished.

"Hi."

"Long day?" I ask.

"The longest." She steps toward the island and smiles. "You cooked. How sweet."

"I'm sensing your sarcasm," I tease and gesture toward the food, "but I assure you this is way better than any attempt at cooking I could have made." I shrug. "Besides, Sammy said it was a rough day and so I wanted to make sure I had your favorite."

She steps toward the table, eyeing the food. "What did you get?"

"Thai. Extra spicy, the way you like it." I grab a container, lifting it with a smirk. "And dumplings, because those were starred twice."

Her eyes narrow. "Starred twice?"

"Yeah. On the menu you have sitting on your desk at the bakery. You told me in Vegas you love Thai. I noticed the menu last time I was in the bakery and snapped a photo of it—just in case. This is *just in case*. So I bought one of everything you had circled on it and two of the dumplings since those were starred twice."

She stares at me dumbfounded.

"What is it, Cookie?"

"You noticed that?"

"I notice a lot of things. I just thought after a hard day's work, you might want food that reminds you of home. Of . . . before all this. Of before me."

Something flickers across her face, something I can't quite name, but it makes me grip the container a little tighter.

She blinks, lips parting slightly.

I expect her usual sarcastic retort, but it doesn't come. Instead, she just looks at me, like she's trying to figure something out. Like maybe she wasn't expecting me to notice.

"You—" She clears her throat, shaking her head. "Since when do you take care of people?"

I shrug, keeping it casual, even though the way she's looking at me makes my chest feel tight. "Since you, apparently."

Her lips press together, and I can tell she's trying not to react. But she does. It's subtle, but it's there—in the way she shifts her weight, in the way she suddenly won't meet my eyes. And I can see the minute she brushes it all off. The second she tries to play whatever this is going on between us as nothing more, nothing less than her fake husband trying to be nice.

Much the same way I've been.

This is dinner. It's supposed to be light. To be easy. To not leave these unanswered questions lingering above us so that it's anything but that.

"Let's eat," I say to try and will that into existence.

"Please. I'm starving." Her smile widens.

But when she reaches for the container in my hand, I pull it out of reach.

"Not so fast, Cookie," I say. "First, you have to do something for me."

Hendrix crosses her arms, already exasperated. "I literally just worked ten hours. If this is some kind of weird drummer initiation, I swear—"

"Nothing weird. Just say: Thank you, Jase. You're the best husband I've ever had, and I don't deserve you."

She stares at me. "You're the only husband I've ever had so that doesn't work." Then, without warning, she lunges.

I laugh, easily dodging her attempt to grab the food, holding it higher. "That's not the magic phrase, Hendrix."

She huffs. "I am not saying that."

"Then no dumplings for you."

Her jaw clenches. "You're such an ass."

"An ass who ordered you dinner," I remind her, taking a dramatic bite of a dumpling. "Mmm. So good."

Her glare could probably set me on fire.

I grin wider. "I can't believe how delicious these are." I make an exaggerated moaning sound just to mess with her.

"Okay, fine!" She huffs. "Thank you, Jase. You're the worst first husband I've ever had, and I definitely don't deserve the emotional abuse of watching you eat my favorite food."

I chuckle. "Not what I had in mind, but you're not exactly one who conforms." At least not anymore and that's fucking awesome in my eyes.

I offer her the container and our fingers brush. Linger. "Thank you for this. For dinner. For noticing. For the laughter."

"You deserve it and then some," I murmur.

Moments pass in silence as we fill our plates with Thai goodness. I take a seat at one end of the counter as she starts to sit on the far end.

"Nope. Get your fine ass over here." Her eyes whip up to meet mine. "Don't you dare sit all the way over there. I don't bite." I quirk my brows and challenge her.

"Lies," she teases but takes the bait and moves her plate next to mine.

I smirk. "Well, not unless you want me to."

She rolls her eyes, but I catch the way her breath hitches. Love that it does.

And just like that, the air between us changes.

It's always been there—that thing neither of us wants to name. The push and pull, the tension that crackles every time we're near each other. But now, sitting here, eating takeout, our knees touching, her lips slightly parted as she stares at the food like it's suddenly the most interesting thing in the world.

I feel it more than ever.

I don't know what to do with it.

But for the first time, I'm not entirely sure I want to fight it anymore.

CHAPTER
forty-six

Hendrix

"STOP RINGING," I CALL OUT TO THE PHONE AS IT RINGS FOR THE THIRD time in the past hour.

Then I laugh.

When have I ever thought I'd complain about being too busy? It's insane. It's overwhelming. *It's awesome.*

I barely manage to balance the piping bag in one hand while reaching for the phone with the other.

"Cookie Cutter," I answer breathlessly, adjusting the phone between my shoulder and ear.

"I'd like to place an order for divorce cookies," the woman on the other end says cheerfully.

I pause, frowning. "I'm sorry, what?"

"Divorce cookies. The special from Gizmo's contest?"

My stomach drops. "Um . . . I think—" *You have the wrong bakery.*

Oh. Shit.

He didn't.

"No, no," she insists. "It's all over social media. Order breakup or divorce cookies—the newest idea from Cookie Cutter—and you're automatically entered to win a meet-and-greet with Gizmo from BENT!"

I nearly drop the phone and it's not because of her high-pitched squeal that follows.

There's no way he did that.

None.

But her squeal and the sudden beep alerting me of another caller on my other line is saying there is. *And he did.*

"Oh, uh—" I scramble to open Instagram on my tablet, my heart hammering as I search for Jase's page.

And then I find it.

A video of Jase grinning, oozing that Gizmo charm, as he explains about the "newest bakery sensation" while showcasing one of my perfectly decorated cookies.

"What in the actual hell?" I mutter.

The customer is still on the line. "So, can I place my order? Does that automatically enter me into the contest?"

I clear my throat, trying to maintain a professional façade despite the fact that my blood pressure just went through the roof. *Divorce cookies?* What in the hell do I even do for those? A broken ball and chain? A cracked wedding cake? Some kitschy slogans?

Jase, I'm going to kill you.

Right after I kiss you.

"Of course. How many would you like?"

After jotting down the details, my eyes bug out of my head when I see my online ordering system ticker begin to escalate one by one and then by tens at a time.

I immediately call Jase. He picks up on the second ring. "Hey. You never call me during the day. Well, you never call me. Only text. Am I in trouble or something?" he asks and chuckles.

Oh, he knows exactly what's going on.

"Your post? Your contest? What the actual fuckity fuck?" I shriek.

"I figured you're helping my career out, so why can't I help yours a little? A quid pro quo. I tried to think of the best way to promote your niche bakery, and then I figured why not use the two best things you have at your disposal? Your cookies and me." When I'm silent, when I sit there dumbfounded and overwhelmed, he continues, "*You're welcome.*"

"I don't even know what to say." I'm both exasperated and invigorated. Like . . . the new orders are populating on my screen to numbers I've never seen right before my very eyes. "Don't you think you should've asked if I can handle it?"

"Probably, but this will force you to hire and get help. Don't worry, I have Nathaniel working on that as we speak."

"He's a lawyer, not a baker."

"He's smart. Resourceful. Writes a mean NDA as you know that will keep everything confidential. I promise he'll come through on this and most likely by the end of the day."

"Jase . . ." I bark out a disbelieving laugh as my head spins.

"Besides, it's not like people divorce a lot—well, this is Hollywood so don't quote me on that—but I figured these are one-time customers that you'll reel into being full-time ones once they taste how fucking good your cookies are. I am the best judge of just how good they taste, no?" His chuckle is suggestive and has me thinking back to last night where that masterful tongue of his spent plenty of time between my thighs. I shiver.

"Leave it to you to crack a joke when you just rocked my world."

"Last night and this morning." Another innuendo that has me shifting my feet. "I have faith in you."

I groan, rubbing my temples. "I can't believe . . . you're—"

"The best husband ever. I know. I might win awards for it, but I don't want to get ahead of myself. We're in the early days yet."

I want to be mad. I should be mad. But another order dings on the bakery's online system, then another, and another.

This is going to be the death of me.

I sigh. "I swear, you're impossible."

"And yet, you keep me around," he teases.

I have faith in you.

Not only is my husband exceedingly skilled at giving me amazing orgasms, but . . . *he has faith in me.* I wonder if he has any idea how much those words mean to me? I shake my head, unable to stop the small smile tugging at my lips as another order rolls in.

"Looks like I'll have to find a way to thank you later then," I say, smiling when I hear his groan.

"You actually think I'm going to say no to that? I'll be waiting . . ."

CHAPTER
forty-seven

Gizmo

THE FIRST CHORD RINGS OUT, VIBRATING THROUGH THE WALLS OF THE soundproofed studio, and I let the rhythm settle into my bones before tapping out the beat on my thigh. It's instinct, muscle memory, the only thing that's ever really made sense to me—music.

Hawkin strums again, frowning at his guitar. "Something's off."

"It's you," Vince says, barely looking up from where he's leaning against the amp, bass resting against his chest. "You always overthink the first few chords."

Hawkin flips him off. "Eat shit, asshole."

"Great, now we're really getting somewhere," Rocket mutters from his stool, playing his fingers over the keyboard.

I smirk, shaking my head as I tap a quick rhythm against the rim of my snare. "We need something dirtier, grittier." I glance at Vince. "Play it heavier. Let it drag."

He follows my lead as I try to show him what I'm hearing in my head, slamming into a darker, more deliberate rhythm. Hawkin and Rocket shift the melody, Vince picks up the bassline, and suddenly, we're somewhere.

I close my eyes, letting the sound settle under my skin. *Yeah. That's it.*

Then, Rocket ruins it.

"So," he says over the music, way too casually, "how's married life treating you?"

I miss the beat. And then still my drumsticks as I level him with a glare.

Vince barks out a laugh. Hawkin doesn't even pretend he's not interested, turning toward me with a slow grin.

"Dude." I sigh, shaking my head. "We're not *really* married."

Rocket waves me off. "Technically, you are. I mean, if you're not thinking you are, I'm sure she'd be fine with being Mrs. Rocket and fulfilling my every fantasy."

My smile is lethal despite knowing he's fucking with me. "So long as you can figure out how to have those fantasies with my drumstick shoved up your ass."

"Worth it," Rocket says and grins.

Hawkin's still watching me, too damn closely. "So? We're back to this conversation again, huh?"

"Yep. Like you three are expecting the answer to change," I say.

"You still pretending it's just casual?" Hawkin asks.

I tighten my grip on my sticks. "It is casual."

Three pairs of eyes stare at me like I've lost my mind.

"What?" I frown.

Rocket snorts. "Oh, Giz."

Vince leans forward, propping his elbows on his knees. "So, let me get this straight. You're 'fake married' to a gorgeous woman who definitely keeps you on your toes, she's living with you, and you're still telling yourself this is just about sex?"

I open my mouth, but nothing comes out.

Which is exactly the reaction these assholes were hoping for.

Hawkin grins, tilting his head. "Holy shit. You like her."

I scoff. "Not in *that* way."

"Oh my God," Vince says, eyes widening. "Jase. Jasey-boy. Our resident love 'em and leave 'em drummer has feelings in *that* way."

I shake my head. "It's not like that."

Rocket smirks. "No? Where do you start your night? In her bed? Where do you finish your night? Still in her bed? I mean . . . sounds like it *is* like that."

My jaw clenches.

Their expressions shift instantly.

Vince lets out a low whistle. "Damn."

Hawkin chuckles. "Yeah, you're screwed, man."

I toss my drumstick at him. He dodges it easily.

"This isn't a thing," I say, forcing my voice to stay level. "Hendrix and I—we're just playing the game. It's working. The marriage serves a purpose to ensure our band can tour. So what if we're having incredible sex to help pass the time?"

Then why do I feel so shitty selling whatever this is between us short with a crappy explanation like that?

Rocket raises a brow. "But?"

I exhale through my nose, dragging a hand through my hair.

But she makes my house feel warmer.

But I know the exact way she likes her coffee.

But I listen for her footsteps when she comes in late.

But she fits next to me, in ways I never thought someone could.

Fuck.

"There's no but," I say, a little too quickly.

Vince and Rocket exchange a look before Hawkin leans in, smirking. "Uh-huh. Sure, man. Keep telling yourself that."

I scowl. "Can we get back to the song now? This new material isn't going to write itself."

"Yeah, yeah." Vince stretches. "But just for the record? There's no shame in wanting more."

I ignore the comment and start the beat again, letting the music drown out the truth I don't want to admit yet.

Because they're right.

I think I do want more and that scares the shit out of me.

Everyone I've ever loved has left me. Scarred me. Hurt me.

I refuse to open myself back up to that, regardless of how good it feels now.

It never lasts.

Ever.

CHAPTER
forty-eight

Gizmo

PUSH OPEN THE BACK DOOR OF THE BAKERY AND LEAN AGAINST THE frame, watching Hendrix work. Flour dusts her apron, and she's focused, piping delicate designs onto cookies. It's late—too late for her to still be here.

Guess I screwed her—and myself—with this whole contest thing. That's why when my surprises show up at any minute, she'll be happy.

"Can I help?"

She startles, nearly smearing the icing, but corrects herself. "You scared me."

"You're busy."

"Somebody created a contest that has made things a tad hectic. I wonder why?" she asks. I'm relieved to hear the amusement in her voice.

I move toward the cookie rack, snatch day-old ones off the rack, and take a bite. So damn good. I groan dramatically. "You're going to make me fat."

"Stop eating my cookies." She slaps at my hand but her smile says she's happy to see me. That makes two of us.

"Hello to you too." I grin as I stop beside her and without thinking, wipe off a smudge of icing on her cheek. She stills, her breath catching slightly, but she doesn't pull away. I take the opportunity to brush my lips against hers.

I mean, if she's going to give it, I'm going to take it.

Sighs come from the other side of the counter. Hendrix jumps back and looks past me. "Hi. I'm sorry, but we're closed."

"They know," I say. "I had Sammy let them in."

She looks at me confused. "What do you mean, they know?"

I grin. "They're reinforcements."

"Jase . . ." There's hesitancy in her voice but relief in her eyes. "You don't even know what I'm looking—"

"They're graduates of the local pastry school, both with experience in cookie designs." I introduce the two ladies who stare at the both of us eagerly. Hendrix shakes their hands and asks them questions about their experience. "They're here to fill your orders. To copy the pattern you've already set . . . while you rest."

Hendrix crosses her arms. "Jase—"

I press a finger to her lips. "Shh. No arguing."

She glares but doesn't push me away.

"We'll go upstairs to your apartment. Stay here tonight. That way if they have questions on anything, you're close by."

"I don't give up control that easily," she murmurs to me. But she catches the amusement in my eyes, the notion of how easily she gives up control to me in the bedroom. "Not the same, Gizmodo."

I bark out a laugh. "Then give them the rundown. Tell them what they need to know. And then they'll take it from there."

Over the next hour, I watch Hendrix go over details and procedures and computer ordering systems with her new employees. There is a quick leaf through of her design binder. A demonstration on how to use the ovens and industrial mixers, although by the faces of the two helpers, they already know how to use them. Hendrix explains the ordering system and emphasizes the attention to detail and perfection she requires. Then she moves to where they dry, how they're labeled, and where to find the prepped boxes.

It's impressive to watch her in her element. Yeah, I've watched her create and decorate, but to see her know her business inside and out is not only incredible, it's also sexy as hell.

The woman is simply incredible in so many facets of the word.

"I'll stay down here with them," she says when she finally finishes. "You can go upstairs and sleep."

"Hendrix. My love," I say with dramatic flair. "I brought them in here to give you a break. To help you. If you stay here much longer, you're going to be icing your feet and creating a subpar product. Trust that they know what you've shown them as well as the skills they already bring into the bakery."

"I know but—"

"No buts." I press a chaste kiss to her lips and can practically feel the exhaustion seeping out of her. "We're going upstairs. They know where to find us. They are capable and talented and you've given them thorough instructions."

She hesitates, but I can see her wavering. The sigh tells me I might have finally won out. "Fine. But if they mess up my cookies—"

"They won't," I assure her. But it takes another thirty minutes and a whole lot more convincing on my part to actually have her on the stairs and heading up to her apartment.

Her steps are hesitant but I keep talking the whole time to distract her. I explain how Nathaniel took care of all the paperwork and payroll for me. How these ladies come seriously vetted with numerous references.

The Type A in her struggles with the notion of giving up control, but I don't let her have an option. This is the way it's going to be.

The apartment is small but cute—it's her in every sense. The muted colors, the warm tones, the tidiness. I can picture her here and the notion makes me both happy and sad to think about her here all alone.

"You have icing in your hair," I murmur as I press a kiss to the back of her neck. "Come on, let me wash it out for you."

"You're going to wash my hair?" She laughs like she doesn't believe it.

"I am. Yes." I reach down and pull her shirt over her head.

Another unexpected first for me.

"Jase . . ." Her voice is thick, drowsy with exhaustion.

"Shh," I murmur as I unclasp her bra and let it fall to the ground. "This is about you."

I rub the muscles of her neck, then move farther down as I knead down her back.

"Step out of your pants for me."

She does as she's told, like a woman who's so exhausted that she can't fight me. There's a part of me that expected to be turned on by this, the undressing her, the having her at my mercy, and while of course, the sight of her naked would turn any man on, I feel something more.

Like I want to protect her.

Take care of her.

Let her know how appreciated she is.

And I don't know how I feel about that as I turn the water on and wait for it to heat up. It's like my head and heart are in a constant battle of opening up and shutting down. Of letting her in and then guarding it back up.

Yet time and again, I let her in when I've never let anyone other than the guys in. That says something, doesn't it?

She blinks up at me, a little dazed, as I help her into the bathtub. She moans softly as she settles.

I go in search for a cup to help wash her hair and at first when I return, I think she's fallen asleep. But I don't stare at her like I want to, I don't take advantage of the trust she's given me either.

She sighs when I pour the warm water over her scalp. She tilts her head back as I work the shampoo into a lather and begin massaging it into her scalp in painfully detailed circles. I rub my fingers into her temples and then to the back of her neck.

This is such a new experience for me, taking care of someone.

Then again, is it? The thought startles me. I took care of my mom for a long time, and maybe I subconsciously stopped wanting to take care of anyone because of that.

Until now.

Until Hendrix.

What does that mean?

"The other day, the day of the gala," she says quietly, her eyes still closed.

"What about it?"

"You were at the homeless shelter. I saw a picture on a gossip site. You were in the food line helping out."

I digest her words as slowly as I respond. "And?"

"Why didn't you tell me that's where you went? Is that where whatever happened, happened?"

I exhale, running my fingers through her wet strands. "I don't tell anyone when I go." It's not a lie, it's just not the full truth. "It's my way of giving back and it's not for public fodder or good press. I never want it to be."

She tilts her head back, eyes barely parting as if the dim light is too much even now. "I'd like to go with you sometime. I mean, if you ever want company. I'd love to help."

Fuck. My chest tightens. No one's ever said that before. No one's ever wanted to be part of that side of my life.

Not that she has any clue how close it hits to home for me.

I nod. "Yeah. Maybe." *I'd like that.*

I finish washing her hair in silence, afraid that any conversation might lead to more questions I'm not ready to answer.

When her hair is done, when she's dressed in a fluffy robe, lying on her bed, I assure her the cookies downstairs are coming along just fine.

And then I crawl into bed beside her, tuck her against my chest, and let her steady breathing and warm body calm my mind.

I should be asleep.

It doesn't come though, because my head is no longer quiet. In fact, it's screaming.

"I'd like to go with you sometime. I mean, if you ever want company. I'd love to help."

How does she keep on giving? Yes, I've helped her financially, but I've uprooted her life, asked her not to crowd mine, and yet, she keeps offering so much to me. *Her kindness, her smiles, her light . . . her body.*

"Need me. Take me. Want me. Use me." And I have. I do. Repeatedly. Uncontrollably.

And then Vince's words roll through my head . . . *again.*

"I remember what it was like to say shit like that—her—when it came to Bristol. Like you want to pretend that fucking ache in your chest isn't there but you can't fucking ignore it."

I've never fallen for anyone before.

But if this is what it feels like, then . . . *fuck.*

CHAPTER
forty-nine

Hendrix

A smirk plays on Josie's lips as she leans on the bakery counter. "Okay, spill it. How is it living with a sex god?"

I snort. "Josie—"

"Don't 'Josie' me." She waves a hand. "You're married to freaking Gizmo. And from what I've seen, from the rumors floating around, the man worships the ground you walk on. So?"

I roll my eyes. "It's . . . fine."

She scoffs. "Fine? I'm going to need more here than just fine. You're new-lyweds. There should be lots of sex. Lots of passion. Lots of late night . . . I don't know." She laughs.

I pick up a cookie and study the design on it to stall. "I don't know what you want me to say."

Josie grins wickedly. "Oh, I know exactly what I want you to say, but fine, keep your secrets."

Secrets.

There are too many. However, she's not wrong. I should be *acting* like a true newlywed. He's actually fun to be around, which has surprised me if I'm being honest. He's insanely nice to look at, so there are no complaints there either. But Jase has thoroughly opened my mind to what mind-blowing sex is like. He's shown me that *Fuck You, Paul* was the one who sucked in bed. *Not literally. Or anywhere else for that matter.* But I now know it *was* him and not me.

And that does bring a true smile to my face.

"I'll tell you this, the women he hired to help me with his ridiculous promotion—"

"Ridiculously sweet promotion," she corrects.

"True. It was. It is. They have helped me tremendously to get all caught up and stay on top of things. I was so nervous about handing over some control to them, but they haven't disappointed me."

They've also allowed me to have a little more breathing room to sink into whatever this is with Jase and enjoy it more. To be able to lie in his arms the next morning, with his heartbeat steady and his breathing even beneath my ear, and think about how he keeps showing up, keeps taking care of me. All this from a man who swears he's selfish, and yet I haven't seen a glimpse of it once.

But he was there when I woke up. The bed wasn't empty like it is at his house. I wasn't sure how he'd be when he woke up, when he realized that we actually slept the whole night together. Would he be quiet? Stoic? Weirded out?

He was none of those. He woke up with a smile on his face and then ran down to get us some coffee while I checked out how everything was in the bakery.

"You drifted off there on me and by the flush to your cheeks it was for good reason."

"He washed my hair the other night, Josie. He sat on his knees and washed my fucking hair."

By the look on her face, it's as big of a deal as I think it is. "You have brought the hot, tattooed rock star to his knees, sweetheart. That's sexier than anything I've ever experienced."

I nod. "How is this my life?" I say it more to myself than to her, but she grins.

"I keep thinking the same thing." She glances over her shoulder to make sure she's out of hearing range of others. "Listen, if he ever wants to promote the coffee shop the way he did the bakery, I wouldn't say no. It's not hair washing but it's just as sexy." She barks out a laugh. "No one has ever complained about skyrocketing sales."

I laugh, shaking my head. "Truth. No complaints here." I glance over to my new employees busy decorating another set of orders. "Business is booming. And yes, you're right, Jase is amazing too." *And I love him.*

Josie watches me for a beat, her expression softening. "But?"

I glance at the calendar pinned to the wall. The date glares back at me, a stark reminder that regardless of how incredible this all feels, Jase is in fact rehearsing for a world tour.

And if he's able to go on that world tour, it means the end of us.

It's like a punch to the gut every time I think about it.

"But nothing." I conjure up a brave smile. "It's just . . . been so overwhelming. How did this even happen?"

"I think it daily, sister, and I'm only getting to live through the great sex vicariously."

"You need help." I laugh.

"I do. I definitely do."

And yet the calendar still sits there. Still taunting that this is only temporary. *No wonder it feels too good to be true.*

CHAPTER
fifty

Hendrix

THE KITCHEN SMELLS LIKE WARM VANILLA AND CARAMEL AS I PULL A fresh batch of cookies from the oven. The dough has browned perfectly, crisp edges giving way to a soft, gooey center. I set the tray down and take a deep breath, letting the scent wrap around me. Baking has always been my therapy, my way of unwinding.

And that's probably why I'm not even at work but I'm still baking now.

My mind is still thinking about that calendar. Still wondering how I'm going to survive this.

Down the hall, Jase's voice filters through the open door, low and steady as he hums a melody. The soft strumming of his guitar follows, each chord measured, precise, then repeated as he tinkers with the composition and adds the other instruments in with whatever he does on his computer program.

Rolling a ball of dough between my hands, I hum along without thinking, knowing the song—or this version of it anyway—pretty much by heart.

The music stops.

A few seconds later, Jase appears in the doorway, his arms crossed as he leans against the frame. "Baking? Even at home?"

I smile. "Trying some new flavors. Want to be my tester?"

"You don't have to ask me twice." He moves to the island and snatches a warm cookie from the tray.

I watch as he takes a bite, his eyes fluttering shut. "Damn. That's . . . incredible."

I laugh. "High praise coming from a guy who thinks peanut butter and pickles belong in the same sandwich."

He smirks, grabbing a butter knife and swiping some icing onto another cookie. "Okay, but hear me out." He dips it in chocolate and then, to my absolute horror, sprinkles cinnamon on top. "Genius or genius?"

I scrunch my nose. "That's a crime."

"Only one way to find out." He holds it up to my lips.

I shake my head, laughing. "No way."

But he wiggles his eyebrows, daring me, and before I can protest further, he swipes a dab of icing across my cheek.

"Jase," I warn.

His grin is pure mischief. "Oops." So is his shrug followed by another dab onto the tip of my nose. "Double oops."

"This isn't a game you want to play with me."

"No?" he asks, but this time, he holds a napkin out to me to help me wipe the frosting off. But just when I go to grab it, he takes his other hand, covered in icing, and smears it down my arm.

I yelp. "You have no idea what you just started," I shriek, grabbing a handful of flour and flicking it at him. A puff of white bursts into the air, landing in his hair, on his clothes—fucking everywhere.

"Oh, it's like that now, is it?" His voice drops low, teasing, and before I can dodge, he flicks some of the softer icing down the front of my shirt in a pattern that would make Jackson Pollock proud.

The next few minutes are pure chaos—flour flying, icing smeared across skin, laughter filling the kitchen as we chase each other around the island. I manage to wrestle a spatula from him, but not before he pulls me against him, both of us breathless, sticky, and covered in sugar.

I look up at him, my pulse hammering. His eyes are dark, his breath warm against my cheek. "You've got icing," he murmurs, his thumb tracing over my bottom lip.

And then he licks it off.

My breath catches. The air between us shifts, laughter fading into something heavier, hotter. His hands settle on my waist, fingers teasing the hem of my shirt.

But just as the moment tilts into something inevitable, I slip in the spilled flour, yelping as I take him down with me.

We collapse onto the floor, laughing as we land, tangled together in a heap, completely sugar-dusted. Jase rolls onto his back, arms sprawled out, staring at the ceiling. "Well, that escalated quickly."

I giggle, shifting so my head rests against his chest. "You started it."

He hums, tracing lazy circles on my arm. "And I'd do it again."

The warmth of his touch comforts me, and for a moment, I forget about everything else. The ticking clock on our arrangement. The way this is supposed to end.

The way I've fallen head over heels for him.

Instead, I wonder, and not for the first time . . . *what would it be like to stay married to him?*

CHAPTER
fifty-one

Gizmo

THE PARK IS QUIET WHEN I GET THERE, THE EARLY MORNING SUN barely stretching over the tops of the trees. Nathaniel is already waiting on a bench, his hands folded, looking every bit the polished lawyer he is. It still feels strange seeing him this way—buttoned-up, controlled—when I remember the scrappy kid who used to chase me through the neighborhood.

He stands as I approach, offering a nod. "Jase."

"Nate." I use the name he hates, still very much like the little brother I am. After what I've gone through, is there any question that I continue to remind him of the animosity I carry like a shield?

We sit in silence for a moment, the tension settling in like a third person between us. Then he clears his throat. "I just wanted to give you a status update on things."

"Please. The walking on eggshells for the past three months is getting a little old."

"Are you really walking on them though?" Nathaniel asks with a look on his face that I can't quite read.

"Meaning?"

"I don't know. You tell me. I talk to Sammy too, seeing as I'm the one writing his checks for you."

"Your point?"

"You're with Hendrix. A lot."

"She's my wife, right? Isn't this what we were trying to accomplish? That everyone, including her bodyguard, sees that."

"Hmm."

"Just fucking say whatever you're *not* saying."

"I don't know. Maybe Judge Watkins is right."

"Fuck that and fuck you." I shove up out of the seat. What the fuck is this shit about?

"And he still acts out when he doesn't want to face facts," Nathaniel murmurs.

I whip around and glare at him. It's too early for this shit, and the last thing I want to do is throw a punch at my brother. "And what facts do I not want to face?"

"That she's a good match for you. That the urge to go out and get shit-faced in a club is different now because you'd rather stay home and laugh with her."

"You don't know the first thing about my life, Nathaniel."

"You're right. I don't. I wasn't allowed to. First, because Dad took me and then because you hate me because he did."

"We're not doing this right now. I came here to see if there was an update about my case, if you'd talked to the judge. Can we stick with that?"

Nathaniel studies me, the muscles pulsing in his jaw. But I can see when he decides to let the fight go. Thank fuck for that.

"I touched base with him yesterday. He made some more favorable remarks about you—noting you hadn't been in the news. I told him how I thought Hendrix was bringing out another side of you that maybe you didn't even know you had, and even I was impressed with how much you've changed."

I nod, waiting for the relief to come. It doesn't.

"You could have told me this over the phone."

"And miss your temper? What fun is that?" he teases.

"This is way too fucking early to put up with this shit."

He clears his throat. "In seven or eight weeks, this could all be over. You'll be in the clear. Able to fully rehearse for the tour, knowing you'll get to go. The charade will be over. You'll be free to go about your normal life."

Free.

The word tastes bitter on my tongue.

"I've requested to set a court date with the judge for his ruling. I'll let you know when it is. Or he might just make his decision and let us know."

"Great."

Nathaniel watches me carefully. "That's good news, right?"

My smile is strained. "Yeah. Awesome."

He exhales, shifting on the bench. "The other reason I wanted to see you was to talk to you about—"

"What did I fuck up now, Nathaniel?" Isn't that what this always comes down to?

"We have to clear the air at some point."

"Over?"

He blows out a sigh that's equal parts frustration and dread. I hate the sound of both.

"The past. Our parents."

"Or we just let it go."

He clears his throat. "That won't fix anything."

"Fixes it just fine for me," I lie.

"Look. Dad was . . . Dad was a dick for what he did. I've told you that from day one."

I snort. "You mean the few weekends I was allowed to come live in your fantasy world where food was cooked, clothes were washed, and you were the kid and not the caretaker trying to hold everything together?"

He meets my eyes and I hate that there are tears welling in them. "Yeah. Exactly that." He hangs his head and draws in a long breath. Despite my annoyance, I begrudgingly sit back down.

"We've tried to do this before—to fix shit—and it never worked. Why dig it up again?"

And we have. On the rare weekends I'd get to live in his life, he'd try to talk to me, but I'd just act out. And then when he'd come to watch the first gigs we played, he'd buy the guys drinks and then try and talk to me, but I'd just down the drink and say it was time to go. Since then, it's been easier to get lost in my job than to fix our relationship.

And for the longest time, I didn't know that I wanted to.

Too much history.

Too much animosity.

And yet . . . he keeps knocking.

Fuck. What am I supposed to do with that knowledge?

"I've always felt like this was my fault," he says quietly.

My jaw tightens as his words slap me. "Yep. I'm the screwed-up brother because you were the perfect one. No wonder he picked you over me. Got it." I start to stand and he yanks me back down to sit.

Can't say I'm too thrilled with that.

"No, you're not hearing me." He leans forward, elbows on his knees. "This is why I became a lawyer. Because of you."

"Sure you did. Used Daddy's money to put you through college while I was busy busking on corners to get enough money to buy Mom her meds."

Sadness fills his eyes and I hate that I want to believe it. This. That he understands an iota of the pain I went through.

I don't think anyone ever could though.

"To fight for people who didn't have a voice."

I start to reply, but he holds up a hand. "No. Quit being a sarcastic fuck and let me finish, will you?" His voice is rough, honest in a way I don't expect. It begs me to listen when otherwise I'd already be walking away. "I didn't speak up that day, Jase. I didn't fight for you like I should have. Like you did for me. I was so worried about having to stay and take care of Mom that I didn't say a damn word and left you to deal with it all yourself."

It's hard to hear those words and believe them.

"Easy to say from your end of the deal, right?"

"Yeah. You're right. It is. But Dad wasn't all sunshine and fucking roses. He was a heavy-handed disciplinarian and a cold son of a bitch. So I got the clothes and the food and the education, but until I had kids of my own, I didn't realize how much he *didn't* provide. And I sure as shit didn't understand how much you could have ever suffered."

"They're just words, Nate."

"You're right. They are. But having kids makes you see things differently. The world changes and for the life of me, I can't understand how the fuck Dad did that to you. How he left you to pick up a mess that was his responsibility."

"And yet you went to visit him weeks ago."

"I went. You're right. Just me. Because it was my turn to finally confront him. It was my turn to explain to him the lives he ruined and the people he hurt and you . . . God, how you deserved better by him."

My chest tightens and a lump forms in my throat. I blink away the tears that burn. I will not let that motherfucker make me cry.

"He left you to fend for yourself in a world much crueler than I could ever have imagined." His voice is quiet, shameful. Loaded with regret.

I don't want to hear it but I can't escape it.

"You were just a kid, Nathaniel." I try to give him the same grace he's given me over the years but fuck if that's not a hard one to swallow.

"So were you," he says quietly. "And I was your big brother. I was supposed to protect you, and I didn't." His voice cracks, and he pushes off the bench, needing to move, to shake off the weight of his words.

Much like I do when emotions become too much.

I watch him, my chest aching. "Why are you telling me this?"

"Because it eats at me every time I see you. Because I note your animosity toward me, and as much as I hate it, I think it should be a hundred times worse. You were just a kid stuck taking care of a severely mentally ill woman. That's not right."

"It is what it is." I shrug but my usual go-to response feels hollow.

Nathaniel nods, his jaw tight. "Maybe next time you go to the shelter, you'll tell me. I'd like to see her."

Bitterness rises in my throat. I've put in the work. The hours. The pain. Why does he get to step in now?

"We'll see," I murmur.

"I understand," he says quietly.

I hesitate, then murmur, "Thank you."

"For?"

"You didn't take care of me before, but you keep trying to now."

He nods subtly. "It's the least I can do."

"I don't think I've ever said thank you."

Nathaniel exhales, shaking his head with a small smile. "Yeah, well . . . don't get all sentimental on me."

I snort, shaking my head as I push to my feet. His words are ringing in my head, though.

"This is why I became a lawyer. Because of you. To fight for people who didn't have a voice."

It's not the first time I've seen Nathaniel show his heart toward me. But maybe it's the first time I didn't walk away from it and ignore him. He's tried over the years to help, to talk, to heal, and it never felt possible.

But today for some reason, I want to believe there could be the *other side* to this. The weight of our past isn't gone, but maybe—*just maybe*—it's lighter. I'd always felt so abandoned by my brother. I used to cry myself to sleep when I was younger. Not because my dad didn't choose me—my anger was too deep for that—but because I lost my brother that day. And life became exponentially lonelier from that day on.

"And I was your big brother. I was supposed to protect you, and I didn't."

How do I let go of that hurt? *Because, fuck, for the first time, I want to.*

CHAPTER

fifty-two

Hendrix

THE HOUSE IS ALIVE WITH NOISE AND LAUGHTER WHEN I WALK through the front door. Music drifts in from the backyard, and I follow the sound, stepping onto the patio to find a crowd of about twenty or so people—men and women—in the pool, at the bar, or at one of the three tables set up for poker.

Jase and his bandmates all sit at the same table, drinks in hand and cards scattered across the surface.

The whole backyard is a lesson in people watching, but it's Jase's table that holds my attention.

It's fascinating watching them interact—like a well-oiled machine built on inside jokes, competitive jabs, and an easy camaraderie that speaks of years spent together. I observe from afar as they rib each other mercilessly, and yet every word spoken is laced with affection.

I lean against the railing, quietly observing. Jase's eyes find mine across the yard, and warmth settles in my stomach. With his simple smile at me, he's invited me into their world.

This is his family. His world. And he's allowing me to step into it. The gravity of that doesn't go unnoticed by me.

"You gonna play, Hendrix?" Rocket calls out, raising an eyebrow. "Or should I say, Mrs. Rocket?"

Clearly, there's a joke there that I don't get. The four of them bark out in laughter and Jase throws something at him in disgust.

"Um. Not sure how I'm supposed to respond to that other than to—" I move toward them and hold up my ring finger and wiggle. The guys erupt in another fit of laughter and razzing. I yelp when Jase pulls me into his lap like I belong there, his arms lazily draped around my waist, and his warm breath on my skin as he nuzzles his chin on my shoulder.

"Hi, Mrs. Gizmodo," he murmurs and presses a kiss to the side of my neck. My body heats at the intimacy of it.

We're at a table with all of his best friends and yet, he quietly lets me know my place, that I belong.

"Hi." I slide my hands over his and squeeze like it's the most natural thing in the world.

"You sure you don't want to play with us?" Rocket asks.

"Nope. I'm good," I say, shifting so my back presses into Jase's chest.

"Why not?"

"For starters, I'd take you all to the cleaners. And then there's the fact that I've been warned about each of you."

Jase puts a hand over my mouth and plays along with my lie. "Shh. Those secrets were supposed to be between us."

Everyone laughs.

Vince, who's already halfway through his beer, snorts. "I, for one, am glad you're not playing. I have a feeling you're right. You'd be handing our asses to us in minutes."

Rocket grins, tossing a chip into the center of the table. "You think?"

"I know," Jase whispers into my neck, sending a shiver down my spine.

I ignore the three smirks directed at me. They're still getting a kick out of the whole fake marriage thing, like it's their personal inside joke that I somehow got roped into. And honestly? It is kind of a joke—until Jase does stuff like this.

Stuff like holding me too easily. Touching me too casually. Acting like I belong in his space.

I clear my throat, pushing that thought far, far away. I turn my attention to Vince and Hawkin as Rocket deals the cards. "I liked meeting your wives at the gala."

Hawkin nods, glancing at what he was dealt and folding on the spot. He tosses them back onto the table. "Quinlan said you were welcomed into the BENT Bitches with open arms."

"I was flattered to become an honorary member."

"Ooh, can I watch your club meetings? I bet those are sexy as fuck—" Rocket says, dodging the poker chip Vince flicks at his head.

"You ain't watching shit," Hawkin says.

I tilt my head. "Is this how it is all the time with you four?"

"Yes." Rocket's grin is mischievous.

"And yet you still have wives?" I tease.

Vince lets out a dramatic sigh. "It's the charm. It's a long, drawn-out process, but we wear them down until they have no choice but to love us."

"More like they exhaust them until they just accept their fate," Rocket adds. "That is why I am still single."

There's more razzing over the comment, but I'm too distracted by the way Jase squeezes my hip and how his lips brush my ear when he says, "Guess that means I still have time to wear you down, huh, Cookie?"

I stiffen, refusing to let the warmth in his voice get to me. "You're not even in the running, drummer boy."

"Ouch." Jase presses a hand to his heart, his laughter ringing out as he looks to the guys for sympathy.

None is given.

"I mean, she's not wrong," Hawkin says, hiding his grin behind his beer.

"Definitely not," Rocket agrees.

Vince just shakes his head. "Poor guy never stood a chance."

"Remind me why I'm friends with you assholes?" Jase asks.

"Because without us, you'd have no personality," Rocket says.

Vince laughs. "And no one to tell you when you're making a complete fool of yourself over Hendrix."

I suck in a breath, my heart doing a weird, stupid flip, but I recover quickly and try to make sure my expression says the same.

Jase's fingers tighten slightly on my waist, but he doesn't take the bait.

Instead, he flicks a chip toward Vince and stretches back in the chair, shifting just enough to make me realize I've been in his lap *way* too long.

"I need to go inside," I blurt out, pushing myself up and off him.

Jase lets me go—too easily, too casually. "Need an escape from these fuckers? That's a daily occurrence for me."

A chorus of "fuck offs" ring out.

"I'll be back in a few," I say and head toward the house.

I just reach the door when a voice stops me.

"So . . . you banging him for the fame? I mean that rock is worth it alone."

I turn to find Rocket's date, Carly, standing beside me, a smug expression on her face.

"Excuse me?"

Carly shrugs, sipping her drink. "Don't shoot the messenger. I mean, it's Jase's schtick, right? Hook up with the hired help for a bit and then move on when he gets bored?" She tilts her head, watching me closely. "No doubt that'll be sooner rather than later. I will say you've lasted longer than most but believe me, I've seen it a dozen times or so. I get you have the ring and the last name, but you'll probably be needing to bake some of those divorce cookies for yourself in the near future."

The words cut through me. *Because that's exactly what people* will *think when this ruse is up.* And I'll get to see and hear it all from social media and looky-loos, enthusiastically, like Carly, rubbing my nose in *my* failure to keep him interested.

I should laugh it off. I should tell her she doesn't know what she's talking about. But bitterness lodges itself in my throat, and I can't shake the sting of her words or the hurt they cause.

I don't want to believe her.

But the truth is, I don't know where Jase and I stand. I don't know if this means anything outside of the arrangement we started with. I mean, I clearly have feelings for him, but is this still a charade to him? Is this more?

I have a feeling I'm not asking him because I'm afraid of the answer. Because even though I've made strides in finding myself again, I can be honest when I say if history dictates itself, I know I'll be the one left hurt. *Again.*

I don't respond to Carly. I just turn and walk away.

But her words are on replay in my head all night.

Over.

And over.

When the game winds down and everyone starts heading out, I keep my distance from Jase. I clean up the kitchen instead of lingering by his side as he says goodbye to all his guests, ignoring the way he keeps glancing at me like he can sense something's wrong.

"Hendrix?" His voice is softer now as he steps up behind me.

I keep scrubbing the counter, pretending I don't feel him standing there. "You should get some sleep. It's late."

"You okay?"

I nod. Lie. "I'm fine."

Jase watches me for a long moment, and I can tell he doesn't believe me. But he doesn't push.

Not yet.

CHAPTER
fifty-three

S OMETHING'S OFF.

I feel it the moment Hendrix walks inside from the backyard, her posture stiff, her smile forced. She doesn't join in the teasing or lean against the counter like she usually does as everyone slowly leaves the house to head home. Instead, she busies herself with cleaning.

With avoiding me.

I let it slide while the guys are here, but when the last of them filters out and the house falls quiet, I find her still wiping down the already-clean kitchen island.

"I'm not buying you're fine. Fine is the kiss of death for a man. So what is wrong?"

She doesn't turn around. "Nothing."

Bullshit.

I push off the doorframe and step behind her, close enough that I see the tightness in her shoulders. "Try again."

She exhales sharply and mutters, "Rocket's date doesn't have a brain in her head."

"Which is probably why he's with her. What does she have to do with you being upset?"

Hendrix slaps the sponge onto the counter and finally turns, arms folded. "She said you have a habit of hooking up with the help and moving on when you get bored."

I stare at her. Then laugh. "That's what has you in a mood?"

She scowls. "It's not funny."

"Which part? The you being *the help* part? Because that's pretty fucking hilarious if you ask me." But by the set of Hendrix's jaw, clearly it isn't funny to her. *Fucking Carly.* I run a hand through my hair and sigh. "Hendrix, Carly has been around for, what? A month? How the hell would she know what I do or don't do?"

Her lips press into a thin line, and I can see the moment she admits to herself how stupid it is to let a woman, *a nobody*, like Carly, get to her. Her shoulders fall. Her cheeks flush. I take a step closer, reaching for her hands, forcing her to look at me. "What's the problem, Hendrix?"

"This is just . . . it's all fucked up, right? You. Me. I mean, this was an agreement, an arrangement . . . no strings attached and then I . . . I don't know how you feel about any of this and the not knowing is making me feel out of control. Like I'm losing my mind. I don't know—"

"Hendrix. Stop." She babbles when she's nervous. I know that. She knows that. "Talk to me. Tell me what's going on?"

She scrunches her nose up and takes a deep breath. "Sorry."

"Don't be." I reach out and brush my thumb over her bottom lip. "Clearly this is about whatever we are?" She digs her teeth into her bottom lip and nods. "If you want to know how I feel, just ask me."

Her throat bobs as she swallows. "How do you feel?"

I laid down the gauntlet and now I'm terrified to pick it back up. Fuck. "I—" *I don't want this to be over. I don't want to go back to life without your chaos mixed with mine.* Instead of answering, I lift the hem of her dress and peel it over her head. "I think you're incredibly creative."

Her breath catches as I trail my fingers down her arms, then thighs until I'm at her feet, unbuckling her sandals, one then the other. "I think you're phenomenally sexy."

Her pulse on the inside of her ankles flutters against my fingertips as I slide my hands back up her legs. "I think you're stubborn as hell."

She exhales shakily as my fingertips play over the apex of her thighs through her panties. "Jase . . ."

"I think," I murmur, lifting her up so she can wrap her legs around my hips and we're eye to eye, "that you know how I feel, but that you also know saying it isn't going to help anything when it comes to us."

You're a chickenshit, Gizmodo.

A fucking chickenshit.

Her eyes meet mine when I carry her, and I hope to fucking God she sees what I feel but can't bring myself to say.

I've loved three people in my life besides my bandmates. My dad picked another life over me. My brother didn't fight for me. And my mom left me.

People I love leave.

I hate how much I now fear that Hendrix will leave me too. I'm fairly certain that will crush me.

"I think this, *you*, has been the single greatest surprise in my life," she says and presses a kiss to my lips. "And I think you taste like beer."

"True."

"And I'm pretty sure I think whatever this is scares the shit out of both of us and that's okay too."

She doesn't protest as I carry her outside, the night air cool against our skin. The pool glistens beneath the landscape lights, but only I can see it since it's at her back.

"And I think"—I walk us right to the edge of the pool— "I think we're doing way too much talking and not enough living."

Her eyes flash with realization. "You wouldn't—"

I smirk. "Too late, baby. Time to Live-A-Little," I shout as I jump in, bringing her with me.

Her shriek is drowned out by us going under water, but her arms never fall from around my neck and her legs find my hips again as we come up for air.

She beats against my chest with one hand while shaking her hair out of her face. "You bastard."

"Yes, but you still love me," I joke before I catch myself. My half laugh falls off as she runs a hand down my cheek and then presses a gentle kiss to my shoulder before looking up to meet my eyes.

There's quiet all around us.

Even in my head.

She exhales, resting her forehead against mine. "Yeah," she whispers. "I do."

CHAPTER
fifty-four

Hendrix

THE SCENT OF BROWN SUGAR FILLS MY NOSE AS I MIX MORE DOUGH. My movements are automatic because my mind is somewhere else. Specifically, skinny-dipping under the stars.

Making love under the stars.

And telling Jase that I love him.

Yeah, *that*.

It wasn't planned. More like it just kind of happened. And when it did, I sucked in a breath and feared the worst—that Jase would do exactly what he said he would—push me away.

But I saw the same affection in his eyes.

I saw it reflected back at me.

He might not be able to say the words, but when his lips brushed against mine, when I sank down on him as our gazes held, I could see it in his eyes and feel it in his touch.

And that has to be enough for me. *For now.*

I squeeze my eyes shut for a moment, then force myself back to a reality I never expected to be mine—not after Paul and surely not after some signed contract punctuated with an NDA.

Love was never part of this deal.

It's not what we signed up for.

But it doesn't change the fact that I feel it.

"Thank you," the last customer still sitting in the café area calls out as they leave.

The chime on the door is the punctuation noting that I'm finally alone. Finally able to lock the door and be out of the public's sight. I lock the door and when I turn around, I freeze.

Vince is sitting on a stool in the kitchen area, his arms crossed over his chest, watching me with an unreadable expression. My two helpers come out of the back office with their purses, whispering excitedly as they sneak glances at him.

Jase may be a part of BENT just as much as Vince is, but no doubt, Vince is more well known.

And my helpers' reactions reinforce that theory.

I wave bye to them as they exit out the back door that clearly Vince came in through and then turn my attention to the man in my kitchen. To one of Jase's closest friends.

His scrutiny unnerves me.

"Vince." I wipe my hands on my apron, keeping my voice even. "Surprised to see you here."

"Figured it was about time I checked everything out."

I guard my expression as I study him. "Are we referring to my cookies or to me?"

He holds my gaze, his eyes narrowed, but he doesn't answer my question. "Seems like business is booming. Must be the BENT magic touch."

I cross my arms. "Or the good cookies."

His lips twitch. "Hmm."

I sigh. Clearly I'm being vetted. "This will be a whole lot easier if you say whatever you came here to say."

He leans forward, resting his elbows on the table. "I'm just curious what you're going to do when this is over."

My stomach tightens. "Excuse me?" *Why am I on the backfoot for the second time in twenty-four hours?*

"The contract." He glances over his shoulder to make sure we're alone before continuing. "The marriage charade. I mean the guys and I are absolutely grateful for you stepping in and helping Giz out, but what's next? Isn't it going to be hard to go back to your normal life now that you've been living in luxury?"

Fuck you. The words are on my tongue, sharp and biting, but I swallow them back. Instead, I force a strained smile. "I wasn't aware my life was any part of your business . . . or Jase's for that matter."

He shrugs. "Actually, it is. That's how we operate. As a team. All for one and all that shit."

"Really? If that's the case, then where were you to stop Jase from getting that reputation that's gotten him in trouble? If you're a team, isn't some of this shit on you and *the guys?*" I ask, mimicking the way he said it to me.

"Gizmo's a grown man capable of making his own choices."

"Exactly." I level him with a glare.

"So what's the plan? Get pregnant and trap him with a baby?" He makes a noncommittal sound. "No, I'm thinking you're more the write a tell-all book to screw us all over type, right?"

"Fuck you, Vince." I don't mince words. *Can't.*

Vince grins like I've just confirmed something for him. "Well, that's a good start, but sweetie, I'm married."

I roll my eyes. "It was figurative."

"No shit." He tilts his head, pauses for a beat. "No one ever wants something from Gizmo without getting something in return. He's too nice of a guy. So I'm asking you to name your price. Give me a figure and if it's within reason, I'll pay it. Then when this is all over, you can go on your merry way and leave him be."

I blink, his words like a punch to the gut. And here I thought Vince was a good guy. His wife was so kind. I actually liked them but now it feels like their acceptance of me was all an act. "I can't believe you just said that."

"Why?" He raises his eyebrows. "It's the truth, isn't it? It's why you agreed to all of this."

"I think you should leave." I point to the door as betrayal weighs me down. This man is so very important to Jase, and if he thinks this of me? If I can't win *his* approval? Then any hopeful chance that I might have with

Jase is gone. "Take you and your checkbook and your insulting allegations and shove them up your ass on the way out."

Vince watches me for a moment, then emits a long, low whistle. "Wow. That's what I thought."

"What is?" I'm tired. I've worked a long day. All I want to do is go back home to Jase. "I'm not in the mood for games."

"You've fallen for him, haven't you?"

I snort. "You think I'm going to tell you shit, after you just accused me of wanting a payoff? Dream on."

A smile ghosts his lips, his eyes softening some. "I can see it clear as day. You're in love with him."

"You say that like it's a curse."

"With Gizmo it kind of is."

Like I need a reminder.

"The question you need to ask yourself, Hendrix, is, if you love him, if you're falling in love with him, what are you going to do about it? Fight for him? Let him go when he pushes too hard? Because he will do just that. Chalk it up to an adventure, to—what does he call it? *Operation Live-A-Little?*"

I open my mouth, but no words come out.

Vince leans back, his expression intense. Serious. "He lives a life where he's never home. People think they know him, that they love him, and are vicious about sharing that love with anyone else. Add to that, we're about to embark on a world tour. How are you going to have your dream here at the bakery while letting him live out his? How is that going to work for you? Have you considered just how hard it is to love a man you don't always see?"

I swallow hard. I haven't let myself think that far ahead. Or maybe I'm scared to.

"I like you, Hendrix. More than I expected and even more with each minute I get to know you better. He's one of my best friends, a brother I never had. If you love him, you'll be glad he has a friend asking these questions and wanting what's best for him. He may be a leap without looking type of guy, but that's because we've already looked out below for him." He stands abruptly, rapping his knuckles against the counter. "Glad we had this little talk."

I watch him leave, but my mind is stuck on his words, his questions.

And I'm not naive in thinking every single one of them is valid.

"How are you going to have your dream here at the bakery while letting him live out his? How is that going to work for you? Have you considered just how hard it is to love a man you don't always see?"

The worst thing? I have no idea how to answer any of them. We live in this bubble at the moment, but when that bursts, *where will I be?*

CHAPTER
fifty-five

Gizmo

R EHEARSAL IS TIGHT, FOCUSED.

It has to be.

We're in the final stretch with the tour looming closer with each passing day. The setlist is locked in. The transitions between songs are agreed upon but still need to be rehearsed more. We aim for seamless when we perform, and we're not close enough to call us that yet.

Could be that I'm a contributing factor to that. My head simply isn't in it.

It should be. Nathaniel let me know the judge has already indicated that he doesn't need a hearing for his ruling. That he'll be making it in the next few days or so.

"No hearing is a good sign," Nathaniel says. "It implies that he's going to give you back your passport and allow for travel."

"Implies. Not a done deal though."

"True. But we're close, Jase. So close I can taste it. Just hang tight for another week or two."

"And then?"

"And then we wait until you're overseas, file for a separation due to irreconcilable differences. More of a she didn't know how hard it was going to be with you on the road type argument."

My gut churns hearing those words. At even thinking of being separated from her. "No. Put it on me. Whatever the reason we break up, put the blame on me. She's going to get enough shit—"

"It has to be on her. You're supposed to be squeaky clean, right? Can't be to blame if you're not."

"Fuck." I sigh into the phone. "That wasn't part of this deal."

"We'll figure it out, Jase."

I pause and then say the words I've been thinking. Words that mean so much more than what anyone else would take them for. "Thank you. I trust you."

It's good news so why do I feel like I'm just going through the motions—singing the notes, keeping the beat going, nodding along when Hawkin calls out adjustments?

My mind is elsewhere, that's why.

On her.

On Hendrix.

On the way she looked at me before I left, like she was desperate to say what's on her mind, but just smiled instead.

I know Vince had something to do with it. He showed up at the bakery, and since then, she's been different. Distant. And I don't like it.

"All right, let's run through Fade Out one more time," Rocket says, tapping on the keyboard keys.

"How about we don't and call it a night instead?" I ask.

"You good, man?" Vince calls from across the room, eyeing me.

"Yeah," I lie. "Fine. Just . . . tired." I drop my drumsticks in my kit bag on the small table beside me, effectively ending the session myself.

"Are we wrapping?" Rocket asks and claps his hands together, his grin widening. "We're wrapping. You know what that means."

Vince grins. "Drinks at Sullivan's to celebrate?"

There's a chorus of agreement, but I wave them off, stretching out my shoulders. "I'm gonna sit this one out."

Vince gives me a look. "Come on, man. It's tradition."

"Yeah, well, I'm breaking tradition."

Rocket smirks. "You getting old on us?"

"Nah, he's just going home to get laid," Hawkin says, causing everyone to burst out laughing.

"Something like that," I say and shrug.

No one presses further, but I catch Vince watching me as I grab my keys and head for the door.

I walk out to the parking lot and don't look back.

I don't need his shit tonight. Don't need his big-brother schtick.

What I really need is her.

Hendrix.

The woman I'm beginning to think I don't want to live without.

CHAPTER
fifty-six

Hendrix

"N**ATHANIEL?**"

He's standing in the entryway to Jase's house looking back at me with a guarded smile. "Hi," he says and steps inside without waiting for an invitation. "I figure it's time we had a chat."

I groan and rub my temples. First Vince a couple days ago and now him? "Oh my God, what is it with you guys?"

Nathaniel raises a brow. "What does that mean?"

"You, Vince, whoever else wants to come and interrogate me next."

"Interrogate you next?"

"Yes. I signed the contract. I did what I was told. I'm well aware of my place and that it's almost time to walk away as previously discussed. I'll keep my promises and everything that came with them. Happy? Good? What else?" Exasperation laces every word just like it's seeped into every bone of my body.

Talking about this makes my throat hurt and my eyes burn with tears. It makes me think thoughts I don't want to fathom about walking out of here and losing a last name I've come to love having.

He studies me for a long moment before tilting his head. "You're sleeping with him, aren't you?"

"No shit." My cheeks heat and my body flushes but it's not worth lying over what I'm sure he can see as plain as day.

"I thought that was part of the deal when you signed the contract."

"No, it was your part of the deal."

"And you went and—"

"My sex life is my prerogative."

"Yes, your prerogative until you demand more money or blackmail or whatever because you went and fell in love with him and then he scorns you before he leaves for the tour."

I stare at him. Blink. "I'm not in love with him," I lie, my voice clipped, trying to save face with Nathaniel for Jase's sake. "Jase is a good guy, but not one I could ever really love. He's too . . . all over the place. Has too many buttons he'll push to satisfy his own needs. I don't think I'd ever be able to trust him. Not while on the road. Not with all the women tempting him. Yeah, definitely not in love with him but more just enjoying the distraction."

The words taste bitter on my tongue, but I keep my expression blank, my walls firmly in place. The last thing Jase needs is to let his brother down after he's trying to rebuild this relationship with him.

Nathaniel exhales, rubbing the back of his neck. "If you say so."

"I do. My life is waiting for me and I can't wait to go back to it."

CHAPTER
fifty-seven

Gizmo

DON'T MEAN TO HEAR IT.

But I walked in the back door to hear my brother and Hendrix talking. Every fucking word.

I'm not in love with him. Jase is a good guy, but not one I could ever really love. He's too . . . all over the place. I don't think I'd ever be able to trust him. Not while on the road. Not with all the women tempting him. Yeah, definitely not in love with him but more just enjoying the distraction.

It shouldn't feel like a knife in the back, but it does. The sharp sting of it burrows under my skin, settles deep in my chest.

I'm not in love with him.

Jase is a good distraction.

A distraction.

I step back, out of earshot, before she or Nathaniel realizes I'm here. My hands curl into fists but I force myself to move. To shake it off.

This was always the deal, right? An arrangement?

But fuck if it doesn't feel different now. *She said she loves me. Was that a lie? A heat of the moment fib?*

I move into the studio, lock the door behind me, and do the only thing I've ever been able to do to cope. I fixate on music.

I write until the lyrics pour out of me.

I write to ignore her texts asking if I'm coming out for dinner.

I write to try and figure out where the fuck to go from here.

But I know the answer. I always have.

Where do I go from here? Nowhere. That's where I go.

On a world tour away from this place. Away from her.

Because once again, I'll be here while she moves on. While another person I love can't love me back.

Yeah, I went and fell for her.

That's on me.

And I hate everything about it.

My phone buzzes. Again. I pick it up, knowing it's going to be her, but am surprised to see Rocket's name on the screen.

"You alive? Or did Hendrix finally kill you in some sex-slave coma or some shit like that?"

"Alive," I mutter, rubbing a hand over my face.

"Good. Then play us the song you've been working on."

"Not happening."

"Oh, so you are a sex-slave then."

I sigh. "Nah. Think I'm over that already."

Rocket whistles. "Wow. Okay."

"You know me. I get bored easily. Same shit, different pussy."

Rocket laughs but it grates, because I know the words I said are a blatant lie. "And here I thought you were beginning to like that ring on her finger."

"No need to get attached," I add and take a sip straight from the bottle of Jack beside me. I hiss at the burn. "They all leave in the end."

CHAPTER
fifty-eight

Hendrix

MUSIC HAS A WAY OF FILLING A SPACE, SEEPING INTO THE WALLS, vibrating through the air until it settles under your skin. It has a way of making you escape the noise in your head and the worry in your heart.

I need all of that and more—and get it—the moment I step into the darkened arena where BENT is rehearsing for the tour.

The steady thrum of the bass, the haunting notes from the keyboard, the powerful yet smooth voice of Hawkin carrying through the mic—it's intoxicating, electric. But none of it pulls me in the way the steady, relentless rhythm of the drums does.

None of it holds me the way he does.

Jase.

There's been distance between us over the past few days. A chasm that feels like it's widening and going to eat me whole as I fall harder for him and he pushes me further away.

But here, he's in his element. Here, we're right back to where we were that first day we met—him, the superstar, and me just a normal cookie baker.

I wish I could say there was more here—to us—but I think that was built on hope and lust and not emotion and love.

But I look at him and my chest aches for more. For him. For the laughter and the love we had what felt like just days ago.

He's seated behind his kit, head bowed, sticks twirling effortlessly in his fingers before he locks in, hitting the beat with a precision that seems effortless. His whole body moves with the music, his arms flexing, his expression distant but so alive.

This is where he thrives.

This is where he belongs.

And I feel the disconnect like a wall between us.

The band is running through their setlist for the world tour, working through transitions, testing out new endings. I hang back near the door, watching from the shadows as they fall into sync with each other, feeding off the energy they create.

Jase doesn't look at me.

He doesn't acknowledge me at all.

I don't know if it's intentional, but it's been building for days.

And now, watching him here, I realize just how much he's already started pulling away.

Rocket hits the keys, shifting into a slower melody, and Hawkin picks up his guitar. The lights dim slightly, the room shifting from pure adrenaline to something heavier. The air changes, thickens.

A ballad.

I recognize it instantly.

It's new. Unreleased. A song that leaked a few weeks ago, one that the fans dissected like vultures, searching for its meaning.

It's raw.

It's about betrayal. About wanting someone so badly it destroys you.

And when Jase finally lifts his head and meets my eyes, my breath catches.

Because I know.

I know, in that split second, that this song, and the way he's decided to acknowledge me now, is his way of telling me what he can't say out loud.

There is nothing more to us than a contract and some convenient sex.

He's choosing this—them, the tour, the life—and he's leaving me behind.

That's what was supposed to happen all along though. I shouldn't be shocked by it. I shouldn't have hoped differently. But his touch told me otherwise. His love language of taking care of me showed the contrary.

And now I'm standing here in an arena feeling so very small, so very unwelcome when all I want to do is understand the why behind it.

But that's for another place. Another time. The texts telling me where he's going and when he'll be home have stopped. The dinners in the kitchen where we'd laugh until we cried or moaned in bliss have ended. It's just . . . over.

The beat slows, his sticks striking softer now, more deliberate. His eyes don't leave mine, even as Hawkin's voice fills the room with soul-stirring lyrics that rip a person open, that tell a story of heartbreak before it's even fully happened.

I swallow past the lump in my throat, past the pain that rises so quickly I don't know how to contain it.

I wanted to believe we were something more.

But watching him now, feeling the weight of that look, I realize—

I may have already lost him.

CHAPTER
fifty-nine

Hendrix

NOTHING HAS BEEN THE SAME SINCE I TOLD HIM I LOVED HIM.

Since Vince and then Nathaniel came to see me.

Since the rehearsal when his eyes owned mine and his heart took a leap back.

It's like we're both tiptoeing around each other, but my heart is on the line while he never gave his to begin with.

At least this is almost over. This charade.

And yet, here I am following Jase as he sneaks out of his own house, clearly avoiding me as he goes.

I can handle the heat the impending divorce will hit me with. What I won't put up with is not having answers. I won't tolerate him avoiding me completely rather than explaining why I saw love in his eyes—felt it in his touch—and then it turned off like the flip of a switch.

It's confounding. Confusing.

And maybe that's why I follow him.

I'll force him to talk to me one way or another because I deserve more than this cold shoulder. I deserve better from him.

I tell myself it's not about jealousy, not about insecurity, but the nagging voice in the back of my mind won't shut up. The way he's taken secretive calls, stopped bothering to communicate with me—in any form—and then just slipped out of the house without a word—it's too familiar. Too cliché.

And pride won't let me walk away without looking him in the face and getting answers.

I keep my distance, trailing behind his car, all while feeling like an idiot as we weave through the city streets.

When he pulls into a public parking lot, I am fortunate enough to find parking on the street a little way back. But I don't have any time to collect myself and question what the fuck I'm actually doing, because he's out of his car and jogging down the sidewalk within seconds.

I hurry behind him and then falter when I see the sign above the door he just walked into.

The shelter.

I stop short, my breath catching in my throat. A different kind of guilt curls in my stomach and twists tight. He's not cheating on me. He's not secreting away for a rendezvous that will be blasted all over *Page Six* and humiliate me. He's not avoiding me because he doesn't want to talk to me. Today, anyway.

He's going to help the less fortunate.

I linger outside for a moment and debate whether I should leave. But a stubborn, desperate need to understand pushes me forward.

Inside, the scent of warm food and disinfectant fills the air. From a distance, I spot Jase as he moves through the space with an ease that says he's comfortable here. At home in a way I've never seen him before. He greets people by name and with a warm smile as he hands out trays. He jokes with a few of the people like they're old friends.

He's . . . this is who he is when no one's watching.

It's a staggering thought and one that wins my heart no favors as it falls a bit harder for him with the revelation.

Without thinking, I move across the space and step up beside him, grabbing a stack of trays like he did to help distribute.

He stiffens when he sees me, his jaw clenched tight. "What are you doing here?"

"Helping."

"Hendrix—"

"You don't get to tell me no."

His eyes flicker with something unreadable, but he doesn't argue. Probably solely because he doesn't want to cause a scene. Instead, he goes back to passing out trays, to making people smile, all while acting like I'm not here.

I pretend not to notice but it stings something fierce.

He talks to the people like they're normal, like they matter. And they do. But what's even more fascinating to me is they all know him. They joke with him, tease him, thank him like this is just a regular occurrence.

Because it is.

And yet, he keeps it hidden.

I want to ask why. Why he won't tell the world about this. Why he keeps his acts of kindness and generosity locked away. But I already know the answer. Jase doesn't do things for show. He doesn't want recognition. This is just . . . who he is.

I'm about to tell him all of this when she appears before me.

The woman is older with wild hair and a familiar tilt to her chin. Her eyes are weary and her cheeks deepen with dimples when she smiles at someone I can't see. She approaches hesitantly, her eyes darting between us, and that's when I hear Jase's quiet "fuck."

"Jase?" I say, both of them turning to look at me, the same expression on both of their faces.

Oh my God. *Is she?* No, she can't be . . . *family,* can she? How could someone in his family be living on the streets and needing food from a shelter?

"Look, I had some unexpected news about a family member that threw me. It wasn't the first time I got news like that, and I'm certain it won't be the last."

Is that what he meant? God, that feels like forever ago now.

My heart shatters for him, because I have an awful feeling this isn't just any family member. How had he described his upbringing? Nathaniel lived with his dad, and Jase lived with his mom.

". . . my mom and me, we did our best."

Oh shit.

Now I understand. The why. The secrecy. The heartache. *The every-thing.* How long has he kept this secret and borne the heaviness of this . . . alone?

Jase's entire body goes rigid. He doesn't say a word. Doesn't move.

The woman—his mother—looks between us, her gaze lingering on Jase with something like recognition, something like longing, but it fades as quickly as it comes. She mumbles something incoherent about people listening to her before turning away and disappearing into the crowd.

CHAPTER
sixty

Gizmo

PANIC CLAWS AT MY THROAT, CHOKING ME AS I PUSH THROUGH THE streets.

She saw.

She knows.

I move faster, weaving between people, desperate to get away before she catches up. Before she asks the questions I can't answer. That I don't want to answer. That says so much more about me than I've ever shared with anyone before.

Before she looks at me with pity . . . or worse, *disgust.*

All I hear is the taunts from childhood, the whispered words from people who thought I couldn't hear them.

Crazy runs in the family.

He'll end up just like her.

That poor kid, doomed before he even had a chance.

That woman must be a drug addict to be that crazy.

I don't stop until I'm blocks away, until the air burns in my lungs, until I can't hear my mother's voice muttering gibberish in the back of my head.

Then I do what I always do.

I throw myself into excess. Into forgetting.

I find the loudest bar and order the strongest drinks. It's the quickest way to silence the war inside me. I knock the shots back one by one, letting the burn settle in my chest and hoping the numbness spreads quickly tonight.

I don't want to feel shit.

I don't want to think about the way Hendrix looked at me, the way she saw something she wasn't supposed to.

"I don't think I'd ever be able to trust him. Not while on the road. Not with all the women tempting him. My life is waiting for me and I can't wait to go back to it." She doesn't love me. She doesn't want me. Same old, same old.

I don't want to think about the way she stood beside me, like she belonged there.

Because she doesn't.

She can't.

She doesn't want this shit.

CHAPTER
sixty-one

Hendrix

WANDERED THE TOWN FOR A BIT. THE CITY OF ANGELS. I FIGURED I'D give Jase time to collect himself, to come to grips with the fact that I know his secret, and then maybe once he did, we could talk about it.

There's nothing to be ashamed of. Hell, he should be prouder of who he is because of it.

But I still figured I'd give him time.

So I sat at the beach and imagined what it was like for him growing up. I searched the internet for mentions of his childhood to see what I could learn—not much—and then felt guilty for doing so rather than waiting for him to tell me himself.

But I was trying to prepare myself for what I'd learn. I was trying to steel myself against making an expression on my face he'd deem as pity or disgust.

All I want is to tell him how much I admire him. That I love him and seeing his truth doesn't negate that. And even though he's pushed me away—doesn't seem to want me anymore—I still think he's an incredible man. Loving him isn't easy, and I may not get the chance soon when he goes on tour, but I want to keep trying. *I want to keep us.*

However, after some time of thinking, I come home to something I thought I'd never see.

I don't know what I expected, but it sure as shit wasn't this.

The pool is packed with half-naked women, their laughter ringing through the air, mixing with the heavy bass from the outdoor speakers. The hot tub is just as bad—bikini-clad bodies pressing in around Jase, hands on his shoulders, in his hair, draped over his lap like they belong there.

And he's drunk.

Completely, devastatingly wasted.

I stand in the shadows for a moment, my heart sinking lower and lower. I learned something real about him earlier—something raw and painful and honest. A glimpse of the man no one else gets to see. A glimpse of his loss.

And to add salt to the wound for ignoring me for days, this is what he does?

This is how he deals with it?

This is what he did on the day of the gala too? Fuck, I read him so wrong that night.

I should leave. Should turn around, walk inside, lock the door, and pretend none of this matters. But I can't move. Can't look away from him, sprawled in the middle of all of them, laughing, drinking, accepting the kisses they're pressing to his neck, his chest . . . as though I'm only a long-forgotten memory. Pretending like nothing happened.

Like I don't exist.

One of the girls tilts her head back in a flirtatious laugh, tracing a finger down his arm. My stomach twists. I hate this feeling. This anger eating at me. This stupid, irrational ache.

How do you fight for someone who doesn't want to fight for himself?

How do you love someone who doesn't want you to?

Jase finally catches sight of me. He grins lazily, lifting his drink in some kind of mock toast. "Hey, wifey," he drawls. "You wanna join in? Or call some of your friends over?"

And that's when I shatter.

I don't reply. Don't give him the satisfaction of a reaction. I just turn and walk away, my hands shaking as I push through the house, ignoring the burn in my chest.

I should have known better.

I knew he would push, but not like this. Cruel. Unforgiving. Devastating.

"You win, Gizmodo."

Because I *do* deserve better.

CHAPTER
sixty-two

Hendrix

DON'T STOP WALKING.

Not when I reach the front door. Not when I climb into my car and put as much distance between the two of us as possible.

I should have never let myself believe in the possibility of us. That he could love me back.

My chest aches, my hands tightening on the wheel as I pull up to the only place that's ever made sense—my bakery. The parking lot is dark, and the closed sign hangs in the window.

My home.

The thought makes everything that happened hurt that much more.

As I get out of the car, I pick up my phone to start a voice text to Jase—my need to tell him what I think of him real and raw—but when I look up, I freeze.

Someone's inside.

Paul.

What the hell?

It only takes me a few seconds to spot his car parked on the opposite side of the street. And only a few seconds more for my fury to form rage, because there's only one reason he might be here and that's to wreak havoc and cause trouble.

My pulse kicks up, a slow, steady dread as I shove open the door. "What the hell are you doing here?"

He smirks, leaning lazily against the counter like he owns the place. "Oopsie. I must have forgotten to turn in this one extra key I had back to you."

"Convenient." I set my phone down.

"Perhaps. Or maybe I just knew it might come in handy." His voice lowers a notch. "I came to collect what's owed to me."

"Nothing is owed to you."

"Yeah, right." His gaze sharpens. "This whole fucking place is because of me. What I don't get is what is he to you? This Jase prick? Your rebellion against me?"

My breath hitches. My body flushes hot, then cold. "No," I whisper, my voice breaking under the weight of my own admission. "He's my everything."

Saying it out loud nearly destroys me. My heart hurts, eviscerated from watching Jase spiral and knowing there's nothing I can do. Knowing that if he can't let me even know about that part of his life without reacting like this, then there never will be anything more between us.

Paul watches me, something close to amusement in his expression. "What? Trouble in paradise?" He laughs. "Like I fucking care."

"You shouldn't be here. You don't belong here. You need to go. Now isn't the time."

"I seem to think that now is the perfect time," he corrects, crossing his arms over his chest. "I want my payout."

"Dream the fuck on."

His smirk widens. "Remember when I had you sign that lease paperwork with me? That we wanted it to be in your name?"

A cold chill slides down my spine. "What did you do?"

"I own fifty percent of this company." His grin is menacing. "You agreed to it. I have your signature."

"That's bullshit."

Paul lifts a brow. "Think what you will. You were the one who didn't read the paperwork. You signed it. That's on you."

I struggle to think rationally while scolding myself for trusting blindly. Funny how life repeats itself. Flustered and overwhelmed, it's like I finally hear what Paul is saying. "Wait. Legal paperwork, signed without a witness? You can't prove it was me. There wasn't a notary here. For all I know, you signed it for me."

He chuckles. "Look at you. Marry a rock star and you grow some brains. When did that happen, huh?"

"The minute I fucking left you," I snap.

His eyes glint with something dangerous. "I'm not going away, Hendrix. I put a majority of my savings into this place and I deserve repayment."

"You took all of my money, Paul. That was my money too in that bank account you drained. Was that not enough for your selfish ass?" I laugh in disbelief.

"You wouldn't have this bakery, these machines, a roof over your head, or any of that money in our account if it wasn't because of me to begin with."

"Save the gaslighting for someone else. Clearly I found a way to make it work."

His chuckle is pure condescension. "Without strong credit, without any banks willing to loan you the funds . . . I call bullshit."

I roll my shoulders and try to process this. Yes, Paul's capital made this happen. Yes, he walked away and didn't ask for the business instead of just money as he probably has every right to. My own personal bank account—my now rainy day savings stowed away in there from my agreement with Jase— is sitting much more comfortable than it ever has been. Wouldn't it just be better to pay Paul back and know I own Cookie Cutter free and clear? To not worry that if say, my business explodes and I get to offer to sell franchise rights as I've always hoped to be able to, he can't come back and take a cut?

I clench my jaw. "Fine. Fair is fair. I'll pay you back the money you put in. Eighty grand." I blow out a breath as tears well in my eyes. Then I lie. "I don't know how I'll come up with the money. You know how strapped I am for cash here, but I'll find a way to give it to you, make payments. I don't know." My stomach twists at the thought.

"Yeah." He scoffs. "You clearly didn't read the agreement, did you?"

"What does that mean?"

"A smart businessman always hedges his bets."

"Speak fucking plain English, Paul."

He pulls a folded piece of paper from his jacket, lays it flat on the counter. "Read what you agreed to."

My eyes scan the words, my stomach turning violently.

"Five hundred thousand dollars?" My voice rises in disbelief as my whole body violently rejects what I'm reading. "Are you out of your fucking mind?"

"No," he says simply, "but there was an off chance this became *a thing*. It had a good premise, good bones . . . and yes, *you* and *your talent*. Someone who would work her fingers to the bone—"

"You motherfucker—"

"So I wanted to make sure I was compensated."

My stomach bottoms out. "I don't have that kind of cash. Nowhere near that. Even if I sold everything in this place, I couldn't pay you that kind of cash."

Paul leans in, his grin widening. "Ah, but your husband does, doesn't he?"

The blood drains from my face. That's what this is about, isn't it? "Leave him out of this." The words are barely a whisper.

"Why? Aren't you the perfectly happy couple?" His voice drips with mockery. "Or maybe this shotgun wedding isn't all it's lived up to be. Should you save some of those divorce cookies he's pitching for you for yourself?"

"I despise you with everything I have."

"Thanks. I love that for you." His sarcasm is like nails on a chalkboard.

"The other option for me is that I sell my story to the tabloids. Tell them how he pursued you and stole you out from under me. How he assaulted me, broke my car window in a jealous rage when you were going to get back with me. With his history, people would believe it."

And so would the judge.

"You're full of shit."

"I know." He holds a finger up. "How about the version where you're just a slut who has slept around from rock star to rock star until you finally found one who'd take you. Desperate for the attention your own daddy never gave you. But the drugs are good and the lifestyle is fast so . . ."

My throat burns. "No one will believe you."

But I know the truth. The public believes anything if the story is spun the right way. And I can't bring the limelight onto Jase. Not now. Not when this is almost done.

Not when my heart already hurts enough.

"Quite the conundrum, huh?"

I take a breath, forcing the words past my clenched teeth. I could sell the wedding ring and the diamond necklace after the divorce. I could . . . I don't fucking know because the thought of parting with Jase's ring is like a knife to the chest. But I can't let this all be for naught. I can't let the asshole in my life ruin things for Jase. "I need time. I . . . I'll figure out how to get you paid."

Paul smirks. "Good girl."

I've never hated a phrase more.

"I'll make this work, on one condition."

"What's that?" he asks smugly.

Shivers chase over my skin as I step closer and load every ounce of vitriol I have in my voice. "My husband is to be left the fuck alone."

CHAPTER
sixty-three

Gizmo

MY CHEST HURTS.

Sure, it's hurt before—from a punch to the ribs or the burn of too much whiskey on an empty stomach—but this is different. Deeper. Searing.

And the panic . . . I can't remember feeling such acute panic since I was a kid. That terrifying fear that overtook me when I'd wake up all alone with no idea where my mom was or when she'd be coming back.

Sometimes it was hours. Other times it was days. A few times it was weeks.

I feel that way now. Devastated but deserving of the pain.

But it's not my mom who's gone.

It's Hendrix.

Maybe because you were a dick, Jase. You pushed until you couldn't push anymore and you got what you asked for. What you tried to do.

She left.

I drag a hand down my face, inhaling sharply as I stare at the mess of bottles scattered around me. The house feels like a graveyard—empty and full of ghosts I don't want to meet again.

I hate it.

Hate the silence, the loneliness, but more than anything, I hate the realization that I did this to myself.

She left.

Can't say I fucking blame her. The shelter. *Her following me.* My mom. *Her knowing.*

Was she in the wrong? Did she invade my privacy?

Yes and yes.

And yet . . . I can't say that I blame her. I'm not exactly an open fucking book.

But it's how I reacted that caused all this. An empty house. Her car gone. She's just . . . gone.

I got spooked. She got too close, I got too scared, and man, I went and fucking fell for her.

I love her.

I love her when I'm incapable of it. I love her when it would be so much better for her sake if I didn't.

I put a forearm over my forehead to hide the light. There were so many women here. So many who were more than willing to be a notch on my bedpost.

But it didn't matter how much I drank to drown the vulnerability, I couldn't have cheated on her with another woman. *I only wanted Hendrix.*

The look in her eyes from across the yard haunted me as I continued to drink. As I continued to let other women's hands touch me. Other women's lips kiss me. *Fuck. I am a complete and utter asshole.* And if paps got photos of last night? Totally fucked. The judge will fuck me over and I'll never get her back. She's right not to trust me. But . . .

All I want is her.

I reach for my phone, my fingers unsteady as I pull up her contact. I don't even think about it. I just press the call button, needing to hear her voice, needing to figure out how to make this right . . .

I freeze.

A voice text sits there from last night. Unread. From her.

No doubt telling me to fuck off and figure out how to finish pretending we're married on my own.

With a sigh, I press play.

Then I listen.

And then my world goes black.

Then red.

CHAPTER
sixty-four

Gizmo

N o. *He's my everything.*

Her voice breaks as she says it and my heart cracks wide open.

There was such conviction in those words that were absent in the ones she told Nathaniel.

No. He's my everything.

Those words repeat in my head as I walk into Josie's Java, and despite protests from the barista at the cash register, I head straight to the back.

I may be impatient as fuck, but I wait for Josie to notice me. The brief conversations we've had in passing over the past few months were enough for me to know this might not be the easiest of conversations.

She has always had Hendrix's back, and I doubt this time will be any different.

Josie's eyes widen when she sees me standing in her kitchen. Her eyebrows lift and her posture stiffens. "Make yourself at home, why don't you?" Sarcasm drips from her lips.

I don't have time for small talk. "The bakery has a sign up. It says 'closed for a few days.'"

"That's the great part about owning your own business, right? Setting your own hours."

"Where is she?"

Josie crosses her arms, already on the defensive. "If she wanted you to know, she would have told you."

My smile is tight, unforgiving. "Josie, I—I screwed up. Plain. Simple. Truth. I fucked up big time, and I'm worried about my wife. I need to find her and make sure she's okay."

"She's fine. She's okay. She doesn't want to see you."

I clench my jaw. "I need to see it for myself."

She stares at me, expression unreadable. "Why?"

A simple question with the most complicated answer I've ever had to give. So much so that the words clog in my throat before I finally force them out.

"Because I love her." *Four words that have never been more accurate.* "I love her, and she needs to know that."

Josie's expression softens, a quiet sound slipping from her lips.

"Please?" I ask, barely holding myself together.

She exhales. I can see her struggle with betraying her friend. "She went home. To her mom's."

"Thank you." Relief surges through me but then I realize, I have no idea where *home* is. "Josie, do you know where that might be?"

"I do." She picks up her phone and scrolls through presumably her contacts to look for it. "And when you get back from groveling for her to take you back, you're going to repay me the favor."

"Sure. Anything." *Just give me the fucking address.*

"A social media post about the café would be great."

She holds up the address for Sandra Wright, and I quickly enter the information into my contacts. I look up and meet her eyes. "You got it."

I don't waste another second. I head straight to the airport, my phone pressed to my ear the entire way.

Halle is on the other end of the first call. She's getting the pilot to the band's jet and whatever it is he has to do to get an immediate departure cleared.

I hang up with her, my head spinning as I listen to that damn voice text from last night again.

And again.

Paul's threat. His attempt at blackmail. The smug fucker.

My next call is to my brother.

Nathaniel picks up on the first ring. "Jase?"

"Why were you at my house the other day? Talking to Hendrix?"

"I came to get her thoughts on how to dissolve the marriage once the court date comes and goes."

I think of the words I heard Hendrix say. The denial of how she feels for me. And . . . then I think of the look in her eyes last night.

How could I have believed she really felt what she told Nathaniel?

She was protecting me. Making me look better in the eyes of my brother. Right?

"And what did she say?"

"I don't know. We didn't get that far. She said she'd only talk about it after the judge ruled. That she didn't want to jinx anything."

"And that was all you came to talk about?"

"What are you getting at?" Nathaniel asks.

Just making sure you're not sabotaging what I have. But the words don't come out. Years of animosity have me thinking them while a newfound attempt to fix what the two of us have broken makes me bite them back.

"Jase?"

I shake my head to clear it. Get my mind back on task. "I need a favor," I say, no nonsense. "I don't want an 'I told you so.' I don't want a damn word."

"Is it illegal?" Nathaniel asks, always the lawyer first.

"No." I sigh. "I need you to draft up a letter. A contract with a payment in the amount of two hundred thousand dollars."

Nathaniel swears under his breath. "Please tell me you're not hiding a dead body."

I bite back the snark. "I need it presented to Paul the Fucktard. Not sure of his last name but Josie at Josie's Java will know it."

"That's a lot of specifics," he jokes but then his laugh dies when I don't laugh too. "For?"

"It has to be in exchange for the release of any and all claim of ownership of Cookie Cutter as well as the sale of any information to the media—"

"What's going on, Jase?"

"Hendrix's ex is trying to blackmail her. He put money into the company but is trying to extort her by leveraging ruining my reputation. And of course, in true Hendrix fashion, she's willing to pay to protect me, to protect the world tour."

"And so you want to pay him off instead?"

"He's asking for half a mil. I'll give him less than half that along with the resignation of all his rights. He'll take it. He's a greedy fuck. And then regardless of what happens between Hendrix and me, he'll be out of her life."

"Regardless of what happens? That sounds like I should know something."

"I love her, Nathaniel." Christ, I said it again and it doesn't hit any easier a second time. "I love her and need to make this right."

"You already screwed up?"

I chuckle. "Yes. And I probably will several more times, but I'm trying. I'll get it right. She's too damned incredible to lose."

His silence is dramatic and unnerving, and I'm just about to say fuck it and hang up. "I'll take care of the ex. I'll make sure you're both covered. And . . . fuck, man, good for you. She's a great woman. I'm . . . proud of you."

I end the call with a lump stuck in my throat and emotions I've never really had before racing through me. *I love her.* I treated her like absolute shit, and she still put me first.

I. Love. Her.

As I pull into the airport, I feel steadier than I have in hours.

I'm going to fix this. I'm going to make this right.

Hendrix is mine.

And I'm going to make damn sure she knows it.

CHAPTER
sixty-five

Hendrix

"**M**OMMA, THE SUN TEA IS DONE."

"That's not possible. It should have an hour more yet," she calls from inside the kitchen. But the liquid in the container looks dark brown from where I stand so I move toward the front wall of her postage stamp-sized yard to check it.

She's always liked it to steep until it's ridiculously strong. I prefer mine on the lighter side.

"It's awfully dark already," I say, and then freeze when I look up to see Jase standing there.

I do a double take.

He's in dark jeans and a white V-neck shirt. A hat is pulled low over his face, his hands shoved deep into his pockets, and his expression is one of pure misery mixed with hope.

Jesus.

I'm sucker-punched, seeing him standing in front of me, in a place that's the complete opposite of him. The man who exists in a world of flashing lights and roaring stadiums is here, on the cracked and crabgrass-dotted sidewalk of my childhood home. He doesn't belong here. He doesn't fit here.

And yet, my heart thrums at the sight of him.

"Hey," he says, his voice rough around the edges.

"What are you doing here?"

Here. In my little space of life that he hasn't touched. Where there are no memories of him woven into every inch of fabric or foot of yard. Not a kitchen island where we made love. Not a frosting bowl we played with. Not a couch where we laughed until we cried. Not a studio in fucking sight.

"I needed to see you." Those words and the broken way he says them gut me.

But he doesn't get to show up here expecting that to erase his mistakes.

"So you tracked me down? Wouldn't a phone call have been easier?" I ask, forcing my voice to stay even and unaffected.

"Yes." He takes a hesitant step closer. "But then again, nothing is easy when it matters, right?"

"What's that supposed to mean?"

He swallows hard. "I screwed up, Hendrix."

Oh God. He slept with one of the women. I think I'm going to be sick.

"Yeah, well, so did I in taking the deal." It's partly to myself, but I'm just so fucking hurt. *Devastated.*

"I disagree."

Yeah well, it's not your heart that has been trodden on, destroyed once again. But I refuse to show him how much he's hurt me. He's already shown me by his actions that he doesn't want me, so why the fuck is he here?

I exhale sharply and cross my arms over my chest. "What did you come here to say, Jase?"

"I love you."

I go still, the words cutting through the thick, humid air, through the walls I've been so carefully rebuilding since I left.

I love you.

That most definitely is not what I expected.

And yet, I ache at hearing it. At feeling the poignancy behind those three words. At knowing I can't let myself believe them, no matter how much I want to.

"Your actions from the last few days, especially last night, do *not* scream love, Jase. No one would do that to someone they love." *I screwed up. Those were the words he started with.* "Sleeping with another woman or women." *I still can't get the visual of all those women all over him out of my head.*

"What? No, I didn't sleep with any of them." His eyes are wide and his voice is shocked. He takes a step closer, hands out. "I promise. I couldn't."

My tongue feels thick in my mouth. "Right. You make a living using words to evoke emotions, so they don't hold as much weight now."

"Hendrix, I swear I did not have sex with anyone last night." His jaw ticks. "But I'm so, so sorry. For being so callous. For shutting you out. And I hate that I did that last night, had those women there, and more so, I hate that you saw *me do that to you.*" He shakes his head, runs his hand down his face. "I—I couldn't do anything more than what you saw. They weren't you. You're my . . . my fucking everything. How can I convince you that I love you? Because I can't live without you."

I don't have an answer. Not a real one. So I throw out the only thing I can think of. "Tell me about the woman at the shelter. Your mom?"

He blows out a breath, his fingers twitching like he wants to reach for something—maybe his hat, maybe me—but instead, he just nods. "You play dirty."

"No. I'm desperate to understand you and for this to work, I need to. In order for you to deserve my love, I have to understand the one thing that made you who you are."

"Okay." He lifts his hat, runs a hand through his hair, and exhales. "My dad left with Nathaniel when I was eight. He chose the orderly, non-troubled kid to take with him and his new family and left the kid who was too loud, got in a little too much trouble, behind. I was left with a mother who was schizophrenic, who would disappear for days on end without warning. That's why I tell you where I am and when to expect me back, so you never have to wonder and wait like I did. It happened gradually, the illness stealing her mind until one day, she left and never came back."

I press my lips together, my heart breaking for the boy he was and for the man he's had to work to become.

"Jase—"

"Let me get it out. Please." His voice wavers. "I was seventeen when it happened. I didn't tell anyone. Didn't want to be put in foster care and sure as hell didn't want to live with the man who left me behind. So I lived at our apartment, deposited the checks my dad sent, and tried my luck at being on my own as long as I could. It was far from easy, but I managed. Made the bet with Rocket, and you know the rest."

I watch him as he speaks, the rawness in his voice unravels me. The hurt. The anger. My love for him.

"I tried to get help for her," he continues. "She wouldn't take the meds. Preferred to be in her own world. I tried to get her committed for her own safety, because being a woman on the streets is dangerous, but that was a disaster and she refused. I volunteer every week, hoping to see her. It's the only way I can make sure she's all right. It's my only chance at hopefully catching a glimpse of the woman I once knew. The woman who once loved me."

Tears burn my eyes, and for the first time in a long time, I'm speechless.

"There's nothing I can say," I murmur.

He emits a self-deprecating laugh. "It is what it is, right? I don't like people to know. It's not for public consumption. A sad story to make an excuse for why I am how I am or to exploit her. Her and her story . . . her plight is only for me to have and hold and suffer through. Nathaniel doesn't even know when she's here. I just . . . I want my world to stay away from hers, because she's under enough pressure. If mine collided with hers, it might break her more than she already is."

"You're a good son, Jase. A good man." *And I love you too.*

I draw in a shaky breath as he tugs at the back of his neck. "I wasn't . . . *I was* hiding it. From everyone. Only the guys know, and so when you showed up there, I felt like I'd been laid wide open for you to exploit. It's not a good feeling, and I pulled a typical Jase. I lashed out. I pushed you away. After I heard you . . ."

"Heard me what?" I whisper.

He looks at me, hurt flickering in his eyes. "After I heard you tell Nathaniel you could never love me, I . . . I guess I was looking for a way to hurt you."

I stare at him as my chest aches and my breath catches. "I told him that because you told me you'd promised him not to get involved with me. I told him that to protect you."

His expression flickers, the hurt shifting into something else entirely.

"And then I heard your voice text," he murmurs. "I heard what you said to Paul—"

"What?" My eyes widen.

"Yes. All of it. His bullshit but more importantly, how I'm your everything. And . . . I knew if I let you walk away from me, I'd lose something that makes me a better person. Someone who means the world to me. *You.*"

The weight of everything settles over us, pressing down on my chest. I stand in my momma's front yard with my heart in my throat, full of so much love for a man I don't know how to hold on to, terrified of being hurt again.

"You scare me, Jase Gizmodo."

He lets out a low, breathless laugh. "You terrify me."

"But . . ."

"But what?" he asks.

"How do we make this work?"

His lips twitch and from one heartbeat to the next, he jumps over the low retaining wall that separates us in one smooth motion. I'm in his arms instantly.

His warmth seeps into me, his heart a strong, steady beat against my cheek as I cling to him.

He leans back, eyes locking on mine. "Let's start by being honest with each other. Let's not assume but always ask for clarification. Let's give each other everything because I believe you can deal with my shit in all its glory." I chuckle. "And then, second by second. Minute by minute. Hour by hour. Day by day. We love our way through the failures, Cookie, so we can reap the rewards."

"Rewards?"

"Marital bliss." He presses his lips to mine and shrugs. "I mean, we already did the hard part, right? The stress of a wedding. The chaos of picking out colors and bridesmaids and—"

"I think marriage is a little harder than a wedding ceremony," I say through a laugh.

"Perhaps." He shrugs. "But I like to think we have this Operation Live-A-Little down to a tee. We try. We fail. We fuck. We make up. We love. We laugh."

"Wow. That's quite a list. Is it always in that order?" I tease.

"It's whatever order we want, Cookie. We make up the rules." He brushes his lips against mine and I feel like my entire world is wrapped around me. "I love you, Hendrix Gizmodo. Seems I can't help myself. Besides, I am your husband, after all."

"I forgot about that part."

He chuckles. "Never again you won't. You're stuck with me."

"No complaints here." I pause and hold his eyes. "Because I love you too."

"Hendrix?" my momma's voice calls out, then she steps onto the porch. Her eyes widen as her hand flies to her chest. "Oh, my stars, is that Jase? Your Jase? Well look at that, for once Natalia was right about something. She just called to tell me you were out here, and I told her she was dead wrong. Shit. I hate when she's right." She waves both of her hands in a *come hither* motion. "C'mon now. Don't be shy. It's about time I meet my son-in-law."

CHAPTER
sixty-six

Gizmo

THE HUM OF THE PRIVATE JET IS A LOW, STEADY VIBRATION BENEATH my fingertips as I stare out the window. The sky shifts from the soft hues of dawn to the deeper blues of morning.

We're heading home. The thought makes me smile.

Hendrix is curled up beside me, her head resting on my shoulder, her breathing deep and even. She's exhausted, and rightfully so. The past few days have been a storm—of emotions, of truths, of figuring out what the hell we mean to each other outside of the lies and contracts and carefully drawn lines that we've both managed to cross over and over again.

I glance down at her and my chest tightens.

She loves me.

I feel lighter. Like the weight I've carried for years is easing and it's safe to love someone.

I reach for the notepad in front of me, my fingers tracing over the creases on the page. I read and reread the scribbled words and half-written lines of the song that has tormented me for months. A song I could never finish, because I never knew how it ended.

Until now.

Until her.

Now, I finally know.

I adjust slightly, careful not to wake her, and pick up my pen. It's time to finish the song. I fill in the missing lyrics, hearing the melody in my head as satisfaction settles deep in my bones.

Sweet surrender, I'm falling now
No more running, no more doubt
Take my heart, don't let me go
I'm yours forever, body and soul
Your touch rewrites my history
Tearing down what's left of me
Every scar, every pain
Fades away when you say my name
I fought too long, now I finally see
Love's not a cage, it sets me free

This isn't just any song.

This is her.

This is us.

This is ours.

Hendrix stirs beside me, her lashes fluttering as she shifts against my chest. She sighs, then snuggles in closer to me. Warming me. Invigorating me. Making me feel whole for the first time in as long as I can remember.

I study her, reaching out to brush away a stray piece of hair from her face. The sleep-drugged, satisfied sound she murmurs has my heart squeezing.

God, I love her.

And for the first time in my life, I'm not afraid to say it.

Not afraid to feel it.

I glance back down at the song, at the words that once felt impossible, and I realize something.

I finally finished it.

Because I finally know what it means to belong to someone.

And I'm never letting her go.

epilogue

Gizmo

Eighteen Months Later

THE SUN ISN'T EVEN UP YET, BUT SLEEP IS IMPOSSIBLE RIGHT NOW ON today of all days.

The anticipation feels like the moment before the beat drops in a song. You know it's coming and yet when it hits, you feel it in every part of you.

The fireplace flickers in front of us, casting soft shadows over the massive living room in our house—*our house*.

The idea still blows my mind that we're here. That she's here. And that we're ten times stronger, better, more in love than I ever thought a person could be.

It's fucking insanity.

And the reason for that overload of sensations is curled up beside me on the couch, her legs draped over my lap, a steaming mug of coffee between her hands. She's barely touched it. Her eyes keep flicking to the television, to the screen where the nominations are about to be announced.

The song. *Our song.*

The one I couldn't seem to get right until she came along.

The one I could hear but struggled with creating until I knew she was mine.

Beauty often comes after struggle.

Those were her words then and they've proven to be true now.

That beauty after struggle, Sweet Surrender, has topped the charts this year, climbed its way into people's hearts, and somehow, impossibly, landed itself in Grammy contention.

And life—our life—has never been better.

The bakery is thriving. Booming even. After we got Paul out of the picture for good, Hendrix threw herself into the business and made it even more extraordinary than it already was. There's even a six-month waitlist for her custom cookies now, and just last week, *Food & Wine* featured her in an article about up-and-coming specialty shops in the Los Angeles area.

I've never seen her shine the way she does when she's in that kitchen, covered in flour, creating magic out of sugar and butter.

And I get to call her mine.

Hendrix chews on her bottom lip, and I reach out, tugging it free with my thumb. "You're nervous," I murmur, amused.

She snorts. "I'm not nervous. You're nervous."

I grin. "You've been gripping that coffee cup like it personally offended you."

She rolls her eyes and sets it down in a show of defiance. "There. Happy? I am not nervous. You're going to get nominated this morning, which is good and bad. Good because that means you're about to be one of eight songs nominated for Song of the Year. Bad because that means it's going to be a mad scramble to find a dress suitable enough to wear to the event."

"Designers will be clamoring to dress you, Cookie."

"Of course they will." She presses a kiss to my shoulder. "They'll want to dress the wife of the songwriter who is going to win."

"Let's not get ahead of ourselves. I haven't even been nominated yet."

"You're about to be though . . ."

And before I can respond, before I can tell her not to jinx the process, the screen changes graphics, and a voice fills the room.

"And the nominees for Song of the Year are . . ."

A list of names scrolls across the screen—all the writers who wrote the hits that kept the world singing this past year—and my chest goes tight, my heart hammering, the world narrowing to this singular moment—

And then I hear it.

"Jase Gizmodo—*Sweet Surrender.*"

For a second, I don't move. I don't breathe.

Then Hendrix launches herself at me, her arms wrapping around my neck, her laughter bright with mine as she presses kisses over my face.

"Oh my God, oh my God, you did it!" she squeals.

Our phones start chirping and ringing like the world has been set on fire. The texts keep coming but there are certain ones that stand out. Specific ones I care about.

> Vince: It's about fucking time. Congrats, man.
>
> Hawke: One helluva song. They finally got it right.
>
> Rocket: It was all Hendrix, wasn't it? Tell her congrats.
>
> Nathaniel: I'm proud of you brother. Mom is too, in her own way too.

The last one puts me in a chokehold like I didn't expect. I squeeze my eyes closed, pull Hendrix close, and hang on for dear life.

"You really did it," Hendrix says against the base of my throat as the texts keep coming.

"No. We did it," I correct and revel in the feel of her against me. My anchor. My beauty on the other side of my struggle. *My everything.*

And we did do it. We survived the odds. We made this work.

"I love you, you know." She leans back and brushes a kiss to my lips.

"I do. I'm one lucky son of a bitch that you do."

"You know what's better than a Grammy nomination?" she asks, mischief in her eyes.

I smirk, my hands sliding down her back as she straddles me, pressing herself flush against me. "What's that?"

She leans in, lips brushing mine, and whispers, "Celebrating."

I grin, rolling her underneath me on the couch. "Time to live a little."

"Time to live and love a lot." She laughs, bright and free, and I know—*I know*—this is just the beginning.

Because for once in my life, I finally got it right.

<h1 style="text-align:center">epilogue two</h1>

Gizmo

Five Years Later

"**D**ADDY, I WANNA GO FAST."

Small fingers tug at mine, insistent, impatient. I glance down at my daughter, Lyric, her dark curls bouncing as she skips beside me, eyes bright, energy endless.

I grin. "Oh yeah? You wanna race?"

She gasps like I've just given her the greatest idea ever, her little sneakers already squeaking against the pavement as she gears up to bolt.

Hendrix laughs beside me, adjusting the strap of her baby carrier, little Ronen sleeping peacefully inside. "No racing in the parking lot. You're going to hurt Daddy's feelings when you beat him."

Lyric pouts but keeps skipping. It's early evening, the slowly falling sun casts long shadows over the pavement. Dinner out was an impromptu thing tonight, but after the long hours we've both been putting in lately, we needed the time to reconnect. To eat without the distraction of toys or orders or a song that just can't wait to be written.

There is nothing that milkshakes and burgers and a simple walk down the street to where the car is parked can't fix. Or at least that was the thought.

I'm jogging to catch up to Lyric, to not let her get too far ahead of us, when Hendrix says, "Jase."

The warning and awe mixed together in her voice has my feet stopping. Almost as if instinct is tugging at a deep, unfathomable bond that can't be erased with time.

Hendrix's fingers brush against my wrist, grounding me as I turn.

And then I see her.

She's sitting against the worn brick wall of the gas station across the lot. She's wrapped in layers too thin for the evening chill, but I know from experience she won't take anything else. She's rocking slightly as she hums a song no one else can hear.

My mother.

The world tilts some and I struggle to breathe as I take steps toward her.

She looks smaller. Frailer. The same though if that makes sense.

Her hair, once wild and tangled, is pulled into a loose ponytail, graying at the roots. Her hands shake as she rubs them together, her nails uneven, and her lips chapped.

She doesn't see me. Maybe she does. I don't know, but I know she doesn't know me. She hasn't in years.

I stand there, my breath caught painfully in my chest, as Hendrix laces her fingers with mine.

Then, the softest voice I know breaks through the quiet.

"Hi," says Lyric.

My mother stops rocking. Slowly, she lifts her gaze, unfocused at first, lost in whatever world she's trapped inside. But then . . . something shifts.

Her vacant, cloudy eyes see.

Not me. Not Hendrix. *But her*. Her granddaughter.

A slow smile spreads across her cracked lips as I struggle with the fear of whether she'll hurt Lyric or lash out and scare her.

But then she speaks and the breath I'm holding loosens.

"Well, hello there," she says, her voice raspy but gentle. "Aren't you just the prettiest thing."

Lyric giggles and my heart cracks.

My mother's expression softens in a way I haven't seen in decades, in a way I thought was lost forever. She doesn't recognize me, doesn't even blink in my direction.

But she sees my little girl.

And in this moment, that's enough.

"Do you like flowers?" my mother asks, her hands trembling as she reaches into her coat pocket, pulling out something delicate and frayed—an old paper flower, tattered and worn at the edges. "I saved this one. For someone special."

My daughter nods enthusiastically. "It's pretty."

Lyric steps forward before I can stop her, before I can break out of being mesmerized to think clearly, and gently takes the fragile paper bloom from my mother's hand.

I don't breathe.

I don't move.

I just watch.

My mother smiles, something distant but peaceful flickering in her eyes. She touches a strand of my daughter's hair like she's touching something sacred. "Beautiful curls," she murmurs. "Like an angel's."

The ache in my chest tightens, a mixture of grief and something impossibly tender.

She doesn't know she's looking at her granddaughter.

She doesn't know she's meeting a piece of me.

But maybe, in some small way, she does.

Maybe her heart recognizes what her mind can't.

My throat burns and Hendrix squeezes my hand.

Then, just as quickly as the moment happened, it's gone.

My mother's gaze drifts again, lost, slipping back into whatever space exists beyond my reach. She hums softly, rocking again, eyes focused on things I can't see.

I exhale slowly, kneeling beside my daughter, brushing my hand over her curls. "Come on, sweetheart. Say goodbye."

She studies me before looking back at my mother. "Thank you for the flower."

My mother doesn't respond. Can't. But as we walk away, I swallow over the lump in my throat, my free hand curling into a fist as I force myself to keep moving, to keep walking.

When we reach the car, Hendrix turns to me, her eyes full of understanding, full of knowing. She doesn't say anything. She doesn't have to.

Instead, she just steps forward, places her hand on my chest, and rests her forehead on my shoulder.

And just like that . . .

The pieces of my broken heart shift.

Not mended. Not fully whole.

But still beating.

Still here.

Still holding on to the people who matter most. The ones who have taught me time and again just how worthy of love I am.

I close my eyes, exhaling as I press a kiss to the top of Hendrix's head, to my nine-month-old son's, and then to my daughter's curls as she leans against me, still holding on to that fragile paper flower.

Maybe my mother will forget this moment.

Maybe she'll never truly know us.

But tonight, for a breath in time, she saw her.

And for now, that's enough.

Did you enjoy Jase and Hendrix in Sweet Surrender?

I hope so. I loved writing their story as much as the other members of BENT.

I wrote Hawkin Play (lead singer) and his story over ten years ago in *Sweet Ache*. Him and his bandmates stuck with me all the time and nagged me to tell their story.

It was Vince Jennings up next in *Sweet Regret*. This book MADE ME fall back in love with writing again. Everything about Vince and Bristol's romance is swoon-worthy. There's something about a man who knows *she's the one* regardless of time apart or years passed.

Then of course was Jase and Hendrix's book that you just finished.

And last but not least is Rocket's book, *Sweet Distraction*, coming this summer.

If you'd like to check out any of my other romances, I write numerous subgenres (sports. billionaires, found family, enemies to lovers, small town, etcetera). You can go to either of these two places to learn more: WEBSITE at kbromberg.com or AMAZON

My books always come with a guaranteed happily ever after—*I just might make you work some to get there.*

As always, THANK YOU for reading!

ABOUT
the author

New York Times Bestselling author K. Bromberg writes contemporary romance novels that make you work to get your happily ever after. She likes to write strong heroines and damaged heroes, who we love to hate but can't help but love.

Since publishing her first book on a whim in 2013, Kristy has sold over two million copies of her books across twenty different countries and has landed on the *New York Times, USA Today,* and *Wall Street Journal* Bestsellers lists over thirty times. (*She still wakes up and asks herself how she got so lucky for all this to happen.*)

A mom of three, Kristy finds the only thing harder than finishing the book she's writing is navigating parenthood during the teenage years (send more wine!). She loves dogs, sports, a good book, and is an expert procrastinator. She lives in Southern California with her family.